# CHANGE OF SEASON

# CHANGE OF SEASON

Anna Jacobs

This first world edition published in Great Britain 2003 by
SEVERN HOUSE PUBLISHERS LTD of
9–15 High Street, Sutton, Surrey SM1 1DF.
This first world edition published in the USA 2003 by
SEVERN HOUSE PUBLISHERS INC of
595 Madison Avenue, New York, N.Y. 10022.

British Library Cataloguing in Publication Data

Jacobs,  Anna
     Change of season
     1.   Australians - England - Fiction
     2.   Family - Fiction
     I.   Title
     823.9'14 [F]

     ISBN 0-7278-5928-5

Typeset by Palimpsest Book Production Ltd.,
Polmont, Stirlingshire, Scotland.
Printed and bound in Great Britain by
MPG Books Ltd., Bodmin, Cornwall.

# One

L ouise stuck her head out of the kitchen door and yelled, 'Mum! Dad's on the phone from New York!' then vanished again.

Rosalind put down the trowel and walked slowly indoors, rubbing the worst of the dirt off her hands. 'Hello? Paul?'

'There you are at last! Hon, it's good news. I'm coming home on Tuesday.'

As he rattled off the flight time, she scribbled it down automatically, then could not help asking, 'How long will you be staying this time, Paul?' He'd been gone nearly six months, dealing with first one crisis then another in the big multi-national company for which he worked.

He didn't even notice the irony. 'About two weeks. Not sure yet which day I fly back. I've got some exciting news and— Oh, hell, there's another call on the line. Look, I'll see you on Tuesday. We'll talk then.'

'Paul, don't—' She stood for ages with the receiver buzzing in her ear before she set it carefully down and went back to finish the weeding. Tuesday was three days away. She had until then to decide whether to leave her husband of twenty-four years or not. And she was no nearer to knowing what she wanted than she had been a month ago when she had first admitted to herself that since his big promotion a couple of years ago their marriage had been virtually non-existent.

The following Tuesday Rosalind watched Paul wheel his luggage trolley through from customs. For a moment he seemed like a stranger, a tall, attractive man whose middle years sat lightly on him – hair still dark, lean cheeks, hazel eyes and neat nose.

Then he clipped her up in a big hug and as her body

1

remembered how it felt to be loved by him, something inside her softened – just a little.

After kissing her, he held her at arm's length to study her face. 'You look good, hon. I like the shoulder-length hair.'

As they went out into the fresh air he stopped to stare around. 'I always remember Western Australia like this, clear and sunny. I'll be able to get a good tan before I go back.'

At home he looked around the house as if he'd never seen it before. 'You've got excellent taste. I really like the way you've done up the living room.'

She had consulted him and sent him a photo, so knew he was sweetening her up. But she didn't say anything, just smiled and went through into the kitchen to get them a coffee. He strolled round the rest of the ground floor, then went to sprawl on one of the new white leather sofas in the living room.

She took the coffee in to him and sat down to pour. 'You said you had some exciting news, Paul. What is it?' She'd rather get the revelation over with. His ideas of good and hers didn't always coincide. He'd been excited by his promotion to chairman's international rover, troubleshooting for the company anywhere in the world that he was needed, but she'd known immediately what it would mean and had had difficulty hiding her dismay. She'd been right, too. Since then she'd seen less and less of him.

He sipped his coffee, looking at her over the rim of the mug. 'Big changes in the offing, hon. Looks like we'll be able to spend more time together.'

'You're getting a posting to Australia again?'

'Hell, no! I've moved to the international scene and that's where I intend to stay.'

She watched him put the coffee mug down and study her. It was an effort to keep a calm expression on her face as she waited for the explanation, which she was already sure she wouldn't like.

After a pause during which he sat chewing the corner of his lip, he said, 'I'm going to be based in England for the next six months instead of wandering the world trouble-shooting for the chairman – *and* they've arranged for you to live over there with me.' Then he went back to sipping his coffee.

She opened her mouth to speak, then closed it again. Think before you speak, Rosalind, she reminded herself, a strategy she'd decided on yesterday. She'd always refused to move around with him and a good thing too, or their children would have had no stability in their lives or education. Until he had joined the giant multinational, Marrill Marr, ten years ago, none of Paul's jobs had lasted more than a year or two anyway, some less. Since then *the company* had dominated his life – and hers too. He'd made several in-house 'career moves' during those years, each to a different part of the world. And now this.

She realized he was looking at her impatiently, waiting for a response. 'But I don't want to go and live in England.'

His voice was low and persuasive. 'Just think about it, hon. The kids have all left home now and—'

'Louise hasn't left yet.'

He rolled his eyes. 'She's about to go to university, isn't she? Which means she's grown up, like Jenny and Tim. Besides, I'm sure your mother would have her for a few months. Lou's seventeen now, past the awkward stage.'

Which showed how much he knew about his children, Rosalind thought mutinously.

'Face it, hon. We're free to live where we please at long last.'

'I live where I please now. Western Australia's a great place.'

He closed his eyes for a moment and sighed as if she had said something unreasonable. 'Don't you *ever* fancy a change?'

'No, not really. I enjoy my life here.' Which was no longer true. She'd felt very lonely during the past year or two. Her children had their own friends and interests nowadays and didn't seem to need her, and she was neither fish nor fowl when it came to a social life – married but without a visible husband.

'Look, Ros, I really do need to live a little closer to the action. And *you* might actually enjoy going back to the country where you were born.'

'I was only two when my parents migrated to Australia. I don't remember anything at all about England. I'd be as much a foreigner there as you are – more.'

'And yet when you write to your sole surviving relative in the UK, you keep promising the old witch you'll go and visit her one day.'

'Well, I will – one day. Just for a holiday. And Aunt Sophie is *not* a witch. She—'

He didn't even try to hide his impatience. 'Quite frankly, you're stuck in a rut here, Ros, and you need to do something about it. You and that little group of friends who all went to school together, not to mention that damned embroidery of yours. In this day and age – embroidery! What a hobby for a modern woman!'

She didn't rise to that old bait. Her embroidery wasn't a hobby but an abiding passion, and she considered raised stumpwork an undervalued art form. She was good at it, too, had won several prizes for her embroidered pictures. But for some reason she'd never been able to fathom, Paul hated her doing it.

His next words were etched in acid. 'I don't want to quarrel, but it's time to tell it as it is. You and I *need* some time together, Ros. We're growing apart. Do you want our marriage to go on like this? Or to end? I don't. Think of it as a change of season, a natural part of life. It might even be fun.' Another silence, then his tone changed. 'Now, how about thinking it over while you make me one of those wonderful gourmet meals. You know I never eat much on the plane.'

That she could do for him, at least.

As she stood up her attention was caught by her own reflection in the glass table top and she stared down in surprise at what it showed. Pastel colours, all of them. Ash-blonde hair, pale pink tee shirt, softly patterned skirt. She didn't look her age, not nearly old enough to have a twenty-two-year-old daughter, but she did look faded and indecisive – and that shocked her.

They walked through to the kitchen together and Paul perched on a stool to chat as she worked, telling her what the chairman had said and how her clever husband had turned a disaster into a profitable deal for the company, thus earning himself a nice fat bonus.

Her thoughts zigzagged all over the place as she put together a salad and nodded occasionally to keep Paul talking. What she kept coming back to – reluctantly, very reluctantly indeed – was that she really ought to give his suggestion serious consideration. The sight of him, the feel of his arms round her had made her feel – well, *married* again.

But the most telling reason of all was: he wanted to put things right between them. That mattered very much to her, because it had begun to seem as if he didn't care.

No, she decided as she served the meal, she didn't want their marriage to end – of course she didn't! – but oh, she didn't want to live in England, either! She had a suspicion that if she once agreed to go, she might not find it easy to come back again.

He was right, damn him, though she wasn't going to admit that yet. Something had to change if they were to stay together.

*But why did it always have to be her?*

The following morning Louise Stevenson got up late, deliberately waiting till her father went out to the golf club before she left her bedroom. Taking a quick shower, she left her hair to dry naturally. It was dark and wavy like her father's, but she was thinking of having her head shaved to a stubble and perhaps getting a gold stud in her nose. Now that she didn't have to conform to stupid school rules, she could have more fun with her appearance. And she had good enough features to get away with it.

Opening the bedroom door she cocked an ear, but there were no noises from below. Her parents didn't realize how much you could overhear from the upstairs landing of an open plan house like this – which could be very useful sometimes. If her mother did go to live in England, maybe Louise would be able to share a flat with her friend Sandy when she went to uni, instead of living at home. She was definitely not going to live at Gran's. Her grandmother's ideas of what was right and wrong were even more out of date than her mother's.

Going back inside her room, she put on a CD and lay back to enjoy the pure heaven of not having to study or worry about exams.

There was a knock on the door and her mother peered in.

'Darling, you promised to clear up your bedroom today. And will you please turn that music down?' She didn't wait for an answer.

Louise scowled. Why shouldn't she have an untidy room if she wanted to? It was her room, wasn't it? The music throbbed through her, making her feel achy inside her belly. Sexy, she decided. She felt sexy. And she wasn't going to wait much longer to do it, either. Virginity wasn't a treasure nowadays and everyone else in her group had done sex. Of course, she hadn't admitted that *she* hadn't, but she felt left out of the conversations sometimes. Reading about sex in books wasn't the same. She wanted to *know* how it felt to have an orgasm.

Ten minutes later her mother stormed back in, switched off the CD player and yelled, 'Get this pigsty cleared up! I'm putting on some washing in five minutes. If your stuff isn't in the basket by then, you can deal with it yourself.' She waited, hands on hips.

Louise sighed and rolled off the bed. 'I'm *supposed* to be on holiday.'

'Five minutes.'

When her mother had left, Louise made a quick phone call then stuffed a few necessities into her tote bag, muttering under her breath. She wasn't clearing anything up today. She was going round to Sandy's where there was no one to nag you in the daytime.

Creeping down the stairs, she held her breath as she crossed the open space near the kitchen. Her mother was sitting there, a mug of coffee cradled in her hands, her back to the world and her shoulders slumped.

What's wrong with her? Louise wondered. Give me half a chance to go to England and I'm off, outa here, bye bye folks, see ya when I see ya.

Giggling softly she made her escape, closing the side door quietly behind her. The washing would be done for her when she returned. It always was.

But that evening when she got back, she found her room hadn't been touched. That really threw her. Her mother must be really upset about the trip to England. It was the only explanation Louise could think of. And if her father saw the untidiness he'd hit the roof and he could be a real bastard if you pushed him too far.

A few streets away, Liz Foxen was also worrying. She could recognize the signs because she'd seen it all before: Bill looking happy and alert, whistling as he did the gardening, giving long explanations every time he left the house. For a clever man, he was remarkably obtuse about other people. It was right what they said about university lecturers – out of touch with the real world. Too busy playing academic politics. Or screwing one another. Or both.

Who was it this time? Some young tart of a student or a new colleague? There had been one or two changes in the lecturing staff this year.

'Oh, hell! I'm fed up with it!' she yelled suddenly, slapping the flat of her hand on the table. This time she wasn't going to take Bill's infidelity lying down, or rather – she paused as an idea slammed into her mind – perhaps she was. 'What's sauce for the goose . . .' she murmured.

Just then the phone rang.

'Oh, Liz!' The voice was hesitant, tearful.

'Hi, Rosalind.' Clutching the telephone receiver in one hand, Liz studied herself in the hall mirror as she listened to her friend. She kept in good trim, didn't she? Worked out at the gym, ate sensibly, dressed smartly. So why did he go after other women?

'Liz, can you come over?'

'Trouble?'

'Mm–hmm.'

Liz sighed. She didn't need someone else's woes on top of her own, but Rosalind had been her best friend since school. 'Put the kettle on, then. But no cake!'

Getting up from the telephone nook, Rosalind made her way to the rear of the house. Her slippered feet made no sound on the tiled floor and she shivered suddenly. It was as if she had no real existence, as if only a ghost had drifted past. A pastel-coloured ghost. Feeling hollow and insubstantial, she filled the kettle and got out the mugs, then went over to touch the vivid green curls of the parsley leaves in her herb pot and stare blindly out of the window.

7

Before the kettle boiled she heard Liz's car.

The two women embraced and as usual, Rosalind felt too tall and well-fleshed next to her friend. 'You look great! I love that outfit. It's new, isn't it?'

Liz twirled round, showing off. 'Yes. I was just trying it on when you rang. Do you think the skirt needs taking up a fraction?'

Rosalind took a step backwards, studied her friend's outline and shook her head decisively. 'No. Don't touch it. It's perfect as it is. Coffee or tea?'

'Coffee.'

When they went into the living room, Liz kicked off her shoes and tucked her feet up underneath her on the couch. 'What's the matter, then? Tell all.'

'Paul wants us to spend the spring and summer in England and – I don't want to go.'

'Well, you've got plenty of time to think about it. What's the panic today?'

'Northern hemisphere spring, not Australian. I'd have to leave within the month.' Rosalind took a sip of her coffee, then stared down at it bleakly. Little ripples were running to and fro across the surface – just like the apprehension shivering in her stomach.

Liz took a sip, made an appreciative murmur and sipped again before she spoke. 'I can't see what the problem is.'

'For a start, it's Louise's first year at university. How can I possibly leave her?'

Liz refrained from saying that lately Rosalind hadn't been getting on with her younger daughter and they'd probably both be happier apart. 'You were there when Tim went to uni. It didn't make much difference, did it? He still bombed out. Where is he now?'

'In America. He's travelling around, working on the sly to pay for it. He rang me last month.' She took another slurp of coffee. 'Anyway, a daughter's different. I was there for Jenny and she got through her degree all right.' Though there had been some anxious times, because Jenny wasn't a top student and had found the business course Paul had insisted on really hard going. 'And anyway, I *want* to be there for Louise.'

Liz leaned forward. 'You're making excuses, Rosalind Stevenson.'

'Well, the truth is, I don't want to go to England at all. And – and before he came back I was thinking of asking Paul for a divorce.'

Liz choked on a mouthful of coffee. 'You can't mean that! Not *you*!'

'I don't know what I mean, but I have been wondering. Only, Paul seems to be – well, making more effort – and he's right when he says we need time together.'

All of a sudden Liz was fed up of humouring her friend. 'It's time you thought of him. You've always put the children first before.'

'I haven't.'

'You have, you know!' Her voice softened. 'You might even enjoy England once you get used to life over there. You should be thankful Paul wants to spend some quality time together. I'd swap places with you any day, believe me.'

Her voice had such a vicious edge that Rosalind realized something was wrong. 'Not – trouble with Bill again?'

Liz nodded, lips tight and bloodless.

'You really shouldn't put up with it.'

'I'm not going to this time.'

'You mean – you're going to leave him?'

'Heavens, no! I'm still fond of the old bugger – too fond for my own good. I just got to thinking that I might give him a taste of his own medicine for a change and see how he likes that. It's simply a question of finding someone I fancy and diving into the nearest bed.'

'You shouldn't joke about something so important.'

'Who's joking?'

The bitterness in her voice worried Rosalind, but Liz didn't mean what she'd said, of course she didn't.

After her friend had left, Rosalind wandered out into the garden. She sighed as she nipped off a few dead leaves. Perhaps something would turn up to prevent her having to go to England. Paul was always changing his plans and rushing off to deal with an emergency for the chairman.

*Oh, please, let something turn up!* she prayed.

\* \* \*

9

That evening their elder daughter Jenny popped in unexpect-edly. 'Hi, Mum! Louise not around?'

'She and Sandy have gone to the movies.'

'Good. I need to talk to you both.' She opened her mouth to speak, then burst into noisy, gulping sobs.

Rosalind hurried across to hug her and pat her shoulders till she had calmed down, not saying anything, simply wait-ing for an explanation.

Jenny finished mopping her eyes. It was her mother she looked at as she said, 'It's Michael. I've left him.'

Paul leaned forward. 'Is he the guy I met last time I was home? Well, it's about time you came to your senses. He's a real no-hoper, that one.'

'What's happened?' Rosalind asked, frowning at him. No need to sound so triumphant when the girl was hurting.

'He's been unfaithful to me and – and he's not even sorry about it!' What's more, when Jenny had confronted him, he'd hit her, though she wasn't going to tell her parents that. She'd known then that the relationship was over. Irrevocably. She wasn't into being thumped. 'The split's been brewing for a while, I guess. Could I stay here? I can't go back. I've got my things in the car.'

Paul gave her one of his icy looks. 'You can't stay for long. The house is going to be closed down. Your mother's coming to live in England with me for a few months.'

Rosalind felt annoyed. She hadn't actually agreed to go yet and he knew it.

'I could look after the place for you,' Jenny volunteered. 'It'd be safer to have someone living here.'

Paul gave a scornful laugh. 'No way. I haven't forgotten the last time you looked after it. That party of yours cost me over a thousand dollars in redecoration, as well as upsetting all the neighbours.'

'But what am I going to *do*? I don't have enough money to pay the bond on a flat of my own, Dad.' She began to sob again.

Rosalind put her arm round Jenny's shoulders. 'I'm not turning my daughter away, Paul.'

'I didn't say I wouldn't *help*. And of course she can stay with us till we find her a flat. But after that, we're closing the house down and we're off on our second honeymoon.'

10

Jenny smiled at them through her tears. 'That's so sweet. *Second honeymoon.* I'm always glad you two are still together. Nearly everyone else's parents are divorced.'

'No chance of that as long as your mother behaves herself.' Paul grinned across the table.

'And as long as you behave yourself, too, Paul Stevenson,' Rosalind retorted.

'Don't I always?'

Jenny laughed. 'You do when you're at home, Dad. We don't know what you get up to when you're overseas.'

He stiffened. 'I work far too hard to misbehave, believe me, young lady. Even if I were that way inclined, which I'm not.'

They both stared at him in amazement, his tone was so sharp.

'She was only joking,' Rosalind protested.

'Well, it's the kind of joke I can do without, thank you very much. I'm unashamedly old-fashioned about jokes like that.'

After the silence had gone on for a bit too long, Rosalind said, 'How about I get us all a drink, then we can discuss what to do?'

Later, when Jenny had taken up residence in the guest suite, Paul sat down beside his wife on the bed and put his arm round her shoulders. 'Feeling better about the trip now? You *are* coming, aren't you?'

'I suppose so.' She'd made up her mind to give it a try, because she really did want to put their marriage to rights. That was the main reason.

He nibbled her ear. 'What am I going to do with you, woman?' As her breathing deepened, he took her in his arms and kissed her. His hands knew all her body's weaknesses, as hers knew his.

And then, of course, she forgot everything else, for he was a superb lover, always had been. Their reunions were fantastic. She missed the sex greatly when he was away. He must do, too, because he was a passionate man.

Maybe they did need a change – and she loved the idea of a second honeymoon.

Four days later the chairman's personal assistant rang from England. Rosalind handed the phone to Paul feeling faintly anxious. The PA only rang in emergencies. She went to sit in the kitchen because Paul hated people listening in on his business conversations.

After a few minutes a shadow fell across her. She looked up and her heart sank. He was looking excited and alert. She knew that expression of old.

He perched on the edge of the chair next to hers. 'Darling, I'm sorry, but I have to get back to London straight away. They've booked me a seat on the six o'clock plane. *Big* crisis.'

'But you've been home less than a week!'

He shrugged. 'That's how things go in this job, and it's exactly why I want you over there with me.'

'That means I'll have to travel to England alone!'

Breath rasped impatiently in his throat. 'I think you'll be able to find your way to the airport from here, and I'll be there to meet you in London.'

'Promise me you'll meet me. *Promise!*'

'I promise faithfully. Now, come and help me pack, eh? Good thing we found that flat for Jenny, isn't it? And your mother's all set to have Louise.' He held her at arm's length and stared at her with mock sternness. 'So you have no excuse for trying to wriggle out of this trip, my girl.'

'I've said I'll come, haven't I?'

He nodded and let her go. 'I'm rather looking forward to having a wife around. Dinner parties, regular sex, theatres and restaurants. We'll have great fun.'

When she got back from taking Paul to the airport, Rosalind took out her embroidery things and set up the smaller spare bedroom as her workshop again. She always put everything away when he came home to avoid arguments and snide remarks. The routine of arranging her things usually helped her to settle down after he'd left – though this time she'd only be here for a couple more weeks herself.

The embroidery worked its usual magic and even when Jenny rang up to complain that the new flat was noisy and Michael was still pestering her to get back together, Rosalind didn't let it worry her. She spoke soothingly and claimed a pan on the stove so that she could end the conversation quickly.

When Paul went away, she always needed a few hours of

peace to reorient her life. Everything was so different without him. And this time she had a lot to think about. She'd agreed to spend the spring and summer in England and wouldn't go back on her word.

But next time someone had to compromise about what they were doing with their lives, it wouldn't be her, she was quite determined about that.

# Introduction to Raised Stumpwork

*This highly individual type of embroidery flourished in its original form for only a few decades of the seventeenth century . . .*

*Its capacity for conveying life and humour, and the way in which it combines many different embroidery and lace-making techniques makes this work an ideal vehicle for modern embroiderers seeking to achieve similar effects in a contemporary idiom.*

*(Barbara and Roy Hirst, Raised Embroidery, Merehurst Limited, London, 1993, p.6 – quotes used with permission)*

## Simulating Life

*The stitches, techniques, threads, fabrics and other materials used to create a raised embroidery are all carefully selected to express, simulate and describe the subject . . .*

*A sampler of this type might be designed with a particular theme in mind – family, nature, the seasons, a period in history, or a particular event.*

*(Hirst, p.60)*

# Two

The twenty-hour flight to London seemed interminable. Rosalind was too tall to be comfortable in planes, even in business class, and could not manage to do more than doze for an hour or two. By the time the plane arrived in London she was exhausted.

Pushing her luggage trolley she walked out into the terminal looking for Paul, pleased at the prospect of being with him again. When she couldn't see him anywhere apprehension began to twitch in her belly. When he'd phoned last week, he'd promised that nothing, absolutely nothing, would prevent him from meeting her at the airport and helping her settle into the English house. So where was he?

She saw a young woman holding one of those signs with people's names on them and didn't look at it, then something clicked inside her brain and she turned slowly back. It said *Stevenson* in ominous black letters.

*He'd broken his promise!*

'Oh, damn you, Paul!' she whispered. 'Couldn't you even do this for me? Does the company have to come first every single time?'

The woman holding the sign looked across at her and nodded in recognition. She was so trim and well-groomed she made Rosalind feel huge and even more dishevelled than before.

'Mrs Stevenson? Paul's wife?'

'Yes.'

The woman stuck out one well-manicured hand. 'You look just like the photo on Paul's desk. I'm Gail Johns from Personnel. I'm afraid Paul's been called away. He's in New York at the moment, actually.'

'*New York!*' Rosalind could hear her voice wobble, couldn't prevent it.

Gail gave her a reassuring smile. 'You don't have to worry. I've arranged everything for you. Let's have a coffee and I'll explain.' She set off across the concourse.

For a moment Rosalind stood watching her, then sighed and began to push the luggage trolley through the crowds. Around her people were hugging one another, some weeping for joy. Children were running to and fro. Everyone, it seemed, was with family or friends. Everyone except her. Only pride kept her head up.

And anger.

The refreshments area was seedy and predominantly brown. The tables had been swiped over casually with a cloth and were still smeary.

Gail brought back two coffees and some food for herself. 'Hope you don't mind, but I haven't had any lunch yet.' She took a huge bite of the sandwich, then got out some papers. 'I have full instructions for you, Mrs Stevenson, all in alphabetical order – so much better than my trying to explain everything now, don't you think? You'd never remember all the details afterwards.'

Her tone was that of an adult dealing with a rather dull child. Rosalind breathed deeply but said nothing. It had been the same when Paul had worked in the company's Australian branch, ambitious young things like this treating her as if she were in her dotage because she was a mere housewife.

'We've found you a house in Dorset. The chairman's family came from there originally and he always speaks well of it. The house is quite large and there's a nice villagey atmosphere, so you should find it easy to make friends. It's only about two hours' drive from London.'

Aligning the papers carefully on the table, Gail dipped into the briefcase again. 'This is the key to the house – front door key only, the others are waiting for you in Burraford Destan. It's a nice little place and really easy to get to, mostly motorway from here. Paul said you'd be all right with the driving.' She raised one eyebrow questioningly.

'Of course I shall.' Rosalind was absolutely terrified of driving in a strange country, but she'd let herself be hanged, drawn and quartered before she'd admit it to this bright young thing.

16

Gail picked up the sandwich again, then glanced across the table with it halfway to her mouth. 'Are you sure you're all right, Mrs Stevenson? You look a bit pale.'

'I'm just a bit – um – jet-lagged. It's a long flight.'

'Well, if you're too tired to drive today, we can easily book you into a hotel.'

Rosalind struggled to *get her head together*, as Louise would have said. 'I – what time is it here?'

'One o'clock in the afternoon.'

Rosalind thought furiously as she adjusted her watch. If she booked into a hotel now, she would fall asleep then wake up in the middle of the night. Paul always said it was better to fit into the day-night pattern as soon as you could after you changed time zones and he ought to know. 'No. I won't bother with a hotel. I've all afternoon to drive down to Dorset, haven't I? So I can just take things easily.' *One step at a time.* Her old motto brought its usual comfort.

Gail devoured the last of the sandwich with a sigh of pleasure. 'That's terrific. Though you'd better stop on the way to pick up some groceries. Paul hasn't managed to get down to Dorset yet and there'll be nothing in the fridge.'

'But I thought – Paul told me he'd approved the house himself.'

''Fraid a few things cropped up and he only had time to set the ground rules. But the agency we use for temporary executive relocation is very reliable and I've shown him the photos. Very attractive house, delightful village. I'm sure you'll like living there. Paul fancies experiencing English village life.' She took another gulp of coffee. 'Dorset is a really pretty part of England. Hills, farms with grey stone walls and—'

She abandoned description with a shrug, which made Rosalind realize that no one from the company had actually checked the house.

'And we have a company flat in London for when Paul can't get down to Dorset. You can get up to town in two hours by train from nearby Wareham, which is pretty convenient. I've got you a good road map.' She unwrapped a piece of fruitcake. 'Don't know why I'm so hungry today. Must be the cold.'

'Is it very cold outside?'

'Freezing.' Gail licked some cake crumbs from her fingers. 'Everyone's saying how late spring is this year. I mean, almost April and no sign of the sun. Even the trees are late getting their leaves.' She glanced sideways, frowned and offered another glib reassurance. 'I'm sure you'll be all right, Mrs Stevenson.'

Miss Efficiency was still talking to her as if she were a doddery old lady and Rosalind wasn't having that. She straightened up and said crisply, 'Well, if you've finished eating, we may as well go and get the car, eh?'

It was a large, comfortable car and Rosalind had no difficulty driving it, though she felt a bit nervous at first coping with the heavy motorway traffic. Then, half an hour later, the engine coughed and spluttered before picking up. A few minutes later, it began to falter again. 'No! Please, no!' Rosalind begged. But the vehicle lost power and began to kangaroo, jerking forward briefly, then losing momentum.

She signalled to move left, cutting in front of a small truck, which blared its horn at her, then pulling off on to the hard shoulder just as the engine died completely. The car rolled slowly to a halt and she sat frozen in disbelief for a moment before opening the door.

Icy wind howled around her. Traffic fumes assaulted her nose. Dark clouds were massing in the sky. What the hell was the matter? The car had a full tank of petrol, so it couldn't be that. She lifted the bonnet, but could see nothing obviously wrong. The battery connections seemed good, the fan belt wasn't slack and no water hoses seemed to be leaking. Beyond that, she didn't know what to look for.

Cars and trucks continued to drone past her and the wind blew icy dampness down her neck, as well as sneaking chill fingers up her sleeves. She hadn't got a mobile phone here yet and could only hope there would be an emergency phone nearby. Locking the car, she began trudging grimly along the hard shoulder, alternately buffeted by the backdraught from passing trucks and mocked by the wind, which continued to tug at her clothes and suck away what little warmth was left in her body.

The phone got her through to the police, who telephoned

the car hire company and then told her someone would be coming with a replacement car, but it'd take a while.

'How long?'

'Sorry, madam. They didn't say. You should stay with your vehicle and if anyone stops nearby it would be safer to lock yourself in.'

So she had to tramp back and wait. She found half a chocolate bar in her handbag and devoured it hungrily, then wished she hadn't because it made her thirsty. Time crawled past and the radio programmes were only half audible because of the traffic noise, so she was left with her own thoughts for company. They were not happy ones.

'Damn you, Paul!' she said aloud.

In Australia that same day, Liz looked at her husband and anger rose like bile in her throat, scalding her with its intensity. She had never felt so furious with Bill before, not even the first time he'd been unfaithful. 'You must think I'm stupid if you expect me to fall for that line.'

'It isn't a line.' But he looked at her warily as he said it.

She leaned her head back and stared up at the ceiling for a moment. 'He does think I'm stupid,' she told it, then looked at him again. 'She's called Marian Hulme and she's just out from England in her first tenured position. She's tall, with dyed blonde hair. And she calls you *William, dear.*'

He went white. 'How did you find out?'

'I can always tell when you're being unfaithful, so I did a bit of snooping, not to mention checking the accounts. You've been wining and dining rather a lot lately. And you shouldn't chat to people in stairwells. I heard everything you said to her yesterday when I was on my way to your office, *William dear.*'

He said nothing, avoiding her eyes.

'This time, however, I'm *not* going to forgive you. Instead, I'm working on the principle of goose and gander, as in sauce for.'

He jerked upright. 'Liz, surely—'

'Surely what?'

'You don't mean that.'

'I do, actually. I've booked myself a holiday. In Hong Kong. Eighteen lovely days. And while I'm there, I'm going to keep my eyes open for a likely new gander – preferably one a little younger than you and with more hair on his head.' She heard the air whistle into Bill's mouth and felt grim satisfaction at hitting him in his weak spot. Heaven alone knew why it mattered so much to him that he was going bald, but it did.

'Don't do that, Liz. I'll – I'll end it at once, and—'

'Oh, but I shall do it. Go to Hong Kong, anyway. I'll have an affair, too, if I can find someone I fancy. And every time you start screwing around from now on, I'm going to take a lover as well. I'm told I'm quite attractive still – even if *you* don't find me so – and I doubt I'll have too much difficulty getting someone to lay me.'

'Liz . . .'

'I leave in two days for Hong Kong.'

His glance was very level. 'I don't believe you about the lover, but if you want a holiday, well, that's all right with me. I'll make sure everything is well and truly over by the time you return.'

'It'd bloody better be.' She smiled then and delivered her coup de grâce. 'Hope you're feeling in a domesticated mood, because you won't be able to eat in restaurants while I'm away. I'm afraid I've cleaned out our account.'

'*All of it?*'

'Yup!'

'You're a nasty bitch sometimes under all that sparkle, Liz. How the hell am I going to manage without money till you get back?'

'I don't actually care.'

She slept in the spare bedroom till she left. And missed him like hell. But she wasn't going to admit that.

As Rosalind sat waiting for deliverance by an English roadside, in America her son put his last coin into a slot machine and reached for the paper cup of coffee. His hand was shaking. Shit, they had certainly pinned one on last night. What had been in that last pill he'd popped? He blinked and risked a sip of the dirty-looking liquid. Oh, for one of his mother's wonderful coffees! That thought made him snort with laughter.

'What's so funny, man?' Wayne appeared next to him.

'I was just thinking of Mum's coffee. It's the best in the whole world.' Tim took another sip. Well, at least this stuff was warm. 'What are we going to do now? I'm skint. And you're nearly out of money, too.'

'We'll have to earn some more.'

'We don't have a work permit.'

'You don't need a permit for what I've got in mind.'

'I don't think I want to—'

Wayne grabbed him by the front of his jacket. 'I'm getting just a little tired of you and your fucking scruples. If you're not happy here, go back home to your darling Mummy. Otherwise, stop moaning and feeling sorry for yourself. We could have earned ourselves some good money working with those guys last night, but oh no, you had to put your foot in it, didn't you?'

'The fat one was a full-on dealer. Serious shit. And he wanted us to push for him.'

'So what? Everyone's into something nowadays, so why not take advantage of that? You've been doing stuff since you were fourteen.' He let that sink in, then added, 'Now, either you're with me or you can piss off and manage on your own. Make up your bloody mind.' Only then did he let go of his friend's jacket, laughing as hot coffee spilled down it.

Tim shuddered at the thought of walking away from Wayne. America – well, the part they were visiting – scared the crap out of him and he wished desperately he'd never left Australia. Even home was better than this nightmare existence, but he wasn't going to crawl back to his father with his tail between his legs. No way. 'I said I was in, didn't I? And you owe me a coffee now, you stupid bastard. You spilled most of mine and that was my last coin.'

Wayne's face slowly relaxed. 'All right, then. One coffee coming up. Now, here's what we do . . .'

It was nearly three hours before another car drew up beside Rosalind, by which time she was chilled to the marrow and bursting for a pee. She had sunk into a dull lethargy, enduring because there was nothing else she could do, too tired now even to think.

A man wearing a cap with the hire company logo on it got

out and she opened the door to speak to him. A flurry of light rain whispered across them, then trailed away into mere dampness, but judging by the dark clouds more was on the way.

'Mrs Stevenson?'

'Yes.'

'John Trevithin. I've got another car here for you. A tow truck will be along in a few minutes to take me and this naughty girl back.' He slapped the car with an affection Rosalind in no way shared.

'Well, I hope you fix the problem before you hire the car out again. I've been sitting here for *three hours* in the freezing cold!'

'Yes. Sorry. There's a motorway services place just along the road. Go and get yourself a meal and a hot drink. You'll feel a lot better then.' He handed her a voucher. 'Compliments of the company.'

She looked at her watch. Half-past four. 'I had intended to get down to Dorset before dark.'

'You'll never make it. Might as well take a break first. Do you good. Not a nice introduction to England, eh, Mrs Stevenson? Never mind. Things can only get better from now on. Enjoy your holiday.'

He didn't look much older than her son, but she felt old today – old, cold and fed up to the bloody teeth. Lips pressed tightly together she started up the car and left him standing there, grinning and waving at her like an idiot. But she did stop at the services to use the ladies', then grab a cup of coffee and a sandwich. Muddy coffee and a pallid sandwich with wilted salad and stringy beef stuck between two layers of anonymous grease. She left half of it.

It was an effort to push herself up again from the small plastic table. She was exhausted and jet lag was making her whole system scream for sleep. But she didn't want to find a motel, just get this endless travelling over and done with, and take possession of her new home.

It grew dark well before she reached Dorset, but she found a petrol station which sold basic foods and bought enough to last her until the following morning. She grabbed another coffee while she was at it and this time it was proper coffee,

22

freshly brewed. By the time she left she was feeling slightly more cheerful. Nearly there now.

She turned on to the Wareham–Swanage road, driving through the darkness with a sense of triumph. According to her directions, Burraford Destan was on the right just past Wareham. If she missed the first turn, there was another soon after it. Yes, there was the sign.

She followed the last of the instructions and found number ten, Sexton Close. She had to stop the car and get out to open the big wrought-iron gates, whose rusty hinges seemed unwilling to move. 'You ought to be here today, Paul Stevenson,' she muttered as she struggled with them. 'For once in your bloody high-powered life you ought to be *with* me.'

The gates gave way at last to her desperate pushing and she got into the car, rolling forward slowly round the circular driveway to the front door as she gaped at the house in the light of the headlights. It really was beautiful, built of some sort of pale grey stone. Even the roof was grey and wasn't covered in slates or tiles but what looked like slabs of stone. A steep gable on the right side of the house looked like something from a small-town Disney movie, and all round the edges of the circular drive were daffodils, scores of them, lit up by the powerful headlights of the car. Her spirits began to lift, though she'd have felt better if there had been lights showing in the windows – and would have felt safer, too.

When she got out, she left the engine running and the headlights on. Outside that charmed circle of light everything looked dark and sinister, but she reminded herself of the self-defence course she had taken. She'd got a commendation for it, too, though she'd never had to use the skills.

Oh, for goodness' sake, she thought, pull yourself together, Rosalind! You're not some fragile little thing to be easily overpowered.

The self-defence instructor had said you never turned your back on danger. Well, she'd just like to see him open this door without turning his back on the garden. 'Come on, come on, you stupid thing!' She fumbled with the lock and turned the key just as rain began hissing down again like a grey chiffon cloak between her and the car headlights.

It took a lot of will power to step forward into the blackness of the hall, even with the car keys poking out between her knuckles as a makeshift weapon. She found a switch and suddenly the place was flooded with light. Weak with relief she leaned against the wall, reassured by the feel of something solid behind her as she studied her surroundings.

It was a few seconds before she gathered enough courage to move forward and begin opening doors. On the left a spacious living room led into a small dining room with a very ugly modern table and chairs, all angles and discomfort. On the right was a smaller sitting room and behind it an office. Kitchen and conservatory were at the rear. She left lights on everywhere because it made her feel better, and put the kettle on while she was in the kitchen. Even instant coffee would be wonderful.

Upstairs, according to the brochure on the house, were 'four spacious bedrooms and two bathrooms' with an 'attic playroom or guest bedroom, plus small shower room'. Well, she'd investigate those when she'd got her luggage in.

She made two quick dashes to the car and when she switched off the headlights and motor, she felt suddenly terrified that someone might be lurking in the bushes, so raced up the steps and slammed the front door shut behind her. Laughing shakily at herself, she shoved the bolt across.

The kitchen was full of steam because the kettle hadn't switched itself off. There wasn't enough water left in it for a coffee, so she filled the damned thing again. Her teeth were chattering and she had never felt so cold in her whole life. She would not cry! She would not.

But she did. She sipped her coffee with tears trickling down her face and plopping into the cup. Realistically she knew Paul couldn't have refused to do his job, but emotionally she felt he had let her down.

She shivered. How cold it was! No wonder her parents had emigrated to Australia. Only then did it occur to her. She was an idiot. Miss Efficiency had said there was central heating. She fumbled for the instructions folder, which said: 'Central heating is switched on from the central boiler, located in the mudroom.' She frowned round. Mudroom? What the hell was one of those?

Suddenly she noticed the door at the back of the casual

meals area next to the kitchen. She'd dismissed it as a cupboard, but perhaps this was the mudroom. It was locked. No key in sight nearby. Back to Miss Efficiency's instructions.

*Keys*, she read. Capital letters, neatly positioned on the page. She could just imagine the immaculate Gail typing it on her computer keyboard, red nails flashing. 'The keys are in the top drawer of the bureau in the sitting room to the right of the front door as you go in.'

Great one! Where else would you keep keys? She found a big bunch of them. 'Aha!' Jangling them in her hand, she went back to the kitchen to try them out. 'No labels on them, of course! Caught you there, Gail Johns! Not good enough. Off with your nails!'

She decided that a mudroom was a utility room, a place for coats and shoes, judging by the hooks and racks. It also contained the controls for the heating system and she left it clucking quietly to itself before trailing wearily upstairs. The quilt in the master bedroom looked fluffy and inviting. Shivering she crept under it without taking her clothes off. Within seconds she was fast asleep.

# Three

In Australia, Louise waited until her gran was asleep then tiptoed downstairs. Honestly, who went to bed at ten o'clock these days? Some of the nightclubs didn't even open their doors until then. She beamed in the darkness as she slipped quietly along the hallway. She was going clubbing tonight with Sandy, who was now settled in her own flat, the lucky tart.

When the front door clicked softly shut behind her, she raised both fists in a silent victory salute, then got into her mother's car. She'd told Gran she had permission to use it. Well, her mother might have said yes if she'd asked. It made sense, after all. But she hadn't asked, because her mother might also have said no.

She'd look after it because she was a very careful driver – a natural, her instructor had said when she'd passed her driving test first time, unlike Tim and Jenny. Mind you, with having to drive on P plates for the first year after passing her test and being under age, she didn't dare drink and drive, but there were other things, less obvious things, that the breathalysers wouldn't pick up – and they could be as much fun as alcohol.

She drove away, turning up the stereo till the bass notes were thumping along her veins. Yeah! This was going to be a great night out!

Audrey Worth lay for a moment in the darkness, wondering what had woken her. When she heard the car drive away, music pulsing loudly from it, she leaped out of bed and pulled back the edge of the curtain to see the tail lights disappearing down the street and the spare parking bay outside her house empty.

'The young minx! I don't know why Rosalind lent her that car. It was asking for trouble. And trouble is what Louise will get from me when she comes home.'

26

Only her granddaughter didn't come home – well, not until six in the morning – by which time Audrey was nearly out of her mind with worry and seriously considering calling the police.

And far from listening to the reprimand, Louise shouted back at her, then slammed out of the house again to go to uni without waiting to eat anything or change her clothes.

'I'm not enjoying her company at all,' Audrey told her friend John when he called in later that morning. 'She's very wilful.'

'I've never understood why you agreed to have her in the first place.'

'You don't know my son-in-law. He'd persuade Eskimos to buy ice, that one would. Well, what can't be cured must be endured, I suppose.' But it was going to be a long six months, she could see that. Very long indeed.

In the evening Audrey once more tried to talk to her granddaughter.

Louise glared at her. 'I told you. I was out with my friends. What is this, a bloody nunnery?'

Audrey tried to keep her temper. 'Don't swear in my house. We agreed when you came that you'd let me know where you were going and what time you'd be back – and that you wouldn't stay out after midnight.'

'Look, these days nothing starts happening till ten o'clock. Did you really expect me to walk out on my friends at midnight? They'd have laughed themselves silly.'

'Yes, I did expect it. For someone who's supposed to be studying, midnight is quite late enough. Anyway, it's not safe out on your own. Young women disappear, get murdered.'

Louise tried persuasion. 'Honest, Gran, nothing starts till late. And I was perfectly safe. That's why I've got the car. We all went for an early breakfast together afterwards. We always do.' An exaggeration. She had never been allowed to stay out all night before. However soft her mother was, she had her sticking points.

Audrey's voice was chill and emphatic. 'Both Rosalind and Paul agreed to my conditions and so did you. You can like it or lump it, but you'll be back by midnight from now on, young lady. And if you're in any doubt about that, we'll ring your mother up and ask her opinion.'

Louise swung round and stamped upstairs. Honestly, you'd think someone who'd left school and started university would be treated like an adult. But no. She had to live with her grandmother instead of sharing a flat with a friend, and she had to be home by midnight. What was this, Cinderella revisited?

Only – if she disobeyed and Gran did contact Mum, they'd find out about the car. Or Gran might tell her father – and she didn't want *him* coming the heavy. He could be a real bastard sometimes – with everyone except her mother, anyway – though he usually managed to get his own way with her mother, as well.

Louise went over to stare out of the window, then realized something and swung round to stare at her bedroom. There were no clothes on the floor, only a large dustbin liner in the corner and it was half full. Where had that come from? She went to investigate.

A strong smell of cheesy socks, dirty knickers and sweaty tee shirts hit her nostrils as she opened it and she gasped in fury. Her clean things were in there, all mixed up with the dirty ones. She stamped down the stairs, dragging the bag with her.

'Gran? What's this?'

'Oh, your washing. I put it all in the bag, dear. I could smell your socks from my room. This is a very small house, you know. I don't intend to wash for you – you keep insisting you're grown up – so if you don't put your things away, I'll stuff everything into a bag.' She had decided this in the middle of her wakeful night.

'But you put the *clean* things in with dirty, so they'll all smell rotten now.'

'You surely didn't expect me to examine your knickers to see which ones had been worn?'

There was no answering that one. 'What am I going to wear tomorrow? I particularly wanted to wear this shirt.'

'Up to you, dear. But if you want to do some washing now, the laundry's free and I have some undercover lines. Your things will be dry by morning.'

Glances locked.

Audrey kept a smile on her face only with difficulty.

Louise didn't even attempt to smile. 'I do not need this.'

28

'Nor do I. In fact, it's inconvenient having you staying here, much as I love you. But I'm sure things will work out once you get used to my ways. You need to remember that this is *my* house.'

The silence was definitely heavy enough to weigh. Cursing under her breath, Louise stormed into the laundry. Before she could sling her clothes into the washing machine, her grandmother was there beside her.

'I can't afford new appliances, so let me show you how to get the best out of this old one.'

Sullenly Louise listened and obeyed. It certainly was an old machine. She looked round. 'Where's the tumble-dryer?'

'I don't need one. They're expensive on electricity and besides, things dry on my undercover lines, even in winter.'

Louise let out an aggrieved sigh. Great! Back to the Dark Ages!

Later, when she had finished her first assignment from university, she wandered downstairs again. Her Gran was watching some dumb documentary on television. The only books on the shelves were romances – Mills & Boon, for heaven's sake, and someone called Georgette Heyer! She picked up one of the romances. 'I didn't know you read this rubbish, Gran.'

'You know enough about romances to pass judgement, do you?'

Louise dropped the book as if it were a hot coal. 'I've never read one in my life!'

'That makes you an excellent judge, then. Anyway, who asked you to read my books – or to comment on them?'

Louise retreated to her room. She was hungry. But she'd put on weight if she ate the things her grandmother cooked. Her stomach growled and she sighed. Maybe she should get some pills to kill her appetite and make her more active. Sandy said they were marvellous. They were a bit expensive, though. She might have to get a part-time job. She switched on her radio and since she and Gran had already had words about noise levels, she turned it down and got into bed. She'd never sleep, going to bed this early. And she'd go mad with boredom in the evenings here.

People who went gallivanting off to England should make

better arrangements for their daughters. Sandy complained about her bedsitter being too small, but Louise would swap with her any day.

It wasn't till she was eating breakfast next morning that she realized she had forgotten to peg out her washing the previous night. She pushed the toast aside with an angry growl and got up to do it. What the hell was she going to wear today?

This was a lousy start to the university year. Absolutely lousy!

The following morning the phone rang and Rosalind ran to pick it up. 'Paul?'

'No. It's me. Sophie.'

Disappointment knifed through Rosalind. You'd have thought your husband would at least ring to check that you'd arrived safely, whether he was in New York or not. 'Aunt Sophie! How lovely to hear your voice. How on earth did you find out where I was?'

'Phoned your husband's company. They didn't want to tell me your number at first, but I insisted.'

Rosalind's smile was genuine. 'I was going to ring you this evening.'

'Well, I didn't want to wait. Look, they told me Paul isn't expected back until the weekend, so I want you to come and visit me for a day or two. You haven't got anything else arranged, have you?'

'No. Well, only sorting out the house.'

'Sort it out next week instead. I need to see you now.'

Rosalind chuckled.

'I'd better warn you. I've got cancer. I don't have long to live, so don't be shocked at how thin I am.'

'Oh, Soph, no!' Tears welled in Rosalind's eyes.

'No maudlin nonsense. I'm eighty-three. Got to die of something. Rather have had a quick heart attack, but there you are.' More silence, then, 'Are you coming?'

'Yes, of course!' *Cancer!* Poor Soph! Paul had been right – Rosalind couldn't have afforded to wait any longer to come to England. Damn him, why did he always have to be right? And why hadn't *he* phoned?

She went to repack her suitcase and set off within the hour, arriving in Lancashire around three in the afternoon after a trouble-free drive along some delightful country roads, then up some busy motorways.

Southport had such a pretty main street she was tempted to stop for a few minutes, but resisted that idea and drove on, following Sophie's instructions.

'This can't be it!' she exclaimed as she pulled up. She checked the number again, but it was correct. Somehow, she hadn't expected Sophie to have such an impressive house. Although it was a terraced house, it was far larger than the one she and Paul were renting and was three stories high, with attics above that. But it was an old house and there was no garage, so she had to park in the street.

As she walked along the path the front door was opened by a complete stranger. 'Am I at the right place? I'm looking for my aunt, Sophie Worth.'

'Yes, this is her house. You must be Rosalind. I'm Prue Daking, a sort of nurse-housekeeper. Do come in.' She smiled conspiratorially and lowered her voice. 'Your aunt's been waiting impatiently all afternoon.'

At the sitting-room door, Rosalind stopped and tried to keep smiling through her shock. Sophie Worth was skeletal, the faded yellowish skin stretched across her bones like crumpled parchment. She was sitting in a wheelchair and didn't get up, just held out both hands to Rosalind, then pulled her close, cheek to cheek, for a moment.

'I'm so glad you've come, dear.'

'I am, too.'

'Prue, would you get us a tea tray?' Sophie let go of Rosalind's hands and gestured towards the comfortable sofa next to her.

Tears filled Rosalind's eyes. She didn't know what to say.

'You can go away again if you're going to weep all over me.'

'You know I always cry easily, Soph.'

'Well, if I'm not crying, you certainly shouldn't be.' She reached out to pat her great-niece's hand. 'I've had a long life and a good one, too. Never married . . .' She grinned wickedly. 'But had a few lovers in my time.'

'*Aunt Sophie!*'

31

'Ha! Shocked you there. Don't know why, though. Did you think we were all sexless in those days?'

Suddenly, Rosalind felt at home. Each time Soph had visited them in Australia, she had felt drawn to her – as she did now. The two of them had corresponded intermittently for years, but Soph had never even hinted at her present health problems.

'What did that husband of yours say when you told him you were coming to see me today?'

'Paul doesn't know.'

'Oh?'

Rosalind shrugged, trying to speak lightly. 'He hasn't been in touch yet. And he didn't meet me at the airport as he promised. If you hadn't told me, I wouldn't even know when he's coming back from America.' In spite of her efforts, her voice wobbled.

'You're too soft with him. I've always said that.'

They both stopped speaking as Prue brought in the tea tray and poured cups for them, her actions quick and efficient, her short dark hair sleek as a seal's coat.

When she'd gone, Sophie continued thoughtfully, 'Paul came to see me – when was it? – two years ago. We didn't get on very well without you to mediate. He stayed for tea, then left for "an urgent business appointment". In Blackpool, he said, but that was just an excuse. He came mainly to value my house and he didn't need much time to do that.'

'Oh, no!'

'Of course he did! Don't stick your head in the sand, girl. He's a businessman. Why else would he visit an old woman he can't abide?'

Rosalind could feel heat creeping across her cheeks.

'Anyway, after he came, I changed my will.'

Rosalind sat up very straight and said stiffly, 'You can leave your money as you like. I don't care about inheriting your property, Soph.'

'Pity, because I've left it all to you.'

'But you said you'd changed your will.'

'I just changed the conditions under which you inherit. My lawyer, Mr Dennison, has all the details.' Sophie gave her niece an urchin's mischievous smile. 'Everything's now left in a trust and your precious husband won't be able to touch a penny of it. You'll get the income, not him, and it must be paid into a bank account that's in your name only. Paul offered to manage my affairs for me, did you know? I told him I could manage them myself, thank you very much.'

'I didn't know any of this.' And the thought of her husband trying to take over Sophie's affairs didn't sit well with her. He not only dealt with their own finances, but wanted to know where every penny went, so that you couldn't even buy him a present without him knowing where you got it from and what it had cost. It was only by saving from her housekeeping money that Rosalind managed to have anything of her own. But whenever she got irritated about this, she reminded herself that he had their welfare at heart.

'Wish I could be there to see his face when the will's read,' Sophie went on. 'He'll be bitterly disappointed not to get his hands on the capital, and you're not to hand the income over to him, either. You're to keep it in your own bank account and spend it yourself. Promise me!'

'Well – if you want me to, I promise. But Paul was probably just trying to help you. He's not quite so – so mercenary.'

Sophie gave her a wry look. 'Of course he's mercenary! If he weren't, he'd not be any good at a job like that. Do you even know how much he earns?'

Rosalind shook her head, unable to meet her great-aunt's eyes.

'Well, don't tell him how much money you get from me. That'll even things up. Anyway, that's enough talking about him. I want to tell you about exactly what you'll be inheriting.'

'I didn't know you were so rich,' Rosalind faltered when the tale was over. She felt quite shocked at the thought of inheriting so much money. This house was the least of it.

Sophie looked smug. 'I did rather well with my investments, if I say so myself, and a couple of friends left me their money.' Her smile faded. 'It's sad seeing your friends die one by one. I'm the last of my circle left. It's time I went.' She picked up a little brass hand bell and rang it. 'I'm afraid I need a rest now. Can't stay upright for too long these days. Get Prue to show

33

you round the house, then you might like to go out for a walk.'

Prue took Aunt Sophie away to the bedroom they'd made out of the old dining room, then came back a few minutes later to show Rosalind to the large bedroom on the first floor, with its square bay window and big pieces of mahogany furniture. 'Don't keep Miss Worth up too late tonight,' she warned in a low voice.

'How is my aunt? Really, I mean.'

Prue shrugged. 'As you'd expect. The doctors have prescribed something for the pain, but she'll only take it at night, because it makes her so dopey. She's a brave woman and I shall miss her when she dies.'

'So shall I.'

'She likes people to ignore her condition as much as possible.'

'I'll do my best. Um – I think I will go out for a stroll. Sitting in a car all day makes me twitchy.'

On her short walk Rosalind passed a florist's and on impulse went inside. There were so many types of flowers available, even at this season, that in the end she asked for a large mixed bunch.

When Sophie reappeared that evening she looked tired, but had changed her dress and tied her long white hair smoothly back at the nape of her neck with a black velvet ribbon. Rosalind gave her the flowers and her face lit up.

'How lovely! Thank you so much, my dear. I've always loved flowers, but I can't even remember the last time anyone bought me a bunch.' She sighed, her eyes blind with memories. 'It used to be men who bought me flowers, of course. I've had quite a few bunches of red roses in my time. But they're all dead now, the men of my generation. They died so quickly. It's the women who're the survivors. Remember that, Rosalind.'

After a light but delicious meal, Prue went to clear up and the other two sat talking for a while until Sophie rubbed her forehead and sighed. 'Have to go to bed again now. Damned nuisance. Need one of those blasted injections. Call Prue, will you? I'll see you in the morning, my dear. There's some rather fine cognac in the sideboard. I can't drink it now, more's the pity, so don't stint yourself. And watch the television, if you like. It won't disturb me.'

But Rosalind didn't watch television. Instead, she sat staring at the flames of a gas fire that imitated burning logs rather well, while cradling a brandy glass in her hands. Sipping occasionally she let her thoughts wander where they would. The room was crowded with mementoes and ornaments, all Sophie Worth's life set out in careful patterns. But when it came down to it, you went out of the world on your own, as deprived of possessions as you'd come into it.

Perhaps, she thought as she got ready for bed, she'd clung to her own possessions too much.

Perhaps Paul was right about her needing a change.

In the morning Rosalind slept late, for her, because she still hadn't adjusted to the time change. When she got up around nine, she found Sophie waiting for her impatiently downstairs.

'Thought you were never going to surface. I was about to send Prue to wake you. Look – I know you spent yesterday driving, but do you feel like a trip out today?' It was typical of her not to bother with the meaningless small talk she had always despised.

'I'd love it, but should you—?'

'I hired a car and driver yesterday. Forgot to tell you last night. The injections make me a bit woozy. I want to go to the Lake District one last time. Will you come with me?'

'I'd love to. But there was no need to hire a car. I could have driven you.'

'Oh, no! Much more fun to let someone else do the driving. This way, you'll see more of the scenery and we can talk properly. I've ordered a big car so my stupid wheelchair will fit into the boot.'

The car was a grey Mercedes with a driver in navy chauffeur's uniform. Sophie giggled and nudged Rosalind as he fussed over them. 'This is doing things in style, eh?'

'Don't you always, Soph?'

The day passed swiftly. They drove north along the motorway to Kendal, then stopped for a while beside Lake Windermere. Rosalind noticed that her aunt was dozing, so sat quietly enjoying the scenery.

'I'd have bought a house up here near the lakes if it wasn't for the holidaymakers cluttering up the place,' Sophie said suddenly.

'You're awake again.'

'Of course I'm awake. Do you think I talk sense in my sleep?' She shifted uncomfortably. 'Need a toilet. One of those bigger ones for disabled folk. Would you mind helping me?'

'Of course not.'

Afterwards Rosalind pushed the wheelchair along the lakeside for a while, worried at how white her aunt's face was. She didn't go far, but found a bench with a lovely view of the water and its fractured reflections of the hills around them. They sat chatting quietly as a light breeze rippled the surface.

'Tell me about your life,' Sophie said abruptly. 'Has it been good for you?'

'Oh, yes. I've made my career out of my husband and family. They're the centre of everything, my whole life and—'

'No!' Her aunt sounded really angry. 'They're *not* your whole life. He's your husband, and important to you, but you're a person in your own right as well. You should have a life of your own and think of *your* needs as well as his. The same with your children. Never forget that.'

Silence sat between them like a chaperone for a few moments, then Sophie sighed. 'Let's go back to the car now. I'm weaker than I thought.'

'Perhaps we should go home?'

'*No!*' Sophie's voice was sharp. She looked at her niece, pleading for understanding. 'This'll probably be my last outing. Let's make the most of it, eh? We'll stop again later and I'll probably have another doze. But that doesn't matter. I'll have seen the hills and lakes again.'

She was very quiet as they drove round by Keswick and stopped near Helvellyn. 'Beautiful, isn't it?' she asked once, then nodded off before Rosalind could answer. She slept most of the way home, too.

Prue took one look at her when they got back and said firmly, 'Bed now, Miss Worth. You're not staying up for dinner tonight, either.'

'Bully!' said Sophie, but went without further protest.

'I shouldn't have let her go out,' Rosalind worried when Prue came back down to join her.

'Well, the doctors would tell you that. But in my opinion she should do whatever she wants. Does it really matter if the outing shortens her life by a few days? She enjoyed it greatly.'

'You're very good to her.'

'Not all my patients are as much fun to be with.' Prue hesitated. 'It's not my place to say it, but you will come and see her again, won't you? She's thoroughly enjoying your company.'

'Oh, yes. I'll come as often as I can. But I'll have to leave tomorrow, I'm afraid, because Paul will be home at the weekend.'

There were tears on Rosalind's cheeks as she drove away from Southport, but she was filled with admiration for Sophie's bravery. Old age was cruel and she didn't know how anyone could face death so cheerfully.

How would *she* face old age? And Paul? It would be worse for him, she was sure. She couldn't imagine him growing old gracefully. He already hated his light sprinkling of silver hairs. But he'd not escape the effects of old age any more than she would. No one did. And it was better than dying young, after all. Or one assumed it was.

She clicked her tongue in annoyance at herself for such morbid thoughts and switched on the radio. It didn't do to dwell on things. She had enough on her plate without borrowing trouble from the years ahead.

Some second honeymoon this was! She didn't think she had ever felt quite so angry at Paul. But she was glad she was here for Sophie, at least.

# Four

It was not until Saturday afternoon that a sleek, dark BMW drew up in Sexton Close and Paul emerged to struggle with the recalcitrant gate. Rosalind had been fidgeting about in the large sitting room with its icy blue decor, because she could see him arrive from there. When she saw the car stop in the street, she debated whether to go out and help with the gates, hesitated then went into the kitchen instead. Let him open the damned gates himself! And let him knock on the door and wait for her to answer it, too.

She heard the protesting screech of the gates being pushed right back, then the sound of tyres on the drive. A car door slammed, footsteps crossed the gravel and someone tried the front door. A muffled curse brought a tight smile to her face, as did the sound of the doorbell being rung, then rung again a few seconds later.

The letter box rattled. 'Ros! Are you there? Ros!'

Only then did she move, walking slowly along the hall towards the front door.

'Darling!' He planted a swift kiss on each cheek. 'Didn't you hear me arrive?'

'No.'

He looked at her, eyes narrowed, assessing the situation. 'In the black books, am I?'

She breathed deeply.

'Oh, give me a proper hug, woman, and stop sulking.' He pulled her into his arms. 'There was nothing I could do about it. The chairman had a crisis on and I had to go to the States. We'd have lost the contract if I hadn't stepped in.'

Something cold shifted uneasily inside her, then perched upon her shoulder, whispering a commentary in her ear. His first remark had been about the latest contract. 'And how are

38

you going on, Rosalind? Are you settling in all right?' she asked sarcastically.

'Hey, don't be like that, hon!'

'You'd *promised* to be there for me at Heathrow, Paul.'

'But, darling, I just explained all that and—'

'There are times when family should come first, family and wife.' She pulled away from him and looked him straight in the eyes. 'Not the chairman, or even the bloody company.'

'Without the company, we wouldn't have all this.' He gestured around them.

She didn't reply to that, didn't say, *But maybe we'd be closer to one another*. She didn't want to start a quarrel. 'Well, now you *are* here, would you like a cup of coffee?'

'Real coffee?'

'Of course.'

'I'd kill for one. You always make the best coffee.'

Suddenly she felt ashamed of her churlish greeting. 'Go and bring your things in, then, and I'll make you a cup. The kitchen's straight through the hall.'

'There's nothing much to bring. I've only got this one bag.'

'What? But you took two suitcases of stuff with you from Australia and you keep some things in the company's London flat. I thought you'd be bringing most of it down here now.'

He pulled her into his arms and sighed. His voice came from just above her right ear, low and persuasive. 'A new problem's cropped up. Look, there's no easy way to say this. I'm sorry, hon, but I can only stay till tomorrow.' Another long, sifting sigh. 'Then I'm afraid I have to go to Hong Kong.'

She jerked back against his arms. 'Hong Kong! *Hong – Kong?* But you said you'd be based in England this year. That's why I came here!' She set her hands against his chest and shoved him away. 'Paul, how *could* you?'

He ran one hand through his hair as he pulled away. 'I've only just found out. Yesterday evening, actually. That's why I'm late. Been to a briefing. Pearson in Hong Kong had a heart attack. Yesterday. Died before they could get him to hospital. I have to go and take over for a month or so till they find someone to head the Asian operation permanently. There are some negotiations at a very delicate stage. I'd have flown out this morning if it hadn't been for you. So you see, I *do* put my family first sometimes.'

A chill spread through her body. 'Then I needn't have come here at all. I'd have been closer to you in Australia. Oh, damn you, Paul, for uprooting me like this!'

She walked into the kitchen and he followed, moving around, peering out of the back window, opening the pantry door, going to investigate the mudroom. He didn't speak, didn't touch her. She knew what he was doing. Allowing her time to come to terms with his news.

Of their own accord her hands attended to the coffee. She was relieved that some part of her was still functioning, because a flock of cockatoos seemed to have settled inside her skull and were filling it with stupid, meaningless noise, shrieking in derision at her situation, her gullibility. Why in hell's name had she expected things to be different here in England? Why hadn't she held out against him? He could hardly have dragged her here by force, after all.

She plonked the cup down near him, splashing a trail of brown liquid across the white surface. 'So I'll be alone here for a whole month.'

'I'm really sorry about that.'

She filled her own cup and stood cradling it in her hands. 'Some second honeymoon this is.'

'I said I was sorry. Be reasonable, Ros. No one could have guessed that Pearson would have a heart attack.'

'I'm going home to Australia, then.'

'You *can* do that, of course . . .'

She didn't take in a single word until he finished, 'But I *will* be back in England for the rest of the spring and summer, I promise you. So why don't you reconsider? We can still be together. I have plenty of leave owing, so I'll take a week off when I get back.'

'*A whole week?*'

'Look, it's hard to get even that at this time of the year. And I've just had some time off, though I spent half of it on planes to and from Australia for your sake, so you needn't get snitty with me.'

'It's hard for you to take leave at any time of year. Any year.' He had loads of paid leave owing to him, months and

40

months of it. And he'd fretted around like a lost soul in Australia during the one week he'd spent there. He'd been *bored*! He seemed to have lost the ability to enjoy himself quietly at home like other men, which was one of the reasons she'd been thinking of divorce. She wanted a companion, not a nominal husband.

He put his arms around her again, tugging at her stiff body until it moved to rest against his and nestling his cheek against her hair. 'Don't go back to Australia, Ros. Please. A month will soon pass. I really do want us to spend some time together.' He kissed her cheek. His breath was warm in her ear and his breathing showed he was aroused.

'I'll see.' She pulled away. She didn't feel aroused. Not at all. A month could pass quickly when you had plenty to do, but time could drag when you were stuck in a rented house in a village where you knew no one. Unfortunately, where his work was concerned, Paul was a reinforced concrete wall. No use beating her head against it.

He abandoned the attempt to make love to her, but was subdued for only as long as it took him to drink the coffee, then went to get his briefcase. He saw her dirty look. 'Just some papers I need to look over today, hon.'

'You can't even give me two full days, can you?'

His voice changed, became steely. 'It's the work I do which pays for all this.'

'Then it pays for things I've never wanted. As far as I'm concerned, you're doing all that for yourself.' She went back into the kitchen and started preparing dinner, banging the pots around. Anything to keep her hands busy.

He didn't follow her and presently she heard the sound of papers rustling in the small office. He'd found that room, all right, and taken possession of it without asking her if she minded.

But as they sat and chatted after dinner, she could feel herself softening, because when he set out to charm, no one was better company than Paul. And when they went to bed the touch of his hands, the feel of his body against hers worked their usual magic.

Whatever Liz said, Rosalind couldn't imagine anything better than their loving.

41

'You're still a damned good lay,' he muttered in her ear afterwards.

'Very romantic!' she teased. 'You're not bad yourself.'

But he was asleep already. She lay awake for ages, listening to his soft even breaths. If they were going to use the word *still*, she'd apply it to her emotions.

She *still* felt angry with him. Very angry.

She *still* felt uncertain about their marriage, too.

After lunch the next day, Paul looked at his watch. 'I'll have to leave soon, hon.'

She could feel her lips tightening.

'You aren't going back to Australia, are you?'

'I suppose not.' But it was for Sophie's sake, not his.

'Good. When I get back, we'll do some entertaining, eh? I owe so many people over here. We've plenty of room for them to stay over. Or the pub in the village has some rather nice en suite rooms, I gather. You could cook some Australian specialities. It'll be fun, make a good impression.'

'I don't see how we can give a decent dinner party here. There's only minimal cutlery and crockery.'

That got his full attention. 'It's supposed to be an executive residence. Everything supplied.'

'It's quite big and the furniture is reasonable, but they've skimped on the kitchen equipment. Six of everything in the crockery line is not enough to entertain with and kitchen gadgets are practically non-existent. There's a hand beater, a plastic grater and a tin opener, and that's about all. I had to buy that coffee plunger myself.'

'Not satisfactory. I'll have a word with Gail and tell her to complain. She's good at that sort of thing.' He grinned. 'It's my bet that in a day or two the agent will get in touch with you and ask your advice about what's missing.'

'What's missing will be you,' she said and could not stop her voice coming out choked, but he was carrying his bag and briefcase out to the car and didn't hear her.

'Look, why don't you go up to Lancashire to see that aunt of yours?' he said as he slammed the boot shut. 'Stay a few days.'

She opened her mouth to tell him that she'd already been to see Sophie, but he was still speaking.

'By the time you've done that and sorted out the house ready for some serious entertaining, I'll be back from Honkers.' He gave her a quick, absent-minded hug. 'Four weeks will pass in a flash. You'll see.'

As she watched him drive away, she knew that wasn't true. Four *days* could seem like an eternity, stuck here on her own, with no family to look after, nothing familiar to comfort her.

In Australia, Jenny Stevenson stood and listened to the scolding from her supervisor with as much grace as she could muster.

'Your heart doesn't seem to be in your work, Jenny,' Mr Bennett said with that solemn expression of his. 'You should remember that you're on probation for six months before we can accept you on our permanent staff – *if* we accept you. It isn't automatic, you know.'

She stared at him in horror. Her father would kill her if she got the sack, and anyway, she needed the money even more now she was renting a flat on her own.

'Is – um, is something troubling you, my dear?'

She stared down at her feet, then realized this was an out. 'I – I've been having trouble with my – my ex-fiancé. We've just split up. I'm sorry. I didn't mean to let my work suffer.' Tears came into her eyes. Michael was still pestering her to get back together again and no way was she going to agree. In fact, he was being more than a pest and had frightened her silly last night banging on her door just before midnight. She'd never go back to him. Never.

The supervisor's voice was more gentle. 'I'm sorry. You should have said something.'

Jenny dabbed at her eyes. 'I'll try to – to do better,' she promised. She really would. However bored she was with office work. However the working days dragged. She didn't dare get the sack without her mother here to help her.

In the middle of the night she woke suddenly. Had she heard something? She lay rigid, listening with all her might.

Before she could get up to look out of the window, there was a crash, which made her squeak in shock and cower in the bed. By the light from the street lamp she saw that some-one had thrown a brick through her window.

It must be a drunk! She got up to peer out of the window, but there was no one outside. And although a light had come on in the flat next door, it winked out again as she looked, and she was left staring at the shards of glass sticking out from her window frame.

She cleared up, but couldn't get back to sleep, well not properly, only doze a little, even though being on the second floor meant she didn't have to worry about someone getting in through the window. And she was late for work while she waited for someone to come and fix a new windowpane.

It was only as she was getting into her car that she had a sudden thought. If drunks were around, you usually heard them talking or laughing. She had heard nothing. But – who else could it have been?

'Oh, no!' Her heart plummeted as she admitted what she had avoided facing until then. There was only one person who bore her a grudge. Michael. He had rung last night and she had shouted at him on the phone, then slammed it down. She felt a cold shudder run down her spine as she suddenly knew for certain it had been him who had thrown the brick.

'What good does it do?' she whispered. 'I'm not going back to him.'

She kept telling him that. Why wouldn't he believe her and leave her alone?

As she posted a letter to her mother, Rosalind noticed a craft shop on the corner opposite and was lost.

She'd only intended to buy a bit of canvas on which to do a small sampler, just to pass the time, but she forgot that as she looked round the well-stocked shelves. And the more she looked, the more the determination grew in her to set herself up for her own type of embroidery, raised stumpwork, the thing she loved doing.

Since Paul had left her here, all alone, it was only right that he pay for the new equipment and materials she would need from the housekeeping account. It wasn't going to come out of her own money this time. And she was not only going to do some new pictures, she was going to take over one of the bedrooms and leave her embroidery things lying around all the time. Just let him complain about her mess again! Ever.

She would send for some of her finished pieces, too, and put them on the walls to cheer herself up. She'd get them professionally packed and airfreighted out. Rebellion burned through her, hot and reckless, and it felt good, damn good, even if it was only a small domestic protest.

When she got home she spread out her purchases, stroking the hanks of embroidery thread and snipping the new scissors in the air. Her eyes became unfocused as she debated what subject to work on. She had several ideas in mind, but a new one blossomed suddenly. The family. Her family. All of them: Paul, herself, the three children. She'd never done a family portrait before. Of course, she'd have to work out a design and create figures which showed their personalities, but she had photos of her children and husband with her. She'd start sketching a layout after tea as she watched television. Sometimes it took a while to get the right composition.

The icy unhappiness inside her began to thaw, though only a little. She was still missing her family and friends dreadfully. She'd never been away from her daughters before and neither of them was a good correspondent. On that thought, she did a quick calculation of time differences and picked up the phone.

Louise answered it. 'Hey, Mum! How are you?'

They discussed university, then Jenny. 'Yeah, she's got over her split with Michael. Well, he was a real dork, wasn't he? I don't know where she finds them! I wouldn't even fancy him if you blindfolded me. What? No, Gran's out shopping. I'll tell her you called. Of course I'm coping with the studying!' Which was a lie. But no one was going to find that out for a long time.

Phew! Louise thought as she put the phone down. Good thing Gran wasn't in. The two of them had had another row this morning. What did it matter if you left a few plates lying around the kitchen? Anyway, what else had Gran to do with her time but clear up?

Louise went to fiddle with the kettle, sighing. The reason she wasn't coping with her studies was that she wasn't finding them at all interesting. *Business studies!* Why had her father insisted on them all doing that sort of degree? Not Arts, he'd insisted, because that was an expensive way of joining the dole queue and he was the one paying for all this, thank you very much. And not architecture, either. There were a lot of young architects struggling to make a living.

Well, she didn't really want to do architecture. She'd only said that to stir him up. She hadn't got high enough scores to get into medicine, even if she'd wanted to, but she had toyed with the idea of training as a nurse. First aid had been a non-academic option at school and she'd enjoyed it very much, been good at it, too. She liked looking after people who were injured, and the bloodier the better. Sandy had slashed her wrist by accident one day when they were fooling around in the kitchen and she'd known exactly what to do. The doctor had praised her efforts, too, which was more than her bloody father ever did.

But Dad had the money, so they had to dance to his tune. Life wasn't fair. But at least those tablets Sandy had got her were working. She wasn't at all hungry nowadays – though her gran hadn't congratulated her on losing the two kilos, just tried to nag her into eating more. Honestly! Her whole family was so far out of touch it wasn't true. If you were fat no one fancied you. It was as simple as that. Thin was in.

The conversation with her younger daughter had relieved some of Rosalind's worries, but it wasn't the same as being there and seeing everyone. She rang Liz afterwards, but there was no answer. She tried several times over the next day or two, but to no avail. And the answering machine wasn't on, either. She hoped everything was all right. Liz had been in a very brittle mood when she'd left.

The next time Rosalind rang Perth, she caught her mother in, which was what she really wanted, and they had a nice long chat, though the question of how Louise was doing brought a stiff tone to her mother's voice. Rosalind debated pushing for more information, then decided against it. She had enough problems managing on her own, was hating the loneliness.

At one point she asked if Audrey had seen Liz.

'Someone said she'd gone away on holiday.'

'Oh? Where?' Liz had said nothing to her about holidays and they always shared their plans with each other.

'Singapore or Hong Kong, I think. Or was it both? I can't remember.'

'But the university term has started. How has Bill managed to get away?'

'Liz was going on her own, apparently. Her mother said she'd been feeling depressed and needed something to cheer her up.'

'I see.' That sounded ominous to Rosalind. Surely Liz wouldn't be putting her threat into operation? It was bad enough Bill being unfaithful, but two wrongs didn't make a right. 'Strangely enough, Paul's in Hong Kong, too, Mum.' She then had to explain about Pearson dying and it being an emergency, and her mother said all the things she'd been thinking, but of course she couldn't agree with them too strongly because that would be disloyal.

'Wouldn't it be funny if Paul and Liz bumped into one another?' she said, to divert her mother's attention.

'It'd be a miracle if they did. That place is so crowded you can hardly move around at more than a shuffle, and you can't even see the people across the street clearly for heads bobbing in front of you.'

Rosalind smiled. Her mother had hated her one visit to Hong Kong. Well, she hadn't liked it much, herself, either. The people were pleasant, the hotels good and the tour guide had been charming, but Rosalind had found the masses of people everywhere claustrophobic after the wide open spaces of Western Australia.

Liz hated being on holiday alone. The hotel in Hong Kong was big and luxurious, but most of the guests seemed to be passing through as part of tours. She'd tried sitting in the foyer, hoping to strike up a conversation with someone, anyone, but people just walked past her.

And as for finding a man, forget it, baby! Most of the guests at the hotel were quite elderly. If she was going to the trouble of having an affair, it had to be with someone decent. At this rate it'd probably be no one, but she needn't tell Bill that. She'd invent some gorgeous hunk and describe the encounters in intimate detail. An American tourist, she'd say. Perhaps she should buy a couple of romance novels, see if they gave her any ideas.

But that evening, a miracle occurred. Someone came up to her table in the restaurant and said, 'What the hell are you doing here in Honkers, Liz Foxen?'

She gaped up at him. 'Paul! But you're in England!'

'I was yesterday.' He glanced down. There was only one table setting. Curiouser and curiouser. 'Isn't Bill with you?'

'No, I'm on my own.'

'Want some company?'

'I'd love some.' It was one thing to swan off and leave your erring husband wondering what you were getting up to, but another entirely for a woman to amuse herself on her own at night in a foreign city.

He sat down and beckoned a waiter.

She watched the man fuss over him. Paul certainly knew how to get good service. Bill always got fobbed off with tables in corners.

Paul looked up and winked at her as the waiter continued to fuss. 'Want me to order for you?'

'Yes. I don't know what half the things are. I was going to have the bouillabaisse.'

'Wouldn't advise it. Not here. The seafood can be very dodgy because the harbour is so polluted.'

'Whoops! I had prawns last night. Do you think I'll live?'

'Oh, yes.'

His smile was warm and his eyes said he found her attractive. Well, it made a change for someone to feel that way. In fact, it felt wonderful.

The food was excellent. A series of small dishes, each perfectly presented, accompanied by superb wines. Too much wine, perhaps. When the meal was over and Paul suggested a cocktail, she found her head spinning as she tried to follow him to the bar.

'I think you've had enough to drink,' he said with a chuckle, steadying her.

She clung to his arm. Lean and muscular. Bill had let himself go a bit lately, was getting a distinct paunch. 'I never could hold my wine.'

'Come on, then, milady, let Sir Galahad escort you up to your chamber.'

At her door he hesitated, then asked, 'Want to meet for a

meal tomorrow evening? I'll be working during the day or I'd offer to show you round.'

'I've booked a coach tour. Going out to see a big Buddhist temple. But I'm free in the evening.'

'Shall we say about eight, then? I'll pick you up here.' He glanced up at her room number.

This was more like it, she thought as she closed the door. Paul Stevenson was a charming bastard when he wanted to be.

It was only then that Liz realized – they hadn't mentioned Rosalind at all after the first round of greetings. Not once. How strange! But then, they hadn't mentioned Bill, either. And of course she wouldn't tell Paul what she had threatened to do. That was between her and her husband.

But it'd been great to have someone to talk to! She was really looking forward to the next evening.

## What is Raised Embroidery?

*Although domestic stumpwork/raised embroidery embraces flatwork and a large variety of stitches, the definitive features of this style might be summed up as follows:*

*The use of 'needlemade fabrics' in the form of needlelace . . .*

*The use of wires and vellum, bound with silk and other threads, to provide texture and decorative relief features.*

*The application of a wealth of supplementary ornamentation in a variety of available materials, including embroidered silk fabrics, pearls, beads, semi-precious stones, real hair, feathers, mica, metal threads/strips, braids . . .*

*The strong use of figurative subjects within an otherwise natural design.*

*(Hirst, p.8)*

# Five

When Aunt Sophie rang a few days later with an invitation to go to Southport again, Rosalind accepted at once. 'As long as you're not too tired for visitors, Soph.'

'I really enjoyed your last visit, dear.'

This time Southport looked grey and unwelcoming. People were hurrying along the pavements, umbrellas much in evidence, headscarves shrouding women's faces into anonymity. She shivered as she parked outside her aunt's and ran through the pouring rain to knock on the door.

When Prue opened it, her face crumpled and tears filled her eyes. 'I tried to catch you before you left this morning. You're –' she hesitated, then finished – 'too late, I'm afraid.'

'What do you mean?' But she knew, really.

'Your aunt died in her sleep.'

As Prue held the door open, Rosalind walked into the hall and stood there. It was a moment before she could speak. 'I can't believe she's gone. Soph was always so *alive*. And I spoke to her on the phone only last night.'

'I'd grown very fond of her, too. More than I usually do with patients.' Prue wiped her eyes. 'Do you want to see her? The undertakers have attended to things – she wanted to lie in her own home, not in a funeral parlour, and I said I'd stay with her. She looks very peaceful.'

'Oh.' Rosalind swallowed. 'Um, Prue – to be honest I've never seen a dead person before.' Not even her own father. 'Maybe I should just – you know, remember her alive.'

Prue put her arm round Rosalind's shoulders. 'If you want my professional opinion, I think it's better to say goodbye properly. There's nothing to be afraid of, you know.'

'Oh. Well, all right.' Feeling shaky inside and wondering

why she wasn't weeping, she who even wept at sad items about complete strangers on the television news, Rosalind followed Prue into her aunt's bedroom, hesitated just inside the door, then walked over to stand by the bed.

To her surprise Sophie dead was still someone she loved. 'She does look peaceful,' she whispered, not knowing why she was speaking in hushed tones.

'Yes. And if it's any comfort to you, I think she was more than ready to go. Though she'd have been sorry not to see you again. Isn't it wonderful that you came to England when you did? That you were able to say goodbye to her properly?'

Rosalind felt a surge of guilt at how reluctant she had been to leave Australia, at how her aunt had been asking her to come and visit for years. 'I'd like to sit with her for a while. On my own, if you don't mind.'

Prue gave her a quick hug. 'Sure. I've put you in the same bedroom as before.'

Rosalind pulled a chair up to the bed and found herself talking to her aunt. 'I'm going to miss you very much, Soph. In fact, I don't know what I'll do without you for the next few weeks.' She blinked her eyes, but no tears came. Why wasn't she weeping?

She sat on for a while, feeling a sense of peace in the quiet, elegant room. Prue was right. It was good to say goodbye properly and, knowing how much her aunt had hated her increasing incapacity, she could not be sorry that Soph's suffering had now ended.

Soon she found herself talking again. 'I'm still annoyed at Paul, you know. He's gone off to Hong Kong. For a whole month. That's why I was counting on coming to see you and . . .' She broke off. She could hear her aunt's answer to that echoing in her head.

*Count on yourself, girl. You're the only person in the whole world you can really rely on.* Soph had said that to her so many times before, but it had never meant as much as it did now, when it was merely an unspoken echo.

She sighed and stood up. 'I'll try, Soph.' Then she went off to ring her mother and tell her the sad news.

Her mother seemed a bit uptight, but Rosalind didn't ask if anything were wrong. She had enough on her plate at present coping here. More than enough. If her daughter was misbehaving, she didn't want to know yet.

The funeral was held two days later. Only three neighbours and the solicitor attended, apart from Rosalind and Prue. When the neighbours had left the cemetery, Mr Dennison came up to Rosalind, leaning heavily on his stick. He looked top-heavy with age, like a tree ready to be blown down by the next gale.

'Could you possibly come and see me in my office this afternoon, Mrs Stevenson, about your aunt's will? I only work two days a week now, so if you don't come today, it'll have to be next week, I'm afraid.' He patted his chest. 'Ticker's not doing too well. Got to take things easy.'

'All right. I'll come today.'

He presented her with a business card, then walked slowly away.

The two women strolled back to the car park in a companionable silence.

'Have you made any plans yet?' Rosalind asked as they got into her car.

'No. But if you like – well, your aunt suggested after your last visit that I stay on for a few days to help you go through the house and see what you want to keep. I know where everything is, you see. I've helped her sort out all her things over the past few months. She was very anxious to leave everything in good order.' Prue paused and sighed. 'I shall miss living there. It's a lovely house, a real home. I suppose you'll be selling it?'

'I suppose so, eventually. I'd like you to stay on for a while. I hadn't really thought about dealing with Soph's things.'

As they went inside, Rosalind stared around. She couldn't believe that this gracious old house belonged to her now and still felt more like a visitor than an owner.

At the solicitor's that afternoon, Mr Dennison summarized the arrangements Sophie had made.

Rosalind nodded. 'Yes, she told me all that.'

He looked at her sideways, as if assessing her, then added, 'She was a bit worried about your husband, even so, worried he'd try to take the money off you, or that you'd just give it to him.'

Rosalind flushed. 'She made her wishes quite clear and you can rely on me to respect them. I'll open a separate bank account for the money.' It upset her that Soph had considered her so much under Paul's thumb. It upset her even more that there had been good reason for that belief.

Mr Dennison nodded. 'Right, then. Do we have your address in England? No? Well, could you just jot it down, then? And your phone number? Good. Now – anything else you want to ask me?'

'Um – about Prue's wages? My aunt wanted her to stay on for a few days, to help me clear things out. She knows where everything is, you see.'

'Just send us a written note when she stops work. Until then, the estate will continue to pay her weekly at the reduced rate agreed upon.'

When Rosalind left the lawyer's office, she decided to go for a walk along the seafront. She needed some fresh air – and some quiet thinking time, too.

She found a series of neat, if uninspired gardens surrounding artificial sea lakes – well, she presumed they were artificial. They were too regular to be natural, surely? It was a cold day, but sunny, and there were few holidaymakers so early in the season.

At one stage she sat on a bench and held her face up to the sun. More changes, she told it.

It continued to smile down at her. What had she expected? it seemed to be asking. Life was full of change. As if to emphasize that, some clouds passed across it and the light went dull before the clouds moved on and everything brightened again.

Rosalind sucked in a deep breath, a breath shaky with grief not only for Sophie, but for herself, for her loneliness and uncertainty, her desperate need to sort her own life out. What did she really want? To become a company wife and follow Paul around the world – or to put down roots somewhere on her own? She knew what the first choice would entail and as for the second, well, she'd been doing that for years. It was the one thing she'd stood up to Paul about. And it wasn't truly satisfactory, either.

Sighing, she stood up and began to walk back to the town centre. Since Paul would not be back for a while, she would make her first priority going through Sophie's possessions.

I'll try to be stronger next time I see him, she vowed as she walked up the garden path. Even if I do decide to become a company wife, I'll make sure I have my own life too. Things like my embroidery. I must. I can't go on like this.

Tim edged forward, his eyes darting from side to side. If the cops caught him – if they put him in prison . . . but the buyer muttered what he wanted, handed over the money and hurried off as soon as he had the small packet. The next sale was just as easy.

When Tim had sold all his packages, he shuddered with relief and walked back to the bar. Handing over the money, he accepted the percentage agreed on – which was quite good pay for an hour's work.

'See,' said Wayne afterwards. 'It was easy. We'll work for a while here, then move on. How about buying me a drink with your profits? And I bought some stuff for tonight. We can share it, if you like.'

'No, thanks. I've got a thumping head. I'm not . . .' Tim paused for a moment as he realized what his decision meant. But he couldn't be any more unhappy than he had been lately, and it was the only real alternative. He looked up and stared at Wayne. 'I'm giving the hard stuff up. It doesn't agree with me.'

Wayne laughed, a sneering sound. 'It's a bit late to stop, isn't it? I mean, you'd need medical help to kick the habit.'

'I've only been using when I could afford it, not every day.'

'You can afford it easily now. Pusher's discount's quite helpful. Quit later, if you must *see the light*.' He tittered as if he had made a joke.

'I want to quit now,' Tim insisted. The haggard, sometimes desperate faces of the people who had bought from him underlined what the stuff did to you sooner or later, demonstrating it better than any films and lectures ever could. 'Look, I'm going back to our room now. Don't bring any chicks home tonight, right? I need some sleep.' He didn't even wait for an answer, just turned and walked away.

Over the next week or two, he pushed drugs only to survive and did try to give the stuff up, to Wayne's great amusement. He slipped up a couple of times, but he did cut it down, way down, and that was a start. His friend, on the other hand, was indulging himself in every new treat that came along and wasn't eating well. Wayne looked thin and feverish, full of energy one minute, sagging around their sleazy little room the next.

Which also kept reinforcing what shit-heads they were to have got themselves into this mess.

Tim bought a money belt and it never left his body, because with his clearer head he had realized that Wayne had been going through his things when he was out and helping himself. As his belt grew heavier, he found another hiding place for his passport and part of his savings, away from their motel. Risky, but who'd look in a neglected cemetery urn?

When he had enough saved for the fare, he was going back to Australia and he was never, ever going to leave it again. He didn't tell Wayne or anyone else about his plans. He was just going to take off one day. He'd already sussed out the quickest way to get to the nearest airport. He'd be gone before anyone realized it, flying to another city before booking his flight home. Oh, yes, he had it all figured out.

Sometimes the thought of home, and of his mother especially, made him want to break down and sob his heart out. He hadn't been fair to her. He'd mocked and scorned her, had encouraged Louise to do the same. His mother didn't deserve that. He desperately wanted to see her and tell her how much he loved her.

Shit! If Wayne saw him crying like this, he'd laugh himself silly. And anyway, becoming sentimental was no way to get out of this mess. Tim knew he had to keep his cool, save his money and run for it when the right moment came.

Louise glared at her grandmother. 'What do you mean, I'm grounded? What do you think I am, a child?'

'Yes, I do. You're only seventeen. That's not grown up in my book.'

'Well, it is in everyone else's. Anyway, I'm nearly eighteen.' And no longer a virgin. But sex wasn't all it was cracked

56

up to be, not by a long chalk. Or else Todd wasn't very good at it. What a let-down that had been!

'You're not eighteen for three months yet. And why didn't your parents let you have a flat if you're so grown-up? Why did they want you to live here with me while they were away?'

'Because my mother is as stupidly old-fashioned as you are!'

'Well, at least Rosalind is polite, unlike her daughter.'

Louise got up and moved towards the front door. 'Grounded, eh? How are you going to keep me in the house, then?'

Audrey gaped at her. 'Are you going to disobey me?'

'You bet. Just watch!' Louise opened the door, swept a mocking bow and walked out, slamming it hard behind her.

Audrey sank down on the nearest chair, legs trembling. She might be old-fashioned, but she wasn't stupid and Louise had definitely been taking something yesterday. She'd been all dreamy and stupid-looking when she'd come home, not expecting her grandmother to be waiting up for her at two o'clock in the morning.

What am I going to do? she wondered. I wish I'd never taken this on. I'm too old for all these confrontations. But I'm not giving in. This is *my* house and as long as she's here, she'll keep to my standards.

The trouble was, what other sanctions could she apply? And how enforce them?

Feeling out of her depth, she went across the street to see John, who was a great comfort to her. He'd told her she was crazy taking Louise in, but he hadn't said I told you so once when he'd been proved right.

Audrey knew if she gave him any encouragement, he'd like to be more than a friend, but she wasn't sure she wanted to live with anyone again. She enjoyed living alone. Her family and friends worried about her, but she had a quiet, happy life – or at least, she had been happy until Louise joined her.

It was nice, though, having John to turn to, to go out with from time to time. Someone who really seemed to care about her problems.

'I'll give Louise a week longer,' she said after talking it over with him. 'If things don't improve, I'll ring my daughter and say it's too much for me.'

'Why not ring the father? He's a damn sight closer to hand.'

'Yes, of course. You're quite right. It's about time he took a hand in the everyday problems of raising of his children, instead of leaving it all to my daughter.'

With Prue's help, Rosalind spent a few days going through the house. She had expected it to be a chore, but instead found it fascinating. Sophie had been a hoarder and there were mementoes dating back to the 1920s and even earlier, the residue of many lives, other members of the family, people Rosalind had never even heard of before.

Soph had put together a family tree and labelled all the photographs, so that her great-niece would be able to identify them. And oh, Rosalind did love those photographs! Album after album of sepia prints, all neatly labelled as to subjects and year – or approximate year in some cases. 'Aren't they wonderful?' she exclaimed one afternoon.

Prue nodded. 'One or two of them date back to the 1860s. That makes a shiver run down my spine. Miss Worth wrote her memoirs, too.' She went to the bookcase and pulled out a huge bound ledger, the sort they had used in old offices.

Rosalind opened the book at random. Soph's familiar spiky handwriting. It should have made her weep, but it didn't. Why hadn't she been able to weep for her aunt? Why was the grief just sitting inside her in a tight bundle? It was so unlike her. 'I shall enjoy reading these.'

'You'd better take them with you, then. You don't want them being carted away with the rest of the stuff.'

'I shan't have anything carted away yet, Prue. I may want – no, I definitely *shall* want to keep some of her things. And I'd like my children to see this place before I close it down. There are some lovely pieces of furniture. I'm going to ship them back to Australia and keep them in the family.'

Before she left, she arranged for Prue to stay on for a few weeks, rent-free, then set off back to Dorset.

She drove slowly. There was so much to think about. What was she going to do about her life? There were still nearly three weeks to go before Paul would return. She had to come to some decisions before then.

\* \* \*

58

Jenny groped through the mists of sleep and picked up the phone. Who could be ringing in the middle of the night? She jerked into full wakefulness at the thought that something might be wrong with her mother in England.

She could hear someone breathing heavily at the other end of the line and yelled, 'Stop this, Michael Lazzoni! You hear me? It won't get you anywhere. I'm not coming back to you and that's that.' She slammed down the phone but within seconds it started ringing again.

She stared at it, her breath coming in gasps, as if she'd been running. What was she going to do about this harassment? She'd asked at the police station, but they said they couldn't really help without proof, and the phone company seemed to think the calls would die down of their own accord. How had Michael got hold of her new number, anyway? She'd only given it to her close friends and had sworn them to strictest secrecy.

When the ringing began to irritate her, she lifted the phone and let it drop instantly, cutting the connection. But it was ringing again within the minute, so she left it off the hook.

Michael was stalking her – there was no other word for it – waiting outside work and staring at her, following her in his car. She didn't know what to do about it, who to turn to. Let's face it, she was scared out of her tiny.

If only her mother was here! Or even her father. She smiled wryly in the darkness. This was actually the sort of thing he'd be the best person to handle. But she couldn't face his scorn. She'd give it a little longer. Surely Michael would grow tired of pestering her?

Soon after Rosalind arrived back in Burraford Destan, the phone rang and Paul snapped, 'Where the *hell* have you been, Ros? I've been calling you for days. I was thinking of getting on to the police to check that you were all right.'

Why hadn't he, then? 'I've been in Southport.'

'But I rang there. Twice. No one answered. I presumed the witch lady was away.'

She felt angry at the way he referred to Sophie and was strangely reluctant to tell him the sad news. 'How's Hong Kong?'

'Great. Busy as ever.'

'Have you run into Liz? She's there on holiday.'

There was a silence, just the sound of the line humming and fizzling.

'Paul? Didn't you hear me?'

'Sorry, bad line. What did you say?'

'I asked if you'd run into Liz.'

'Why should I have done that?'

'She's on holiday there.'

'There are rather a lot of people in Hong Kong, as you know from your own experience. Bloody millions of them, actually! Wouldn't be my favourite place for a permanent posting, I can tell you. Anyway, never mind all that. Tell me how you're getting on with the house. Have you sorted things out with the agents? Some rather important clients will be in town next month. I'd like to give them a country weekend. You'd better explore the district, see if there are any stately homes nearby. Those Americans adore them.'

When she didn't reply immediately, he asked sharply, 'Ros, are you listening?'

'Yes. I'll see what I can do. The agent's authorized me to buy some more equipment.'

'What do you mean, you'll see what you can do? Is there some problem I don't know about?'

She hesitated, but she had to tell him sometime. 'Yes. There is rather. Aunt Sophie died last week.'

Silence, then, 'Did she leave you anything?'

She slammed the phone down.

When it began to ring again, she waited for eight rings before picking it up.

'Ros?'

'Yes.'

'We got cut off. Is something wrong? Why did it take you so long to pick the phone up again?'

'We didn't get cut off, actually. I put the receiver down. I've just lost a relative I loved very much and all you asked about was what she'd left me.'

Silence again, then, 'Hell, don't take things to heart, Ros. You know me. I'm the financial manager of the family.'

'Not this time you aren't.'

His voice became very soft. 'What – exactly – do you mean by that?'

She smiled as she told him. And afterwards, when he started complaining, saying they'd have to try to overset the will's conditions, she didn't slam the receiver down, but replaced it gently in its holder. It started to ring but she didn't pick it up. Instead, she poured herself a glass of her aunt's cognac and raised it mockingly. 'Well, Soph, you'd be pleased with me today. The new independent Rosalind's first act of rebellion.' Small, but immensely satisfying.

The next day her embroideries arrived from Australia. They felt like old friends. She carried them into the large sitting room and hung them on the wall, stacking the tacky prints they replaced in a corner of the attic bedroom with their cartoon-like blue roses hidden.

Much cheered, she began working on the new embroidery, the family group. Her preliminary sketch was of Paul, taken from a photo she'd brought with her. She'd tried to draw his figure several times, but it hadn't come out as she'd wanted. Now, still angry with him, she tried again. And it was so right, so absolutely right.

It would go in the centre, of course.

She started work on the head first. Muslin face, lightly padded. Dark brown embroidery silk for hair, boyishly tousled. Predator's stance.

At that thought, she stopped stitching. *Predator?* Paul wasn't a predator. He was just – a little aggressive and opportunistic.

*He's a predator! Admit it.* The voice in her head sounded like Sophie's.

OK, she told it. You're right, really. He is a predator. But there have been times when I've been glad of his strength. And at least he's looked after his family – in his own way. He's not like some men, going off having affairs, behaving irresponsibly.

She continued sewing. Sometimes she had to make two or three heads to get the face right, but not this time. At first try she got Paul right. He was to be an arrogant figure, arms folded, dominating the foreground, standing on his own. Why had she not realized before how dominating he was? Funny how the embroidery seemed to be helping her to see things more clearly than usual.

Was she going to continue letting him rule the roost? Her small act of defiance yesterday was not going to change much. She shook her head ruefully. She'd never been good at dealing with him in the past, why should she be any better in the future?

But on that thought she looked up and promised Sophie's hovering shade she'd continue to do what she could to stand up for herself. She'd at least try. She felt better for that, as well as apprehensive.

# Heads and Faces

*The head is usually the first part of the human figure to be embroidered on the ground fabric or applied to it. The soft-sculpture technique . . . is both versatile and lively . . .*

*Obtaining a head that is of a correct size for the design is often a question of trial and error . . . Insufficient soft filling will result in a flat, uninteresting face . . .*

*It is more important to create the desired impression than to copy slavishly from the design source.*

*(Hirst, pp.42–6)*

# Six

During the next few days Rosalind spent a lot of time thinking about her situation and relationships as her clever fingers built up the figure of Paul in her embroidery. This wasn't at all like one of her usual pictures, it was – it was more a search for understanding, she decided during a stormy afternoon, watching the rain march across the hills towards her, then splatter against the windowpanes of the bedroom she used as her workroom. This wasn't just a pleasurable activity, but a necessity, and it was taking far longer to do than usual because she seemed to be spending a lot of time staring into space, lost in the dark tangles of her own thoughts.

When the figure of her husband was finished, she held the square of material at arm's length and stared at it in amazement. Such a strutting, arrogant creature! And yet – it was Paul!

Was she being cruel to him, creating a caricature? No, she decided reluctantly, she was being truthful, using her artist's eye. Paul's experiment had backfired on him. Change of season, he'd called this visit to England. Change of perception, it seemed to be for her – about herself as well as him.

She set the piece aside for a while because working on it was so traumatic. She couldn't face doing herself or her children yet, not if their figures were going to reveal as much as Paul's had.

For the next embroidery she chose a charming thirties scene with children playing in a park, based on one of Soph's old photographs. It was a relief to work on that after the wrenching emotion of doing Paul.

She was no longer sorry she'd come on this trip, because it meant she had said farewell properly to Soph. And the money she'd been left made her feel better about herself, more confident somehow.

It fretted her that Paul was so far away and contacted her so infrequently, because she wanted, no, *needed* to discuss their future. They hadn't talked enough in the past, not seriously, anyway. Improved communication could only strengthen their relationship in the long run, even if it was painful. Twenty-four years together must mean they were basically on track as a couple. Paul wasn't like Bill Foxen, after all.

Liz let Paul swing her round the dance floor and gave herself up to enjoyment. She had danced with him before, of course she had, but it hadn't felt like this, as if they were alone in the universe. Other faces blurred around them. She looked up and found him smiling down at her.

'Enjoying yourself, Liz?'

'Oh, yes.'

'Me, too.'

As he pulled her closer, Paul could not help wondering if Liz had meant what she'd said to Ros about 'sauce for the goose'. He had dismissed the idea then, but what was Liz doing on her own here in Hong Kong if she hadn't meant it?

He shouldn't think about such things, definitely not. Rule number one: never foul your own nest. But the feel of Liz's small firm breasts against his chest, the smell of her perfume, the pleasure of her company and intelligent conversation – well, they were all having an inevitable effect. He only hoped it wasn't too noticeable.

It was. Liz smiled as she nestled against him and felt his arousal. She wished the dance would go on for ever. Even if it was only Paul, it was good to feel a man get hard because of her, especially a man as attractive as this one. She had seen the other women in the restaurant looking at him. Well, look all you want, ladies! she thought triumphantly. Tonight, he's mine.

That made her blink. Whatever was she thinking about? He wasn't hers. He was Rosalind's. Her best friend's husband, for heaven's sake! What sort of woman was she to fantasize about him, press herself against him like this? She pulled away, only too aware of her own body's reactions. And his.

'I think this is getting too – too . . .'

He didn't let go of her hand, didn't stop moving in time to the music. 'I'm enjoying myself, Liz. Very much.'

She swallowed hard, then the words crept out of their own accord. 'So am I.'

'Then why stop?' He pulled her closer and started dancing again. She couldn't resist the invitation behind those words, because it was balm to her pain.

Any more than he could resist following up on her unspoken consent. A man's sexual needs were so much more pressing than a woman's.

One fine but cold day Rosalind decided not to sit around and mope today. A really long walk would do her good.

The neighbours, who had invited her in for morning tea once, had told her about the wonderful scenery you could only see properly on foot, all signposted for walkers, apparently. The lady at number seven had even lent her a book of walks, graded from easy to energetic. Rosalind decided to try something of medium distance to begin with, flipping through the book. No, a mile wasn't enough. Three miles would be just right. That would tire her out and then she'd maybe get a good night's sleep, for a change.

Lovely, she told herself as she set off. But she'd never been one for solitary walks, or solitary anything, come to that. She was really missing her circle of friends, not just Liz, but the others she'd known for years, the ones she went to the theatre with, or out for cosy little feminine lunches. Her mother, too.

With the sun shining and a moderate wind blowing her along, Rosalind did feel better for a while. The countryside was truly beautiful and there was a blaze of daffodils in gardens and even along the sides of the road sometimes. There were clumps of purple aubretia, too, forming an attractive contrast with the yellow, and often tumbling out of crevices in the grey stone walls that edged many of the gardens.

She passed picturesque cottages which would look good in an embroidery, even stopping to photograph one or two. But her fingers were so cold with her gloves off that she messed up one snap and had to do it again.

The inhabitants of those cottages probably had more sense than she did and were staying inside, keeping warm. Only idiots went for walks on freezing cold days like this.

She was an idiot. Definitely.

The walkers' trail had been clearly marked so far, but suddenly the path split into three and there was no indication as to which way she should go. She pulled the guidebook out of her shoulder bag, but could get no help from it. Shrugging, she stuffed it back, wrapped her scarf more tightly round her neck and turned left because that looked the most used of the three tracks.

It twisted down a steep slope into a small wood. Leafless trees surrounded her and bare brown branches swept at the grey overcast sky like giant brooms, while the skeletons of last year's leaves were still piled in hollows. When did the new leaves come out here, for heaven's sake? It was April already, allegedly spring.

The sun went in and suddenly everything seemed to take on a sinister feel. Charcoal clouds raced one another across the sky and the landscape lost every vestige of colour. Here in the woods there were only greys and browns and muddy hues – earth and rock and decay. She glanced up anxiously, hoping the rain would hold off until she got back.

One moment she was striding along at a cracking pace, the next she trod on some gravel and felt it roll beneath her feet. She scrabbled desperately to keep her balance, found only other loose stones and cried out as she lost it completely. She felt herself falling awkwardly and called out again. But only the trees heard her.

As she hit the ground, the breath was slammed out of her and she lay half-stunned for a moment. There was no sound to be heard, apart from that damned howling wind and her own ragged breathing. Her ankle hurt. She moved it cautiously and couldn't help moaning as pain clamped its teeth into her. Was the bone broken?

She made an attempt to get up, yelping as she tried to put some weight on that knee and bumped the ankle. And suddenly, it was all too much. She fell back on the ground, with sobs forcing themselves up her throat in painful bursts of harsh noise. She could lie here and die of exposure and no one would know, or even care.

Delayed grief for Sophie hit her in a secondary wave and

she lay there weeping helplessly, her head pillowed on her arms, sobbing out her misery on the rocky ground.

On that cold spring day, Jonathon Destan also decided to go for a walk. He'd been meaning to check out the unfenced bit of land above the grove and at least string a token wire barrier across it with a *Private – Keep Out* notice before the summer influx of tourists. Several walkers had taken a wrong turn the previous year and had then treated the grounds like a public park, leaving litter and other, more disgusting, signs of their passing.

He strolled slowly across the gardens and paused to look back at the house, his gaze softening as it always did. He loved his home. It was as much a part of him as his own body and he didn't intend to let anyone take it away from him. Well, Isabel had no reason to break the family trust – even the courts had recognised that, since everything would go to his elder son in due course – but his ex-wife had certainly taken all his spare money in lieu. He didn't know how he was going to manage. He'd tried to think of some way to earn money because the days of landed gentry living on their rents were well past. Only – what was he qualified to do except manage this small estate?

He sighed. He wanted to support his two sons and pay for a good education, of course he did, but he also wanted them to have Destan Manor as their inheritance. Not an old ruin no one could afford to maintain, but a beautiful home that had been lived in by the same family for several centuries. A wave of bitterness washed through him. What he had really wanted was to bring up his children here and potter along, keeping the place up to scratch – but Isabel, no doting mother, had taken his sons away from him out of sheer spite and the bloody courts had supported her.

From further up the slope he heard a noise he couldn't place and stopped to listen. It sounded like – oh, hell, it was! – someone was sobbing! He moved forward a little, peering cautiously through the trees to see a figure huddled on the ground, a woman. Her whole body was shaking with the passion of her weeping.

The last thing he needed just now was to get involved in

someone else's troubles, but he couldn't force himself to move on. She sounded so very unhappy. And she was lying in the place the family always called Araminta's Grove, because one of his ancestors had loved that quiet spot above all others. He'd taken refuge here himself a few times during the quarrel-filled year before he and Isabel had split up. In late spring there were bluebells under the trees and in summer it was a place of filtered green light and whispering leaves.

He studied the woman. She definitely wasn't from the village. He knew all the permanent residents by sight. Another tourist gone astray, no doubt. But it was a strange place to let out her grief. And a strange time of year for walkers.

The sobbing went on and on. Dammit! I can't leave the poor bitch like that, he thought. He went right up to her without her even noticing him, cleared his throat and asked, 'Can I help you?'

She didn't hear that, either. In the end he had to bend and touch her shoulder, repeating his question.

'Oh!' She jerked upright in shock, then whimpered in pain and clutched at her leg. 'I didn't hear you coming,' she muttered, turning away to brush futilely at her face with her sleeve. But that didn't prevent more fat tears from overloading her eyes and tracking down her wet cheeks.

Oh, hell, how could you leave anyone in such anguish? He knelt beside her cradling her in his arms. 'Shh! Don't. Whatever it is, we'll sort something out. Shh, now.'

Gradually, the soft comforting sound of his voice penetrated her distress and she began to calm down. As she realized she was sitting weeping against the chest of a total stranger, she gulped a few times and managed to stop sobbing. But when he looked down, Jonathon saw that she was still clutching his rough jacket as if it were a lifeline. Perhaps it was.

Her hair was fair, a sort of ash blonde, fluffy and longish. Not dyed, as his ex-wife's had been, but quite natural in colour. This close, he could see a few silver hairs among the pale strands and he had a sudden urge to run his fingers through its softness. It smelled of shampoo, just as her skin smelled of fresh soap, not make-up.

Who was she and what was she doing on his land?

As she shivered, he became more aware of the practicalities

of the situation. He could feel an increasing dampness in the air and when he looked up, he could see heavy rain clouds piling up. 'It's going to pour down soon. Let's get you to shelter, hmm?'

'I can't walk. I think I've sprained my ankle.'

'Is that why you were crying?'

Her eyes fell. 'Partly.' She drew in a deep breath that still quivered with suppressed sobs. 'And – and you won't be able to carry me. I'm too big.'

'Let's get you standing up anyway, then we'll work out what to do next. The ground's too damp and cold to sit on. Put your weight on your sound foot and try to hold the other in the air. Now, give me your hands.' Holding her gently, he pulled her to her feet.

She tried to muffle a whimper as she bumped her ankle and that again touched something inside him. 'There's my brave girl,' he whispered, holding her upright against him.

'You're very tall,' she muttered.

'Yes. Bane of my life.'

'Mine, too.'

'You're not tall.' He could give her five or six inches, he reckoned. Even his sister was taller than she was, at six feet.

'I'm a hundred and seventy-eight centimetres.' She saw his look of puzzlement. 'About five feet ten. That's a big disadvantage for a woman. My husband says if I ever put on weight I'll look like a carthorse.'

He took an instant dislike to the husband. 'With a face as pretty as yours, you could never look like a horse and you don't appear to be carrying any extra weight to me.'

She blinked at him as if she didn't believe him.

'Now, we need to get you to the house before the heavens anoint us. If I put my arm round you, will you be able to hop?'

They tried it for a few paces, then she sagged against him. 'I – could we rest a minute?'

'Of course. Lean against this tree.' He had a sudden idea. 'Look, we've got an old bath chair in the stables. I could push it up here and get you back to my place in it if you don't mind a bumpy ride. Can you hold on for a minute?'

'Mmm.'

70

She watched him run down the hillside with long-legged confident strides. What a bony man he was, taller than Paul and much thinner. He had a nice face, though. Kind. Lovely brown eyes, soft as a doe's, and a long sharply-chiselled nose. It was the sort of face you'd trust instinctively. And how lucky that he'd found her. She blushed bright red as she remembered *how* he had found her, lying sobbing on the ground like a stupid child. Feeling absolutely washed out, she leaned her head against the tree trunk. The injured ankle was throbbing, her good leg was aching from supporting her whole weight and she was so cold she couldn't even think straight.

A few minutes later her rescuer reappeared at the bottom of the slope pushing an ancient bath chair made of basketwork which had frayed in places on a frame that was well rusted. It squeaked in continual protest as he pushed it up the hill, but it didn't fall to pieces.

'Voilà, Madame!' He flourished a bow. 'Your carriage awaits.'

She could not help smiling at his triumphant expression. With his help, she hopped across to her unlikely chariot and collapsed into it, groaning.

His voice was gentle. 'Ankle hurting?'

'Mmm.'

'Hold on, then.'

The going was rough and the jolting hurt, but soon the path levelled out, becoming marginally smoother. Now they were on crazy paving which led between unkempt lawns to a house half-hidden by trees. Her rescuer was panting, but laughing exultantly, too, as if this was all a merry adventure, and she found her spirits lifting.

Only when they got closer did Rosalind realize how old the house was, or how large. 'What a lovely building! Do you really live here?'

'Oh, yes. We Destans have been at Burraford since the Middle Ages – though the main part of the present house dates only from the early seventeenth century.'

'You have the same name as the village?'

'It's called after us, actually. My ancestors took over here after the Norman Conquest.' He chuckled as he added, 'Somewhat forcibly, I'm afraid. The previous owner had been

71

killed at Hastings. Burrh means a fortified place – near a ford. The river's on the other side of this house. The original keep was much closer to the water.'

'How wonderful to know your family's history so far back!'

'In some ways it is, but there are down sides to it all. These ancient piles cost the earth to keep up, even small places like mine.' And they attracted social climbing women, who then tried to gut them of their valuables – and Isabel would have succeeded, too, if he hadn't come home early by sheer chance, and caught her and her lover stuffing bags full of the smaller pieces of silver into her car. He pushed the memory of that dreadful encounter away hurriedly. He had not realized he had it in him to grow so furiously angry, let alone to punch someone on the chin. 'Houses like these are draughty in winter and stuffy in summer, but—'

She finished for him. 'But you love it.'

Her smile was soft and gentle. He felt warmed by it. He'd like to make her smile more often, wipe that sadness from her face. 'Yes. I do love it. And so far we Destans have managed to keep our home for ourselves, not hand it over to the National Trust.' Though for how much longer, he wasn't sure. He realized she was shivering. 'But I shouldn't stand here talking. You need to get warm. Would you like to come inside? Do you fancy a cup of tea?'

'I'd kill for a hot drink.'

'Then you've arrived at the right place. I rather pride myself on my skill as a tea maker.' He trundled the bath chair to the foot of the front steps and an old dog appeared, wagging furiously and nudging his hand for attention. 'Sit, Dusty! Stay!' He turned to grin at Rosalind. 'This old fellow is a cuddle hound – never has been interested in hunting or guarding things, just likes to coax cuddles out of people. Wait there a mo. I've even got a pair of crutches somewhere from when I broke my leg. They'll be easier than hopping.'

She sat staring up at the house as the first drops of rain landed gently on her cheeks. It was built of what she now knew to be grey Purbeck stone, with the steep stone roof that seemed typical of this part of the world. Three stories high only, with a gabled wing jutting forward at one side and four windows along each floor of the main block. There was an extra-tall window in the middle above the entrance, probably to light the stairwell. The gardens needed attention and the front door needed painting, but that didn't destroy the charm and it looked like a home, not a showplace.

He came striding out to join her, brandishing the crutches and beaming. 'Here we are. Just in time.' Easing her out of the chair, he helped her make her slow, painful way up the steps. As he was closing the front door, the rain stopped teasing them and came down with an express-train roar.

'Thank goodness you found me,' Rosalind said shakily. She paused, finding the crutches unexpectedly hard to manage.

He noticed and laid a gentle hand on her arm. 'No need to hurry now we're under cover. I'll adjust them once we've got you sitting down.'

The room he helped her into was so perfectly proportioned that for all her discomfort she could not help exclaiming, 'Oh, how beautiful this is! Just look at that plasterwork!' The furniture was old and well used, big easy pieces you could sink into, and everywhere there were objects to catch your eye: an unusual ornament, a painting, an elegant piece of furniture.

He guided her towards a sofa. 'There. If you sit with your leg up for a while, it should help the swelling. I'll go and make some tea, shall I? I haven't any live-in staff, just a woman who comes in three times a week to clean.'

'Tea would be lovely.'

'Earl Grey all right? No, it's a bit early in the day for that – how about English Breakfast?'

'Perfect.' Not the time to tell him you were a coffee addict and all types of tea tasted more or less alike to you. Rosalind wedged herself into the corner of the high-backed sofa and gave herself up to enjoyment of the room. Nothing really matched, but everything seemed to cohabit happily. Each piece of furniture her eyes lingered on was a treasure begging further inspection. Old polished wood – dusty in parts – exquisite inlay work, carving, ornate brass handles. She didn't know where to look next. She could spend a whole day in here and still not have studied everything!

Footsteps on the polished boards of the hall, accompanied by the pattering of the dog's paws, heralded her host's return. He set down a wooden tray carefully. 'Brought you some

biscuits. Chocolate. I hate plain ones. They look so anaemic.'
Deftly he poured her some tea. 'Milk? Sugar?'

'Just a little milk. No sugar.' She balanced the cup in her
hand while he fetched a small table.

He turned back to the tray and picked up a lumpy tea towel.
'I put some ice in this. Thought it might help your ankle.'

'How kind.' She watched him adjust the compress with deft
fingers.

He picked up a plate. 'Biscuit?'

'No, thanks. I have to watch my weight.'

'You're kidding.'

'Thin is fashionable and my husband likes me to – to keep
up to date.'

She saw him make a moue at that statement – was it because
she'd refused the biscuits or because she'd admitted that she
watched her weight to please Paul. She realized suddenly that
she wouldn't have cared herself if she'd put on a bit of weight
and she spent a lot of time watching others eat food she'd
cooked and longed to eat. She glanced back at the biscuits,
set out on an old linen doily with hand-worked edges. He'd
gone to some trouble. What harm would one biscuit do? 'Well,
perhaps just one. Sweet things are supposed to be good for
shock, aren't they?'

His face brightened and he passed the plate over, then took
one for himself and bit off half of it with great relish, saying
indistinctly, 'So, tell me what you were doing in our grove.'

'Trying to find the public footpath so I could get back to
Burraford.'

'You're living there?'

'Yes. Temporarily, anyway. We're from Australia.'

'I guessed that from your accent. Who's "we"? You and
your husband?'

'Yes. When he's at home. Which isn't often. He works for
a multinational company and travels a lot.'

'You must be living in the old Harris house in Sexton Close,
then.'

'I don't know about any Harrises, but I do live in Sexton
Close. Number ten. How did you know?'

His grin made him look about twelve years old. 'I know
everything that goes on in the village. My sister sees to that.

She lives just behind the church.' He saw that his visitor wasn't listening and followed her gaze. 'That's Araminta's picture.'

'If it weren't for my ankle, I'd have my nose pressed against the glass.'

'It is rather jolly.' He unwound his long legs and went to lift the framed embroidery off the wall, setting it down on her lap. 'Here. Take your time.' He took another biscuit and leaned back in his armchair, smiling as he saw she had forgotten him completely.

'This is a very fine example of raised stumpwork,' she said at last. 'About 1670, I'd guess, though there isn't a date on it. The last corner, after her name, is unfinished. What a pity! Did she die? Do you know who this Araminta was?'

'One of our most loved ancestors. She lived all through the Civil War, kept the Roundheads from destroying the place, then died suddenly at the age of fifty-two from a fever. My sister found this in an old chest in the attic, together with Araminta's diary and account books. We had the embroidery framed because we both love it.'

'No wonder. It's a particularly clever use of materials and look how realistic the figures are. And the animals. You could almost stroke that little dog. I've seen photos of pieces like this in books, but this is the first time I've met one face to face.'

'You sound very knowledgeable.'

She shrugged. 'Well, I do a bit of embroidery myself.'

'This sort?'

'Mm-hmm.'

'You've done actual stumpwork pictures?'

She couldn't help smiling at his eager tone. 'Oh, yes. I've got an attic full of them at home in Australia. And I've brought one or two with me – just to make the rented place a bit more home-like.'

'No room left on the walls at home, eh?'

She blushed and fiddled with the edge of the frame. 'Well, not exactly. Such things are not to everyone's taste.'

He looked at her, eyes narrowed. Who had criticized her work and made her so apologetic about it? The damned husband again, probably. 'We have a colour photo of this one, for insurance purposes. Would you like me to have a copy of it made for you?' He watched her face light up. She was lovely when she smiled.

'Oh, would you really? I'd love that. And – and if I could come back with the photo and make notes on the stitches she used. She was a very skilled needlewoman, your Araminta.'

'Of course you can. I'll show you round the rest of the place too, if you like, when your ankle's better. But for the moment, I think we ought to get you to a doctor. That ankle doesn't seem to have gone down at all.' He took the picture from her and brought back the crutches. 'Just let me adjust these.'

She looked down at her leg, the light fading from her face. 'It is rather swollen, isn't it?' It was throbbing. So was her head. How far could she have crawled if he hadn't found her? The thought made her shiver. There was no one to miss her or come looking for her. She could have been stuck overnight and died of exposure out there in the woods.

He helped her up and measured the crutches against her. 'That's better. Now, I think you should see old Doc Barnes. Is there someone you want to call to pick you up?'

Her voice was toneless. 'No, there isn't anyone. My daughters are in Australia and my husband will be in Hong Kong for another few weeks.' And she had no idea where Tim was, any more than he knew she was in England.

'Then I'll drive you myself, wait till you've seen Doc and take you home afterwards.'

'I couldn't put you to all that trouble. If you'll just call a taxi, I'll get out of your way. Though I'd appreciate it if I could borrow the crutches.'

'It's no trouble. Honestly. I'll pop in to see Harry while I'm in the village.'

'Harry?'

'My sister. Short for Harriet, which she hates. She's a widow – not the merry sort, still grieving. Lung cancer, it was. Went on rather a long time and Phil was a decent chap, didn't deserve to die like that.' He took a deep breath and shook off those memories. 'You stay there and I'll bring the car round the front.'

The doctor examined the ankle, then strapped it up tightly, speaking in curt phrases as if he didn't have time for whole sentences. 'Nothing broken. Bad sprain. Keep off your feet for a few days and you'll be all right.'

Rosalind stared at him in dismay. 'But I can't!'

'Can't what?' He had already opened the door and gestured to Jonathon, who was sitting outside, to come and help her out.

'Can't stay off my feet. There's only me. What am I going to do?'

Jonathon tried not to say it, but the words were out before he could stop them. 'Harry and I will look after you.'

She turned to him. 'But I can't ask you to – we'd never even met until today . . .'

He shrugged. 'We're blocking the doorway. Come on. We'll discuss it on the way to Harry's.'

People were staring at them, so she tucked the crutches under her arms and swung painfully and slowly after him. The receptionist wanted her to sign some papers and by the time she got to the car, she felt as if her armpits were on fire.

When he climbed in beside her, she said faintly, 'I think I'd rather go straight home, if you don't mind.'

He looked sideways at her as he started the car. Hell, she was as pale as a ghost. 'All right. I'll phone Harry and ask her to come over to your house for a council of war, if that's all right with you. She'll find a way to help you.'

'You're being so kind, and to a complete stranger.' Rosalind leaned her head back against the car seat with a sigh.

Jonathon drove as smoothly as he could, very conscious that she was in pain. There was something about her that touched him. She was so soft and vulnerable, with that swollen trembling mouth and those gentle blue eyes. And anyway, if you couldn't help someone in trouble you weren't worth much as a human being. Why was she here alone in England when her home was in Australia? And why was that damned husband of hers living in Hong Kong if they'd come to spend the summer here? It didn't make sense.

What was he doing getting involved? That made even less sense. Jonathon smiled ruefully to himself as he parked in front of her house and went to open the gates. Well, if nothing else she'd taken his mind from his own worries, making him feel pleasantly philanthropic – and actually, he liked her.

He really did. Such a transparently honest face. There didn't seem to be many people like that around nowadays.

Harry would like her, too, he decided hastily, not letting himself linger on his own reaction to her, though it was the first time since his highly acrimonious divorce that he'd been attracted to a woman in any way at all. Which was probably a good sign. Well, it would have been if the woman in question hadn't been married.

He got her settled on the couch and then said, 'Won't be a jiffy. I'll just phone Harry.'

# Seven

Harriet Larcombe was so intrigued by her brother's call that she agreed to join an immediate emergency conference about how they could help this Rosalind Stevenson cope for the next few days. As she put the phone down, she wondered what Jonathon was doing getting involved with a complete stranger? This female must be a gorgeous piece to make him break his vow of abjuring all womankind except his sister.

Only Rosalind wasn't a gorgeous piece, Harry saw instantly. She was a gentle person, the sort others often took advantage of. There was nothing striking about her as there had been about Isabel, who had so ravaged poor Jonathon's life. Nor was this woman trying to attract a man, for she spoke openly of being married. So it was just Jonathon, who had a chivalrous soul, rescuing a damsel in distress. But perhaps this little adventure would stop him brooding so much on the past and put him in a more positive frame of mind about the future. He hadn't been truly happy since the boys had left and she knew he still missed them dreadfully, even two years after the divorce.

'Why don't you move in with me for a few days, Rosalind?' she offered when she saw the two of them looking at her for guidance, as people often did. 'I've got plenty of room.'

Rosalind shook her head, smiling at her visitor, who was a mere six feet tall compared to her brother's six feet three, but equally thin and with the same bony, aristocratic face. 'It's very kind of you, but no. My family will want to contact me and – and my husband prefers to ring me, since he's such a busy person.'

'Why, if he's in Hong Kong and you normally live in Australia, are you here in England on your own, if I may ask?' Harry had been puzzling over this.

'Paul thought he'd be settled in England for the summer on a special project, so he insisted – I mean, he *asked* me to come over here, too.' Rosalind blushed at her slip, but neither of the others seemed to notice. 'Then the man in charge of the Hong Kong office died suddenly, so Paul has had to fill in until they can appoint someone.'

'Bit rough on you.' Harry decided they couldn't be short of money if the husband had that sort of job and mentally revised her plans for helping Rosalind to include paid assistance that would benefit another of her protégées. 'We could ask Alice Tuffin to come in each morning for an hour or two until you're functioning again, if you like. Her services are very reasonable and she'll do your shopping for you as well as your housework. I've always found her extremely reliable, if rather outspoken.'

'What a lovely name! It sounds like something out of Beatrix Potter.'

'It's a local surname. She was a Bugg before she married and that's a Dorset name, too.' She shared a conspiratorial smile with her brother and confided, 'The Buggs insist they've been in the area for much longer than the Destans and they may be right. There's a reference to a Thomas Bugg in Araminta's diary.'

'He was put in the stocks several times for drunkenness,' Jonathon added with a grin, 'but we haven't mentioned that to Alice.'

Harry glanced at her watch. 'Look, I have to go soon, but I can pop across here for the next afternoon or two to get your evening meal. The more you rest that ankle, the quicker you'll be walking on it again.'

Rosalind leaned back with a sigh of relief. 'I can't believe how kind you're both being to a complete stranger!'

'Oh, it makes us feel nice and virtuous. Christian duty and all that. Now, do you want me to bring anything downstairs for you before I leave?'

'My embroidery, if you wouldn't mind.' She had to explain what she was working on to Harry and Jonathon, who then inspected the embroideries hanging on the wall.

'I say, you *are* good,' Jonathon said instantly. 'As good as Araminta.'

Harry looked at the pieces, head on one side. 'When you've recovered, I'm going to coax you into donating one of these to the fête. We raise funds once a year for the old folks' centre.'

'Oh, I'd be happy to donate one – if you think someone will want to buy it. They're not to everyone's taste.'

She'd said that before, Jonathon thought, frowning. How could she possibly have doubts about such gorgeous work?

They settled Rosalind in the living room with the gas fire bubbling away in the grate and her embroidery to hand.

'I've got a committee meeting at three for the fête,' Harry tossed over her shoulder as she strode out. 'But that'll be over by five at the latest. See you then.'

Jonathon lingered for a moment or two longer.

'You've both been so kind,' Rosalind said.

'Oh, Harry enjoys playing lady of the manor now I haven't a wife to fill that role.'

'Is such a thing still needed?'

'Well, not really, but she's convinced everyone in the village that things would go to pot without her help, and she does do a lot of good, so who am I to deny her these little pleasures? Are you *sure* you'll be all right on your own?'

'Yes, of course I will.'

'Right-ho, then. I'll see you tomorrow.'

Rosalind listened to the front door close, then picked up her embroidery. But the weeping and the fall had exhausted her. Within minutes she put her bits and pieces down and let her head fall back on the soft pillow Harry had found for her.

When she awoke the afternoon light was dimming gently outside and Harry had just returned to prepare her evening meal. 'I'll take the sandwiches you didn't eat for my dogs, if you don't mind. You won't want them as well as an evening meal.' She bustled around, making an omelette and salad, clearly not keen to linger, but she did stop to study the pictures on the wall again. 'These are truly lovely. Are you sure you can bear to part with one for our fête?'

'Oh yes. I've got plenty of them at home. I won't give you one of these because they're my favourites, but I'll send for one of the others.'

'Well, we'd be very grateful.' If it didn't fetch too high a price, Harriet might even bid for it herself. She didn't know why those embroideries attracted her, but they did. Each seemed to tell a story, as well as being a work of art.

It occurred to Rosalind as she lay in bed that it had been a good day in a strange sort of way. The burst of weeping had been very cathartic and she'd made some friends. She really liked Jonathon and Harry, who were so direct and honest.

And that embroidery at Destan Manor was glorious, simply glorious. Fancy getting the chance to study a rare old piece like that! She was looking forward to going round the house, too, when she was better. Who knew what other treasures were hidden away there?

Yawning she snuggled down, feeling better than she had since her arrival in England.

The Hong Kong office was organized so efficiently that it was easy for Paul to keep things on an even keel with minimum input. This looked like being one of the easiest assignments he'd ever had, boring even.

'What have you got planned for tomorrow?' he asked Liz that evening as they ate dinner together. If it was a coach tour, he wasn't going to get involved. He was simply not the sort to be driven round in a herd of sheep-like tourists and told what to look at.

'I thought I'd wander round the shops, stopping for a coffee, you know the sort of thing. Why?' She hoped he had a better suggestion because she was finding it hard to fill the days, could not afford to buy anything else and was sick to death of coach tours. All day she had been looking forward to seeing Paul and having someone to talk to.

He smiled at her. 'I'm at a loose end too. We could catch the Star Ferry over to Kowloon and then wander round together, if you want.'

'Are you sure you can spare the time? I thought you were here because of an emergency?'

'Well, it turned out that my late lamented colleague had good staff and ran things efficiently. So long as I go into the office each day at some stage, I can easily take time off. It's no part of my brief to interfere with something that's running well. The chairman trusts me absolutely to judge that sort of thing.' He glanced sideways at her. 'If you *want* some company, that is? You said you had another week here. But perhaps you've made other plans?'

She stared at him across the dinner table. She almost asked why he was suddenly seeking her out, when they'd been disagreeing about things for years, but bit back the words. She'd always enjoyed the sparring, now she came to think of it, been exhilarated by it. Perhaps he had felt the same. She was glad he hadn't taken her dancing again tonight, though. His lean, muscular body pressed closely against hers had affected her far too much. He really was a splendid specimen of manhood. That hadn't occurred to her before, but it did now – rather too much for her peace of mind.

If she hadn't had such a big row with Bill, made such a point of getting away to think about where their marriage was going, she'd have returned to Australia early and avoided temptation altogether, but she had shocked Bill rigid and wanted him to stay shocked. Why the hell had she booked such a long holiday in one place, though?

Paul reached out and brushed away a lock of hair that had fallen over her forehead, a small intimate gesture that made a shiver of awareness run through her. 'You have lovely hair, Liz. Always so dark and glossy. And no grey in sight.'

The shiver did another lap of her body and settled in her belly. For a moment she couldn't breathe.

'Shall we not share a few days?' he asked.

Did she take that at face value, or was he offering her more? She looked sideways at him and he smiled, a lazy, sexy smile. He *was* offering more, definitely. For a long moment she hesitated, tempted, so very tempted, but trying to think of Rosalind. Then she sighed and gave in to the urges that had been humming through her all evening. 'Why not? I'd really welcome some company.'

He raised her hand and pressed a gentle kiss into the palm, a kiss which seared her skin.

'Why not, indeed?' he echoed, still holding her hand, eyes gleaming. 'We'll keep our encounter to ourselves, though, shall we? We don't want to hurt other people.'

She had always wondered if Paul were faithful to his wife during those long absences and now she'd found out. *Oh, Rosalind, I'm sorry, but I can't resist this.* After all, what her friend didn't know wouldn't hurt her and Liz could certainly trust Paul to keep quiet, just as she would herself. She would still tell Bill about the affair, of course, but not the name of the man.

Oh, hell, she needed an affair for so many reasons, not just to get back at Bill, but to reaffirm that she was still an attractive woman. You had to wonder if there was something wrong with you when your husband kept being unfaithful.

She smiled at Paul as he led the way out of the restaurant. From then on, neither of them mentioned their spouses.

It took Rosalind a long time to wash and dress the morning after her accident, and she had to sit down on the bed afterwards for a rest. When she had recovered a little, she eased herself slowly down the stairs on her backside, one tread at a time, then pushed herself upright on to the crutches.

The kitchen seemed a million miles away, so she unlocked the front door ready for her new helper before she started the slow trek to the back of the house. After a scrappy breakfast of cereal she went into the sitting room, grunting with relief as she eased herself down on to the sofa.

Someone knocked on the front door, opened it and called, 'Hallo–o? Alice Tuffin here. Mrs Larcombe sent me.'

'Do come in!'

A small woman with faded sandy hair, of the body type always labelled wiry, came and stood staring down at Rosalind, head on one side.

'I'm so glad you could come and help out, Mrs Tuffin.'

'Call me Alice.'

'And I'm Rosalind.'

A quick shake of the head at that Aussie egalitarianism. 'How long do you want me for, Mrs Stevenson?'

'A couple of hours a day for as long as it takes my ankle to get better – and Mrs Larcombe said you might do my shopping for me, as well.'

Another nod. 'Wages?'

'Whatever you think right.'

'Seven pounds an hour is what Mrs Larcombe pays me. Shall I make you a cup of tea before I start?'

'I prefer coffee. Do you know how to use a plunger?'

'One of them things you press down?' Alice shrugged. 'There's not much to it, is there? How much coffee do you put in?'

'Two measures. Get yourself a cup, too.'

'I might as well try it.'

The coffee was not a success with Alice, who grimaced and said it was too strong for her, but was clearly pleased to have been offered it. 'I'll stick to tea from now on,' she said firmly, staring round the sitting room in an assessing sort of way.

By mid-morning, the downstairs rooms were clean and Rosalind knew all about Alice's invalid husband and four strapping sons.

'Eat me out of house and home, they do,' Alice wound up fondly.

When she had finished attacking the housework as if she had a personal grudge against dust, she came in with another cup of coffee and lingered to stare at Rosalind's embroidery. 'That's going to be a nice little picture, that is.'

'Oh – er, thank you. It's my hobby. Embroidery, I mean.'

'I like that old-fashioned lady you're doing now better than the picture on the wall there – though that's good as well.'

Rosalind liked it, too. She hadn't even considered working on the family portrait. Doing Paul's figure had left her feeling bewildered about her husband and marriage. It was as if she had never really looked at him before, as if he were a stranger. Besides, she wasn't certain who to do next – in fact, was having second thoughts about finishing the picture at all. That wasn't like her. She usually chose a subject and then forgot everything else while she worked on it.

When Alice had left, Rosalind fell asleep again and woke feeling not only refreshed but more cheerful. She phoned Prue, explained about her accident and checked that everything was all right in Southport. Prue had found a daily job, so Rosalind gave permission for her to continue living at the house.

She really ought to put the place on the market, but somehow she didn't want to. Not yet, anyway. Her great-grandparents had lived there and she was absolutely determined to show it to her children, to give them a sense of the family's history. The house had passed to her grandfather and then to her uncle. Her father had been the younger son and had emigrated to Australia in his early twenties, not expecting to inherit anything. When his elder brother had died unmarried and childless, the house had gone to the only girl of the family, Sophie. It made Rosalind feel strange to have the weight of family inheritance on her shoulders and she could not help wondering how that affected Jonathon, who had so much more to look after for the next generation.

In the late afternoon, there was a knock at the door. Rosalind called out that it was open and Jonathon came in, carrying a basket.

He uncovered it to show a casserole dish. 'My sister's famous boeuf bourguignon. She's had to rush off to Winchester. Her daughter's just miscarried, poor thing. Everyone in the family sends for Harry when something goes wrong.' Even Isabel had done that last year when the boys had got a bad dose of flu. Couldn't ask the boys' own father to help, though, could she? She was still trying to keep them apart, hated the fact that they loved not only him, but the house here.

'It smells lovely,' Rosalind said, smiling. 'Um – I don't suppose you'd care to stay and share it with me? I'd love a bit of company.'

He hesitated, sniffed the casserole with exaggerated relish and nodded. 'All right. There's supposed to be enough for two days, but if I bring round a take-away tomorrow evening, perhaps that will make up for my eating half of this now?'

'It certainly will.' She fumbled for her crutches. 'Look, come into the kitchen. I have some vegetables and rolls in the freezer and we could do some jacket potatoes in the microwave.'

'You can sit and give orders, but you're not doing anything yourself, milady. I'm not the world's best cook, but I can follow instructions and I have a very stylish way of heating frozen vegetables.'

When the meal was ready, Jonathon slapped his hand against his forehead in mock anguish. 'Oh blast! I am an idiot! I should have brought some wine with me. A red to complement the beef.'

'Don't panic. I have some. It's in the dining room inside the sideboard. We ought to have opened a bottle earlier to let it breathe, but there are a few nice Australian reds there and

86

I don't mind drinking one that hasn't breathed if you don't. Choose any you fancy.'

She hauled herself across to the table. She was definitely not going to win a gold medal for crutch-hopping. Her body seemed to get heavier every time she moved. Her foot was still swollen, though not as badly as it had been yesterday, and she didn't think it wise to put any weight on it yet.

As she subsided into a chair, she banged her ankle on the table leg and let out a muffled whimper.

He was there kneeling beside her in an instant. 'Let me help you.' He pushed her and the chair carefully into position, brought a footstool for her from the living room, then carried over the plates of food. 'Start without me while it's hot. I'll just open the wine.'

But she didn't start without him, of course she didn't. She hoped she had better manners than that. In fact, she wasn't all that hungry and although the food was good, she put down her knife and fork when the plate was half cleared and looked at him apologetically.

He smiled. 'It's all right. You won't get spanked if you don't clear the plate. Besides, you're not doing much to work up an appetite at the moment, are you?'

'I feel guilty, though. Such lovely food. And such good company, too.' She stared at him. He stared back at her. The silence lasted too long and the very air between them seemed to tingle.

'I'll take your leftovers home for Dusty,' he said at last. 'He much prefers human food.' He studied her with a sympathetic expression. 'It's getting you down a bit, isn't it, being an invalid?'

She nodded.

'And you were weeping when I found you yesterday. Your other troubles won't have gone away overnight. I don't mean to intrude, but if you ever want to talk about it – well, I'm here.'

'Thank you.' But she couldn't confide in him. It would seem disloyal to Paul. She had intended to confide in Sophie, but had left it too late. So she would just have to work through things herself.

'Come on! We'll have dessert in the living room.'

'I couldn't possibly eat anything else.'

But he brought in a packet of fancy chocolate biscuits, laughing at his own weakness for them, and she found herself taking one and nibbling it while he ate four or five.

As the evening passed she found herself chuckling quite often over his nonsense. Jonathon was – well, he was uncomplicated and fun. She could feel herself relaxing, laughing, expanding somehow in the warmth of his company, and couldn't remember the last time she'd enjoyed herself so much. She supposed she was quite a simple person, really – or at least, Paul always said she was – and she liked doing quiet, companionable things best of all.

And even when Jonathon had gone, the house seemed full of warmth still, as if the laughter they'd shared was clinging to the walls and wafting round the rooms.

The following afternoon, Jonathon came round to make sure Rosalind liked Chinese food and to let her choose from the take-away menu. It seemed quite natural for him to stay and make her a cup of coffee.

When the phone rang, he called, 'Shall I get it?'

'Yes, please.' She'd forgotten to bring the portable phone in with her.

'Hallo?'

A voice bristling with indignation said, 'Who's that?'

'Jonathon Destan. And you are . . . ?'

'Paul Stevenson. I was trying to contact my wife.'

'She's here, but she's hurt her ankle. Hold on for a moment and I'll take the phone through to her.' He walked into the living room, rolled his eyes at Rosalind and mouthed. 'Your husband.'

She waited till Jonathon had closed the door behind him before she spoke. 'Paul?'

'Who's that fellow?'

'A friend. He and his sister have been helping me. I've sprained my ankle. If he hadn't found me when I fell, I'd have been in serious trouble, because I couldn't walk and I was miles from anywhere.'

'Did you have it X-rayed?'

'Jonathon took me to a doctor. It's just a sprain.'

'Who exactly is this fellow? One of the locals?'

'The lord of the manor, actually. And his sister lives here in the village.'

'Oh, well, that's all right, then.'

She could feel herself bristling. 'What do you mean – *that's all right*?'

'I just wondered what a man was doing answering your phone.'

'I don't like your tone, Paul. If you don't trust me by now, there's something wrong between us.' She could hear him breathing more deeply, as if restraining anger, so said lightly, 'Now, what can I do for you?'

'I rang to see how you were, of course.'

'I'm well enough, apart from the ankle.' And apart from feeling depressed. And apart from worrying about Tim, for some reason she couldn't fathom.

'I've been thinking about your aunt's money. That house of hers should be worth a nice little sum. We can sell it and—'

'I told you – everything's in a trust. I get the income from it, but I can't touch the capital without the trustees' approval.'

'Yes, but I'm sure you'll be allowed to sell the house. And anyway, I've been thinking about it all. I know a good lawyer. We'll set him on to see if we can overthrow that trust.'

'I don't want to do that.'

'Look, Ros, you know you don't understand financial matters. Nor did your aunt. She was probably senile towards the end. She seemed completely dotty when I saw her, the things she said. Should be quite easy to prove that. Leave me to—'

Rosalind slammed down the phone on him for the second time in her life and when it rang, she didn't pick it up. Jonathon opened the door and found her glaring at the phone, making no attempt to touch it.

'Get cut off, did you?'

'No. I put the phone down on him, actually. Sometimes my husband can be very infuriating. Will you take that thing back into the kitchen, please? And – and don't answer if it rings. I shan't speak to him again tonight.'

When Jonathon came back with the coffee he said nothing about the phone that was ringing again and she was grateful for his forbearance. 'Tell me about your children. What are they called?' She could imagine him as a father, teasing, joking, throwing little children up in the air.

'Giles and Rufus. They're old family names, Rufus hates his, but it's a tradition in our family, so he'll jolly well have to put up with it.'

As he talked, she thought how unfair it was that he had so little access to his sons, but not once did he say anything against his wife.

He smiled as he finished his tale. 'The boys are coming down to Destan for the fête. I'll introduce them to you.'

Jonathon was the easiest person to be with, she decided later as she slid into bed. Unlike Paul. What had got into her husband lately?

*What had got into her, too?*

Darkness rustled and whispered outside as the wind teased the branches near her window into a lazy ballet. She lay watching the shadows on the curtains and it was a while before she faced the truth and answered her own questions. There was nothing really different about Paul lately, but her perception of him had altered.

And *she* had changed since her arrival in England, was still changing.

She would get the embroidery out in the morning, study it, think about the other figures. It had taught her so much about her husband. Perhaps it would do the same about herself.

She was a little worried about where all these changes were leading. Only – whatever became of her, she couldn't wish them undone. She felt better inside herself than she had done for years. Much better.

# Emotion

*Much intricate and ingenious stitchery is used for foliage, flowers, birds, fountains and buildings on seventeenth-century raised embroidery, but the whole is brought to life by the small human figures and the stories they represent. Humour, pathos, anger and many other emotions are depicted . . .*

*(Hirst, p. 38)*

# Eight

P aul slammed the buzzing phone down and stood glaring at it, breath rasping in his throat. What the hell had got into Ros? He paced up and down the hotel room, chewing one fingertip and trying to work out how much money the old witch would have left her. He was itching now to get back and sort it all out. What a time to be away!

The phone rang and he picked it up. 'Ros?'

'No, Liz. Watch broken down, has it?'

He glanced at his wrist. 'Oh, shit, I'm supposed to have picked you up ten minutes ago, aren't I? Sorry. I was talking to Ros on the phone. That old aunt of hers has died and left us all her money, but it's the most idiotic will – she's set up a trust fund and no one can touch the capital. And when I suggested contesting the will, Ros hung up on me. I don't know what's got into her lately.'

'She'll be upset. She was very fond of Aunt Sophie.' Liz waited for a response to that, an acknowledgement of Rosalind's grief, but clearly her words hadn't even penetrated. Heavens, he might be a good lover, but he was the most self-ish man she'd ever met. How had Rosalind put up with him all these years? She'd rather have Bill any day.

*Rather have Bill!*

That realization shocked her rigid. Bill wasn't as good-looking as Paul, wasn't nearly as good in bed and was an unfaithful bastard – but he was infinitely nicer to live with. Well, she thought, one decision made. We soldier on. 'Sorry, what was that you said?'

'I said Sophie Worth was senile,' he repeated.

'I don't know what you're worrying about. Rosalind still benefits, even if the money has to go through a trust fund. I shall enjoy having a rich friend. Now, why don't you meet me downstairs? I'm famished.'

He went straight down and stood in the lobby waiting for her. When she came out of a lift, he watched her walk across towards him, admiring the vividness of her colouring and the energy of her stride. 'You keep yourself in damn good trim, you know.'

'I work out at the gym.'

'Ros could do with toning up a bit,' Paul mused, still looking at Liz. 'Perhaps you could persuade her to go to a gym when we get back?'

'I've enough on my plate keeping my own body in order, thank you very much. And I think Rosalind is just right for her height. The scrawny waif look wouldn't suit her at all. Now – are you intending to eat or not?'

'Of course I am – and after dinner I'll apologize properly for keeping you waiting.' His voice was husky with innuendo.

'I shall insist on that.'

But she was beginning to wonder if this affair was really worth it, and guilt was beginning to creep in.

She didn't have to psychoanalyse the man, for heaven's sake, just enjoy his rather dishy body and his company. Given the circumstances, he wasn't likely to tell anyone about their affair – which was a good thing, because Paul Stevenson definitely wasn't worth losing her best friend for.

Paul waited three days before ringing his wife again and this time kept the conversation carefully neutral, making no reference to the fact that Ros had put the phone down on him last time. Liz was right. She would have been upset and perhaps he had been just a tad tactless. 'How's the ankle?'

'Getting better now, thank you. The swelling's going down nicely.'

'Good. Good.' She still sounded miffed, probably not liking being on her own in England. 'So what have you done about the house? Is it ready to entertain in yet? We can start thinking about our first house-party, if you like. I can phone people up from here and invite them, set it up for my first weekend back, perhaps.'

'The house is all right, but I'd rather not plan anything until after you get back, if you don't mind – after all, I am fairly immobile still, and anyway, you may only be with me for a couple of days.'

'Ouch! I really upset you there, didn't I?'

'You've upset me in a few ways lately, Paul. But I dare say we can talk it through when you come back.' She was absolutely determined to get their relationship on a better footing before they did anything else.

When he had put the phone down, Paul grimaced. Talk what through?

Then he smiled. Ros was one of the best hostesses he'd ever met, a good listener who drew people out and made them feel interesting, exactly the sort of wife he needed for the next stage in his career – but he wouldn't tell her about the other changes that were on their way for a while yet. It'd take a lot to get her to move away from Western Australia permanently, so he'd have to plan his campaign rather carefully.

In the middle of the night the phone rang and Jenny was awake instantly, heart pounding. She didn't answer it, of course. She'd learned not to do that. When the ringing stopped, she took the receiver off the hook and lay there listening to the dialling tone. On and on. The humming sound nearly drove her mad in the tiny bedroom of this horrid flat, so she unplugged the phone from the wall.

Michael had left a note on her car windscreen at work yesterday, asking her to meet him for dinner to talk things over. He'd written that he still cared for her and wanted her back in his life. She hadn't replied to the note, didn't want to speak to him or see him ever again.

Let's face it, the rotten bastard had got her well and truly spooked. She didn't dare go out now at night unless a friend picked her up and came back with her while she searched the flat. Not that that took very long, what was there to search? But it made her look such a wimp and she didn't like that.

When the phone rang the following evening, Jenny looked at the clock. *He* didn't usually ring this early. Taking a deep breath she picked up the phone. 'Yes?'

'Hello, love, how are you?'

'Mum!' Relief flooded through Jenny. 'How are you getting on?'

'I'm fine, though I've sprained my stupid ankle. Have I caught you at a good time for a chat?'

'I've always time to talk to you, Mum. Goodness, I'm missing you.' More than she'd expected to and not just because of this nastiness with Michael, either.

'I'm missing you, too.' They chatted for a few minutes, then Rosalind asked, 'Look, could you do something for me, love? I don't want to ask your gran, because I think she's got enough on her plate with Louise.'

Jenny rolled her eyes at the ceiling. Her mother didn't know how right she was. Gran had more than enough on her plate. The last time she'd seen her sister, Louise had boasted about using her mother's car and doing what she wanted with her life, in spite of being forced to live with an old lady who needed a reality implant. The two of them had had a big row about that, but Jenny hadn't been able to make her sister see sense. 'So, what can I do for you?'

'I need some more of my embroideries sending over to England, and I want them airfreighted here, however expensive it is. I know it'll be a bit of trouble, but do you have time to go to the house and get them for me – and fairly quickly? It's only a question of taking them to the same shipper as before. You don't need to do the packing. These are unframed pieces.'

'No problem. Is someone over there interested in them?'

'Well, sort of. There's this fête coming up in the village and I've promised to donate one.' Besides, she missed her pieces. It had surprised her how much she missed them. At home, when Paul was away, she'd sometimes pull down the carefully colour-coordinated pictures from the walls and put her embroideries up instead. 'Do you have a pencil?' She listed the pieces she wanted, knowing exactly where each was stored in the attic.

'That'll be easy. I'll go over tomorrow after work and pick them up – Oh no, I don't have a key any more.' Her father had taken her key when she'd moved out, saying it wasn't good security to leave keys lying around in houses where no-hopers could get hold of them.

Her mother's voice sounded happy and more confident than usual. 'Borrow your gran's key again. And Jenny . . .'

'Mmm?'

'Get one cut for yourself while you're at it. I don't happen to agree with your father about that.'

'Oh. Well, all right. But don't tell Dad or he'll hit the roof.'

Rosalind chuckled. 'What he doesn't know won't upset him, will it?'

'You don't usually go against his wishes.'

'Well, maybe that's going to change from now on.'

'How are you managing on your own if you've hurt your ankle?'

'Oh, it's only a sprain and it's getting better slowly. I'm developing a very elegant limp now. And I've made some new friends because of the accident.' She was also getting a lot of embroidery done – and seeing Jonathon regularly, so that he felt like a friend of many years' standing by now. She suspected he was lonely, too. What a lovely man! He'd taken her for a drive yesterday to Weymouth and back and they'd had a delightful afternoon out. She couldn't believe how beautiful and unspoiled the Dorset countryside was. She realized her mind was wandering and pulled her attention back to what her daughter was saying.

'I don't know why you don't put your pictures on the walls at home, Mum. They're so beautiful. When I get somewhere proper to live, I'm going to beg one off you. I love them.'

'You could have had some ages ago!'

'I didn't want to risk them when I was sharing with Michael.'

'I'll let you choose one when I get back.' Rosalind took a deep breath. 'And I agree. I'm definitely going to put some up permanently. I don't know why I haven't insisted before. Your father will just have to lump it.'

When Jenny put the phone down, she shook her head. Dad would find some way to stop her mother putting up the embroideries. He always got his own way. Though how anyone could call her mother's work 'amateur', as he did, she didn't know. The only word that did those pictures justice was 'exquisite'.

*   *   *

On her way home from work the following day, Jenny called at her gran's for the key, and of course had to stay for a cuppa. Louise was nowhere to be seen, thank goodness, and when she asked about her sister, Gran looked unhappy, so things mustn't have improved. Jenny had had it with Louise, absolutely had it.

After that, since it was late-night shopping, she stopped to get a key cut for herself and pick up a newspaper. She wanted to look at adverts for flats. She was thinking of moving – and of changing her phone number again. Trouble was, if Michael had found her once, he could keep on finding her.

On sheer impulse she bought herself a scratchie coupon – she never had any luck with them, beyond winning an occasional couple of dollars, but she liked having one in her purse. She always kept it for days, dreaming of what she would do with her winnings and waiting until she felt a lucky moment come upon her. Then she would scratch the coupon and examine the numbers. It was a fun thing to do, a licence to dream.

Her parents' house seemed dark and menacing when she approached it at night on her own. She made absolutely certain no one was around before she got out of her car, glad when the movement sensors switched the outside lights on. Unlocking the front door as quickly as she could, she darted inside and slammed it shut behind her. It was the work of seconds to dial the correct number into the security system, but she still felt nervous. How her mother had stood it here alone this past year – well, as alone as you got with Louise still living at home, which was pretty much alone – she didn't know.

I've never really liked this place, Jenny decided as she walked up the stairs, switching lights on everywhere. The house where she'd grown up had been much more home-like. This one had too many big, echoing spaces.

She had to steel herself to slide the loft ladder down and go up into the roof storage area, which had only a couple of bare bulbs to light things up. They threw a lot of spooky shadows, but luckily, her mother had everything in pin-neat order and she found the embroideries immediately, sorting out the ones to send, then packing the others up carefully again.

Carrying them down to the kitchen, she hunted in vain for something padded to wrap them in, so went back up for a bath towel. She stopped for a moment to finger the top embroidery and admire the scene on it. Her mother seemed to get the essence of her subjects. Jenny had loved art herself when she was at school, been good at it, too, but of course, her father hadn't let her study it in upper school.

As she was locking the front door carefully behind her, a voice said, 'Hi, Jenny!'

She jerked round in horror. She should have realized that the outside lights being on meant someone was around. *He* was standing there smiling, looking smug.

'Michael!' She tried not to show her fear, but it came slamming into her belly, grappling its way up into her lungs and making her feel short of air. She shot a quick glance around. There was no one in sight on the street – well, people in this district went everywhere by car, didn't they? Would the neighbours even hear her if she yelled for help?

He was barring the way. 'Why didn't you answer my letter, Jen?'

'We'd said all there was to say. Why do you keep phoning me, Michael?'

'I don't remember phoning you.' His smile said he'd enjoyed doing it, just as he was enjoying tormenting her now.

She grew angry. 'I know it was you, Michael. And there's no way I'm going to get back together with you. The sooner you accept that, the sooner we can both get on with our lives.'

His smile slipped and he grabbed her shoulders, pulling her towards him. Although she twisted about and shoved at his chest, she couldn't break his hold. 'Let me go!'

In response, he dug his fingers more deeply into her shoulders.

'You're hurting. Let me *go!*' She kicked his legs and he stopped smiling as he shook her so hard she bit her tongue.

'Why are you doing this?' she whispered when he stopped. 'What do you want?'

'I want to remind you how well we go together.'

She saw his intention in his eyes and froze for a moment. *He was going to rape her!* He pressed himself against her and she could feel his erection pressing into her. He was bigger than she was and much, much stronger. 'Don't, Michael!' she pleaded. 'Please don't do this.'

'That's not what you used to say.' He laughed then. 'Now, we can do it the hard way, or—'

Just then the unlikely happened, the best miracle of her entire life. The woman next door looked over the fence. No warning, just a face suddenly appearing.

'Oh, it's only you, Jenny. I saw the lights and heard voices, and I knew Paul and Rosalind were away, so I—'

Before Michael could say or do anything to stop her, Jenny screamed out, 'Call the police! This man's threatening me.'

The neighbour took one look at Michael's furious face, gaped in horror at the hand upraised to slap Jenny and yelled, 'Stuart! There's an intruder next door! Get the dog! Tommy! Here, boy!' There was the sound of claws clicking on brick paving and human feet thumping as someone ran towards the gate.

Michael shoved Jenny away from him. 'You'll be sorry for this, you bitch! I know where you live and work. It's only postponed.'

He strode out of the garden and Jenny collapsed against the car, sobbing in mingled relief and terror. Angela Coppin came rushing round, followed by her husband and their big Doberman, woofing and pulling at its lead. There was the sound of tyres squealing and a car driving away.

Angela rushed to put an arm round Jenny, shushing her like a baby. 'You're all right now. He's gone. How lucky I peeped over the fence to check who it was!'

'Very l–lucky,' Jenny managed, but she couldn't stop shaking.

'I'll go and call the police,' Stuart said. 'I couldn't see the number plate on his car, unfortunately.'

'No, don't call them!' Jenny clung to Angela, still shuddering. 'We won't be able to prove anything. He'll say I misunderstood what he wanted, that he was only trying to kiss me. He – he used to be my boyfriend, you see, and he can be a very convincing liar.' As she knew to her cost. How she could have thought herself in love with someone like him, she would never know. 'He's stalking me,' she admitted in a small, shamed voice.

'But you can't just let him get away with it,' Stuart declared.

Angela looked at her husband and shook her head to stop him saying anything else. 'Come into our house for a minute or two, Jenny. You're still shivering.'

'There's my car. Oh, and I've dropped my mother's embroideries.' She bent to pick them up, relieved that they hadn't been trampled on. 'I couldn't bear anything to happen to them.' She clutched the unwieldy bundle to her breast, tears still rolling down her cheeks, wishing desperately that her mother were there. Or even her father.

Stuart held out his hand. 'Let me have your car keys. I'll put the embroideries in the car boot then drive it round to our place. You're in no fit state to get behind the wheel.'

So she found herself sitting in their lounge, explaining what had been happening during the past few weeks and weeping again as she did so. She'd never had much to do with the Coppins family, and knew her father was rather scornful of them because they were into caring for the environment and were members of what he called 'the brown-rice brigade', but they were being very kind to her now.

'Haven't you had anyone to talk to?' Angela asked gently as the flood of confidences subsided.

'Not really. It only started after Mum left.'

'Well, if you want my opinion, you need to get away from Perth. Get right away for a while, somewhere he can't find you, then he'll turn elsewhere for his nasty pleasures. I read an article about stalkers.'

'I can't afford to go anywhere. I'm only a trainee manager and the pay's lousy. Besides, I'm not due any holidays yet.' Jenny tried to pull herself together. 'Look, you've been very kind. I won't let him catch me in a vulnerable spot again. I'd better go home now.' But when she stood up she burst into tears again, afraid to drive off on her own, afraid to go into her flat even, in case he was there, waiting for her.

'We'll drive you back,' Stuart said firmly, seeming to understand her fear without being told. 'You can ride with Angela in our car and I'll drive yours. We'll see you safely inside your flat, too, and check that he's not hanging around.'

'But I can't ask you to – it's right across town.'

'You didn't ask. I've got daughters of my own. I wouldn't

like to think of them being so vulnerable.' If he'd been on better terms with Paul Stevenson, he'd have rung him up to tell him what was going on – but you couldn't get close to someone who was never there. Funny sort of marriage that was, with the husband away all the time. Though Rosalind was pleasant enough.

When they had left her, Jenny fastened all the doors and windows in her flat and sat down in front of the TV. But she was too locked in her own thoughts to notice what was on the screen. She felt reasonably safe now because there were people within screaming distance. In fact, there was always someone moving about nearby until the small hours of the morning. The noise had driven her mad at first; tonight she was glad of it.

But if Michael had followed her once and caught her on her own, he could do it again. You couldn't be on your guard every second of the day. You couldn't stop going out, either – and you had to come home each day and worry about whether he was waiting for you.

What the hell was she going to do?

Jenny met her friend Carla after work the following day and they went for a drink, which led to a visit to a food hall for a quick, cheap meal. Afterwards they went back to Jenny's flat together, because she didn't dare go home on her own.

'You know, you really ought to call in the police, Jen,' Carla said as they walked up the concrete stairs. She had been saying that ever since she'd found out about the attempted rape.

'What can they do? I can't prove what he was *intending* to do, can I?' She hadn't slept properly the previous night and today her supervisor at work had had a word with her about late nights and their effect on work performance. He clearly thought she was partying on. *In your dreams, Mr Bennett!* she thought sourly.

At the flat door, they both stopped dead and Jenny clutched her friend as terror cramped through her. 'I didn't leave the door open. I wouldn't.' She stared at it. 'The lock's broken. He's smashed it.' She hated to put it into words, but it had to be faced. 'He – he may be waiting for me inside.'

'You'd have thought someone would hear the noise.' Carla glanced sideways.

'Yes.' Jenny's arms and legs felt all stiff, as if they'd never move or bend again.

Her friend sucked in a breath, then whispered, 'You peep inside and I'll stay here, ready to scream for help.'

'I don't want to.'

'You *have* to. We can't stand out here all night. Go on! He can't rape two of us and he can't lock you inside, not now he's smashed the door.'

Jenny gulped and forced herself to move. It took a huge effort to set one foot in front of the other. She was going to be sick. She felt faint. What if he jumped out at her? What if she was so scared she couldn't scream?

Pushing the door fully open so that he couldn't hide behind it, she waited a minute, listening, then exchanged glances with Carla before stepping inside. If Michael did pounce on her, she was sure she'd not be able to run away. Terror had already fused her knees into stiff unyielding lumps.

As she looked round and realized what had happened, a sob wrenched its way out.

From the doorway, Carla yelled, 'What is it? What's wrong?'

'He's wrecked the place.' Jenny looked round the normally neat living area and burst into tears. All the furniture had been thrown about and her brightly-coloured cushions had been slashed. In the kitchen area, food was scattered across the floor, margarine trampled into flour and sugar, with drinking-chocolate powder scattered artistically across it all in a question mark. Broken eggs were lying in a slimy shell-strewn mess in one corner and some bananas had been ground into pulp at the other side. And there was a strong smell of urine.

Carla called from outside, 'Jenny! *Jenny!* Are you all right?'

'Yes.' But her voice was only a hoarse whisper and it was a moment before she could get it to come out more loudly. 'There's no one in the living area. I'm going into the bedroom. Stand nearer the front door so you can hear me.'

Carla appeared in the opening. 'Shit! The man's a lunatic.' She brandished her mobile phone and jerked her head towards the other door. 'Talk as you go and if you stop talking, I'll start screaming and call the police.'

Jenny went into the room. 'There's no one here, but oh, God! Carla, it's such a mess.' She was weeping helplessly now. 'I'm looking in the wardrobe – nothing here, either – just the bathroom to check now – oh, the bastard! What a mess!' All her make-up had been ground together in the sink and all her perfumes poured down it so that the place was full of a cloying stink. 'He's not here – you can come in.'

Carla walked through the small flat, muttering to herself as she inspected the damage. 'He's sick, that man is, really, really sick. *Oh, my God! Look at that.*'

Jenny turned reluctantly towards the bed. Her best underwear was arranged on top of the covers, as if a body were wearing it. Black lace bra and panties, the suspender belt she'd bought because *he* had said it was sexy. Why the hell hadn't she thrown that away? And there was a condom standing ready by the bedside. But where her heart would have been, just below the black lace bra, a carving knife was sticking up in a pool of red.

'Don't touch anything.' Carla dialled the 000 emergency number on her mobile.

It took an hour for someone to turn up, during which time Jenny jerked in fright at every sound of footsteps in the stairwell, even though Carla had wedged a chair under the front door handle.

The policeman was brisk and factual, examining everything, then calling into the station for someone to come out and investigate more thoroughly. 'It's a sicko,' he said into the phone. 'A real sicko.'

It was three hours before the investigation team had finished with Jenny, by which time she had repeated the sordid details of her affair with Michael and her troubles since they'd broken up, going over it so many times she felt like a record stuck in a groove.

'Do you have somewhere else to stay tonight?' the woman officer asked as they prepared to leave. 'We'll send someone to make this place secure, but you shouldn't stay here on your own from now on.'

'I – yes, I can go to my gran's . . . Oh, but she hasn't got a spare bed now.' She stood there, feeling utterly dumb, unable to think of an alternative.

'Come round to my place and crash on the floor,' Carla offered. 'Sue won't mind. You can think of something more permanent tomorrow.'

Jenny could only nod. 'I'll pack some things.' She took plastic bags and stuffed every garment she could find that was untouched into them, emptying her drawers and her shelves. She didn't want *him* coming back to finish creating mayhem. And she didn't want to come back here herself, either. Not ever.

It wasn't until the following morning, as they were getting ready for work, that Jenny remembered her mother's embroideries. How lucky she'd forgotten about them and left them in the car boot! As she was fumbling in her bag for her keys, she found the scratchie. Well, she certainly didn't feel lucky at the moment! Still, she got out a coin and scratched off the coating.

As she studied the numbers, she gasped and checked everything again. But she hadn't made a mistake. 'Five thousand dollars!' She raised her voice to yell, 'Carla, I just won five thousand dollars on a scratchie. Oh, I don't believe this!' Then she was weeping again and her friend was comforting her.

'But why are you crying, you idiot? You've won some money. That's good news, for a change.'

'Because this is the answer, don't you see?'

'Call me stupid, but I don't see. Five thousand dollars isn't exactly a fortune.'

'It's enough to get me to England. I'm going to stay with Mum.' Michael wouldn't be able to reach her there or even find out where she was.

'Wow! Good idea.' Carla went back to her breakfast, waving one hand at the phone. 'Be my guest. Phone her now and tell her.'

Jenny picked up the receiver, then put it down again. 'No. I'm not giving her the chance to speak to Dad. He'll say no for sure and she always does as he tells her. I'm not even going to tell Gran.' She hugged her arms around her chest. 'I'm shit-scared, Carla. That policeman was right. Michael's a real sicko. I'm leaving the country. And if that means that bastard's won, well, he's won.'

'What about your job?'

'I'll tell my supervisor what's happened. I think he'll understand. He's been asking me if anything's wrong. And if he doesn't give me leave, I'll quit.' It was better to be alive and unemployed than dead – or raped – or both.

After Carla had left, Jenny rang work and told them what had happened, then phoned the detectives. Before she could say anything about her plans they asked her to go to the police station and answer some more questions.

What they said made her even more determined to leave Perth. Michael had an alibi. Well, of course he did. Two of his sleazy friends had sworn he'd been with them at the hotel drinking, they'd gone there straight after work and stayed until closing time. And a barman remembered seeing him, because he'd complained about a wrong order, but the guy couldn't decide on the exact time for this, as things had been pretty busy around then.

Jenny looked the female detective in the eyes. 'I knew you wouldn't be able to prove anything, but I swear to you it's him.'

'I believe you.'

The male detective looked at her thoughtfully, then nodded. He was inclined to believe her, too. The suspect was a cocky bastard and had smirked the whole time they were interviewing him. He *smelled* bad, as far as he was concerned. And the victim was as nice as that guy was suss. 'We'll keep an eye on him from now on. Your parents' neighbours gave us a clear description, even to the colour and make of his car. We both believe you, Jenny.'

'You do?'

The female detective smiled at her. 'You've got that sort of face, Jenny Stevenson. Honest. So what are you going to do? You'd be best getting away for a while, if you can.'

Jenny managed a near smile. 'I'm going to England to join my mother.'

'Your ex won't know her address?'

'No. It's a rented house. She went there after I broke up with him.'

'Perfect. Leave us your contact details, though.'

It was not until she was sitting on a plane that Jenny remembered the note she'd scribbled to her gran and forgotten to post in her hurry to get away. It was still in her pocket. Oh, well, she'd ring from England. She snuggled down in the seat. She hadn't felt so safe for a long time. Soon she was asleep.

# Nine

The sun was low in the sky and it had been a balmy spring day. Rosalind walked slowly round the gardens of Destan Manor with Jonathon, a short stroll, so as not to overstrain her ankle. Dusty trailed behind them, sniffing at this and that, wagging his tail whenever someone looked his way. Rosalind felt more at peace with the world than she had done for a long time.

She bent to caress a patch of vivid purple aubretia that tumbled over a low, grey stone wall above a clump of bright daffodils, then half turned to smile at Jonathon. 'These are so beautiful, aren't they? I think I'll do a Dorset garden in spring as one of my next pieces, with an art-nouveau kind of lady in the centre, slender and elegant with sweeping skirts that tangle into the flowers till you can't tell which is which.'

'That sounds beautiful.'

'It's good sometimes to escape into fantasy art – though I enjoy capturing reality, too.'

She also enjoyed talking to someone who understood her references. Paul would have asked what she meant, Liz would have told her to do something from the twentieth century, and her children would just have shrugged and said, Yeah, yeah, very nice – no, Jenny might have been genuinely interested. But Jonathon, well, he seemed tuned into the same cultural things as she was. It was one of the many things which made him such an easy and pleasant companion.

As they reached the end of the alley, he took hold of her hand and swung her to face him. 'I've been trying not to say this, but I can't hold it in any longer. Rosalind, dearest Rosalind, you do realize I've fallen in love with you, don't you?'

She stood and stared at him, mouth open. She had sort of realized it, she admitted to herself, but she had not let herself face up to it, or to her own feelings for him. She was attracted, definitely attracted, though she couldn't understand how this had happened. She had not encouraged him to be more than a friend, because she was not the sort of person to be unfaithful. Only – she had seen so little of Paul during the past year or two, and he seemed to have changed . . . and Jonathon was so . . . She didn't let herself finish that thought.

Gnats drifted past them in a cloud, trailing a thin wailing sound that seemed to express exactly how she felt. She could not be less than honest with him. 'Oh, Jonathon, why didn't I meet you twenty-five years ago?'

His voice was soft. 'You were at the other side of the world and actually, I took a while to settle down, rebelling against the burden of all this.' He waved a hand towards the house. 'Then Dad died suddenly and it all came to me, so I had no choice. Later I fell in love with Isabel and I think she loved me at first, I really do! Though it's hard to be sure now, after all the acrimony.' He stared into the distance. 'Only, I wouldn't wipe out my sons any more than you'd wipe out your children. We've both reaped the pleasure of children from our marriages, even if other things haven't been – wonderful.'

As she met his solemn gaze, she tried to find the right words to answer him, but failed because her thoughts were in a total tangle.

'Well, we've met now, Rosalind, and I don't think you're indifferent to me.' He took her other hand and raised it to his lips, gazing into her eyes, trying to gauge her response. He saw only confusion.

Her voice was breathless, soft as everything else about her. 'You must think I'm stupid, but I hadn't realized until now how you felt – or how I felt, either. No,' she corrected, determined to be absolutely honest. 'I had realized, but I just hadn't faced it. I've never even looked at another man before, you see.'

He nodded. 'You seem like the sleeping princess sometimes, slightly out of touch with reality. You're not happy with Paul, though, are you?'

She stared blindly at the masses of colour around them. She didn't want to acknowledge that Jonathon was right, but that would be cowardly, something the new Rosalind was trying very hard to avoid. 'No. I'm not happy with him and I haven't been for a long time.' She closed her eyes for a moment before saying the rest of it and facing things squarely. 'He's good in bed, but not much use as a husband and father. Well, you can't be when you're never there. And where he's heading now isn't where I want to go. I'm not even sure I can pretend any more, let alone follow him.'

Silence whispered around them for a few moments, then she stretched out one hand to touch his cheek briefly. 'I *am* attracted to you, Jonathon, but I've been married a long time and we've both been faithful, so Paul and I do share a bond of loyalty, if nothing else. I can't just – walk away from everything. Your marriage is over, you're cut off from your children and I can tell how that hurts you. If I left Australia, came to live in England, I might cut myself off from mine, and I don't think I could bear that.'

And besides, Paul cared enough about their marriage to arrange this second honeymoon, even if it had gone awry. She had held on to that thought through her anger with him and the damned company.

She let her hand drop and walked on. Jonathon walked with her, not interrupting, allowing her time to think. Dusk closed in around them, hiding the flush on her face, encouraging more confidences. 'Paul and I have admitted that we've grown apart and we've agreed to try to – get closer again. I have to give it a chance.'

'And you're not the sort to have an affair.' To him it was part of her charm. 'But would it upset you greatly if I kissed you? Just this once? I've been longing to for days.'

Without waiting for an answer, he drew her into his arms, holding her for a few moments to gaze down into her eyes. Love shone brightly in his face.

When he bent his head to kiss her, she gave in to temptation and with an inarticulate murmur, she put her arms round his neck. She did not hold back because she wasn't going to do this again and wanted something to remember him by. When they stopped kissing, she rested her head on his shoulder and let him hold her for a long time.

At last he pulled away. 'May I remain your friend, Rosalind? I promise I won't pester or embarrass you about this.'

'You *are* my friend.' She swallowed a hard lump that was sitting in her throat. How quickly she had grown to love this man. *Love him?* Yes, this was love. She couldn't imagine life without him now, couldn't even contemplate going back to Australia and never seeing him again!

But she didn't voice those thoughts because acting selfishly would mean hurting Paul and her children. She reached out to hold Jonathon's hand, allowing herself that small pleasure, and together they strolled back through the softly shadowed gardens.

By now he knew her real preferences, so made her some coffee and said in a more normal tone, 'My sons will be visiting me for the fundraising fête. They come every year.'

She was glad to talk of something else. 'I shall look forward to meeting them.'

He stared down into his cup. 'Isabel doesn't like them staying here – she wants to stop all the family traditions and get Giles to break the trust when he grows up, but the more she keeps them away from Destan, the more the boys seem to love it.' He gave a wry smile. 'There's an extra fascination in the forbidden, don't you think? They come here every year at this time. That's part of our divorce agreement. They think the fête is enormous fun.'

'I'll look forward to it all. Perhaps you'd like to bring them round to tea?' Twelve-year-old boys on their best behaviour could be delightful. Or utterly ghastly, if they were in an off mood. She could remember Tim at that age, before he'd withdrawn from any closeness with her.

'I think it'd look better if I gave everyone tea here – you, me, Harry.' Because he knew Isabel questioned the boys when they got back and would love to find an excuse to keep Giles and Rufus away from him in future.

As they drank their coffee and chatted quietly, Rosalind saw how his glances sometimes betrayed his feelings and wondered if hers did the same. She was very conscious of his body – and of her own. How short a distance his hand was from hers! She kept wanting to kiss him again. Or at least hold his hand.

But she didn't.

And neither did he.

\* \* \*

Tim took the money back to the dealer and handed it over.

'Where's the rest?'

'What do you mean?'

'I give you fifty packets. There's money here for only forty. Where's the rest?'

'I don't have any more.' Tim's mind raced back to his hour on the street. Wayne had come up to chat to him. They'd been laughing and horsing around a bit. Surely his friend hadn't robbed him?

Who else could it be? No one else had touched him, and a serious thief would have taken all the dope.

'Someone must have picked my pocket and—'

'Do you think I came down in the last shower of rain?' The dealer beckoned and two figures stepped out of the shadows.

Tim backed away, but the two men dragged him outside. One of them flung him hard against the wall, then punched him several times. When the fist slammed into his gut again, he was violently sick, unable to control himself.

'Shit!' said a voice up above his crouched body. 'This bastard just puked all over my shoes.'

'Kick him in the balls.'

Tim curled up, trying to protect himself. 'Please, no! I won't . . . It was an accident, losing those packets.'

A foot slammed into his back and pain exploded everywhere. 'I make fuckin' sure you don't have any more accidents, man! And you don't push for no one else in this town. Got it?'

He screamed, but they ignored that and continued to beat him till he felt himself losing consciousness. He was sure by then that they intended to kill him.

He woke early next morning, surprised to find himself still alive and lying in an alley he didn't recognize. It took him a while to drag himself painfully to his feet, for every inch of him seemed to hurt. Although people were passing the end of the alley, they didn't come to help but hurried away when they saw him staggering around.

He leaned against a wall and began to weep, but it didn't make any difference. No one came to help him. After a while, he stopped sobbing and staggered towards the street. Oh, hell, what was he going to do? Those bastards had emptied his wallet and money belt. Or someone else had.

He was only sure about one thing: he had to get out of town fast. He didn't even dare go back to confront Wayne and pick up his clothes.

At first he stumbled blindly along the streets, but he found a ten-dollar note in an inside pocket and a stop at a burger joint for two cups of strong coffee helped him pull himself together. Another stop bought him some aspirin and the pain receded a little. It took him a while to work out what to do, but the only safe place he could think of was the cemetery, so he went there and hid among the tombstones, shivering every time he heard a car drive past.

Come nightfall, he'd retrieve his money and passport and leave town.

He was going back to Australia, even if he had to ring up and grovel to his father for the rest of the ticket money. And once he got there, he was never, ever going to leave it again.

After another disturbed night lying worrying, Audrey went into her granddaughter's room and stared at the smooth, wrinkle-free bedcovers. Seven o'clock in the morning. Bed not slept in again. And no threat seemed to have any effect on Louise's increasingly nocturnal habits.

The girl did clear up after herself now and do her washing more or less regularly. But that was a minor victory. Set it against Louise's blatant refusal to keep reasonable hours or let her grandmother know where she was going – not to mention a certain glassy-eyed look the last couple of times she'd come in late – and Audrey knew she was beaten. As for studying, well, she suspected Louise was cutting classes as well, but couldn't prove it.

It's time for someone else to take over now, she decided. John's right. I've given it a fair go, but I don't intend to make a martyr of myself.

She waited until about four o'clock, to allow for time differences between the UK and Australia, then picked up the phone and rang Paul's head office. It took a while to persuade them to give her his number in Hong Kong, but she did, because she was absolutely determined. Though he wasn't going to like her telling them there was a problem with his younger daughter, she knew. Well, too bad. There *was* a problem.

When she got through to the hotel in Hong Kong, she fell lucky. Paul answered his room phone at the second ring. 'Yes?'

'It's Audrey here.'

'Ma-in-law! Hey, nice to hear from you. How are things?'

She grimaced as his voice took on that over-jolly, patronizing tone he always used with her. How she hated it! 'Not going well, so we'll not waste time on chit-chat. Paul, I can't cope with Louise any longer. You'll have to make other arrangements for her.'

He sighed. 'Have you rung Ros? The children are her business, really.'

'No, I haven't rung her and I'm not going to. You're nearer to Perth by a few thousand miles than she is. I'll expect you to fly down here at the weekend. You can take Louise away then. I've had more than enough of that young woman.'

'Look, put her on the phone and I'll have a very strong word with her. I promise you, I'll make her so afraid she'll—'

'Not good enough, Paul. I'm sixty-seven not twenty-seven. I can't cope and dammit, I won't even try any more. You have until Saturday to fetch her.'

He scowled at the phone. Stupid old cow! 'I can't make it on Saturday, I'm afraid, Audrey.'

'Then I'll have to call social services, say she's unmanageable and ask them to take her off my hands. She's not eighteen yet, after all. I think they'll be interested.'

'*You wouldn't!*'

'I would, actually. I don't want police raiding my house looking for drugs or—'

'*Drugs?*'

'I'm pretty certain she's taking something.'

'I'll be there on Saturday. Don't tell her I'm coming. Let me surprise her.' He'd surprise Liz, too, while he was at it. He'd missed her since she'd returned to Perth, missed her astringent conversation and sexy body. She'd been very firm about not continuing the relationship, but he was sure he could persuade her to see him while he was there. They'd been good together in the sack. If only Ros were more proactive about sex like Liz was.

As he put down the phone, anger sizzled through him and

he thumped the pillow with one clenched fist. Bloody kids! You gave them the best of everything, private schools, expensive holidays, bicycles, and who knew what else – and what did they do to thank you? Went off the rails. Abandoned their studies. Ran off to America. Oh, hell, his youngest daughter doing drugs like her brother. *Why? Where had he and Ros gone wrong?*

He sat down on the edge of the bed, chewing his lip. Unfortunately Audrey was right to ring him. This was not something Ros would be able to cope with. In fact, Ros must have been weaker than he'd thought on the discipline side. First Tim, now Louise. And even Jenny had chosen a no-hoper of a guy when she was let loose on the world, though she'd had the sense to realize that and leave the fellow, at least.

He was going to nip this present mess of Louise's in the bud right away, but first he had to figure out what you did with a seventeen-year-old rebel in Hong Kong.

It was not until he was getting ready for bed that an idea struck him. He began to smile. Yes, that should sort it out nicely.

The following day he strode out of Perth airport and hailed a taxi. At Audrey's he paid off the driver and turned to find his mother-in-law waiting for him at the door. They didn't waste time on greetings.

'Louise is still asleep,' Audrey said in a low voice. 'She didn't get back until about four o'clock this morning.'

Something caught his eye and he didn't follow her inside. 'What the hell is Ros's car doing here?'

'Louise has been using it. She said Rosalind gave her permission.' Audrey's heart sank. Oh no, not more lies! And Paul looked so grimly angry today she hardly recognized him.

'Ros definitely didn't do that.' She'd have told him if she had. She'd told him every other goddam detail of her preparations for England in those boring letters she wrote weekly when he was away. She hardly ever used emails, and hadn't bothered to get online in England. He was going to drag her into the twenty-first century, even if she screamed all the way. He pushed those thoughts aside. He had to deal with his daughter first.

'Tell me the details about Louise.' He listened in growing fury, then said in a tight, clipped voice, 'You stay here and I'll go upstairs. This may take a while. You were absolutely right to send for me. You – er, might like to put the radio on. There will definitely be some shouting.'

As he opened the door of Louise's bedroom, he stared around in disgust at the mess. Dirty clothes on the floor, litter everywhere. By the side of the bed was a cotton thing that looked like a shoulder bag made from a flour sack, so he upended it on the desk by the window. A small packet of what looked like herbs fell out. He sniffed it. Pot. Pray that was all she was on. But there were a few pills, too. He didn't know enough about drugs to guess what they were.

He began to search the drawers and all the time his daughter slept peacefully behind him, looking as innocent as the child she had been not long ago. There was also a packet of condoms. Bile rose in his throat. His daughter screwing around. At seventeen! How had she got into all this?

He stood by the bedside, contemplating the child who had always been his favourite, the one who looked most like him. She appeared innocent and pretty still, sprawled on her side with one hand curled beneath her cheek. But she wasn't innocent, she was spoiled, dirty. He bent closer and saw the ring in her nose, the streaks of dirty blonde on one side of her hair. She looked so tarty that for a moment disgust rose like vomit in his throat. Then he reached out and shook her – hard.

'Hey! Wh–what? *Dad!*' She jerked upright in the bed. 'What are *you* doing here?'

'Your grandmother phoned. It seems, Louise, that you've been upsetting her, as well as burning the candle at both ends.' He flicked one finger towards the things on the desk.

She gasped and stared at him, her eyes large and frightened, but didn't say anything.

'I thought you had a little more sense, but you didn't waste much time following Tim's example, did you?'

Her voice was sulky. 'Everyone does something nowadays. It's only dope.'

'And the tablets?'

'Amphetamines. To help me keep my weight down.' They gave you the most lovely feeling of energy and optimism, too.

115

Pity they were so expensive. 'They're not hard drugs, Dad.'

'I don't expect *my* children to do *any* drugs. Hard or soft.'

She laughed, a shaky nervous sound. 'They're no worse than alcohol. The law's stupid. This is the twenty-first century, not the—'

She didn't finish what she was saying, because he slapped her across her face, hard, then slapped her again.

After an initial screech, she cowered down on the bed, sobbing noisily.

'I've never hit you before, Louise. Perhaps I should have.' He reached out and held her at arm's length, forcing words past the anger that seemed to have solidified in his throat. 'Now listen, and listen well, young woman.' He gave her another shake for emphasis. 'I learned my lesson with Tim. I overlooked this and overlooked that – and he carried on mucking around. Heaven knows where he is now – whether he's still alive, even.'

She looked at him in horror.

'Surely that possibility had occurred to you? America can be a dangerous place. He hasn't been in touch for months.' And Paul worried about that, though he hadn't said so to Ros.

Louise stared up at her father and waited for more harsh words – or more slaps. He shook her again, but less violently, then said in a tight, angry voice.

'I'm *not* going down the same path with you, Louise. I trusted Tim to grow out of his silliness and he ran away instead, got in deeper. You have a simple choice ahead of you, really simple. Behave yourself – and I'll be watching closely, so don't think you can pull the wool over *my* eyes as you have your mother's – or get out of my life and family this minute. I shan't give you a second chance, either.'

She could only goggle at him. *Get out of the family!* He couldn't mean that. But she saw the grim determination in his eyes and realized with a jolt that he did.

He leaned forward until his face was almost touching hers. 'Do you believe me? Do you believe that I mean *exactly* what I say, Louise?'

She nodded, gulping.

He moved back and stood there with arms folded. 'Right then, it's entirely your choice. If you don't toe the line from now on, I'll cut you off from the family within the hour – and push you out of your grandmother's front door myself.'

The chairman would have recognized him. The chairman really approved of the way Stevenson cut through the crap when it was necessary. So would one or two cheating managers whose thieving Paul had uncovered, and whom he had sent packing there and then.

But Louise had never seen her father like this and was, quite literally, terrified. 'D–Dad, don't!'

He looked at his watch. 'I'll give you exactly one minute to decide, Louise. Not one second longer. After all, it's a very simple choice.'

She started sobbing.

'And weeping won't make any difference at all.' Implacable, he waited until she capitulated – as he'd known she would.

# Ten

Rosalind picked up the phone. 'Yes?'

The voice was hesitant. 'Mum? Is that you?'

'Jenny! How nice to speak to you.' Rosalind glanced at the clock. She was meeting Harry in five minutes and they were going to have coffee with the organizers of the auction. Didn't people always ring up for a chat when you were in a hurry?

'Mum – oh, Mum, I'm in England, at the bus station in Poole. Can you come and pick me up?'

'*In Poole!* Jenny, what have you *done*?'

There was the sound of sobbing at the other end. 'It's not what you think, Mum. I – please can you pick me up? I'll tell you about it then.'

'Yes, of course. Where did you say you were?' But although she would be glad to see Jenny, Rosalind's heart sank.

She cancelled everything and drove into Poole. Her anger vanished as she hugged her daughter and saw how haunted and jumpy Jenny was looking, not to mention how much weight she had lost. 'What's wrong? Have you been ill?'

'Not exactly. I'll – explain later.'

Jenny picked up her big suitcase and Rosalind took the piece of cabin luggage out of her hand.

'That one's got some of your embroideries in, Mum. I had the rest shipped out – these two may be a bit crumpled, but they're safe, at least.'

Why should things not be safe? What had been going on in Perth? Rosalind looked sideways at her daughter, not attempting to start the car. 'Tell me.'

Jenny's face crumpled. 'It's Michael. He's been – oh, Mum, he's been stalking me. He kept phoning at all hours. I couldn't get a proper night's sleep unless I unplugged the phone. And then he broke into my flat and trashed everything. I've been

118

terrified. If your neighbours hadn't turned up when I was getting those embroideries for you, he'd have raped me.' And every time she thought about that, she wanted to curl up into a ball and scream herself into oblivion.

Rosalind felt horror trickle through her as she took Jenny in her arms, shushing her and patting her back as she had done when her daughter had been a child. Now, Jenny was five feet nine and a woman grown, but she needed holding just as much as the child had.

When the tears had subsided and Jenny had blown her nose several times, they looked at one another.

'You aren't – angry with me, Mum?'

'Only with Michael. But how did you get the money for your fare, love?' If it was from her mother, it'd have to be paid back at once. Rosalind knew Audrey had very little to spare.

Jenny gave a hiccupy laugh as she explained about her timely win. 'I took the money and ran, Mum. Fled for my life. I was terrified. I thought – no, I *knew* he was going to kill me if I stayed in Perth.'

'*Kill you?*'

Jenny nodded. 'The policeman said he was a sicko.' She explained about the underwear laid out on the bed, the knife and mock blood.

Horror kept Rosalind silent for a moment. 'You did the right thing, then. But Jenny, if you'd rung and explained what was happening, I'd have sent you the money for your fare earlier.'

'I thought of that, but Dad didn't want any of us to come here with you. He'd have persuaded you not to help me – or arranged something else. Only, you see,' her voice quavered, 'I needed *you*. Do you mind very much?' She reached across to take her mother's hand.

'I don't mind at all, not now I understand.' Rosalind squeezed the fingers that were quivering against hers. 'And your father doesn't dictate everything I do.'

Her voice was so quiet and sure Jenny stared at her in surprise. 'He usually tells you – well, he tells us all what to do.'

Rosalind stared down blindly at the steering wheel. 'I've let him do that in the past, to my shame. But he won't be giving me quite so many orders from now on – or at least, if he does, I won't be obeying them.'

'You sound different.'

'Yes. I think I am. We can talk about that later, though. We're both shivering, so let me get you home. The country-side round here is gorgeous. There's nothing like pretty scenery for soothing the savage breast.'

When they got to Burraford, Rosalind settled Jenny in front of the fire with a big mug of coffee and tried to ring Paul, breaking her normal rule of not disturbing him when he was working on a project. But although it would be the middle of the night in Hong Kong, he wasn't in his room, and the hotel receptionist said he was away for the weekend. Which seemed very strange. He didn't usually take holidays when he was working on a project. 'I'd like to leave a message, then. And tell him it's extremely urgent . . .'

That evening Jonathon decided to ring Rosalind simply because he wanted to talk to her. Another few days and his sons would be here, and after that her husband would be back. Oh, hell, he didn't want this interlude to end, this brief idyll when they'd forged a friendship and fallen in love.

'Hello?'

He smiled at the way her voice always sounded as breathy and uncertain as a young girl's. 'It's me, Rosalind. Do you fancy going to the pub for a drink?'

'I can't, I'm afraid. My daughter's just arrived from Australia. Jenny, the eldest. She's been having trouble with an ex-boyfriend.' She lowered her voice. 'He's been stalking her and she's very upset.'

'Anything I can do to help?'

'Not really.'

'I shall miss you.' He didn't have to spell it out that her daughter's arrival meant their closeness had ended sooner than they'd both expected.

'Yes. I shall, too.' She didn't dare talk more openly to him. She had done nothing to be ashamed of – *Nothing but fall in love*, that truthful little voice said inside her head – but even their public friendship would have to be lower-key now. And perhaps that was a good thing. Though it didn't feel like a good thing.

When he had put the phone down, Jonathon poured himself

a whisky, then went to pace up and down the long gallery upstairs as he did sometimes when he was upset. The creaking floorboards suited his mood today, as did the frayed hangings and worn carpets.

At first he was angry that the daughter had come, then he got annoyed with himself because stalking was a very serious matter and any mother worth her salt would naturally drop everything to look after that daughter in those circumstances. But the thought of not being with Rosalind hurt even more than he had anticipated.

'Oh, sod them all!' he told the last bit of amber liquid in his glass. 'I've never had any luck with women.'

Well, at least the boys were coming down the following weekend. That was something to look forward to. And he'd get Harry to invite him, Rosalind and the daughter round for coffee. He had to see his lovely, gentle darling sometimes, to make sure she was all right, at least. He poured the rest of the whisky down in a gulp and went to refill his glass.

Not even his divorce had made him feel this bad emotionally, because by then all affection between himself and Isabel had been gone and he'd only been left with anger at her rapaciousness – and relief at being rid of her.

The house creaked and shifted around him and the ghosts of his ancestors rustled past, as they always seemed to do when he was alone in this room. Thin spindly people like him and Harry, with sad narrow faces. He never quite knew whether he was imagining them or whether they really did gather round him, but they felt real enough. And certainly, when this mood came upon him, Dusty grew uneasy, whining and twitching at the shadows. But dogs were like that. They could sense your mood – and perhaps see your family ghosts. He looked down at the furry face and wagging tail. Dogs didn't pretend. They gave their love wholeheartedly and unconditionally. As he'd like to give his.

For once, he drew no comfort from the sense of solid continuity to Gilles D'Estaing, who had carved out his own territory in the conquered foreign land of England, or to the many ancestors who had allowed their name to be twisted into a more English sound. He raised the glass, drinking a silent toast to Araminta Destang, his favourite ancestor, who had saved the estate from destruction during the Civil War. 'Paul Destan!' he toasted next. The poor fellow had lost an arm at Waterloo, but had gone on to sire four sons. And had made the final name change.

Jonathon went to look for some more whisky, opened his reserve bottle and drank Rosalind's health, trying to ignore the tears trickling down his face. Who said men didn't cry? He'd cried when the court had awarded custody of his sons to Isabel. And he was crying now.

How was Rosalind feeling? Was she missing him? Would she weep into her pillow tonight?

In Australia Paul Stevenson paced up and down the hall of his own house. Louise was in bed after a very unpleasant day, having cried herself to a complete standstill as he and Audrey had gone through her room with a fine toothcomb, exposing the evidence of her peccadilloes, which were not as bad, thank goodness, as he had feared. Though he hadn't said that to her. No, he had acted as if she were ripe for the gallows and he the hangman, while she had wept and sobbed and promised him whatever he demanded. 'Take out that bloody nose ring for a start!' he'd roared, and when she'd done so, he'd tossed it into the rubbish bin.

And while he had ranted on at Louise, Audrey had sat there and watched, tight-lipped. He hoped she was upset behind that stoical mask. She should be. She had failed lamentably and she knew it, the silly old bat. But at least she hadn't wept on him as his daughter had.

God, how he hated snivelling women! And although Louise had promised faithfully not to misbehave any more, he wasn't going to leave her in Australia in a flat. You couldn't trust seventeen year olds. You needed to watch them all the time. His two youngest had taught him that, by God they had, and he didn't intend to fail with Louise as he had with Tim. She was going to grow tougher and she was going to do well in life. He hated other people boasting about how successful their grown-up children were, hated being unable to match tales with them. Hated most of all the thought that *his* children had grown into fools and wastrels.

For the first time he wondered if Ros had been right and it

had been unwise to take her away at precisely this time in Louise's development, then he shrugged. It was essential to his career that his wife loosen her ties to Perth. That had to come first. Perhaps he should have let Louise come to England with them, then? On reflection, he supposed so – and would have done if he had known all the facts. But he hadn't really wanted a teenage daughter hanging around. He still didn't.

Hell, he was horny tonight. Solving a crisis always had that effect on him. And Liz was only a few hundred yards away. He listened. Not a sound. Louise had been so exhausted she'd barely made it up the stairs before tumbling into bed. Maybe he could arrange something? He could sneak out to Liz's place if Bill was at one of his meetings – or he could meet her in the garage here so they could screw themselves silly on the old couch. Worth trying. He always thought better when he wasn't in lust.

He went into his home office and picked up the phone.

Louise, who'd been lying in bed pretending to be asleep and worrying about what her father intended to do with her, heard the sound of the phone and sat up. Who was Dad phoning at this time of night? If he thought he was just going to dump her on someone else, she wanted to know about it.

She crept into her parents' bedroom and picked up the receiver carefully. She'd listened in a few times from here. The phone system was in excellent order because her father had brought the company back several times to fix things like echoes on the line or clicks from other extensions. As long as you didn't make a noise and put down the receiver *after* the other person, no one knew you were listening in.

Her father's voice. 'Liz?'

Louise frowned. What was her father phoning *her* up for? Liz was her mother's friend and he didn't get on all that well with her.

'Paul?'

'Who else?'

'I thought we'd agreed not to get in touch.'

'I'm here in Perth.'

A hiss of indrawn breath.

'Any chance of seeing you?'

'No.'

123

'Liz, baby, we're good together. You know we are.'

Louise listened, stunned. Her father's voice had gone all warm and smarmy, the way it did when he was charming someone. But this was *Liz* he was talking to, her mother's friend, and from what he had said . . .

'Surely we can seize an odd moment or two to satisfy our mutual needs? You said Bill was a second-rater in bed. You said you were never satisfied with him. I think you were quite satisfied with my performance, though.' He chuckled softly.

Louise wrinkled her nostrils in disgust. How gross, to screw her mother's best friend! And *he* called what she'd done bad!

'I thought I made it plain that I don't want to continue the affair. The last thing I want to do is hurt Rosalind. I must have gone crazy in Hong Kong, but I'm not crazy any more. It's over. Finito.' Her voice softened for a moment. 'It was great, it really was, but it's finished. Enjoy your life.' She put the phone down without waiting for an answer.

From below, Louise heard the sound of a phone slamming down, set the handpiece gently in its cradle and hurried into her bedroom, lying with her back to the door so that her face was hidden. Who'd ever have thought it? *Liz and her father!* Oh, wow!

Wait till Tim heard about it. She sighed. She did miss him. The two of them had always been close. They were both into *living* – with a capital L. Jenny was a wimp and Mum was just a doormat. A nice doormat, but she still let everyone tread on her. Though actually Dad was a lot kinder to her than anyone else, so he must have some feelings for her – if not enough to stay faithful.

When she heard footsteps in the stairwell, Louise closed her eyes and started breathing slowly and evenly. He came in to check, of course. He'd said he would and he always did as he'd threatened. He'd told her that if she so much as put her nose outside the house without his permission, she wouldn't get back inside again. A shiver ran down her spine. He meant it, too. Indignation followed the shiver. Who was he to preach at her when he'd been cheating on her mother? Probably for years.

Tim had hinted at that sort of thing before, said he'd seen Dad out with a young chick once in Sydney, but she hadn't believed him. She did now. Oh, she wished her brother were here to talk to! He was the only one who understood her.

And she wished she knew what her father was going to do with her. The thought of him tossing her out, so that she had to get a dead-end job and manage on her own, definitely did not appeal. Why should she anyway, when her father was rich? Well, comfortable. So OK, she'd have to toe the line for a bit and that didn't really appeal, either. Those oldies forgot what it was like to be young and full of energy. Well, she was full of energy when she took those pills, but how the hell was she going to manage without them now? She'd lost a lot of weight and she looked good. She'd kill herself if she got fat again. Nobody loved you when you were fat.

A tear trickled down her cheek, followed by another. If only Mum was here. Dad was never as bad when Mum was around.

The following morning Paul woke Louise at six, dragging her from the bed, having had an idea about how he could start the new regime. 'Come on! I'm going running, so you're coming too. I want you where I can keep an eye on you.'

'*Running!* But I – Dad, stop! Hey, I don't do things like that.'

His smile made her shiver. 'You don't think I'm going to leave you alone in the house, do you, Louise? You must think I'm a fool.'

'But I haven't had any breakfast!' She hadn't eaten anything at all yesterday and she was hollow inside.

'You don't get breakfast until afterwards. One exercises on an empty stomach. Hurry up, or I'll drag you outside in your pyjamas. You'll need shorts and a tee shirt – and wear some joggers that aren't simply a fashion statement.'

His expression was so grim she hurried, slumping down breathlessly in her seat as he drove them down to Cottesloe beach. He'd put her mother's car away and brought out his own. Normally she would have loved riding in it. While he'd been away, she'd even toyed with the idea of borrowing it and taking it for a spin, but had not quite dared.

She shivered. A light rain had begun to fall and it was chilly. It was autumn now, after all. 'Can't I just stay in the car and watch?'

'Certainly not. I thought young women liked to keep themselves fit and trim. You're always worrying about putting on weight. Maybe this is the answer. Those pills certainly aren't.'

'I've kept my weight down without any of this exercise crap.'

His gaze was as chill and assessing as a meat inspector looking at a carcase. 'You're slim, yes, but grossly unfit.' He gave her upper arm a squeeze and pulled a face at its lack of muscle tone, then slapped her thigh. 'Flabby! To look good, flesh needs to be firm.' He got out of the car. 'Come on! I'm going to run up and down the beach where I can keep an eye on you and if I see you stop moving, you're in deep trouble. You can do a hundred yards running and a hundred yards walking until I tell you to stop. That's how beginners start training.'

Anger burned in her, but she kept her mouth closed and did as ordered. She'd watched Tim blurt out defiance and get nowhere with it. Her bastard of a father always had all the answers. At first she did run, thinking she might as well get some benefit from this, but soon her feet felt like lead, an iron band settled round her chest and she could only stagger along. But every time she looked along the beach she could see him staring at her, so she didn't stop moving.

When he came jogging over to see why she'd slowed down, he looked fit and energetic for all he was nearly fifty, and she could see a couple of young women giving him the eye. She was panting and puffing, was soaked to the skin, felt like death warmed up, and no doubt looked it, too. She hated him – *hated* him!

'You're in worse condition than I thought. All right, I'll make it a short session today. It's nearly breakfast time. We'll go home and shower, then we'll find a café. There's nothing to eat at home.' How different it felt without Ros's efficient organization!

Louise brightened. This was more like it. She loved having breakfast in a café.

But when they got there, he ordered for her – fresh fruit salad and a low-fat muffin – not even asking what she wanted.

'Couldn't we have croissants?' she begged, trying to make her voice as girlie-soft as she could.

'Full of grease and calories. You are about to get fit, young lady, really fit.'

He didn't even look up from his newspaper as he spoke.

Louise sat there, fuming inside but not daring to interrupt him. She was so hungry she ate the bloody muffin and picked up the crumbs from her plate with a dampened fingertip.

When he'd read the paper from cover to cover, he leaned back and studied her. She hated it when he did that. You could never outstare him.

'I've decided to take you to Hong Kong with me, then on to England. Since I can't trust you on your own here, I'll find a cramming school for you in England.'

Her initial surge of joy turned into leaden horror. 'A *school!* But I've left school.'

'You obviously left it too soon, before you were mature enough.'

'But I'm not going to be in England long enough to do any proper studying.'

'And did you do any proper studying here? Your TEE results were pretty pitiful. I had to pull a few strings to get you on that course, you know.'

She slumped down in her chair glaring at him. 'But I've started the course here now.'

'Don't worry. I'll arrange a deferral. Or find you somewhere else to study. You do need some qualifications, I agree.'

They drove home in silence, then she went up to sit in her bedroom while he made phone call after phone call. At first she stood behind her bedroom door and listened to his voice floating up the stairs. Shit, he certainly ordered people around! After a while, she grew tired of business talk, put on some music and turned it up loud, trying to lose herself in the beat.

She nearly jumped out of her skin when he erupted into the bedroom and switched the CD player off. 'No music. Get a book and come downstairs where I can keep an eye on you.'

'What do you think I'm going to do, climb out of my window?'

He slapped her face, leaving her speechless with shock.

'I don't think you've quite realized, Louise, how angry I am. Or how little latitude you have. Now, find yourself a book

127

– no, not a rubbishy spy novel, something worth reading – and come downstairs. We'll be leaving Perth tomorrow. You can spend this afternoon packing. We'll pick up the rest of your stuff from your grandmother's later on.'

'I've never been to Hong Kong,' she ventured after sitting for a while staring at the travel book he'd provided, a dull thing on ancient temples in Indonesia. Her mother had used something from it for an embroidery. It had looked good, too. 'What is there to see? What shall I pack?'

'This won't be a tourist visit. We'll be going on from there within a few days to England, so pack for the English spring. A bit like our winter.'

She huffed one shoulder and pretended to read. Stupid pictures of Asians in silly costumes. Who cared about such things?

He turned back to his own book, but his mind was on other things. He'd have to find her a minder for the next few days while he tied up the loose ends at the Hong Kong branch, but that should be quite easy in a place where labour was cheap. He smiled grimly. She was in for a few shocks, one way or another, his darling little daughter was. All his family were.

He was about to take charge properly. Should have done it years ago, should have *insisted* on Ros moving to New York or London. Well, better late than never.

Rosalind examined the embroideries Jenny had brought and pressed them carefully. They hadn't suffered any damage, thank goodness. She invited Harry round to choose one – and couldn't resist inviting Jonathon, too, feeling guilty but looking forward so much to seeing him and spending a little time in his company.

Jenny hardly left her side all day. 'I'm sorry to hover – I'm a bit nervous still. It hasn't got through to my emotions yet that I'm safe. Do you mind?'

'Not at all. I'll try to ring your father again.'

When she didn't get Paul, she tried her mother and what Audrey had to tell her made her feel quite sick with shock.

Jenny, who had been watching, waiting to have a quick word with Gran, came up and put an arm round her mother as she put down the phone and stared around blankly. 'What's the matter? Mum! Talk to me, please, Mum!'

Rosalind let Jenny help her to a chair because her legs had turned to rubber. 'Did *you* know Louise was misbehaving?'

Jenny avoided her eyes. 'I knew she wasn't studying much. And that she'd got in with a strange crowd.'

'You should have told me.'

'It's a bit hard for one sister to tell on another. I did talk to her, try to make her see sense, but you know what Louise is like.'

'She's been using my car, as well. Told your grandmother I'd given her permission.'

Jenny nodded unhappily.

'And –' Rosalind had to take a deep breath even to get the dreadful admission out – 'your grandmother says she's been on drugs. *Drugs!* At seventeen!' And sex, too – her mother had found condoms in Louise's drawers. 'I *told* your father she was too young to leave on her own.'

'Too immature, you mean. She's like Tim, greedy for life. Take, take, take.' Jenny was still worried about her mother's pallor. 'You can't babysit her for ever, Mum. She has to go out and face the world sometime, even if she mucks things up. It's the only way she'll learn. Shall I make you a coffee?'

Rosalind stared at her blindly, without answering. When the doorbell rang, she didn't even seem to hear it, just continued to stare into space and pleat the material of her skirt.

Jenny went to open it and found herself facing two strangers, both very tall and bony, obviously related. 'You must be Jonathon and Harry Destan.'

'Yes, we are. And you're Jenny?' the woman said. 'You look so like your mother.'

'Yes, I suppose I do. Look, come in. I'm afraid Mother's just had a bit of a shock.'

'What's wrong?' Harry nudged her brother as she spoke because he looked as if he was about to rush off to find Rosalind. Luckily Jenny was gazing towards the kitchen not at her visitors.

'Not – news about your brother?' Harry inquired. They both knew how worried Rosalind was about her son.

'No. Mum phoned Gran and found out that my younger

sister had gone off the rails a bit and my father'd had to fly down to sort things out.' Jenny led the way into the family area near the kitchen. Her mother was still sitting there, but when she saw the visitors she stood up and tried to remember her duties as hostess.

'Harry, Jonathon. Do come and sit down. I'll – um, get you some coffee and . . .' She stopped and shook her head, saying hoarsely, 'I'm sorry. It's not a good time just now. Could you come back tomorrow?'

Only when they'd gone did it occur to Rosalind that if Paul was in Perth he'd probably be at home. Even before the front door had closed on her visitors, she was picking up the phone. 'Paul! Oh, thank goodness I've caught you. How's Louise?'

'Subdued. Look, I'll tell you all about it when I get back. It's not the sort of thing to discuss on the phone.'

She had to know. 'Mum said drugs – and sex.'

'Yes to both.'

'Oh, Paul!'

'I'm dealing with it, Ros, all right?' His voice was impatient. 'Louise and I are flying out to Hong Kong together tomorrow. I'll keep her with me there and bring her back to England next week.'

'Yes. Yes, of course.'

'There's another call on the line, Ros . . .'

She grew angry at his patronizing tone. 'Let them wait.' She took a deep breath. 'I'm afraid I have some other news. Jenny's here in Dorset with me.'

'*Jenny!* What the hell is *she* doing there? Has she lost her job? My god, what have I ever done to deserve such stupid, useless children?'

Rosalind thumped the kitchen surface and shouted down the phone, 'For once, just shut up and listen, Paul! Jenny's ex-boyfriend has been stalking her. She's been in danger and terrified. He tried to rape her, then he broke into her flat and trashed it.'

Silence, then, 'Did she call in the police?'

'Yes, of course. They haven't been able to prove anything, so they said it was better she get away for a while. He – he must be deranged from what he did. *They* reckon he is, anyway.'

'Shit! That's all I need! How did she get the money to fly to England? Did you send it her or did Audrey lend it her?'

'Neither. She won it on a scratchie.'

'She *what*? She should have stayed there and faced him out.'

'Are you mad?' She explained the exact state of Jenny's bed and the carving knife.

'Then he's definitely crazy. I told you he was a no-hoper. And you say the police can do nothing?'

'Nothing. Michael had set up an alibi. She says he's quite clever about such things.'

'He was never clever enough to impress me. Well, it looks like we'll all be playing Happy Families in England for a while, Ros. *You* should enjoy that, at least. So much for a second honeymoon.'

She ignored the gratuitous sarcasm. And she would not, she knew, enjoy having Louise around. Or even Jenny at the moment, when she was discovering so much about herself. She'd just settled into a quiet happy routine and – oh, face it, she was missing Jonathon's company already. 'Do you, um, want to speak to Jenny?'

'Yes, of course I do. I'll get the details and see if there's anything I can do to help the police.' He had a few contacts. Or no, maybe he'd set someone on to watch that sick bastard full time. He wasn't having anyone thinking they could get away with stalking his daughter.

She passed the phone to Jenny, who was standing nearby looking apprehensive.

'I'm not going back!' Jenny hissed as she took the phone.

'Of course not.'

'Hello, Dad – Yes, well, I—' She rolled her eyes at her mother.

Rosalind patted her daughter's shoulder in encouragement, then wandered out into the back garden. The grass was damp and looked very green. The next-door garden was full of trees, some with fat buds on them, nearly ready to burst into leaf, but there were only two trees here, both cropped to within an inch of their lives, standing stiffly on guard at each rear corner of a square of manicured lawn which had a foot-wide flower bed all round the fence edge. Daffodils alternated with aubretia

131

with ruthless geometric precision, courtesy of a fortnightly gardener, who didn't like you 'meddling'. She really missed having her own garden.

When she went back inside, Jenny was sitting in a corner, looking upset. 'How was I to have known Michael would turn out like this? Honestly, Dad is the most unreasonable man I ever met! It's never *his* fault if things go wrong, and he doesn't have any sympathy for anyone else's troubles. You'd think I'd encouraged Michael to stalk me just to annoy Dad.' She jerked to her feet. 'I think I'll go for a walk into the village.' She was desperate for some fresh air and she'd be quite safe here. She had to keep reminding herself of that, reminding herself to get on with her life. 'Do you want anything from the shops?'

'Yes, I do, actually . . .'

When her daughter had left, Rosalind went up to her work-room and took out the embroidery of the family. She picked up the sketch pad and began to rough out her own figure, with a few glances in the mirror. Vulnerable, submissive, too soft for her own good. She was beginning to see that now. Could she show it all in her embroidery? She didn't know, but she was certainly going to try.

When she had cut out the paper figure, she studied herself in the mirror. Her face was more determined than the one in the sketch – but that was now. This picture was going to show how she and her family had been for all those years. If she embroidered it, she would understand it all better. She didn't know why, but she would. Placing the paper figure next to Paul on the embroidery, she studied the effect. Heavens, that was so *like* him, the best figure she had ever done. She was startled every time she looked at it.

After a minute, she frowned and moved her own figure, settling it eventually at the far left side of the embroidery. Yes. That was where she belonged. Not next to him. Not together. They hadn't really been together for quite a while. She could see that now, as well. And she'd do herself in pastel colours, to contrast with the bold dark colours of Paul. She looked down at herself. Why did she always choose such faded colours?

She'd been too quiet about things and far too reasonable.

Jenny was right. *He* wasn't at all reasonable. And neither were the children, not even Jenny. Had she been a bad mother, brought them up wrongly? She'd loved them all, done her very best for them, but – she had to admit it, though it hurt like hell – her love and care hadn't been enough. Tim and Louise had both gone off the tracks, and Jenny – she gasped in horror as she realized it – Jenny had followed in her own footsteps, going out with a dominating man.

Well, everything was going to change. For both her and for Jenny. She would think of her own needs as well as theirs from now on, and never ever again would she fall in with others' wishes if they felt wrong for her.

A sad smile curved her lips for a moment – *change of season*, Paul had said about this trip. She'd not been able to get that phrase out of her thoughts. Change of every bloody thing, it seemed to her.

He wasn't going to like some of the changes, but that didn't make any difference. They had happened now, were still happening and evolving. No one could turn the clock back.

She didn't even want to try.

# Eleven

Rosalind decided she needed to do something to cheer Jenny up and take her mind off her worries. 'Want to come and look at my inheritance from Aunt Sophie?'

'But I thought it was at the other end of the country?'

'It's a small country, love. Southport is six or seven hours away by car – you can do part of the driving if you like. After all, you'll want to see a bit of England while you're here, surely?'

Jenny's face brightened. 'I'd love to see it.'

'I'll give Prue a ring, then let Harry know we're going away for a few days. We'll get back for the fête, though.' She was picking up the phone even as she spoke. 'Prue, just to let you know – my daughter Jenny and I are coming up to Southport for a few days. We'll be there sometime tomorrow afternoon. My elder daughter, yes. It's a long story. Tell you when I see you.'

And a minute later, 'Harry – Jenny and I are heading north for a few days. You couldn't come round and choose an embroidery now, could you? It need only take a few minutes. Yes, I'm definitely feeling better, but we're both a bit down in the dumps, so I thought a trip would cheer us up.'

As she put down the phone, Rosalind saw her daughter's amazed expression and grinned. 'I'm learning to act more decisively – well, trying to.'

Jenny hugged her. 'About time, too, Mum. You go for it!' But would her mother stay more decisive once her father arrived? Jenny doubted it. She knew from her own experience how hard it was to stand up to him.

At the other side of the village, Harry put down the phone and nodded in satisfaction. That'd get Rosalind out of poor

134

Jonathon's hair for a while. He was moping around like a sick puppy worrying about her. Poor old thing. Still, the boys would be coming to Burraford soon and that'd take his mind off Rosalind.

She slung on a raincoat and drove over to Sexton Close, humming tunelessly under her breath. She didn't really like this part of the village. Full of newcomers. And the houses were the sort which tried to look bigger than they were. Places for yuppies, she always thought. Still, the occupants would come to her fête and spend their money with carefully calculated generosity. They always did. Liked to show themselves as part of the village. Ha! You had to be born here to be really part of it. Though some did fit in after a while. Rosalind was that sort – well, she would be if she were free to stay – which she wasn't. Damned pity, that.

When Rosalind spread out the two embroideries, Harry beamed in delight. 'They're absolutely gorgeous,' she said at last, touching one of the figures gently. 'How can you bear to part with them?'

Rosalind shrugged. 'I have plenty more. They only sit in the attic at home. And besides, it's in a good cause. But you'll need to have whichever one you choose framed. I'll pay for that, of course, part of my contribution. Sarah at the craft shop will get it done for you.' She gestured towards the paintings on the wall. 'Something like that for a frame – you can take it with you, if you like, to show her.'

Harry nodded, but her attention was still on the embroideries, which had surprised her with their beauty. She had wondered if the two on the walls were the best of the crop, but these others were just as good to her untrained eye, and showed how skilful her new friend was. Her friend George Didburin was going to be very interested in them indeed, she was sure. She picked one up to examine details more closely, fingering the figures and backgrounds. 'I don't know how you have the patience to do this, but they're fine efforts, damned fine.'

In the end she chose a picture in sepia tones of some slum children of Edwardian times, who had a little dog leaping about beside them. Bare feet, ragged clothes, with that hollow look that long-term poverty gives sometimes, and yet still full of mischief. 'How did you get the dog to look so alive and frisky?' she marvelled.

'Not easily. That's the third dog figure I made. The other two were rather wooden looking. But this one seemed OK.' Rosalind sneaked a surreptitious glance at her watch. 'Is this the piece you want, then?'

'If you don't mind.'

'Take it.' She had expected to feel upset at losing it, but she didn't. Jenny's troubles were serious, worth getting upset about. These embroideries were simply a hobby – well, a bit more than that, but she was the only one who truly cared about them. It'd be nice to know one had found a good home with someone who loved it enough to bid money for it. If anyone did bid. She saw Harry looking at her in concern and dragged her attention firmly back to the present.

'Yes, we will be back in time for the fête. I wouldn't miss it for anything.'

Harry nodded. 'It is pretty popular.' In fact, her fête was getting a solid reputation, because she focused on quality, not silly bouncy castles and such rubbish. Old-fashioned country games like skittles, which she'd played in her youth. The tourists loved them. And the local kids loved to run them, which convinced the outsider kids that they weren't – what was that word young Jim Tuffin had used the other day? She'd forgotten it again. She was out of touch with this modern slang.

'Jonathon opens up his home on fête day, too,' she told Rosalind, 'donating the entrance money to our charity, plus there are a few houses in the village with rather nice gardens which are also open. We run horse charabanc trips from the fête to Destan House. Take one lot of people over, dump them and fetch the previous lot back. No hanging around or wasted journeys. The trick is to offer the grockles lots of things to do, so that they don't have a chance to be bored.'

'Grockles?' Jenny queried.

Harry grinned. 'Tourists.'

'I love the word. And the fête sounds good,' Jenny said. 'If I can help out in any way, just ask.'

Harry looked at her, decided she meant it, then looked at her watch. 'Look, I'm sorry to take the picture and run, but

136

I have a few million things to do. And thank you, Jenny. I'll definitely take you up on that offer.'

When Harry had left, Rosalind smiled at her daughter. 'Let's set off today and stop overnight on the way up. The Wye Valley is supposed to be lovely – we could find somewhere to stay in Shrewsbury. Brother Cadfael country.'

Jenny beamed at her. 'Wonderful. I'd love to see Shrewsbury.' She and her mother were both Brother Cadfael fans – and even Louise didn't scorn those books, though she usually read novels with more modern themes than a medieval monk who was also a detective.

What was her younger sister doing now? Jenny didn't envy her spending time with their father when he had one of his snits on.

Paul listened to the phone ringing out again. 'Where the hell is she?' He opened his office door and the secretary assigned to him looked up inquiringly. 'Keep trying this number, will you?' He rattled it off. 'I need to speak to my wife.'

There was no reply by the time he was ready to go back to the hotel. Nor had Louise and her minder returned. He paced up and down his office, fretting. What the hell had got into his family? Why were they doing this to him?

When the minder eventually brought Louise back, the woman was obviously annoyed and his daughter was wearing her sulky look – though that tarty blonde patch had been re-dyed to match Louise's dark hair, thank goodness.

'What happened?' he demanded, cutting through the polite phrases.

'Your daughter wished to go elsewhere. We had a small – disagreement.'

Louise let out a long aggrieved sigh. 'I only wanted to go on the harbour cruise.'

'Your father wished you to do otherwise,' the woman said quietly, but her face had a steely look to it, which was why she had been hired.

Paul suppressed a quick memory of Liz, laughing beside him on one of the cruises, then lying under him in bed. He was having a lot of trouble getting Liz out of his mind. She was some woman. That wimpy Bill didn't deserve her. 'You're not here to go touristing,' he told his daughter curtly.

'But it's such a waste if I don't see *anything*!'

He turned to the minder, whose official title was personal trainer. Bloody expensive, but sharp enough to read the agenda behind the overt reasons for hiring her. 'Did she do her exercise after you'd been to the hairdresser's?'

'Yes, sir. We kept active.'

He grinned. He intended to make sure Louise was so tired every night that she slept soundly and thus didn't give him any trouble. Last night she'd nearly fallen asleep over dinner.

As if to reinforce his satisfaction, Louise yawned and sagged against the wall. The minder gave her a poke. 'Good posture, Miss Stevenson. We've already discussed its importance.'

Louise's scowl deepened, but she straightened up.

Back at the hotel Paul gave his daughter ten minutes to get ready for dinner and smiled at the look of panic on her face. He got through his own ablutions with his usual speed and tried the phone again. Nothing. And the answering service wasn't even on, though he'd told Ros to fix one up. But that was Ros all over. Dreamy and impractical. Heaven knew what she'd have done without him – and the thought of someone else managing her money was still worrying him. The sooner he got back to her and sorted that out the better.

The lawyer he'd consulted hadn't been too optimistic about overturning a trust when the money from it went straight to Ros. But Paul wanted to know what she was *doing* with all that income. When she'd told him how much it would be approximately, he'd felt sick. She was probably wasting it. She'd always spent far too much on books and embroidery equipment. As if he didn't know what she got up to while he was away. He'd seen those pictures of hers stacked up in the attic. How many hours had she wasted on that old-fashioned rubbish? He intended to clear them out when they got back, give them to some charity. If any charity wanted them.

And when they moved to the States, embroidery would definitely not be on the agenda. He'd get her to join a health club, get her body into shape. Firm. Like Liz's.

He pressed the redial button and the phone rang again, on and on. Dammit, where was she?

The day of the fête dawned cool but fine. They had got back the previous day after a golden interlude in Southport and Rosalind was feeling in need of exercise. She peeped into her daughter's room, but Jenny was still asleep, curled up into a tight ball like a child, with her long fair hair spread out on the pillow. She always had needed a lot of sleep, but she was looking so much better now, thank goodness, though she still grew a bit jumpy after dark.

From the look of the early morning sun, it was going to be fine for the fête. Good. Rosalind grabbed an apple and set off, intending to pick up a newspaper. There were people bustling about the village already and an air of expectancy everywhere.

When she got back, Jenny was sitting frowning over a cup of tea.

'Something wrong, love?'

'Dad rang. Woke me up.'

'Oh?'

'He was in a foul mood. Why does he have to be so – *jarring*? You and I were away for four days and we didn't have a single cross word. Anyway, he says you're to ring him the minute you come in.'

'Oh, does he?'

Jenny looked at her in surprise. 'Aren't you going to?'

'No. Why spoil a lovely day?' Paul never rang unless he wanted her to do something, and what she intended to do today was go to the fête.

'He'll be furious.'

Rosalind shrugged.

After breakfast Jenny came down in jeans and shirt, with a sweater tied round her waist.

Goodness, she looks so like me, Rosalind thought and felt quite awed, remembering the tiny baby whom she had adored on sight. She blinked as fingers snapped in front of her face and she saw her daughter laughing at her.

'Wake up, Mum! I've asked you twice what time you want to leave.'

'Oh, well, whenever you like.'

As they walked into the village together, Jenny asked, 'Can we go and see Jonathon's house?'

Rosalind looked at the cars turning off the main road to park in the field and the people strolling up and down, pointing to the 'quaint' houses and the 'cute' things in the shops. 'Not with hordes of other people there. I'll get him to show us round another day, just you and me. It's a lovely house and full of beautiful objects.'

Jenny glanced sideways. 'He's been a good friend to you, hasn't he?' She felt like a voyeur at the expression on her mother's face, the tight controlled sadness quickly replaced by that bland look her mother used as a barrier against her father when he was in one of his fusses. But why did her mother need a barrier now? Surely she hadn't fallen for this Jonathon? No, that was unthinkable. Not Mum.

'Harry and Jonathon have both been good friends to me,' Rosalind said carefully. 'Though he was the one who found me when I fell, of course.'

'You'd have been in trouble if he hadn't.'

'Oh, I dare say I'd have managed to crawl for help.' She took a deep breath and summoned up a smile from somewhere. 'Well, let's get into it. At least we live close enough to come home if we're bored.'

But they weren't bored because Harry pounced on them as soon as they walked through the gates of the school yard. 'Going to treat you like locals, I'm afraid. I need someone to help out in the tea tent. Would you mind, Rosalind? And Jenny, would you help out at the skittles? I've got my nephews setting them up for people, but I need an adult to collect the money. Meg Loder's let me down again – not that it's her fault – her youngest is always catching something.'

Still talking at the top of her voice, she led Jenny through the groups of people. 'These are my nephews – Giles and Rufus.'

Jenny smiled at the two boys, both at that thin pre-puberty stage of bony limbs and jerky movements. They were very like their aunt and father. 'You'll have to explain to me what's going on. I don't know anything whatsoever about skittles.'

They stared at her solemnly, then nodded as if she'd passed some unseen test. 'All right,' said one. 'It's not hard, really.'

'I'll be off, then.' Harry left her in charge of a small table and cash box with a float of change.

The two boys hovered next to her. 'You're Australian, aren't you?' one of them asked.

Jenny grinned. 'Too right. G'day, mate.'

'I say, do people really say that?'

'Sometimes.'

And from then on, whenever there were no customers, they plied her with questions about Australia, which Giles was 'doing' for a geography project and which the other boy seemed equally fascinated by.

Just before lunch, two young men appeared in front of Jenny.

'Phil Ross,' said one. 'Here to relieve you.'

The other bobbed his head. 'Ned Didburin. Mrs Larcombe sent me to guide you to food. She's got refreshments set out for the helpers in that old green tent at the rear.'

'Oh, good! I'm starving.'

He began to stroll along beside her. 'Is that an Aussie accent?'

'Mmm.'

'Thought I recognized the twang.' He looked at her sideways. Pretty. And gentle-looking, as if she had no malice in her. He liked the looks of her. 'Um – you wouldn't like to come for tea with me later when the auction's over?'

Jenny stiffened. 'No. No, thank you.'

He gave an exaggerated sigh. 'Something I said or do I just not appeal?'

She looked at him warily. He had a kind, open sort of face. She didn't want to upset him. 'Just – something someone else did. I – haven't quite recovered.' To her horror, her voice trembled.

He looked aghast. 'I say – sorry to have roused the sleeping tiger.'

'N–not your fault. You couldn't be expected to know.' She hurried off before he could say anything else, but she was trembling still and couldn't face a crowd of people, so wandered down the main 'street' of activities. But there were people everywhere, people she didn't know, who made her feel nervous as they pushed against her, so she turned back

141

and made her way reluctantly towards the green tent.

Ned Didburin watched her go, upset by the real fear he had seen on her face.

Later, it seemed as if fate was smiling down on him for once, for he ran into her again, this time looking even more distressed as two young guys – from London by the sound of their accents – had her cornered between two displays and were trying out their wit on her.

'Sorry lads, the lady's with me!' he called out, striding forward and hoping they wouldn't cause trouble. He wasn't a physical type and never had been. For a moment it was touch and go, then one of them shrugged and moved off.

The other hovered, frowning in puzzlement at Jenny's distress. 'Only 'avin' a bit of fun, you know, gel. Didn't mean to upset you.'

She turned her back on them, not wanting anyone to see the tears of relief that had started flowing the minute Ned had come to her rescue.

'They really didn't mean any harm,' he said softly from behind her.

She looked down at the handkerchief he had pushed into her hand and shook it out, swallowing hard as she mopped her wet face. But the tears continued to flow. 'S–sorry,' she managed.

'It must have been bad, whatever it was that upset you,' he said gently. She was still gulping and trying so desperately not to sob that his heart went out to her. 'Look, no one can see you with me standing here, so if it helps to cry it out, go ahead and water away.'

She was caught between a sob and a hiccup of laughter. 'You must think I'm a fool.'

'No. I don't, actually. The ones I think are fools are the people who keep their emotions under wraps and get all het up inside. Terrible for the old health. I was brought up that way, but I've found my way out of it now.' Thanks to an ex-girlfriend, to whom he would be eternally grateful.

She found the sound of his crisp English voice vaguely comforting. The tears had stopped now, so she mopped her eyes and blew her nose, then looked down at the handkerchief in dismay. 'Oh, I'm sorry. You must tell me where you live and I'll wash it before I give it you back.'

'All right.' He fumbled in his pocket and produced a business card, delighted to have an excuse to see her again.

*Edward Didburin, Didburin Fine Arts, Dorchester.*

She held out one hand. 'I'm Jenny Stevenson.'

'My friends call me Ned.' He clasped her hand, trying to think of an innocuous question. 'And what are you doing in Dorset, Miss Jenny Stevenson from down under?'

She gave him a half-smile. 'I'm taking a bit of time off to – to recover. I'm a management trainee, graduated last year.'

'And do you enjoy managing things?'

'Not really.' She shrugged. 'It was Dad's idea of a good career for me.'

'You're staying round here, then?'

'Mmm. Dad's rented a house in the village. Mum's been here a while, but I only arrived a week ago. It's a lovely part of the world, Dorset. I'm really looking forward to exploring. Mum and I just spent a few days in Southport – at a relative's house.'

He wanted to stay and talk to her. She was so soft and fair and feminine looking, and apart from that golden tone to her skin, not at all what he'd imagined an Australian girl would be like. But a quick glance at his watch made him exclaim, 'Oh, hell! Got to go to the auction. I'm here on duty for my father, I'm afraid. Got to bid on one or two pieces. Unless – you wouldn't care to come with me, would you? It's jolly interesting.'

She looked at him doubtfully. He was only a little taller than she was, with thinning brown hair which would probably leave him bald by the time he was forty. He had kind blue eyes, not gleaming black ones, and for some reason she felt safe with him. 'That would be nice. I want to go to the auction anyway, because Mum's got an embroidered picture in it. I want to be there to give her support. She's worried no one will buy it.'

'Not the slum children thing?'

'Yes.'

'But that's a *gorgeous* piece. It's the main thing I've been sent to bid on, actually.' Another glance at his watch. 'Come on, then. Let's go and see what happens to it.' And when he caught hold of her hand so they didn't get separated, she didn't draw away, but let him race her off to the auction tent, where they both arrived breathless and laughing, collapsing into two empty seats at the end of a row just as the bidding began.

Rosalind sat down at the back of the auction tent and tried to look as if she were studying the catalogue. Not that she was here to bid for anything. But she had to see what sort of person bought her picture and what price it fetched.

Harry mounted the dais, ready to get things rolling. She gave a nod of satisfaction at the turnout, then smiled at the plump, bald man who had come to sit beside her, saying something that made him smile, too. After Harry had introduced him, he tapped a hammer to quieten people down and the auction started.

It was an hour before Rosalind's embroidery came up for sale, and she was delighted to hear the woman behind her whisper, 'Wish I could afford that one. It's gorgeous, isn't it? Bound to go for tons of money.'

'Mmm. Must be an heirloom piece. Don't know how anyone can bear to part with it.'

'Doesn't say so in the catalogue. Says it's a modern piece in the Jacobean style of raised stumpwork.'

'Let's start the bidding at fifty pounds,' the auctioneer called.

Rosalind gasped aloud. Start at *fifty*!

But no one bid, so the amount went down to twenty pounds, then fifteen. She could feel her face going red. Perhaps Paul was right. Perhaps people didn't like that sort of old-fashioned stuff nowadays.

Then someone raised a hand and the auctioneer pointed a finger towards him. 'Ten pounds I'm bid. I'll take it in fives from now on.'

Only a few seconds later, he pointed again. 'Fifteen, lady in the blue coat.'

From then on the bidding climbed steadily and Rosalind sat there in a state of shock.

'A hundred pounds.'

'Hundred and twenty.'

'Hundred and seventy.'

144

'Two hundred. Any advance on two hundred?' The auctioneer looked around. 'No more bids? Right then, going once,
going twice, sold for two hundred to the gentleman in the
fawn jacket. Now, the next item is . . .'

Rosalind got up and stumbled out of the tent, avoiding
people and slipping between the big auction tent and the
smaller grey tent next to it, desperate for a moment to herself.
*Two hundred pounds!* Her picture had fetched two hundred
pounds and several people had wanted to buy it! Joy filled
her and pride, too. If someone had paid all that for her embroidery, it wasn't worthless!

'You all right?'

She looked up with a smile. 'I'm fine. Just a bit overwhelmed. Jonathon, did you see how much my picture
fetched?'

'I did indeed. Congratulations.'

Without knowing quite how she got there, she found herself
in his arms, hugging him and when he bent his head she kissed
him back because it seemed the natural thing to do.

Jenny, who had followed her mother outside to congratu-
late her, stopped in shock at the sight of the entwined figures
then tiptoed away. That was no kiss of friendship, that was
the kiss of a man and woman who really fancied one another
– or loved one another. Her mother's expression had been
radiant as she'd turned to greet Jonathon and he'd been beaming down at her.

Oh, heavens, she hoped Dad never found out. He'd go off
his face.

She walked to and fro at the other side of the tent, waiting
for Ned to finish paying for the picture and thinking about
what she had seen. She didn't blame her mother for being
tempted by a nice man like Jonathon Destan – her father had
treated her like an idiot for years – but she hoped this wouldn't
break up her parents' marriage.

Another thought occurred to her, a much happier one. Her
father would be furious when he found out how much the
embroidery had fetched and how many people had bid for it.
If her mother didn't tell him, then she would. Maybe from
now on, he'd stop criticizing her mother's hobby.

The other thing, the attraction to Jonathon Destan, was just a passing fancy, surely? Perhaps her mother had needed that to stiffen her spine. Good for the old morale to know some-one fancied you.

Which brought Jenny's thoughts back to Ned. She really liked him. He wasn't good-looking, but he was kind and fun. Not at all like Michael – or her father. She not only felt safe with him but he made her chuckle with his wry remarks.

Turning, she saw him coming towards her and smiled. When he held out his hand, she put hers into it without hesitation.

# Twelve

Rosalind spent the morning feeling nervous as she waited for Paul and Louise to arrive. When she saw his car turning into the drive, she was conscious of a strong desire to flee. She didn't want to see him. Or Louise. She sighed and remained in the bedroom.

A couple of minutes later, a voice called, 'Mum! Dad and Louise are here!'

'I'll be down in a minute, Jenny. Can you open the front door?' She had deliberately left it locked like last time, so that he wouldn't be able to take her by surprise.

It wasn't until she heard voices in the hall that Rosalind went downstairs. Paul was so busy ordering Louise to fetch the rest of the luggage in, he wasn't even looking at his wife.

Louise tossed a 'Hi!' in her mother's direction, then slouched off.

'I'll come and help you.' Jenny pushed her sister out of the door.

Paul put his arms round Rosalind and gave her a quick hug. 'Well, woman, I'm back now for a while.'

'Good.' But it didn't feel good. It felt as if a trap had closed around her. 'Come and have a coffee.'

Louise came back in, hesitated, then at a nudge from Jenny put the luggage down and went over to hug her mother properly. 'Fancy us all being here in England together.'

'Not quite all. Tim's not here.'

Louise's eyes filled with tears. 'I miss him.'

'Well, you've got Jenny and me, so you won't exactly be lonely.' To her surprise, Rosalind saw Louise shoot an uncertain glance at her father.

'We'll see about that.'

The air was suddenly full of tension.

147

'Louise has let us all down,' Paul said, giving his daughter one of his icy looks. 'Behaved badly to her grandmother, *stolen* your car and used it, and worst of all, got into drugs.'

For heaven's sake, Rosalind thought, why is he making such a drama of it? He's already told me this on the phone.

'I haven't decided yet what to do about her, or whether I can even trust her to behave if I leave her here with you.'

Louise looked so unhappy that Rosalind went straight across to put her arm round her, feeling the initial stiffness give way to a convulsive hug. 'Well, until you have decided, she's here and I shall be able to enjoy the company of both my daughters.' While he, no doubt, would be going away within a day or so, even if he did intend to use this as his base from now on. Oh, Lord, she was doing more talking inside her head than she was with her mouth. She had to stop this.

As they sat and drank coffee, Rosalind realized she and her daughters were carefully watching Paul and guarding what they said. He was the only one who seemed at ease as he told them about Hong Kong and the project there. 'The chairman doesn't hang around when a new man needs selecting.'

Later, he went upstairs to change. When his wife didn't follow, he called down impatiently, 'Rosalind? Aren't you going to come and unpack for me?'

She didn't really want to be alone with him. Aware of her daughters' eyes on her, she gathered her strength together for the first minor confrontation. 'I'm busy down here at the moment. If you stick your dirty clothes in the linen basket, I'll put a wash on later.'

There was silence from upstairs, no sound of movement, even.

Louise stood up. 'I – I'd better unpack, too.' She saw her mother and sister's surprise. 'He can get grouchy if you – if you—' She burst into tears.

Rosalind, who had never seen Louise so cowed, went to put her arms round her again. 'Well, before you do go up, let me say again how lovely it is to see you, even if I don't approve of what you've done.'

Louise stared at her for a moment, eyes wet with tears. 'I'm glad to see you, too,' she said in a gruff voice, then glanced upstairs. 'I'd better go and unpack, though.'

When she'd gone Jenny looked at her mother and whispered, 'What's he been doing to make her so meek?'

'I don't know.' And she definitely didn't like it. Louise had misbehaved, and badly, but it seemed wrong to knock all the spirit out of her. She had always been such a lively child.

Paul came clumping down the stairs and went to dump some things in 'his' office. 'Not a bad house, really, is it?' he asked from the kitchen doorway.

Rosalind, who'd been talking quietly to Jenny, broke off and nodded. He turned away again.

'He always expects us to jump to attention, doesn't he?' Jenny asked softly.

'He does, rather.' Rosalind heard him go into the living room and her heart started pounding in her chest. She had left her embroideries up on the wall for the first time ever.

'Ros? Could you come here a moment?'

'Don't let him take them down,' Jenny whispered.

'I won't.' She took a deep breath and walked into the living room. 'Something wrong?'

'Why have you brought those?' he demanded, pointing to the embroideries. 'You know I hate the damned things.'

'Since you weren't here, I decided to please myself. I happen to like having them around.'

He had already unhooked one. She took it from his hand and put it back on the wall. 'Leave it, Paul.'

'There were already pictures up, a matching pair, which went well with the decor of this room, so there was no need for this. How did you get them out here so quickly? What did that cost, eh?'

'I don't see why you're making such a fuss about something so unimportant.'

Their eyes met, held, then a look of scorn came over his face. 'What do you think people will say if we have those old-fashioned things displayed on the wall? I thought you had a bit more sense than that, Ros, I really did. What you do in your own time is one thing, what you show the world is quite another ball game.'

'Apparently I haven't any sense at all, because I love to have my pictures hanging where I can see them and I don't care what other people think.'

149

'Well, they're coming down when people visit. They're too amateurish.'

Jenny appeared in the doorway. 'They're not amateurish at all, Dad. They're beautiful.'

He turned to glare at her. 'You can keep out of this, young lady.'

'I don't see why. I like looking at them, too, and those prints were trashy. Besides, I don't think Mum will tell you, but one of her embroideries fetched two hundred pounds at a charity auction two days ago. There was intense bidding from several people, but a fine-art dealer bought it – to sell in his gallery.'

'You're making this up.'

'Why on earth should I?' Jenny went to put her arm round her mother's shoulders, feeling the tension there and angry that he had been so unkind within minutes of arriving. 'I'm very proud of Mum. And everyone here has *admired* her embroideries. People did at home, too. There's only you who doesn't like them, actually.'

The silence was heavy with menace. 'Well, I definitely don't. And I have to live here, too.'

Rosalind intervened. 'How long are you staying this time, then, Paul? One day? Two? I think you can put up with them for that long.'

'I'm leaving tomorrow.' He saw the scorn on her face and snapped, 'Well, I have to report in, don't I? I've brought our younger daughter down for you to keep an eye on, so I did *put family first*, contrary to what you accused me of last time. But now I have to go up to London to make a full report to the chairman about Hong Kong.'

Rosalind's voice was without inflection. 'Yes. Of course.'

'But I'll be spending the weekends down here from now on, so I should have some say in what I have to look at.'

Did he never give up? she thought wearily, wondering if this was worth it. There was a knock on the front door before she could answer him.

'I'll get it.' Jenny was worried about the anger on her father's face. Why was he being so brutal about her mother's embroideries? 'Oh, Mrs Larcombe! How lovely to see you! Won't you come in? Mum and Dad are in the living room. You haven't met Dad yet, have you?'

Harry marched forward with her usual aura of energy and purpose to plonk two kisses in the air above her friend's cheeks. 'Rosalind! How are you today?'

After the introductions, they sat down to chat while Jenny went to make some coffee.

'Nice girl, that,' Harry said. 'Big help on the skittles.' She turned to Paul. 'You must be very proud of your wife.'

'Must I? Why?'

'Why, because of those.' Harry waved one hand towards the wall. 'Damned fine work. A much smaller one fetched two hundred pounds at the fête.'

His smile had quite vanished. 'Amazing. But some folk will buy anything to support a charity.'

Harry stared at him incredulously, then turned to Rosalind as if he had not spoken. 'I popped round because George Didburin wants to come and see you about your work. He's interested in representing you. All right if I give him your phone number and address? You do have other pieces for sale, don't you?'

Happiness surged through Rosalind. 'Yes. And I'd love to talk to him.'

'You don't need to huckster your work around,' Paul snapped and changed the subject.

Harry was not to be deflected. She held up one hand. 'Just a minute!' before turning to Rosalind again. 'Did you mean it about repairing Araminta's embroidery for us?'

'Of course I did.'

'Who's Araminta?' demanded Paul. 'And why can't she repair her own embroidery? My wife's not a damned sewing woman!'

Harry guffawed. 'Araminta's one of my ancestors, seventeenth century, and your wife offered to repair an embroidery she did. It's a rather valuable piece.' She'd taken an instant dislike to this man, who reminded her of her stockbroker – good at his job, she'd guess, but would tread on anyone to get a profit.

It was with relief that Rosalind showed Harry to the door ten minutes later, because Harry gave as good as she got, was impervious to subtle insults and was quite prepared to be downright rude to Paul.

151

On the doorstep Harry leaned close to Rosalind and whispered, 'Don't let that husband of yours put you down!' Then she winked and raised her voice. 'George wants to make your embroideries the centrepiece of his next needlework exhibition. So don't give away any of them from now on – except one to me for next year's fête, of course.'

Rosalind stood by the door watching her friend stride down the drive, then summoned up her new-found inner strength and went back inside the house.

I don't even want to see Paul, she thought. Guilt shot through her at the memory of Jonathon kissing her, congratulating her, being glad for her. She stopped moving for a moment till it faded. *He* didn't bark orders at her and disparage her embroideries.

Paul appeared in the doorway of the sitting room. 'Ros? For heaven's sake, are you going to stand out there all day?'

She sighed and went in to continue the battle.

By afternoon Rosalind was near screaming point. Paul was in his office, fiddling with something on his laptop. 'I – um, think I'll go out for a walk,' she told her daughters. 'Anyone else want to come?'

Louise shook her head. 'Dad'll want me to go jogging soon. That's enough exercise for one day.'

'You – jogging?'

'Yes. It's his idea of rehabilitation.' Louise started fiddling with the handle of her mug. 'And I have lost some flabbiness, even in the short time since we started. He hired this personal trainer for me while we were in Hong Kong. I thought she was just – you know, a minder for the naughty girl. But she really was a personal trainer and she taught me all sorts of things. So I might keep the exercising up. See how I go.'

'You look all right to me, love. You've definitely lost weight, however you did it.'

'Oh, Mum, I'm just thin. I don't have any tone. And –' she blushed – 'I lost the weight because I wasn't eating. I was – you know, taking these amphetamine pills. They were wonderful. You don't feel at all hungry and you're simply bursting with energy – but I wasn't *seriously* into drugs, whatever Dad says! I was just – you know, trying things out. Pot isn't a hard drug. Everyone smokes it. It ought to be legalized. It's no worse than alcohol.'

'So they say. I'm not so sure. They wouldn't ban it for nothing.' Sadness gripped Rosalind suddenly. 'Tim used to smoke it, too, didn't he?'

'Yes.' There was silence, then Louise looked over her shoulder and asked in a low voice, 'You haven't heard from him, have you? I mean, I know he wouldn't contact Dad, but I hoped he might have at least written you a card. Just to let you know he's OK and all that.'

'I haven't heard a thing since that last postcard, which you saw.'

'Are you worried about him?'

'Very. I worry about you all. But Tim – well, he could be dead and I –' her voice broke – 'I wouldn't even know it.'

Louise was near tears. 'He isn't! He can't be!'

There was silence, then Rosalind went to find Jenny, who was reading a book in the conservatory. 'Do you want to come for a walk, love?'

'No. Not just now, thanks. Ned said he might ring.' Jenny didn't want to get heavy with anyone, but it'd be nice to have a date or two.

'I'll go on my own, then.'

Paul came in. 'Go where?'

'Out for a walk. And to pick up a couple of things at the shops.'

'It's going to rain. Take the car.'

She was always surprised at how little he used his own feet. Oh, he trained in the gym. And jogged. Religiously. But he rarely walked anywhere for the pleasure of it.

She didn't take the car but picked up her umbrella instead. And when the rain got heavy she went to sit in the little café in the village.

Jonathon came in and saw her gazing sightlessly through the rain-streaked window. It seemed like the answer to a prayer to him, for he had been wondering how to contact her.

She saw him and her sad expression lightened as she gestured to the seat next to her.

Beaming, he hurried across. 'On your own?'

'Yes. I'm the only real walker in the family. When it started to rain, I took shelter here.'

'Mind if I join you for a cuppa?'

'I'd love it.' She realized her voice had been too warm and looked down at the table, saying more temperately, 'Please do.'

When his pot of tea and chocolate cup cakes had arrived they sat in silence, then he said, 'I miss you dreadfully, Rosalind.' He didn't look at her, just stirred his tea round and round.

She could not be less than honest with him. 'I miss you, too.'

Another silence. 'Harry says you're going to repair Araminta's picture for us.'

'Yes. I'd like to do that, actually. Perhaps you could bring it round to the house sometime?'

'Or you could come and get it?'

'You must be sick of people invading your house. Harry said the horse charabanc was full every trip on the day of the fête.'

'I enjoy having people round, actually. It can get very lonely with the boys away. And I left showing folk round to Mrs Durden-Jones, who runs the local historical society. She knows nearly as much about the place as we Destans do, but she puts it across better and handles the groups better, too.' He leaned forward and said conspiratorially, 'I'm a failure at handling crowds, actually. I'm too soft with them.'

She sighed. 'I've been too soft with everyone, I think.'

'How's it going? Now your husband's home, I mean. How's it really going?'

A shrug was the only answer and seeing the distress on her face he started talking about the fête instead, telling her how pleased Harry was about the takings, which looked like creating a record.

As they were parting Rosalind said, 'I miss you so much, Jonathon dear.' Then, as if terrified by what she had said, she turned and rushed off.

# Thirteen

Paul answered the front door. 'Yes?'

'George Didburin.' The man on the doorstep was plump and bald, but held himself with casual confidence, was dressed immaculately and spoke with that drawling, educated accent which is peculiarly English. He proffered a business card and waved one hand towards his companion. 'My son and partner, Ned. We're looking for Rosalind Stevenson. She's expecting us.'

Paul took the card and examined it cursorily, not at all impressed by the accent or appearance of his visitor. 'Ros! It's that art fellow for you.' He was annoyed at all this fuss over his wife's hobby, felt betrayed by it. Who'd ever have thought people would get excited about bloody embroideries?

Still, if there was money to be made from it he'd better make sure no one cheated her. She hadn't the faintest idea how to push for the best bargain. He held the door wider. 'I suppose you'd better come in.'

George stepped into the hall, taking in far more than was immediately apparent. Good-looking chap, Stevenson, but the smile didn't reach his eyes. He wondered what the wife was like. He hadn't had a chance to meet her after the fête. Ned said she was pleasant but with no sparkle. Well, sparkle or not, George hoped she had some more pieces like the one of those children. Very touching scene, that. Brilliant needlework, too, with some unusual uses of materials. But it was the artistic style that made it valuable, the eye for a composition. He hoped the other pieces were of the same quality. It had been a while since he'd discovered a new talent.

Rosalind hurried down the stairs, wishing the art dealer had come after Paul had left. She advanced across the hall, with

155

her right hand outstretched. 'Mr Didburin? I'm *so* pleased to meet you.'

Why didn't she tell him how humbly grateful she was for his interest while she was at it, Paul thought, watching her closely. Honestly, she was such a fool. Look at her body language. Even a blind man could read it. She was putting all the cards into her opponent's hand before the game even began.

George presented Rosalind with a business card – you had to be careful nowadays when dealing with a husband and wife, treat them equally and all that, and anyway he was here to see *her*, not that cold fish beside her. He clasped her hand in both his, holding on to it for a minute as he studied her. Well, at least her smile reached her eyes, but what the hell was she nervous of? People didn't usually find him intimidating. Then he saw her glance flicker uncertainly towards her husband and back again. Ah.

'Shall we go and sit down, Ros?' Paul prompted, his voice impatient.

'Oh, yes. Yes, of course. Do come this way, Mr Didburin.' She led the way into the sitting room and indicated a chair.

George didn't even see her gesture because he'd noticed the pictures on the wall. 'Do you mind?' He didn't wait for an answer but walked across to examine them. 'Aaah!' He was not aware he had made an approving noise, not aware of anything except the pieces. They were exquisite. Oh, yes! Abso-bloody-lutely exquisite.

Excitement filled him, rushing along his veins and bringing a slight flush to his fair complexion. There was nothing to beat the thrill of discovering a new talent, nothing. And such an unusual talent, too. Her pictures weren't just pretty, they had guts. That was the only way he could phrase that indefinable something that meant an artist had captured some essence of life, some wonderful essence that would bring people of discernment flocking to buy their work.

'What do you think?' Paul asked as the silence dragged on and the guest made no attempt to take a seat.

George continued to ignore him. He stabbed a finger towards an Elizabethan lady in full costume with a miniature ruff, wondering how Mrs Stevenson had managed to do that

156

so accurately on such a small scale. 'This one is pretty and will sell, but this other –' he stabbed a finger at an old lady sitting on a park bench, looking suspiciously at the world as she watched some children play – 'is masterly. You should stay away from the pretty scenes and capture Life – with a capital L. It sells better.'

Rosalind flushed. 'Oh, well, I—'

'Could you tell us a bit about yourself, Mr Didburin?' Paul cut in smoothly. 'We're happy that you like the embroideries, of course, but what are your credentials for handling my wife's work? Or for passing judgement on them?'

Rosalind stared at him in horror.

There was the sound of a phone ringing, footsteps, then Louise called, 'Dad! It's for you. The chairman.'

Paul froze in instant response to that magic word, murmured something which might have been an excuse and left swiftly, pausing to hiss at his wife, 'Leave any negotiations about prices to me.'

Embarrassment reddened her cheeks. He had sounded like a schoolmaster ordering a pupil around – and a scornful schoolmaster dealing with a stupid pupil, at that.

'I'm afraid I prefer to deal directly with the artist,' George said mildly to Rosalind, feeling sorry for the poor downtrodden woman. 'I like to develop a *personal* relationship with my clients. No intermediaries.'

She felt overwhelmed with embarrassment at Paul's all-too-obvious assumption that she could not handle things herself. 'I'll explain that to my husband, because I'd prefer to deal directly with you, as well. If you're going to buy more of my work, that is.'

'I hope I am. Do you have much completed?'

'About fifty pieces. But most of them are back in Australia.'

He nodded, smiling gently, exhilaration still coursing through him. *Fifty!* Oh, yes! He had definitely made a find. 'If they're as good as this lot, I won't guarantee to make you rich, but I will guarantee you recognition of your talent. And a fairly steady income.'

'Oh.' She went pink with pleasure. 'Are you sure I'm – well, good enough?'

He looked at her incredulously. She really meant it. She was that uncertain of herself. 'Yes, very sure. I'm a bit of an expert on embroideries, actually. And these are really first-rate.' It was about time for a revival of interest in this particular form of needlework.

'Dad's one of the top experts in Britain on raised stump-work pieces, actually,' Ned put in. 'In Europe, even.'

George smiled deprecatingly at Rosalind. 'Bit of a passion of mine, embroidery. And in my judgement, Mrs Stevenson, you have considerable talent.' He paused, unable to think of a tactful phrase. 'Do you really want your husband to negotiate prices in advance for you?'

'I'm not sure what you mean by that.'

'Well, let me try to explain how I usually work before you decide. Prices are a delicate point until I've got you established as an artist. I'd much rather take a few of your embroideries – about twenty or so would give me enough for a good display – pay you a retainer and then arrange an exhibition. In the meantime I'll show your pieces round and gauge reactions, though I'm pretty sure your stuff will take.' He patted his chest. 'I get a feeling here when I discover a new talent. I've got it now. Strongly.'

Delight flooded through her. 'You make me feel very happy, Mr Didburin, with your expert appreciation. And I'd definitely like you to handle my work. I couldn't work with someone I didn't – well, trust and respect. The embroideries mean too much to me.'

'Call me George. And –' he remembered what her husband had called her – 'you're – Ros, is it?'

'No. Only my husband calls me that. I prefer my full name, actually – Rosalind.'

'Rosalind it is, then. Can you get the other embroideries sent over from Australia?'

'Yes.' She hesitated. 'But there are a few I don't want to sell. They mean too much to me.'

'Would you consider showing them anyway? We could put a "sold" sticker on them. If they're good, they'll help draw people in.

'I – yes, why not?'

'How soon can you have them here?'

'Oh. Well. I can phone my mother. She'll go round to the

house and take them to the shipper. They'd be here within the week, I should think, airfreight. They're not framed or anything, though.'

He sighed in delight. 'Great! I'd prefer my own framer to deal with them anyway. She's one of the best in the country for embroideries! Give me a call when they arrive, then bring them over and have lunch with me in Dorchester. I'll show you round my little gallery.' His eyes twinkled and he lowered his voice. 'On your own, perhaps?'

'Yes, definitely.' Paul was probably packing already. The chairman never rang just to say hello.

George got up and went to examine the pictures again, the framed ones on the wall, then the unframed ones on the dining-room table, for those Jenny had sent had arrived now. He was still standing near the latter when his host came back.

Paul consulted his watch. Was that fellow going to spend all day gaping at these bits of cloth? He needed to set off for London and would do so as soon as these two had left. That fellow was damned rude. Hadn't even turned round to acknowledge his host's return. He waited a moment, then prompted, 'Well, what do you think?'

'I like them very much.'

'How much are they worth?'

Rosalind interrupted. 'It's too soon to tell that, Paul. I'm sending for some of the others from Australia before we settle anything with Mr Didburin.' She was ashamed of how nervous she felt, how hard it was to stand up to Paul.

'There will be no discount for quantity,' Paul said severely.

George stared at him, absolutely gobsmacked, then said in a chill tone, 'It's not a question of *quantity* with works of art as wonderful as these, Mr Stevenson. When the others arrive, we'll put on a display in my gallery, invite a few selected buyers from the trade and a few of the top collectors, and that'll help us gauge the market.'

Paul snorted in disgust. 'I prefer to talk prices *before* I begin a contract.'

George had had enough of this. He walked across and looked his host firmly in the eye. 'But I shan't be signing a contract with *you*, Mr Stevenson. I'll be dealing with your wife. She's the one with the talent.'

At the sight of Stevenson's outraged expression, Ned hastily converted a choke of laughter into a cough, hiding his face in his handkerchief and clearing his throat loudly before he dared take it away.

'Nonetheless, I am the one with business understanding in this family and if I'm not satisfied with the terms, we'll take them elsewhere.'

Shame stiffened Rosalind's backbone. 'Paul, I'm quite happy with what Mr Didburin wishes to do. How can he decide anything when he's only seen a few of my pieces?'

The look he gave her was icy, then he glanced at his watch again and clicked his tongue in exasperation. 'I have to leave right away. The chairman wants a full briefing, then we have a shut-up, lock-up planning session for a few days. Very well, then, Didburin, we'll leave it at that for the moment. Nothing agreed to. Nothing to bind either of us. We'll send for some more stock. Negotiate when that arrives.'

George closed his eyes in pain at that word. *Stock!* What a philistine this man was!

'I'll see Mr Didburin out while you start packing.' Rosalind led the way hastily towards the front door. The men exchanged curt nods of farewell, then Paul ran up the stairs two at a time, whistling under his breath, a busy, tuneless sound that meant he was already mentally far away.

As they walked into the hall Ned wondered how best to ask to see Jenny. Hearing footsteps he glanced sideways and there she was. 'Jenny, hi!' he called, forgetting the others in his pleasure at meeting her again.

She had been deep in thought but smiled at the sight of him. 'Ned! How nice to see you!' He had told her he might phone and she'd been hoping he would, because she was desperate to get out of the house and spend time with someone of her own age who was pleasant and uncomplicated. You could cut the atmosphere here with a knife since her father's arrival.

Ned moved towards her, taking her hand, holding it as his father had held Rosalind's, in both his own, because he wanted to touch her. 'I was going to phone you, then Father said he was coming over, so I tagged along. Your mother's other embroideries are absolutely wonderful.'

Jenny beamed at him. 'I hope you told Dad that.'

'Yes.' He hesitated then whispered, 'I don't think he believed us, though. He started talking about "no discounts for quantity" and "not signing a contract" – that sort of thing.'

She began to look anxious, which was not what he'd intended.

'But your mother stood up to him,' Ned added hastily.

Her eyes were wide with what was surely disbelief. 'She did?'

'Well . . .' He sighed. He didn't want to lie to her. Not now, not ever. 'Sort of. She slid sideways, so to speak, and managed to postpone a decision – on his part, not on hers or ours. We would definitely like to develop your mother as an artist. And I think she'd like us to represent her.'

'Dad won't admit to himself how good she is.'

'Well, luckily he got summoned to the phone and we were able to set the ground rules while he was out. My father has a top reputation in the trade. He'll deal fairly with your mother, I promise you.'

She betrayed the same nervous embarrassment as her mother had. 'Oh, I'm sure he will. It's just – well, Dad might interfere.'

He saw that his father and Mrs Stevenson were watching them from the front door and got to the point. 'Look, my father's going to have lunch with Mrs Larcombe after this. He's got a bit of a soft spot for her, values stuff for her every year for the fête, then has a post-mortem on prices afterwards. I wondered if you'd take pity on me and come out for a pub lunch or something while they're nattering.'

'Oh. Well, I don't know.'

'Just to the pub and back,' he urged gently. 'You'll be quite safe with me there.'

'You – understand? It's not you, it's . . .' Her voice trailed away and tears filled her soft blue eyes.

'I can guess. A little.' He laid one hand on his chest and put on a mock-solemn expression. 'I promise you I'm trust-worthy and reliable, Ms Stevenson. In fact, I can get refer-ences to that effect. In triplicate. Or centiplicate – if there is such a thing. I'll take a lie detector test, too, if that helps.'

She gave a gurgle of laughter. 'Now you're being silly. All right. I'd love to come and have lunch with you. You go ahead and I'll meet you there.' She didn't want her father interfering.

'See you in half an hour, then? At the Destan Arms?'

'Lovely.'

She watched him stride along the drive. He seemed so nice and uncomplicated. Surely she wasn't making a misjudgement this time?

'What was all that about?'

Jenny jumped in shock and turned to see her mother smiling at her. She had been miles away. 'I'm going to have lunch with Ned at the pub.'

'Good. He's a nice boy. I like him.'

'Boy? He's not a boy. He's . . .' She broke off, realizing how little she knew about him.

'His father is a close friend of Harry's, so I'm sure you'll be safe with him.'

Jenny leaned her head against her mother's shoulder for a moment, in wordless acknowledgement of her understanding. Then she pulled away. 'I've got to go and get ready. Come and help me choose something to wear.'

'All right. But we'd better be quick. I have to do your father's packing.'

The thought of Paul leaving filled Rosalind with relief. She had never expected it to be so difficult to get on with him. Had he changed so much in such a short time?

Or had she?

As she waved him off a short time later, worry and guilt sat heavily on her. But she did not intend to let him negotiate with George. Definitely not. She smiled faintly. And she hadn't done too badly at standing up for herself – for a beginner. She would improve with practice. She was determined to.

And Paul would adjust too, learn that she wasn't to be ordered around.

Surely he would?


Tim tried to phone his parents from a public phone in a large city, and the answerphone gave his grandmother's number, so he phoned her instead. He was amazed when she told him his parents and sisters were in England, but delighted. It was so much closer and he could afford the air fare without having to beg help from his father.

When he got off the plane at Heathrow, he fretted his way through customs and then tried to vanish into the crowd as quickly as possible, because officials made him nervous. Not that he was carrying anything. He wasn't that stupid.

He had no luggage to collect, since he'd lost everything he'd taken to America except the passport and money he'd hidden in the cemetery. His hand luggage contained a change of clothing and not much else.

He found his way to the coach station and bought a ticket to the stop nearest his parents' village, then waited for the coach, leaning against a wall, his head still aching and that ever-present need for a fix gnawing at his belly.

I'm on the last stretch now, he told himself. I can hold out. Once I'm with Mum things will start to improve. He needed quite desperately to see her. And even if the old man was around, seeing him wouldn't be a problem for long. It never was.

Rosalind dialled her mother's number, delighted to hear Audrey's voice. 'Mum?'

'Darling! I was just going to call you. How are you?'

'I'm well. Mum, I've got such good news! An art dealer has bought one of my embroideries for two hundred pounds – that's over five hundred dollars!'

'Goodness!'

'And – and he wants to see the rest of my work. He says he can sell them for me. He really likes them.'

'Oh, Rosalind, I'm so happy for you! You have a real talent there and it deserves recognition.'

Rosalind beamed at the phone. 'Could you go and get the rest of the finished embroideries from the attic for me and have them shipped out as soon as possible? You've got my credit-card number. Use that to pay for them.'

'Yes, of course I can. I'll get John to help me.' She took a quick decision. 'Rosalind – I have some other news for you.'

'Oh?'

'Tim phoned me. From America.'

'Tim did! *Tim!* Oh, Mum, is he all right? I've been so *worried* about him, absolutely frantic.' Tears welled in her eyes. Paul refused point-blank to discuss their son, got angry if she so much as mentioned his name, but not mentioning Tim did not stop her worrying about him.

Audrey took a deep breath. 'I'm pretty sure he's in trouble.'

That didn't surprise Rosalind. She had felt for a while that something was wrong. She wondered sometimes if she was fooling herself when she got these premonitions, or if all mothers felt like that at times. 'I wish I could see him.'

'You can. He's on his way to join you in England.' She waited for an exclamation of pleasure, but there was nothing, no sound at all. Had they been cut off? 'Rosalind? Are you still there?'

'Yes, Mum. I just – I can't help it. I . . . Oh!' She turned blindly to Louise, thrust the phone at her, then collapsed on the telephone seat, sobbing loudly. She had been out of her mind with worry, but now she knew he was all right, it had all come bursting out. He was alive, her Tim was alive – and coming to join them in Burraford. Oh, it was the best news she'd had for a long time! The very best.

Louise held a short, excited conversation with her grandmother, then put the phone down and hovered beside her mother, who was still sobbing loudly. In the end, she couldn't bear to see such pain, put one arm round the heaving shoulders and gave her mother a big hug.

After a while, she coaxed her into the living room. 'I'll get you a cup of coffee, shall I?'

'Please.'

'Tim will be all right, you know.'

'Yes. But it's been so long. What has he been *doing*?'

When Louise set a mug down beside her mother, she, too, had suspiciously bright eyes. 'I've missed him,' she confessed. 'And I've been worried about him, too.'

Then they both wept, putting their arms round one another and sobbing for ages. It didn't occur to Rosalind until much later how close she had felt to Louise at that moment. Or how much comfort her daughter had been to her, as if she were another adult, a friend.

She was deeply relieved Paul had not been there to mock her foolishness, though – and that she would have Tim to herself for a while before her husband came back.

\* \* \*

164

In the Destan Arms Jenny and Ned chatted carefully, both feeling rather self-conscious. Neither paid much attention to the food, but each paid a lot of surreptitious attention to the other.

'Would you like to come out with me one night?' he asked. 'For a meal or to the pictures – or they have some good shows at the theatre in Bournemouth sometimes.'

'I . . .' The thought of going into Bournemouth at night with someone who was still a virtual stranger made her feel nervous, much as she liked Ned. 'We could go out for a meal perhaps. Here? It's a nice pub. Just – chat, get to know one another.'

'Whatever you like, Jenny. Just as long as I can see you. How about tonight? In fact, let's just stay here for the rest of the day.'

That made her chuckle and feel warm inside. 'Are you sure about coming here? You'll have to drive over from Dorchester again.'

'It'll be more than worth it to see you.'

She let him take her home, but didn't invite him in.

And the news that was waiting for her inside made her feel even happier. Tim was safe! The three women opened a bottle of wine and drank his health, not even waiting till the evening meal.

'We'll drink to your embroidery, too,' Jenny said, raising her glass. 'Here's to my famous mother.'

'To your embroidery, Mum!' Louise echoed. She took only a small sip and put her hand across the top when Jenny tried to refill her glass. 'Wine's not good for the figure or for my fitness level.' To her surprise, she was enjoying the jogging.

'We're not going back to that dieting stuff again, are we?' Rosalind asked with mock severity. 'I don't want a daughter who looks like a stick insect topped by a skull, thank you very much.'

The entente cordiale faded a little. Louise scowled at her mother. 'What I want is—'

Rosalind stood up, her mood of euphoria evaporating suddenly and exhaustion setting in. She needed to be on her own now. 'I don't really care what you *want*, Louise. Other people have needs, even mothers, and it's about time you

165

noticed them. You don't live in a vacuum, you know. You're part of a family.'

Louise's voice was aggressive. 'Well, I don't think—'

'Your father's left a long list of instructions about what you're to do with yourself for the rest of the week. I've put it on your dressing table. I agree with him absolutely about the need to watch you carefully. I think I've been too soft with you in the past. I don't feel quite as soft any more. You should understand that. *Everyone* should understand that.'

She saw them both staring at her in amazement, mouths gaping in shock. 'I'm going up to my room now. I need a bit of peace and quiet. I don't want disturbing unless it's an emergency.'

The sisters exchanged glances as she walked out of the room.

'He's pretty rude to her sometimes,' Jenny whispered, 'but she's learning how to fight back at last.'

'He's pretty rude to everyone. But that's not my fault. And anyway, she should have stood up to him years ago.'

'Oh, yes? Like you stood up to him when he found out about your cavorting?'

'You just mind your own bloody business, Jenny Stevenson!'

Although the row was very loud indeed, their mother didn't come down to stop the quarrelling, as she usually did. And when the shouting had petered out and they had both – separately – got themselves a cup of coffee, Louise looked upwards and asked, 'Do you think she's all right?'

'I don't know.' Jenny remembered her mother kissing Jonathon Destan at the fête. They had both looked so right together, so tender. Suddenly she felt tired. Her mother wasn't the only one who needed a bit of peace. 'I think I'll go up and get ready for Ned. He'll be here soon.'

Louise was left with the television. And her own thoughts. Anger was still simmering inside her, but she didn't dare poke her nose outside the house. Her father's scribbled instructions had been very specific about that. Here she was in England, but not where there was anything going on. No, she had to be stuck in the middle of nowhere being treated like a child. It was sickening.

Then she brightened. But Tim was coming. Things would brighten up when he arrived. They always did. He'd work out a way to get round these stupid restrictions, though she might keep up with the running, persuade him to join in, even. Her body was getting firmer, developing quite a good shape, actually. She didn't like to admit that her father was right about that, but he was, the bastard. She picked up the half-empty bottle of wine, pushed the cork in and put it in the fridge.

In her room, Rosalind shut her ears to the noise from below. To help her resist the urge to go down and tell them both off – which had never done any good in the past and was not likely to do any good now – she went and got out her embroidery.

She sat for a moment or two staring at the pretty art-nouveau scene, not really seeing anything, still trying to control the confusion inside her head. When she felt calmer, she put that piece away and took out the family portrait. Concentrate on Life with a capital L, George Didburin had said. Well, this family portrait was no pretty scene. Her own figure with its wishy-washy pastels upset her – but it was true to life – or at least, true to what she had been for so long. Paul's figure continued to disturb her, too.

She would never exhibit or sell this piece. It was for her and her alone, and it was going to reflect her whole life, which was turning out to be a failure in so many ways. When she saw it all more clearly, surely she'd know what to do about it?

*Jenny*, she thought. I'll make a start on Jenny's figure today. She got out her family photos and the sketching materials, but ruined several drafts. The happy smiling girl in the photo was not the Jenny of today or the younger Jenny of her memories. She closed her eyes, trying to visualize the figure she needed and suddenly realized how nervous her elder daughter often was. In fact, Jenny always had been slightly nervous of life.

She took out a fresh piece of paper and this time the sketch grew beneath her fingers like a thing alive in its own right. When she put her pencil down, she stared at it, knowing it was good, really good. Or it could be. But would she be able to translate the drawing into an embroidered figure? Well, she could only try. Carefully she cut the sketch out.

Now, where to put Jenny? As if of its own volition, the figure settled at the back of the scene, standing by itself. Only it was the wrong size to go there, so she took another piece of paper to sketch it smaller. Yes. That was right. Poor Jenny. As alone as her mother.

No, Rosalind frowned, Jenny had not been quite alone. There had been the dog. Zip had been more Jenny's than anyone's, spending a lot of time cuddled up to her. She had taken him for walks, fed him and looked after him very responsibly, even when she was quite small. And when Zip had died at the age of thirteen – why did dogs live for such a short time when they could be such a comfort to people? – there had been a cat, because Paul had refused to have another dog. Sasha, the cat had been called. A nice creature, again devoted to Jenny. But when Sasha had been killed by a car, Jenny hadn't wanted to get another cat. She had begged and pleaded for a dog. And her father had continued to refuse, even though it would hardly have affected him.

Guilt shot through Rosalind. I should have let Jenny have her dog, she thought, I really should. I was wrong. Paul wasn't around half the time, even then. If we'd got a dog while he was away and presented him with a fait accompli, he'd not have been able to do anything about it. Or would he? You never knew with Paul. He could be quite ruthless at times, not against her, of course, but against other people. She frowned. No, she was fooling herself. He was ruthless with her, too – though he meant it for her own good. At least, she had always believed he did. Now she was not even sure of that.

Under her fingers – such clever fingers tonight – Zip took shape, almost as big as Jenny because that was how he came out, and then the cat, slightly smaller than the other two, but certainly not cat size. They had been such a comfort to Jenny, those animals. It was right to show them larger than life. And all three of them were looking away from Paul. Funny, that. But she had come to believe lately that her needle didn't lie, so she didn't attempt to change the figures.

She knew it would upset Jenny if she saw this portrait – well, it hurt Rosalind to do it – but she continued working.

168

She heard Jenny call farewell and go out with Ned. She heard the television blaring from downstairs. When Louise came up to bed, calling out good night, she answered, but didn't go out to see her.

Later Jenny came home, humming as she ran upstairs. She hesitated outside her mother's workroom, but went to bed without coming in. Which suited Rosalind at the moment.

The house fell silent. She didn't go downstairs, because she wasn't hungry, just consumed by impatience to get the figure done. At one point she got herself a drink of water from the bathroom, but continued sewing until her eyes grew too tired to focus. And by that time, the essence of Jenny had been captured.

Only then did she go to bed, feeling drained and sad. Her last stray threads of conscious thought were of her son. She hoped Tim would turn up soon. Even if it did add to the discord in the house. He had never been easy to deal with but she had to see for herself that he was all right. Not until then would she be able to do his picture.

And if necessary she'd find a way to keep Paul off their son's back. She must learn to stand up for her children, as well as herself.

# A Question of Scale

*A researcher can be confused, as well as charmed, by the profusion of pictorial and decorative detail on stumpwork embroideries, and also by the strange absence of scale. Flowers, insects, animals and trees jostle for position in scrapbook fashion and mix indiscriminately with fountains and fish, country mansions and castles, and costumed figures, as well as lions and leopards, all in an improbable English countryside, where the sun and moon shine at one and the same time.*

*(Hirst, p.10)*

# Fourteen

The phone rang as Rosalind was passing through the hall.
'Yes?'

'Mum?'

The voice was so wobbly it took her a minute to realize who it was. '*Tim?* Is that really you, darling? Where are you?' Tears started pouring down her cheeks, tears of such relief and joy that it was hard to focus on what he was saying.

Louise came pounding in from the kitchen at the sound of her brother's name, trying to put her ear close to the phone and listen in. Jenny hung over the banisters.

'I'm in Poole, Mum. At the coach station,' Tim said.

'Wait there. I'll come and get you.'

'How long will it take you to get here?'

'An hour, perhaps less.'

'There's nowhere comfy to wait, nothing to do. Look, there's a shopping mall across the road. I'll go in there and get a cup of coffee. I'll meet you in an hour near the mall entrance that's opposite the coach station. And Mum – it's great to hear your voice.'

'It's great to hear yours, love.'

Louise grabbed the phone, but he had already put it down. She glared at her mother. 'You *knew* I wanted to speak to him!'

'There isn't time for chatting. We have to leave at once.'

'Well, you bloody might have let me say hello, at least.'

'If you don't apologize for speaking to me like that, I'll not even take you with me to Poole. Do you really think you can be polite to your father and rude to me?'

Louise's mouth fell open in shock. She had never seen such an expression of determination on her mother's face.

'Well? I'm still waiting for an apology.'

171

'I'm sorry. I didn't think. I – I didn't mean to upset you, Mum.'

'Well, you did upset me. I've lost count of the times you've upset me by your rudeness in the past year or two, and I simply won't take it any longer. Do you understand that?' Her voice was still quiet, but steely in tone.

'Yes, Mum.'

'Now go and get ready.' Rosalind raised her voice. 'Jenny? Are you coming with us to meet Tim?'

'Wouldn't miss it.' As Jenny walked back into her bedroom to grab her coat and bag, she could not help grinning and making a triumphant fist in the air. Wow! Her mother was really getting tough.

She paused. No. Not tough. Mum could never be tough in that sense and had spoken as quietly as she always did. But she was starting to stand up for herself – not waiting till she was goaded, like before, and then bursting out with a hysterical-sounding protest. This time she had spoken straight away, as soon as the put-down had started, and had stayed in control of herself. About time, too.

As she came downstairs, Jenny suddenly remembered her date. 'Oh, can you just wait a minute, Mum? I want to cancel my date with Ned. I'm not going out with him on my little brother's first night back.'

Tim put the phone down, then went into the shopping centre, where he bought a cup of coffee and sat watching the crowds.

When an hour had passed he went to the entrance and found his mother and sisters waiting, looking anxious and scanning the crowds. He hurried across to them, tried to hug them all at once and then said in a shaky voice, 'Get me out of here.'

'Where's your luggage?' Rosalind asked.

'Lost.'

It seemed a long walk to the car. Tim sank into the back seat of the car and huddled down. 'I'm exhausted!' He was holding tears back only with great difficulty. It was so wonderful to see them. So fucking wonderful.

'So where have you been in America?' Louise asked. She was sitting next to him in the back of the car, worrying about how ill Tim looked.

172

He shrugged. 'Here and there.'

'But where exactly?'

'We wound up in New York.' Which was a lie.

'You and Wayne?'

'Yeah. But we split up.'

Silence.

'It's lovely to see you, Tim,' Jenny ventured from the front seat.

He nodded, but didn't say anything.

'I'm absolutely delighted to have all the family together again,' Rosalind said softly.

Tim jerked forward in his seat. '*All* the family? Dad's not down here, is he? Oh, God, I can't face *him* yet!'

Rosalind frowned, wondering why she had said 'all'.

Louise laid a hand on her brother's arm. 'It's all right. Dad isn't here just now. The chairman called and he rushed off to London again like a tame little piggy-wig. He won't be back for a few days, because he's going to some sort of live-in planning meeting.'

Tim buried his face in his hands, relief making him shake. 'Thank goodness! Oh, thank bloody goodness!'

In the front, Jenny and her mother exchanged astonished glances. In the back, Louise sat and worried some more.

By the time they reached the village, Tim had calmed down again.

'This is it,' Louise said, waving one hand scornfully. 'Burraford Destan. Dad's English country dream. Centre of the bloody universe it isn't.'

'It looks wonderful to me. Peaceful and full of real people.'

She stared at him. What had happened to make Tim welcome the idea of living in a dead-end hole like this? She would get it out of him later. He always told her things.

Liz stared at the doctor in horror. 'No! I don't believe it. We had tests, lots of tests. I can't have children. We tried for years. It must be something else, gastric flu maybe.'

The doctor sighed. She hated to see women react like this to the news that they were pregnant. 'According to your records, the tests showed you weren't highly fertile because you don't produce many eggs, but you could definitely conceive. Your husband was in a similar position – under-fertile – which made it very difficult for you.'

'But we've never taken any precautions, not since those tests. And I've never got pregnant.' She had boasted about that to Paul, who had produced some test results giving him a clean bill of health and had then boasted in return that he chose his partners very, very carefully and she had no need to worry about catching anything, if she wanted to really enjoy sex without those bloody condoms.

The doctor cleared her throat to bring her patient's attention back. 'There's no mistake. You are definitely pregnant.'

Liz buried her face in her hands. She hadn't let Bill near her since she'd got back. And although it was only a short time and she'd only missed one period, she was feeling wretched, nauseous all day. She had gone to the doctor for help, worried that she'd picked up a virus in Hong Kong. She hadn't even asked what the tests were for, just let them take her blood and urine, then gone back another day to find out what was wrong.

'It isn't my husband's child,' she said in a voice still muffled by her hands. 'I'll have to get rid of it.' Her voice rose hysterically. 'I'll have to!'

'Ah.' The doctor steepled her hands. 'Well, if you really want to do that, we can discuss it later, but it's too soon to make a decision.'

Liz raised her head and glared at her. 'What do you mean, too soon? What else can I do? And surely the sooner we do something the better?'

'You could tell your husband and ask him to accept the child. After all, he wanted children too, or he wouldn't have gone for the tests.'

'That was a long time ago. And he wanted his own children, not another man's.' Bill had flatly refused to consider adopting, becoming aggro at the mere idea. Telling him about this child would mean her accepting his screwing around, as well as his accepting her little affair and its consequences. She'd never get an edge over him after this. *If* he accepted the child. *If* she decided to have it. *If* they managed to stay together. Oh, hell! What a bloody mess! She groaned aloud.

The doctor shook her head and gave Mrs Foxen a moment

or two more to pull herself together. Patients never ceased to amaze her by the complexities of their emotional and sexual lives. 'Well, it's still too soon to think of an abortion. You tried for years to have a child and at your age this may be your final and only chance. My advice is to go away and think it all over very carefully. Take a few days. We don't need to rush into anything.'

Liz stared at her. It was good advice – for other people. She could see that. But *she* could never have this child. Still, you had to go through the formalities, the rigmarole and procedures the medical profession had set up. If the doctor wanted her to wait, there was nothing she could do about it. Just as she was about to agree, however, a thought struck her. 'I don't think I can hide it from my husband for much longer. The sickness is so violent in the morning he's bound to guess.'

'I can give you something which may help. But it probably won't stop the sickness completely.'

Liz accepted the prescription and walked out to sit in her car and try to come to terms with it all. She was going to get rid of it, of course she was. Oh, hell! What a stinking, rotten mess!

When they got back to Sexton Close Tim gulped down a coffee, smiled faintly at the empty mug and looked at his mother. 'I used to dream about your coffee, Mum. It's still the best in the world.'

Rosalind gave him a quick hug as she passed. 'Well, now you can drink it till it comes out of your ears.'

'Yes. I can.' He tried to smile. Didn't succeed.

'Have something to eat.'

'I'm not really hungry, Mum.'

'Just a snack, then. To please me.'

'OK.' He picked at some food, then pushed the plate away. 'What I'd really like is a bath. I must smell awful. I've been in these clothes for days.'

'What happened to your own stuff?' Louise asked.

'Stolen.'

Rosalind hadn't commented, but he did smell pretty high. 'I'll find you something of your father's to wear.'

'I have a tracksuit that's unisex,' Louise volunteered.

175

'Thanks.' He trailed up the stairs without even looking at her.

'Shall I clear your stuff out of the spare bedroom?' Louise asked her mother, trying to be helpful.

'Why?'

'Well, why do you think?' She sighed. Honestly, her mum could be so vague. 'Tim's back. He'll need somewhere to sleep.'

Rosalind fixed her with a cool gaze. 'There *is* another bedroom free. The attic. If you don't think it's suitable for your brother, you can move up there yourself. I have my room all set up as I like it, so I see no need to change things.'

Louise opened her mouth, caught her mother's eye and shut it again. 'I'll go and make the bed up in the attic for Tim, then, shall I?'

When she had gone clumping up the stairs, Rosalind looked at Jenny and for a moment her courage faltered. 'He looks so ill,' she whispered. 'He's nothing but skin and bone.'

Jenny had seen people looking like that before, at university. 'I think – it's only a possibility, mind – but he might be seriously addicted to hard drugs. Or just coming off them.'

Rosalind closed her eyes and took a few slow breaths. 'Yes. That had occurred to me, too. But he's not going to take drugs in my house.' She began to fiddle with things in the kitchen, trying to find something to keep her busy. 'How about a roast chicken for tea?'

'Fine.'

'I'll defrost one.'

She sat and listened to the microwave pinging and whirring as it defrosted the chicken, listened, too, to the sounds from upstairs. The bath lasted a long time, then slow footsteps climbed up to the attic.

A short time later Louise came into the kitchen. 'He's fallen asleep.' She looked a bit miffed. 'He had a shower, lay down on the bed, grunted at me and fell asleep.'

'Perhaps that's what he needs most.'

'I wanted to *talk* to him, ask him about America.'

Jenny made a choky little noise to show her disgust. 'You always think about what you want. Try thinking about what other people need for a change.'

'Has Mum been talking to you?'

'What about?'

'What you just said.'

Jenny looked at her in puzzlement.

'Oh, forget it!' Louise stamped out of the room.

They took it in turns to go up and check, but Tim slept all through the rest of the afternoon and the evening, too. Feeling drained, Rosalind had a nap as well, something rare for her, waking with her son's name on her lips.

The girls stayed up till ten o'clock, then went off to bed, yawning. Rosalind hesitated in her bedroom doorway, then shook her head and went to work on her embroidery. She could not sleep yet. She sat there quietly with the door open, listening to the sounds of her daughters getting ready for bed, tossing and turning about, then falling asleep.

About one o'clock she went to bed herself, but lay there wakeful worrying about her son. In the end, she gave way to temptation and tiptoed up the attic stairs in her bare feet.

Louise had left a lamp on at the side of the bed. Tim was lying sprawled across it in the way he always had done, even as a very small child.

As she watched, he opened his eyes, jerked upright and stared around him in what looked like sheer terror. Not until he saw her by the door did he sink back on the pillows again. 'I thought it was all a dream and I was back there again.'

She went to sit by the side of the bed. 'Do you want to tell me about it?'

He reached out for her hand and they sat holding one another for a few minutes. She saw tears on his cheeks, then he sniffed and looked at her. 'Yes. I do want to tell you about it – some of it, anyway. But – do you really want to know, Mum? It isn't nice. I'm not proud of what I've done.'

'You're still my son.'

He smiled through his tears. 'And you're still the best mother in the world. I wanted you dreadfully when – when things went bad.' Then he began to tell her.

She sat very quietly, holding his hand but not interrupting, not even allowing herself to exclaim in shock.

When he had finished, she simply gathered him in her arms and held him for a long time, rocking him slightly. Only after he pulled away did she move again.

'I've stopped taking the drugs, Mum.'

'Do you need help with that? I have plenty of money now. I can get you into a clinic—'

'*No!*' He took a deep breath and tried to smile, but failed completely. 'I don't want to be shut up anywhere. Can you understand that? Even the plane – and the bus – made me feel bad. What I want to do is spend as much time as I can in the fresh air, in quiet places. Like beaches. Or woods.'

'Well, there are plenty of places like that round here.'

He didn't seem to have heard her and the confidences were still pouring out of him like pus from a boil. 'When it gets bad, Mum, when I'm hanging out for the drugs, I go out and walk till I'm exhausted. It helps. If I can live here quietly for a while and get my head together, I think I'll come through it.'

'Well, no one will stop you going for walks. I did it myself when I was first here because I missed home so much. But I warn you, I shall try to feed you up.'

He shrugged. 'I don't seem to feel hungry.'

'But you'll eat a little – to please me?'

'Are you sure you're not a Jewish momma?' he teased with a brief return of his old self.

'In the sense of feeding you up, I'm as Jewish a momma as they come, so beware.' She watched his smile fade. 'Look, I'll go and get you a tray. I won't bring a lot of food, but you must eat something.'

When she got back, he was staring blankly into space. She set the tray in front of him and sat down. 'I'll feel better if I see you eat something.'

So he forced down two of the delicate sandwiches, and drank half the glass of milk. Then he looked at her pleadingly. 'If I eat any more, I'll chuck up.'

She took the tray. 'Do you want to get up or stay here?'

He sounded surprised. 'I think I can sleep again. I'll have a pee, then come back.'

'It's not the most comfortable bed on earth.'

'It feels pretty wonderful to me.'

'Then I'll leave you in peace.'

Before she went to bed she wrote a note to Louise and propped it at the foot of the attic stairs, warning her to let Tim sleep, then she went to bed. She thought she'd never sleep herself, but her exhausted body had a different view of that and she didn't wake until ten o'clock.

She found all three of her children gathered in the living room looking sad. She decided to think and act positively. 'When I've had something to eat, would anyone like a ride to the nearest beach?'

'Sounds great,' said Tim. He could just sit quietly and look at the water.

'All right,' said Louise. 'I can do my running there, I suppose. I'm getting quite fit, Tim. You could join me when you've picked up a bit.'

'Yeah, sure.'

'I think I'll stay here,' Jenny said. 'I'm not much into beaches.' And she was finding being with Tim a strain. He looked so miserable it hurt her to see him, because every time he came into a room, she was instinctively expecting the old Tim, the one who bounced round the house, talked rebelliously and couldn't even sit quietly to drink a cup of coffee.

'If your father rings,' Rosalind said quietly to Jenny as they left, 'don't tell him about Tim yet.'

'No.' She could understand that.

But Paul didn't ring.

And they were all glad of that.

In fact, Rosalind was so dreading Paul's return that she was even thinking of taking Tim up to Southport before he came back and staying there with him. Tim seemed to need to be with her. He didn't say much, but often sat nearby watching her. He particularly liked watching her embroider and he was the only one to whom she showed the family picture she was working on.

He stared at it for a long time. 'Shit, you're good. You've got that sod down to a tee.'

'And myself,' she said with a wry smile. 'All pale and wishy-washy.'

He studied her for a minute, then shook his head. 'That was the old you. You've changed. You're still quiet – but you're more – more colourful.'

She treasured that compliment.

# Fifteen

A few days later, Jenny went quietly upstairs, listened to see whether Tim was awake and heard the sound of low voices. Her younger brother and sister sounded as if they were having another heart-to-heart, so she went and wandered round the back garden, restless, worried about her mother and unsure what to do with herself. As usual she felt to be the odd one out, though Tim was a lot kinder to her than he had been in the past. It was just that he and she had never been close and now she didn't know how to bridge the huge gap yawning between them.

She needed to talk to someone about her feelings for Ned, only Louise and Tim seemed to have monopolized her mother's attention.

Was she ready for another relationship? She didn't know, only felt she didn't want to lose him.

On an impulse, she picked up the phone. 'Ned?' Already she was relying on him, turning to him. Their relationship seemed to have progressed so quickly. She smiled. That was because they were right together, easy and open in one another's company. Strange, how quickly she had realized that – and had not even needed to ask if he felt the same way.

'Jenny? Hi there, o gorgeous one!'

She didn't waste time on chit-chat. 'Ned, are you doing anything for lunch?'

'Not if there's any chance of seeing you.'

'I thought I'd catch a bus into Dorchester, have a look round the shops – and whatever else there is to see. But I don't want to – to . . .' Her voice tailed away.

'It's a wonderful idea. Come and meet me for lunch, then go off and do your own thing for the rest of the afternoon. If you can hang around till five-thirty, I'll drive you home after

180

work and take you out for tea in Burraford as well. Might as well make a day of it.'

'You're too kind to me, Ned.'

'I enjoy your company, Jenny. You know that.'

When he put the phone down, Ned was beaming.

'Good news?' his father asked.

'Yes. Jenny's coming over to Dorchester to have lunch with me. You don't mind, do you? It's not likely to be a busy day.'

'No, I don't mind at all.'

He wanted to talk about her, mention her name. 'She's great company, Jenny is.'

His father looked at him over the top of his half-glasses. Not like Ned to chat about his girlfriends. What he saw on his son's face made him sound a warning. 'She's very like her mother, though. Too soft for her own good.'

Ned stared in surprise. 'Don't you like her?'

It wasn't a question of liking or not liking. He wanted a stronger sort of woman for his son, because Ned was soft, too. The sort of gentle person who kept getting hurt. There had been one or two young women in the past whom George would have cheerfully strangled. He saw that his son was still looking at him, waiting for an answer. 'I'm not sure whether I like Jenny or not. I've hardly exchanged two words with her. But you seem taken by her.'

'I am. Very.'

'Well, that's what matters then, isn't it? But don't rush into things, eh? And don't forget the appointment in Weymouth this afternoon.'

'No. Of course not. But that isn't till three.' He turned away, smiling to himself. *Don't rush into things!* He'd been gone from the moment he first set eyes on Jenny Stevenson at the fête – and he rather thought she had fallen for him quite quickly, too, he couldn't think why.

Jenny turned up at the gallery around twelve and found Ned hovering near the door. She was surprised when he kissed her hard on the mouth by way of a greeting, but instinctively wound her arms round his neck and reciprocated with interest.

When the kiss was over, they both suddenly realized how public their situation was and pulled apart, each a little pink.

'Like that, is it?' she teased softly.

'Yes, it is like that. Very much like that.' He offered her his arm. 'I thought I'd show you round the gallery, then we'd go to the pub round the corner. It's my favourite watering hole.'

'Do you always eat out in pubs?'

'Most of the time. I don't booze at lunchtime, of course, but I still like the feel of a pub – and when you go to the same place regularly you get to know people. Besides, Karen at the Nag's Head does the best sandwiches in town. Huge. Full of goodies. Just wait till you see them. Now, come and have a look round.'

The gallery was larger than she'd expected, crammed with interesting and beautiful things. Half of them were antiques, half were works of art. Some embroideries were displayed in one corner. They were pretty, but not as telling as her mother's, somehow. At the rear, two larger rooms were each devoted to a show by one artist. Jenny wrinkled her nose at the dark landscapes in one room. At least, she thought they were landscapes.

'Don't you like them?'

'Not really. They make me feel uncomfortable.'

'They're supposed to. Landscapes of nightmare, the artist calls them. I'm always surprised at how well his stuff sells.'

'People read a lot of horror novels nowadays. These follow the same trend, don't they?'

He looked at her with surprise as well as respect. 'Good girl. Absolutely right.'

She flushed. 'I used to like art at school.'

'Then why did you take business studies at university?'

'Dad.'

'Ah.'

By the time lunch was over Ned had come to the conclusion that something was wrong. He took Jenny's hand. 'Want to talk about it, whatever it is?'

She smiled, then the smile faded and she looked at him wistfully. 'I do rather. Do you have to go back to work now?'

'I have to drive over to Weymouth to see some stuff we've been offered. You could come with me, if you don't mind sitting in the car while I'm wheeling and dealing.' He grinned. 'It's an old lady actually, with a cupboard full of rather nice ornaments. Shouldn't take more than half an hour to value them.'

'I'd like to come with you.' He made her feel – hopeful, loved. She blushed at the last thought and was glad he didn't ask her to explain the blush.

It was a quiet drive. Ned didn't make conversation just for the sake of it and Jenny was lost in her own thoughts. But both were glad to be together.

He dropped her reluctantly on the seafront at Weymouth while he went off to see old Mrs Trouter. Jenny watched him drive away, then turned to study the town. She fell instantly in love with the huge stretch of windswept promenade and after a cursory inspection of the famous statue of George III, which Ned had dutifully pointed out to her, she set off for a brisk walk.

A few people were sitting huddled in shelters, for it was a cool day, showery and with more rain to come, judging by the clouds piling up. The place was almost deserted and even the sand looked as if the rain had washed it down. She welcomed the wind, cold as it was, feeling cleansed by it, liberated briefly from her worries. Throwing back her head, she sucked in the salty air. If there hadn't been people around, she'd have run along the sand, skipping and dancing like a child.

When she looked at her watch she realized she was late so ran all the way back, arriving at the statue breathless and pink.

'You look gorgeous,' he said and pulled her towards him for another kiss. His eyes were full of promises.

She smiled and nestled against him for a moment. It was right between them, it really was – only she needed to tell him about Michael now.

On the drive back to Burraford, he turned the car down a small side road and stopped on the verge. 'Look!' he pointed to the left. In the distance, on a mound of land nestled at the bottom of the rolling folds of the Purbeck Hills, was Corfe Castle.

They got out and she stared, entranced. 'Oh, wow! This has got to be one of the most picturesque places in all England. It's like something out of a movie. Is it real?'

He was pleased with her reaction. 'So real I'll take you round it one day.' There were many things he'd like to share with her. He hoped she liked Dorset, for he could never think of living anywhere else.

A shower had just passed and the sun had come out, together with a rainbow, but there were more clouds looming. Silence settled between them and he saw the anxious look reappear on her face. 'Tell me what's worrying you,' he said quietly. He put his arms round her, so that she was leaning back against him, not facing him.

She looked at the rainbow and its colours began to blur and run together. Only then did she realize she was weeping – silently, helplessly, the pent-up anguish of the past few weeks overflowing at the sight of all that beauty.

'Tell me,' he said again, holding her close, hurting for her. 'What did this bastard do to you?'

'He – he . . .' And suddenly the words were pouring out of her in harsh spurts of shame and pain and guilt. 'Why did he pick on me? What did I do wrong? I've never understood what I did *wrong*!' she wailed when the story was told. By this time, her face was muffled in his chest.

He rocked her against him. '*You* didn't do anything wrong. The policeman was right. That bastard was sick. You were just in the wrong place at the wrong time.'

'It doesn't – put you off me?'

'Never.' When there were no more confidences, he suggested they get out of the car and stretch their legs. After a short walk, they came back and leaned against it, watching another rainbow. 'That one's ours,' he said softly.

As she turned a glowing look on him, he admitted to himself that he loved her. Deeply. The sort of love which led to a life-time together. But he wasn't sure she was ready for that so he didn't speak of his feelings.

Rain hissed down suddenly and they laughed as they both dived for shelter in the car, then sat there for a while longer, hand in hand, looking out through the miniature rivers on the windscreen at the rainswept landscape and the romantic ruined castle below them.

She leaned across to kiss his cheek. 'Thank you for listening and understanding. You're a lovely man.'

He eyed her speculatively. 'Then you like me enough to keep going out with me, me and no one else?'

184

'Yes, definitely.'

'That's smashing!'

He gaped, for she was quite convulsed with laughter. 'What's the matter?'

'That word. *Smashing*. It sounds so corny. I didn't think you Poms still used it.'

'Well, we do. And it *is* smashing that you're going to continue seeing me. In fact, it calls for a celebration.' He allowed a pregnant pause. 'And I have just the thing.'

'Champagne?' she joked. 'Caviar? Red roses?'

'No, this.' He produced a bar of chocolate from his pocket, wrapper torn and crumpled, with pieces missing from one end. 'Want some?'

She chuckled, feeling light and happy again. 'Definitely. I didn't know you were a chocoholic.'

'Unfortunately yes.' He patted his waist – not fat, but not thin either.

'Well, I'll let you into a secret.' She leaned closer. 'I adore – chocolate.' She linked her arm in his and leaned her head against his shoulder, letting him feed her piece by piece, letting the damp wind blow through the open car window now the shower had passed, so that her hair fluttered around her face. She had the strangest conviction that her troubles with Michael were blowing away, too, in that soft damp wind.

Then the heavens opened again and they had to close the car windows quickly.

She was flushed and pretty, so he kissed her. He was, he decided, going to marry her one day if she would have him. Definitely. But he'd better not say anything about that yet. He suspected she needed a little more time to recover.

It took only a few days for Tim and Louise to start bickering. She wanted to be with him – he wanted to be alone. Or he wanted to be with his mother.

When Louise started to complain to him about being cut off from the world in a dead-end dump like Burraford, he turned on her, terrified the rot had set in with her, too – for he felt himself to be rotten now, terminally sick like a fungus-ridden tree. He would lie there in his narrow bed, half-awake, imagining he could feel pieces crumbling away, a fingernail here, a toe there, hair, ears – there were lots of bits you could lose and still keep stumbling along in a semblance of life. So when Louise complained about this lovely, peaceful place, he glared at her and it was a moment or two before he could force any words through the haze of anger. 'You don't know what you're talking about, you stupid – *you child*!'

Her anger was as swift to rise as his. 'I do know, too. And I'm not a child any more. You're not the only one to have done drugs, you know. And I've had sex, too. Lots of times.'

'Well, I'm not doing drugs now and I never will again. What have you been on?'

Sulkily she told him.

He sighed with relief. 'You've not got really hooked, then? Not on the hard stuff?'

'On the allowance Dad gives me?'

He sighed in relief and grasped her arms, so that she had to look him in the face. 'Look, Lou, I've seen what happens to drug users – and I've seen the sort of lowlifes who make money out of the suckers. I'm not going to be a sucker again and if I ever see you doing drugs I'll tell Dad right away.'

She jerked away. 'Well! Thanks for nothing, Big Brother!'

He looked at her, sad and solemn. 'There's nothing clever, either, about giving sex away for kicks. They sell it on the street every day. That sort of sex is a cheap commodity.' His voice softened. 'You should wait till there's some love going with it. That's what makes it really special, worthwhile.' He had been fond of a girl once, though she'd got fed up of him. And who could blame her?

Louise snorted. 'Ha! Who believes in love and romance these days? You don't think Mum and Dad are in love, do you? I want to *live*, not stifle to death in a cosy little house!' She stormed off.

He went to find his mother and sit quietly, watching her work in the kitchen, so efficient, so clean, so *warm*. 'If you're worrying that I'll be a bad influence on Lou, Mum, I thought you might like to know that I'm trying to talk a bit of sense into her.' He tried to please her by forcing down one of her new-baked scones, but couldn't finish it, so slipped half of it surreptitiously into his pocket to be flushed away later.

'Thanks, Tim love. I am worried about her, I must admit.

She's been very foolish, but your father's too harsh with her. Perhaps some of what *you* say may get through.'

He studied his coffee gloomily, thinking how little it had meant to him when people tried to talk sense into him, how eager he had been to follow Wayne to America – eager enough to steal the money. His mother didn't know about that and he hoped she would never find out, either. 'I don't think anything helps really, except a dose of Capital L–I–F–E. Why didn't Dad let Lou go nursing? That's what she really wanted. It'd have suited her, too. She's always –' he managed a faint smile as he remembered – 'been good at mopping up blood and gore – usually mine.'

'Paul wouldn't even countenance it. And in those days I had no money of my own, so I couldn't help her.'

'But you do now . . .' He let the words trail away suggestively.

She nodded. 'Yes. But I'll only do something if it's what she really wants to do and if she'll promise to give it a fair go. No good will come from pushing her down another blind alley.'

'Yeah, that's for sure.' He looked sideways at her. She'd changed. Was more sure of herself now, though still quiet. He liked that about her, needed it.

Only – how would she be when his father came home? How did a gentle person cope with a bully like him? Tim was thinking seriously of asking his mother for a loan and getting the hell out of this place before his father got back. Very seriously. Only, he couldn't seem to get around to planning it yet. All he wanted to do was to rest. And be with his mother. It was hard enough managing without the drugs. He couldn't manage without her yet.

Next time Tim and Louise had a spat he threw at her, 'That sort of life, little sister, leads to young kids dying in back alleys from an OD. Drive-by shootings. Crims with guns. Hunger and dirt and old people with hopeless faces waiting to die.'

'I don't believe you. I won't. There's *got* to be more to life than this!' She waved one hand scornfully.

'Of course there is, but not if you're greedy and in a hurry to grab things. Like I was. I didn't make it to the nice parts of America, where the normal people live and exciting things happen.' Thanks to Wayne and his 'connections'. And would staying here bring trouble to his family? That still worried Tim a lot in the endless hours of fidget-filled darkness, tangled sheets and equally tangled thoughts.

'Well, I don't want to get into that sort of sleaze, Tim, of course I don't. But there must be *something* more interesting than business studies. I'll go mad if I have to go back to that, right round the bloody twist.'

'Why don't you try nursing? Talk to Mum about it.'

'Ha! What good would that do? She always does as Dad tells her.'

'Mum has money of her own now. If she thought you really meant it, she'd help you.'

Louise looked at him and frowned, not sure whether to believe him or not. 'I'll think about it.' But she didn't believe her mother would stand up to her father about something like that, didn't dare believe it. Because she'd be too disappointed if it didn't happen.


When Jonathon rang early one morning Rosalind spoke to him briefly, not realizing that her voice had softened and an involuntary smile had crept over her face.

'How's it going?' he asked. 'Enjoying having your son back?'

'Just a minute.' She went to close her bedroom door. 'It's not going all that well. Tim's – damaged. That's the only word for it, Jonathon. Damaged. Badly. And I don't know if I can put the pieces together again.'

'Let me know if I can help. In any way.'

'I'd be hammering on your door, don't worry. But there's nothing anyone can do that isn't being done. They say time is a healer in cases like this. I just – well, I hope they're right.'

Tears welled in her eyes so she said goodbye in a voice that came out choked and put the phone down before she started crying in earnest. Jonathon would understand her abruptness. He always understood things. She wished – oh, she wished desperately he could be here to help her through all this. She felt so alone.

She thought of her husband and grimaced. These mammoth

planning sessions for the company went on for ages some-times. Paul hadn't rung, so he didn't even know Tim was back. Not that he'd have come home for that. She wasn't sure he'd be much help in the future, either. His way had never been right for Tim. That was why she hadn't called him.

And although it was good that Paul had got Louise inter-ested in exercise, he was still insisting on her going back to the same university course. That wouldn't work, she was sure. Louise was a doer, not a thinker. Why could Paul not see that?

Not long after that Audrey rang, sounding querulous. 'For days I've been expecting someone to call about Tim. I presume he arrived safely?'

'Oh, Mum, I should have rung you. I'm so sorry. I'm sorry for *all* the trouble we've caused you lately.'

'It's not your fault, love. But I'm too old for all these fusses now. I said so to John only yesterday.'

'Not too old to have a boyfriend in tow,' Rosalind teased.

Audrey's voice softened. 'No. Never too old for that. Do you like John?'

'Yes. Very much.'

'Good.'

Rosalind waited for the news she'd been expecting for a while, but it didn't come. 'Well, I must go now. Lovely to speak to you.'

Audrey's voice was suddenly urgent. 'Don't let those chil-dren run rings round you, Rosalind. Stand up to them as well as to Paul. *You* have needs, too.'

'I am standing up for myself,' Rosalind assured her mother. 'Well, starting to.'

'Good. Don't expect to change completely in a few weeks. Bye!'

That night Tim let himself quietly out of the house shortly after midnight. The girls were sound asleep, but Rosalind heard him leave and wondered about stopping him, then shook her head. No. He'd said walking helped him cope with the with-drawal symptoms. And this wasn't an inner city, after all. He should be safe enough in the quiet Dorset countryside.

She knew she would not get back to sleep till she heard

189

him return, so she got up and went to her embroidery, her usual refuge and comfort.

Jenny's figure was finished, so this time Rosalind drew Tim – drew him as the thin, anguished creature he now was, not the lively young lad he had once seemed, for he had been unhappy underneath for a while now. She only needed to do one sketch. As she stared at it, she knew it was right, terrifyingly so. As instantly right as Paul's figure had been.

When she heard Tim come in again two hours later, she made no attempt to conceal the fact that she was up.

He came into the back bedroom, bringing a cold damp smell with him, but looking more at peace with himself. 'Can I see what you've done today?'

She leaned backwards and gestured to the partly-finished piece. 'I'm still working on the family portrait. It's not going to be a pretty one. I'm trying to see us as we are.'

He was silent for a moment or two, studying it, then nodded. 'It's good. That's Jenny to the life. Christ, Dad's an arrogant shit! But you're not like that figure any more.' He touched the pastel-coloured Rosalind, standing sideways, looking at her family with a faintly anxious air. 'You used to be, but not now.'

'Mmm. I know.' She hesitated, then confided, 'Actually, I'm thinking of putting another me back to back with that one, a more brightly coloured figure, sort of like a Siamese twin, looking out at the world.'

'Worm turning?' he asked softly, not looking at her.

'Yes.'

'Good. About time.'

He went back to studying the embroidery. 'It's a good one of Zip, too. Funny how he was always Jenny's dog, isn't it? What about me? Have you done a sketch of me yet?'

She pulled the piece of paper out from underneath the pad and passed it to him.

He was very quiet, studying it intently, then nodded and handed it back. 'It's excellent. You've got a real flair for this sort of thing. You're good enough to do portrait sketches. I dare say you'll become very famous with your embroideries, then I'll go round boring everyone about my clever mother.'

She smiled, but her thoughts were still on her sketch of him. 'You look a bit young here, that's all.'

'Don't change it. Not if you want the truth. I feel young sometimes, young and stupid. And yet old, too.' Tears were running down his cheeks. 'Oh, fuck, why am I crying? What a wimp!'

She'd found a book about drugs and getting over them on a shopping trip into Poole, had gone there deliberately to see if she could find something to show her how to help him. 'You have to expect mood swings and a very emotional state while you're detoxifying. It's part of the process.'

He grinned through his tears. 'Found a book on it, have you?'

'Yes.'

'You and your books.' He looked down at his wet, cold feet. 'Well, this one's bloody right, I can tell you. Only, I don't know how I'm going to cope with it all for much longer. It's – it's like something gnawing away at me, this need. I'm even snapping at Louise and all the poor little bitch wants is to be with me.'

'Thanks for trying to talk sense into her.'

'I'm not sure I got anywhere – well, not very far, anyway.'

He looked at his mother, naked anguish in his eyes. 'You don't deserve kids like us, you know.'

'You're my son, Tim. I love you whatever you do.'

She was always glad afterwards that she'd said that to him. Always.

He came over to her and put his arms round her, laid his cheek against hers and said in a choked voice, 'I love you, too.' They stood silently for a while, then he yawned and pulled away. 'I think I'll manage to sleep now. See ya, Ma.'

'Don't call me that,' she said automatically and saw him smiling at her. But she couldn't seem to smile back. Tonight everything felt too charged, too sad.

Paul was called out of a meeting for an urgent phone call. It wouldn't look good, this. But it'd have looked worse to refuse to take the call.

The receptionist directed him to a phone booth in the foyer. 'Hello?'

'It's me, Paul.'

'Liz?' Her voice had been husky, anxious. 'Is there a

191

problem?' Not his mother-in-law! That'd send Ros scurrying home to Australia and he'd never get her away again.

'I'm pregnant.'

The world seemed to lurch around him. 'You *can't* be!'

'I am. I was a bit surprised myself.'

'You *are* going to get rid of it?' Silence. 'Liz?'

'I'm thinking about that.'

'What do you mean, thinking? Haven't you seen a damned doctor?'

'Yes.'

'And . . . ?'

'She wants me to think it over for a few days, then she'll help me if I still want an abortion.'

'I thought you were sterile.'

Her voice wobbled. 'So did I.'

'Well, I don't see a need for us to upset Ros over this.'

Suddenly Liz wished she hadn't rung, didn't want to speak to him any more. What had she expected from Paul Stevenson, for heaven's sake? Support? Warmth? She should know by now what he was like. 'I just thought you should know,' she said wearily. 'I'll deal with it.'

'If you need any money—'

There was a sudden buzzing. The bitch had put the phone down on him. He stood there, anger roiling through him. Suddenly he thumped the wall with his clenched fist. He didn't need all this hassle! He had a living to make, a career to get on with. Had the whole world gone mad lately?

Liz did not find the doctor's anti-nausea remedy much use. Oh, it gave her time to get to the bathroom before she threw up, but it didn't do much else. So when Bill came out of the spare bedroom where he was still sleeping, opened the bathroom door and stood there watching, she knew the game was up.

Another wave of sickness hit her and she had to concentrate on hitting the toilet bowl. When she had finished, she washed her face and went out into the bedroom to face him.

He was sitting at the dressing table, arms folded. 'That's not an upset stomach. You're pregnant.' His voice was flat and definite, making a statement, not asking a question.

'Yes.'

'Hong Kong?'

She nodded and padded across to slip under the bed covers, shivering with the after-effects of the vomiting.

'Cup of tea any use?'

She looked at him and saw he meant it. Tears flooded her eyes. She had not expected kindness from him, given the circumstances.

When he came back, she accepted the mug of tea gratefully, sipping it and holding its wonderful warmth between her hands while she waited to see if it would stay down. After a minute, she tried another sip, saw him watching and explained, 'Sometimes there's a double whammy with the sickness. I have to be cautious.'

He held out the plate of biscuits. 'Want one of these? I read somewhere that a dry biscuit helps.'

She shook her head, tears scalding down her cheeks. 'Stop being so damned kind!'

'Well, I'm not going to beat you up, you fool, but we do have to talk.'

'Yes. If it's any consolation, I went to see the doctor, told her I wanted to get rid of it. I don't expect to land you with – with someone else's offspring.'

'Bit drastic that, isn't it?'

'Yes. But I couldn't see any other choice. And she s–said – she said to think it over – and I thought what a load of crap, why doesn't she just sign the bit of paper? Get rid of it quick before anyone finds out. But last night I dreamed of it – a little boy – and he s–smiled at me – and I knew I couldn't do it, couldn't kill him.' The dream child had looked too much like Rosalind's son, Tim, as a child. But if she did have it, how was she going to manage when Bill left her because she hadn't had to earn a living for over twenty years?

He looked solemn, stern, not at all like the easy-going man she normally lived with. 'Don't do anything yet. I'll need to think about it, too.' At the door he turned. 'Do you know who the father is, by the way, or did you just screw anyone?'

She threw the mug at him then, scattering hot tea all over the quilt. 'Of course I know who he is! I only screwed one person, dammit! Unlike you!'

He didn't duck but the mug fell short, smashing against a chair leg and breaking into dripping pieces of fractured clay. When the door had closed behind him, Liz couldn't take her eyes off that mug. Was her life going to fall into pieces, too?

She wished she hadn't phoned Paul. What was the point in telling him about the baby? Did he really think she'd go shouting her mouth off to Rosalind, her best friend?

More tears flooded her eyes and she mopped at them with the edge of the sheet. She felt ashamed of what she'd done, desperately ashamed. Burying her head under the covers, she wept again.

But Bill didn't come back to comfort her.

# Sixteen

Tim felt really bad that day. He spent most of it in his room, sweating and resisting the urge to scream, to smash things, to take out his body's agony on anything and everything. And he succeeded in keeping control. A small victory. Well, each day was a small victory at the moment, wasn't it? What was it his Mum always said? One step at a time.

But what terrified him was: they said you never lost the desire, never, whatever you did. That the need for a fix always haunted you. And he didn't think he could take a lifetime of this.

There was a tap on the attic door. Louise poked her head round it. 'Want a cup of coffee?'

'Yeah. Thanks.'

She came back with two mugs and a plate with a piece of cake on it. 'Mum said you might like to eat something.'

He looked at it with loathing. 'And there again, I might not.'

'Shall I dispose of it for you down the toilet? We can pretend you've eaten it.'

Somehow that idea was loathsome to him. He had even felt guilty about flushing away the piece of scone the other day. 'No. I'm not going to lie to Mum.'

'Everyone else does.'

'What do you mean by that?'

She shrugged. 'Shan't tell you.'

He lay back, rolling his eyes at the ceiling. 'I'm not in the mood for childish games. If you can't talk sense, go away and play at getting fit.'

'What do you mean "play"? I *am* getting fit.'

'Well, go and get fitter, then.'

Rosalind, crossing the landing with some clean towels,

heard the sound of them quarrelling and let out a growl of exasperation. Sometimes Louise did more harm than good, with Tim in this fragile state. She put down the towels and went across to the attic stairs, the small noise her slippered feet made on the bare wooden treads masked by the raised voices above her.

Just as she got to the attic door, she heard Louise yell, 'Well, Dad does lie to her all the time. He's having an affair with Liz at the moment. Mum's best friend. And he's probably had lots of affairs before that. He's even more of a shit than we thought.'

Rosalind stood in frozen horror on the stairs. *Liz and Paul!* It couldn't be true! It just – it wasn't possible. She didn't move away, though, couldn't, because she had to know the truth. Louise wouldn't say something like that without a reason.

Tim's voice was low and scornful, amazingly like his father's. 'I don't believe you. Even *he* wouldn't – not with Mum's best friend. I've seen him with young chicks a couple of times, not with older women. And how did you find out about it, anyway? You must have made a mistake.'

'I overheard him phoning her, talking about being together in Hong Kong, asking her to meet him for a screw.'

Rosalind believed it suddenly. She put one hand across her mouth to hold the shock and pain inside. There was the sound of someone moving inside the attic, then Louise yelping in shock.

Tim's voice came out in jerks, as if he were shaking his sister. 'If you ever – say one word – about this to Mum – I'll kill you myself.'

'I haven't. I wouldn't.'

'You'd bloody better not.'

There was silence now from inside the room. Rosalind looked round blankly, realized where she was and tiptoed down the stairs, forgetting the pile of towels she'd put down on the landing. She had to get out of the house, couldn't face anyone yet, could hardly face her own thoughts even. She went quickly into her bedroom, snatched up her handbag and rushed downstairs, passing Jenny on the way.

'Are you all right, Mum? You look—'

The front door slammed and there was the sound of a car

engine. As it faded away into the distance, the house became silent. Too silent.

Why couldn't they all be happy, like other families? Jenny wondered as she went into her own bedroom.

Eyes half-blinded by tears, Rosalind drove out of the village more by instinct than by good judgement. Then suddenly she could go no further, so she pulled the car up at the tree-shadowed end of a lay-by, switched off the engine and sat there, back to the world, bowed over the steering wheel. The tears she'd been holding in overflowed, rolling down her cheeks.

So many pieces had suddenly fallen into place, like tumblers clicking inside a lock, which then let the door swing back to reveal the hidden things behind it. Nasty things, growing like poisonous fungi in the dark.

Paul *had* been unfaithful! She knew it with an utter certainty as she sat alone in the car. But why with Liz? *Liz, of all people!* Any woman was bad, but her best friend . . . She started sobbing again.

It had happened in Hong Kong, of course. They had both been there at the same time. Liz had sent only one postcard and hadn't replied to Rosalind's letters since.

She suddenly remembered a silence on the phone once when she'd mentioned Liz to Paul. And how her friend – who was not now her friend, who could never be her friend again – had declared before she left that she was going to get her own back on Bill. Sauce for the goose, she'd said.

'But why use *my* husband to pay him back?' Rosalind whispered. 'Oh, Liz, how could you do that to me? *How could you?*'

Was Liz just a one-off aberration? For a moment Rosalind tried to cling to that hope, then shook her head slowly and sadly. No. A man like him couldn't cope without regular sex. And even he wouldn't be unfaithful for the *first* time with Liz. When he was home he was always so lusty, wanting to make love every day. Twice a day sometimes. He loved sex. So did she. It had been hard to get used to the periods of enforced celibacy.

She let out her agony in a raw, moaning sound. Oh, what a credulous fool she'd been! All those years she had made their marriage and their family the centre of her life. Even when Paul began to go away for long periods, she had tried to adjust, to be a supportive partner, to be a good mother. Dammit, she had tried so *hard*.

Rain spattered against the car windscreen, then worked itself up into a frenzy, pounding on the metal roof. She welcomed the cacophony because it shut her in, gave her a sense of utter privacy. Even when the tears had dried on her cheeks, she sat on, with cars droning past behind her back and rain pattering down more gently now. She didn't know what to do. Her whole life had just fallen apart.

*No,* said Sophie's voice inside her head. *Not your whole life. He's your husband, but you're a person in your own right. You have a life of your own, needs of your own. Never forget that.*

'He might not be my whole life,' Rosalind told the hovering shade of her aunt, 'but he's a damn big part of it, Soph.'

Traffic thundered past, wind blew so strongly that the car rocked with the force of it, but Rosalind didn't notice. The main thing she had to decide was – should she forgive him? No, even that was not the full pattern of her truth. She admitted it to herself at last. The main thing was, did she really *want* to stay with him now?

She didn't think so. Not when she'd experienced the warmth and companionship of another sort of man.

Only – how could she break up her family?


The following day Jenny met Ned for lunch. As she ran towards him, he held out his arms and gathered her close, swinging her round.

'Oh, hell!' he said suddenly, stopping and looking down at her. 'I can't hold it in any longer, Jen. I love you. I want to marry you.'

She stared up at him, her mouth open in shock, then gradually a smile crept across her face.

'Trust me to blurt it out,' he said. 'I meant to propose all romantically, only the sight of you coming towards me was too much. I couldn't wait a second longer.' He raised one of her hands to his lips to kiss it, then did the same to the other. 'Oh, Jen, you will say yes, won't you?'

She flung her arms round his neck. 'Of course I will. I can't imagine what you see in me, but yes, Ned, I love you, too. And yes, I will marry you.'

A woman bumped into them and muttered something about 'cluttering up the pavement'. Ned came down from his rosy cloud for long enough to guide Jenny into the pub and sit down in the corner with her.

'I don't know what to say,' he admitted. 'Except that I don't think I've ever been as happy in all my life.'

'Me, too.'

They ordered sandwiches, which neither of them finished, and drinks, which they left almost untouched on the table. They said very little, just smiled at one another and held hands and told each other the things lovers always have said, yet which always seem new and wonderful to each couple.

As the lunch-time rush ebbed, Ned realized what time it was and grimaced. 'Should have been back at the gallery an hour ago.' He pulled her to her feet. 'Come on! Let's go and tell Dad our news.'

'Now?'

'Yes. And later we'll go over to see your mother.'

As they walked into the gallery together, Jenny suddenly felt shy. Ned's father peered out of a door at the back, waved one hand in greeting and waited for them to join him.

'What time do you call this?' he demanded in mock anger.

Ned beamed at him. 'I completely forgot the time. I've been proposing, you see, and Jenny has just agreed to marry me.'

George gaped at his son. 'Goodness me! Well, you *have* taken me by surprise.' He gave Jenny a bear hug, muttering, 'Great! Great!' in her ear as he patted her back. 'I'm delighted about this and my wife will be, too.' Then he held her at arm's length. 'Welcome to the family, Jenny, my dear. I hope you two will make each other very happy.'

He went on to give Ned an even more crushing hug, pounding him on the shoulders repeatedly. 'About time, you young scamp, about bloody time. Your mother's been fretting for a year or two.' He winked at Jenny. 'Wants grandchildren before she's too old to enjoy them.'

She blushed. And wondered if many other fathers hugged their children so naturally. She would make sure Ned hugged theirs. She could not remember her father hugging any of them.

Ned detached himself, grinned and put his arm round her again. 'A bit premature, to think of grandchildren, don't you feel, Dad?'

'OK. We'll wait a bit for that.' That lad looks older, George thought in surprise. No, not older, more mature, more – decisive. He gestured to the phone. 'Do you want to tell your mother or shall I?'

'I will.' Ned took the phone and pressed the automatic dial key. 'Mum?' He pulled a face. 'No, I'm fine. Look, Mum, will you *listen*?' He took a deep breath. 'Jenny and I have just got engaged.'

There was a shriek at the other end of the phone. George rolled his eyes at Jenny and grinned as a gabble of words had Ned nodding and murmuring.

At one stage he passed the phone to Jenny so that she could 'meet' his mother.

Afterwards, he said, 'We need to buy an engagement ring, Dad. All right if I take the rest of the day off?'

'Be my guest. It's not every day my only son gets engaged. Do you want to look at our antique stock of jewellery first? Or are you going to buy a new ring?'

Ned looked at Jenny questioningly.

'I think I'd like a new one, if you don't mind.' She wanted everything to be fresh and new in this relationship.

'I don't mind at all. We'll go and hunt round the shops.' He was already guiding her towards the door as he turned to his father. 'Oh, and Mum wants us all to do lunch tomorrow, to celebrate. Will you book a table?'

'Fine.'

When his son had left the gallery, George picked up the phone again. 'Stella? No, he's just gone. We can talk now.'

'How did he look?'

'Absolutely besotted.'

'What's she like?'

'Gentle. Pretty. Looks as besotted as he is. They're clinging to one another like a pair of damned leeches.' He chuckled. 'Ah, young love! Yes, one o'clock tomorrow, usual place. Don't overdress. She's not a fashion plate. And don't overpower her

200

with your enthusiasm for grandchildren. She blushes easily.'

When he put the phone down he leaned back and smiled around him. 'If she makes him that happy, she'll do,' he told his favourite statuette, a bronze art-nouveau lady with flowing skirts and hair. Pulling out a large handkerchief, he blew his nose vigorously.

Jenny arrived home at tea time looking windswept but happy. Ned came into the house with her and they both went upstairs to see Rosalind, who was in her workroom.

She turned to greet them, hoping the make-up had hidden the redness of her eyes. Then, as she saw the linked hands, the beaming faces, she guessed what had happened and tried to respond joyfully to their news. It had been so long since she'd seen that happy look on her daughter's face that she didn't want to spoil things now by confiding her own troubles.

She led the way downstairs, calling to Tim and Louise to join them and opening a bottle of wine for a toast.

After they had chatted for a while, Tim excused himself. He had been very quiet, but had smiled at Ned and sipped some wine.

Rosalind watched him go, trying to hide her anxiety. Seen next to Ned, he seemed blurred, no more than a shadow in their midst. And surely he was getting thinner?

Louise looked at her mother and pushed herself to her feet. 'I'll go and – and see if he's all right.' She turned to her sister and gave her another hug. 'I'm really glad for you two.'

Rosalind tried to sound hearty and happy. 'We'll need to tell your father. I'm sure he'll be delighted.'

'Yes, I suppose so.' Jenny looked at Ned, then back to her mother. 'We can wait till Dad's finished this conference thing, though, can't we?'

'Yes.' Which meant Rosalind would have to wait for her own confrontation with Paul until after that. And she didn't know whether to be glad or sorry. Relieved, probably. She had a lot of thinking to do. Finding out about his unfaithfulness had thrown her emotions into turmoil and she wasn't sure what she wanted any more.

'Would you mind if I went out to the pub with Ned for dinner? Would Tim mind, do you think?' Jenny wished he would, but doubted it. Her brother seemed only half-aware of the world around him.

Rosalind felt a sense of relief. 'No one will mind at all, love. Just go and enjoy yourselves.'

Ned came to hover in the doorway of the kitchen while Jenny was changing. 'Any sign of the other embroideries arriving?'

'What? Oh. Oh, yes. They arrived a few days ago. I forgot to tell you.' She led the way into the dining room. She hadn't even opened the box. 'Why don't you take it with you tonight, Ned? You and your father can have a look through them, see what you think.'

'Don't you want to open them yourself? Check they're all right?'

She made a huge effort to concentrate on business. 'No. I've – um, got something on my mind just now. Don't sell any till I've told you which ones I want to keep, though.'

Ned looked sideways at her. Under the make-up her eyes were reddened. It was probably something to do with Jenny's brother. He had a lot to answer for, Tim Stevenson did. But he looked as if he were paying for it. He looked awful. Like an AIDS sufferer, all hollow-faced and big-eyed, his body a series of sharp angles.

'I know your father will look after them.' Rosalind pushed the box towards him with her toe.

'He definitely will. I'll pick them up when I bring Jenny back. I don't want to leave something so precious in the boot in a pub car park. I'm really looking forward to seeing them.'

He glanced over his shoulder to check they were still alone and his face became solemn. 'Um – Jenny told me about – about that fellow Michael she used to be with – and what happened in Perth. I just wanted you to know that she'll be quite safe with me.'

Ned's tender concern for her daughter was another spear stabbing into Rosalind's guts, but the years of putting on a public face at Paul's functions stood her in good stead. 'I know she will.'

She waved them goodbye, then pleaded a headache, leaving Tim and Louise to get their own tea. They had obviously made up their quarrel, but both were subdued.

*    *    *

About ten o'clock she heard Jenny come back and help Ned carry the box of embroideries out to the car. Afterwards there was a long silence from the hall, filled with faint rustlings and murmurs, then the front door closed behind Ned, and Jenny then went straight to bed.

About eleven o'clock, Louise went to bed, too.

Tim stayed downstairs watching TV, then went up to the attic about midnight.

About two o'clock, he woke Rosalind as he crept out. To her surprise he took her car. She usually kept the keys in her handbag in her room, but now she remembered that she'd left it on the hallstand tonight, she'd been so upset. Was he insured to drive the car? She didn't know. The company had leased it for her.

She couldn't get back to sleep, but lay and worried about him. Well, she always worried when he went out at night, but somehow, tonight, she felt more worried than usual. As if – oh, she didn't know what she thought. She didn't know anything any more.

But why had he taken the car? He usually went walking.

Eventually she dozed a little, then woke up and saw grey smudges against the cloud-filled darkness of the sky. Nearly dawn. She rose and went up to Tim's room, thinking he might have come in while she'd been asleep.

He wasn't there.

She peered out of the window. Neither was her car.

After frowning at the untidy attic, she searched all the surfaces, sighing in relief when she realized his things were still there and there was no sign of a farewell note. She'd been desperately worried that he might take his own life, he seemed so lacking in hope sometimes. There were no clues to his absence, none. The bed had been lain on, but not slept in. The radio was still muttering quietly to itself. Irritated by its faint rasping noise, she went and snapped it off, then went back to her own room.

Where was he?

In the shower, she thought she heard the car and ran into the bedroom dripping wet, only to see the man next door turning into his drive. Disappointed she trailed back to the shower, which was still hissing away.

When she was dressed, she went downstairs to make some coffee, but could not galvanize herself into doing anything useful after that, so sat on alone in the quiet kitchen, hoping to hear the sound of Tim's key in the front door.

But he didn't come back. And the sky was fully light now.

She threw away the cold coffee that half-filled her mug and made some more. He'd never stayed out so long before.

*Something must have happened to him!*

She felt a quick lurch of terror in her belly. He might be lying somewhere in pain, suffering from withdrawal symptoms like those described in her book, or he might have been driving carelessly and had a car accident. 'Please let him be safe,' she whispered. 'Just let him be safe. Never mind the car, it's Tim who matters.'

Time trickled past and the second mug of coffee grew cold. She considered making more, but couldn't focus on such mundane things.

*Where the hell was her son?*

# Seventeen

L iz was standing in the kitchen waiting for the kettle to boil when the phone rang. She picked it up listlessly. The early morning nausea was not as bad today but she still felt pretty ghastly. It was a wonder that women ever had more than one baby, she decided, a triumph of instinct over common sense. 'Yes?'

'Hi there. How are things? Can you talk?'

She glance quickly round, but Bill was still upstairs. 'What do *you* want?'

'Just to find out how you are. Have you – er – dealt with that little problem?'

'Not yet.'

'Need any money?'

'No.' She hesitated, then malice made her add, 'I'm thinking of keeping it, actually.'

His voice grew hard and angry. 'I'll deny everything.'

She felt perverse, not wanting to make it easy for him. 'But will people believe you? Rosalind, for instance? Plenty of hotel staff saw us together – that barman who made the beautiful cocktails. I can easily prove we were together if I have to – and then there's DNA testing. That could show a lot.'

His voice sounded incredulous. 'You're going to *tell* Ros? And you call yourself her *friend*?'

'I'm a better friend to her than you are a husband, you rotten sod. I've betrayed her once. How many times have you betrayed her?'

A sound made her glance round and she saw Bill standing behind her, his face like stone. He walked forward and took the phone from her hand, shouted, 'Go to hell, Stevenson!' then slammed the receiver into its cradle. After breathing in and out deeply several times, he finally raised his eyes to look at Liz. 'I'm disgusted by what you did. Utterly, totally disgusted.'

'You're a fine one to talk.' But her protest sounded weak and unconvincing, even to herself.

He stared at her for a moment, then shrugged. 'I've broken my marriage vows, yes – several times. But I've never betrayed my best friend and, strange as this may seem, I've never stopped loving you. What's more, I've dealt fairly with the other women. They all knew the score, knew I wasn't about to break up my marriage.' His voice grew thick with revulsion. 'How could you do it to her, Liz? *Rosalind Stevenson*, of all people? The gentlest, kindest person I know. How could you even think of it?'

She was sobbing now, her whole body shaking with the violence of her feelings. 'I don't know. I don't *know*, dammit! I think I went mad for a time. I was furious with you and so bloody bored up there in Hong Kong. I was even thinking of coming home, that's how bored I was, only I wasn't going to give you the satisfaction. Then Paul arrived and turned on the charm – and that bastard can be very charming when he wants, believe me. And I fell into his arms like a ripe cherry. Only *you* ripened me, you know you did.'

She looked up for long enough to hurl at him, 'Don't you think I'm sorry? Even without this.' She gestured towards her belly. 'Don't you think I feel like the lowest kind of – of worm, doing that to my best friend?' The minute the plane had taken off coming home from Hong Kong the guilt had started to nag at her, and she'd been amazed that she had even thought of having an affair with Rosalind's husband.

When her husband didn't speak, she asked, 'You aren't – going to tell her, Bill?'

'Me? Of course I'm not. What do you think I am?'

She covered her face with her shaking hands. 'Sorry. I know you won't. I don't know why I said that.'

'Will *he* tell her?'

'He's managed to keep all the others from her,' she said in a dull voice.

'*All* the others?'

'Yes. It appears he's made quite a hobby of it, says he enjoys the variety.'

'He was just making use of you, then.'

'Yes.' After a moment, she stood up, wanting to escape, unable to stand his calm scrutiny and the scorn in his eyes, but she stumbled and would have fallen headlong had he not jerked forward to catch her. Then she started sobbing loudly, clutching at him, calling his name. 'Bill, Bill, Bill!' On and on. She couldn't stop herself.

He sighed and closed his eyes, keeping hold of her, patting her shoulder occasionally. She was right. He had to take some share of the blame, he knew that, but could he take another man's child along with it? She was still weeping helplessly against him, the whole of her small body shaking, her eyes drowned in tears. The only other time he'd ever seen her weep like that was when they'd told her she was not likely to have children.

'Shh, calm down, Liz. This isn't good for you or the baby. We'll work something out – together.'

She looked up, hope dawning in her eyes. 'Bill?' she said again, uncertainly this time.

'Don't – push things.' His decision was made, really, but he didn't want to say it out loud yet.

She stared at him, not daring to voice her hope in case she broke the fragile gossamer threads that were drawing them together. After a moment, she laid her head against his shoulder with a weary sigh and they stood there in silence.

Finally he muttered, 'Oh, hell, I don't want us to split up, Liz.'

'Neither do I.' She huddled against him, praying for a miracle.

'And I definitely don't want to kill a baby.'

Another silence. Much longer this time. She hardly dared breathe as it dragged on.

Then, 'You'd better be a bloody good mother, though.'

The old Liz revived enough to ask, 'Will you be a good father?'

He nodded, holding her at arm's length and looking very solemn. 'I like kids. I always have. I was wrong about not adopting. But you're not to tell anyone it's not mine. Ever. That's my only condition.'

'I won't. Oh, Bill, I promise I won't.'

Then she was weeping again, tears of joy this time, and

they were kissing one another as they hadn't kissed for years, hungrily, needily. Excitement flared between them and they started tearing at one another's clothes as they sank down together on to the soft vinyl of the kitchen floor.

Flesh against flesh, stripped of all barriers, they started to grow together again.

Tim drove through the darkness and when it started to rain he didn't switch on the windscreen wipers, laughing as he nearly ran off the road. Maybe that was one way to end it? But something made him switch the wipers on and slow down just a little.

He came to Poole, eventually. Everything looked quiet, but when he got down to the docks area, there were signs of life, lights here and there, the odd person walking or stumbling along.

He stopped the car and got out, waiting till a man came along and asking bluntly, 'Where's the action?'

'Piss off.'

The words were slurred and Tim could smell the beer on the other's breath. He stepped back and watched the man stumble away. Patient now, because the end of his agony was in sight, he waited for someone else.

This man tried to avoid him, but when Tim repeated his question, 'Where's the action?' the fellow stopped and stared at him suspiciously.

'You want to score?'

'Yes.'

After a careful scrutiny of both him and the surrounding area, the man nodded. 'You're in luck. I've got some. Cost you, though.'

Tim fumbled in his pocket. His mother had had quite a stash of money in her handbag, thank goodness.

When he got the stuff, he had to say, 'I've lost my equipment.'

The fellow laughed. 'Cost you some more.'

Tim paid, then walked away, twitching now for a hit. The only question was where. He didn't want anyone interrupting him.

He remembered the pub in the village. It was further than he really wanted to go, but still, it'd be deserted at this hour of the night and the car park was hidden from the road.

He got into the car and drove off again, this time switching the windscreen wipers on immediately and even humming along to the radio. Not long now. Just a hit now and then so that he could think straight, get his life in order. If you controlled the habit, it wasn't so bad. It was when you let the need control you that it was dangerous, and he'd proved he could live without it most of the time.

Rosalind felt as if she'd been sitting in the kitchen for a very long time when Louise got up and joined her.

'Ooh, Mum, you gave me a shock, sitting there so still!' She was dressed for her run and had already begun the warming-up exercises. She finished and realized her mother hadn't moved. 'You all right?'

'Tim hasn't come back. He went out last night, took my car. He left about two o'clock and – he hasn't returned.'

'He might have stopped somewhere for breakfast.'

'Where? This isn't a large city, with cafés open all hours. This is a small village, with one Olde Worlde Tea Room that doesn't open till ten.'

'Perhaps he stopped off at a garage for a coffee or something.'

'I can't see that, somehow. He's been avoiding other people ever since he got here.'

'I'll go and check his room.'

Louise ran upstairs, there was silence, then the sound of her coming down again slowly. 'His loose change is lying on top of the chest of drawers, just as it was last night when we were talking. I kept staring at it, seeing the patterns of the coins while we talked. It hasn't been moved. So he can't have stopped anywhere for breakfast.'

Fear dug its claws right into Rosalind's guts. 'What if something's happened to him?' She gave a shamefaced laugh. 'I expect I'm just getting worked up over nothing. He probably stopped the car somewhere and fell asleep. He'll be back soon.' Surely he would?

Jenny, who had been woken by Louise's footsteps pounding up and down the attic stairs, came into the kitchen in her dressing gown. 'What's wrong?'

'Tim went out last night and took Mum's car. He hasn't come back.'

'Oh.'

'I should have taken him straight back to Australia,' Rosalind worried. 'Gone with him and made him seek proper treatment. I *will* when he gets back. In fact, we'll all go home. I'm fed up of living here, with your Dad popping in for an odd day. And now, well, he'll only rub Tim up the wrong way, he always does. I'll book our fares as soon as Tim gets back.'

Jenny and Louise exchanged worried glances.

The words *if he gets back* might have been written in fire around the walls.

'I don't want to go home to Australia. Not now,' Jenny said. 'Ned and I have only just got engaged and – well, I'm not going back.'

Rosalind went across to hug her. 'I've plenty of money. You can rent a flat in Dorchester or somewhere. I just – think Tim is in danger if he doesn't kick his habit. I have to *do* something. Help him.' Save him.

Louise didn't go out for her run. Half an hour later she looked at the clock again. Nine o'clock. 'Oh, Mum, where *is* he?'

Another hour passed, long tedious minutes dragging by between short bursts of awkward conversation.

'Should I ring the police, do you think?' Rosalind asked suddenly.

It was Louise who spoke. 'It wouldn't hurt. They could tell you if there'd been any accidents, couldn't they?'

So Rosalind found the number and dialled the nearest police station. To her surprise, they took her seriously. 'Has there been an accident?' she repeated.

'No, ma'am. What sort of car did you say it was?'

She told them, impatient now to get off the phone in case Tim was trying to ring home. The car had probably broken down, that was all.

'And the number of the car is?' the voice pressed. 'Thank you. And your address? If we hear anything we'll get back to you.'

She put down the phone and turned to smile shamefacedly at her daughters. 'He's probably just broken down. If he didn't

210

take any money, he'll not be able to ring us.' She picked up her handbag from beside the phone. It felt too light. She peered inside. 'Anyone seen my purse?'

There was dead silence.

She looked from Louise to Jenny and back again. 'He wouldn't have. He wouldn't.'

So they searched the house carefully, but there was no sign of her purse.

'I probably left it in the car,' she said uncertainly.

Louise shook her head. 'You're very careful with your purse, Mum. Ever since it got stolen that time.'

Tears filled her eyes. It seemed all too obvious that Tim had taken it.

Louise came and put one arm round her, guiding her into the kitchen. 'I'll make us all some fresh coffee, shall I?'

But most of the coffee sat in their mugs till it went cold. And it didn't occur to any of them to eat anything.

At midday, still with no sign of Tim and no word from the police, Rosalind could stand it no longer. 'I'm going to ring your father. Ask his advice about what to do.' At that moment she had completely forgotten about Paul's affair with Liz, forgotten everything except her anxiety for her missing son.

'Yeah,' Louise nodded. 'I'll say that for him – Dad usually knows what to do in a crisis.'

The secretary was insistent that she couldn't possibly disturb Mr Stevenson, whereupon Rosalind stopped being polite and yelled, 'This is a matter of life and death, and if you don't fetch my husband now, I'll have to send the police to do it.'

There was a gasp from the other end, then, 'I'll see what I can do. I'll call you back.'

When the phone rang a few minutes later Rosalind snatched it up. It was Paul and he was furious. 'What the hell do you mean by ringing me here, Ros? You know I'm working.' Twice now this had happened. What would the chairman think?

'It's Tim. He turned up a few days ago. He'd got himself into trouble in the States. Drugs.'

'*What?*'

'He was trying to kick the habit, and I *know* he hasn't taken anything since he's been with me. Only –' she had to gulp back the fear before she could put it in words – 'now he's

211

taken my car and – and disappeared. My purse is gone too. Should I call in the police and tell them?'

'What do you mean "disappeared"?' Paul questioned her with the skill he usually brought to his work, drawing more details out of her. What he discovered made him splutter with rage. 'The stupid young bastard! What did he think he was playing at? And why didn't you let me know before?'

'If you can only mouth off at me, I'll put the phone down,' said the new Rosalind. 'For the last time, should I or should I not call in the police and tell them everything? I think – I feel sure he's in trouble. Serious trouble.'

'Not yet. I'll come straight home. It'll take me about two hours. Don't do anything at all until I get there. Not a single thing. Is that clear?'

'Yes.'

When a car turned into the drive a couple of hours later they thought it was Paul and all three of them went rushing to the front door. But it was a policeman. He had a woman with him, not in uniform, but she looked like some sort of official, too.

Rosalind took one look at their solemn faces and guessed what they were going to say. So when blackness rose around her she let herself slip into it gratefully.

From a long way away she heard Louise's voice. 'She's coming round. Don't stand too close. Let her recover before you say anything.'

A mutter of voices.

Rosalind didn't want to open her eyes, but she knew she had to. Had to face it. Had to.

She was surprised to find herself lying on a sofa in the living room. How had she got here? Louise was kneeling beside her, there was a wet cloth on her forehead and Jenny was standing behind the couch, gripping it with white-knuckled hands. Rosalind felt their anxiety and their support even before she looked across to the two strangers sitting stiffly on the other sofa.

'He's dead, isn't he?' she asked. 'Tim's dead.'

They nodded.

'Sorry,' said the woman.

'How?'

'Overdose. He was sitting in your car behind the pub. You'd contacted the police earlier about it, if you remember, asking if there'd been any accidents.'

Rosalind tried to take it all in. It was the sort of thing you heard about on the TV news. She always felt sorry for the families. And why wasn't she crying? Shouldn't she be crying? Only there were no tears, just a huge block of ice forming slowly inside her, layer upon chill layer.

After a while, she found she had to know one thing above all others. 'Did he – feel any pain?'

The man shook his head. 'Shouldn't think so. I don't think he'd even have realized what was happening. And it must have been very fast. The – er – needle was still in him.'

'Probably the heroin was too pure,' the woman said, 'and he gave himself an overdose by mistake.'

Rosalind couldn't speak or move, still trying to come to terms with the idea that her son was dead. They didn't try to pester her with any more questions, thank goodness.

At last, she forced herself to sit up properly but she couldn't think what to do or say next.

Jenny slipped round to sit on the sofa beside her. Louise came and perched on the sofa arm at her other side.

Rosalind reached out to touch them, needing to make contact. Jenny was weeping. Louise looked frozen, stricken.

Another car drew up outside and someone pushed open the front door. 'Ros! Where are you, Ros?'

'That's my husband,' she told the police officers quietly, relief surging through her. For once Paul had put his family first. She found that comforting. If anything could be comforting on a day like this.

'We're in here!' Jenny called, her voice breaking on the words.

He stopped in the doorway and glared at Ros. 'I told you not to call in the police till I got here! Do you never bloody think before you act?'

It was Louise who got up and stood toe to toe with him. 'Don't you talk to Mum like that! *We* didn't call the police in. They came to tell us that Tim's body has been found in the car.' Her voice wobbled for a minute, then she forced

213

herself to continue. 'He's *dead*! So don't start throwing your weight around, because we don't need any aggro from you today!' Then she collapsed against her mother, sobbing wildly.

Rosalind put her arms round Louise and watched her husband. He looked stunned. She was glad he was here, but she didn't want to go to him, just wanted him to take charge. She continued to hold Louise and patted Jenny's hand from time to time with her other hand.

'Tim's – dead?' Paul's voice was the merest scrape of sound. Rosalind nodded.

Paul couldn't move for a moment. Tim dead. His son. His only son. And the last time he'd seen him, they'd argued, shouted – said dreadful things to one another. He shuddered and tried not to think of that.

The policeman seemed to materialize at his side. 'Come and sit down, sir. You've had a bit of a shock.'

Paul shook the hand off his arm and found his own way to a chair. 'Tell me the details,' he said in a harsh voice very unlike his usual light baritone. 'I need to know – the details.'

So they repeated them.

He tried to focus on the police officer as he listened, but his eyes kept sliding back to Ros, sitting with a daughter on either side of her, weeping, being comforted. Why was no one trying to comfort him?

The woman cleared her throat. 'I'm sorry to do this to you, sir, but someone will have to come and identify the body.'

Paul stared at her in horror. 'But you've just told us he's dead, so you must know already who he is. What good would it do for us to go and see him?' And with a shock, he realized that for the first time in a lot of years he couldn't do what was expected of him. He just – he simply couldn't. 'You shouldn't even ask it of us, dammit.'

Rosalind surprised them all by standing up. 'I'll go and identify the body, officer. I *want* to see my son.' She had to, in order to accept that he was dead. Her boy. Her baby. Her agonized young man of the embroidery.

Louise stood up, too. 'I want to see him, too. I need to – to say goodbye.'

Jenny shook her head in response to their questioning glances. 'I'm sorry. I c–can't face it.'

'We'll take you in the police car, Mrs Stevenson,' the police-woman said quietly. 'And bring you back afterwards. We'll get your own car back to you as soon as possible.'

'I'll get the leasing company to change it,' Paul said at once. 'You won't want to drive that one again.'

Rosalind looked across at him. He sat down, shook his head blindly and put it in his hands without saying a word. He didn't attempt to speak to her, let alone comfort her. And she found she had nothing to offer him, either.

She looked at her younger daughter and put an arm round Louise's shoulders, feeling Louise's arm round her waist. Together they walked out of the house with the police officers.

When they'd gone, Jenny scowled across at her father. 'You couldn't even help her do that, could you?'

He glared at her. 'You didn't go with them, either.'

'I'm not her husband. You are.'

She went to phone Ned.

Paul sat there and tried not to weep. He had not wept since he was a small boy and it'd do no good now, no good at all. He kept seeing images of Tim, hearing faint echoes of their many quarrels – and wishing he had seen him alive once more.

In the end he went and poured himself a large whisky. It was the only comfort he could think of.

By the time Rosalind got into the police car, the news was all over the village, because one of the Tuffins had found the body.

Feeling upset about the dreadful news, Harry drove over to see Jonathon. Better if she told him about it so that he didn't give himself away. She came straight to the point. 'Have you heard?'

He was working in the big formal dining room, sanding the floorboards in preparation for a new coat of stain. 'Heard what?'

'Heard about Rosalind's son?'

'Tim? No. What's he done now?'

'He hasn't done anything. He's dead. Drug overdose.'

Jonathon stood up, turning white and clutching at the nearest wall. 'Dead?' he whispered. 'That poor lad's dead?'

'Yes. Alice Tuffin told me. Her eldest son found the body in the car park behind the pub. This morning. Just sitting in the car, she said. She thought I'd want to go and see Rosalind. But – well, I thought I'd better come and tell you first.'

'Oh, hell and damnation! Hasn't she enough to bear with that selfish brute of a husband? Does she have to bear this, too?'

'Tim was twenty, that's all. Twenty.' Harry looked at her brother. 'Got any gin?'

'Yes.' He escorted her through to the small sitting room he used in winter to conserve fuel. 'Sit down. I'll get us both a drink.'

They sipped at gin and brandy respectively, sitting in silence. Once he got up to put some more wood on the fire. Once she opened her mouth as if to speak, then closed it again. Nothing you said made any difference at a time like this. She'd found that when her husband had died, had often wished her kind friends would just go away and leave her to grieve in peace. But she sat on in case Jonathon needed her.

'What hurts,' he said at last, 'apart from the tragedy of a young life lost, is that I have no right to go and comfort her. And I can't see that damned husband of hers being much use at a time like this. Can you?'

'He'll probably deal with the practical details very efficiently – which will spare her that trouble, at least,' Harry said. There were a lot of details to sort out when someone died. 'I'll call in on them tomorrow, if you like, then let you know how things are going.'

He shook his head. 'I'll call myself.' He had to make sure Rosalind was all right.

'We'll go together, then. It'll look better, don't you think?'

He raised his eyes to stare at her. 'You know, don't you? How I feel about her, I mean?'

'Oh, yes. Sticks out a mile. Well, to me it does. Pity she's married. I like her, too. Bit soft for her own good, but nice. Heart's in the right place.'

But for once Harry was wrong. Paul Stevenson wasn't dealing with anything efficiently. While he sat and waited for his wife to return, he drank a whisky quickly, then poured another

216

one to sip, drowning his grief in gulps of amber comfort.

By the time the car turned into the drive, he was sitting in an owlish stupor and Jenny was fiddling around in the kitchen, trying to keep herself occupied while she waited for Ned to arrive. She went into the hall, expecting her mother and Louise to be in floods of tears, but they weren't. They were very still and white. For the first time ever she saw a faint resemblance between them, something about the way they held their bodies.

She took their coats, hesitated, then whispered, 'Dad's drunk. In the sitting room.'

Rosalind looked in to see Paul slumped down in an armchair, snoring, a glass with an inch of whisky in it tilting dangerously in his hand. And was glad. She didn't want to face him yet. Not about anything.

'What shall we do?' Jenny whispered.

'Nothing. Leave him to sleep it off.' She switched the sitting room light off again, turned back into the hall, hesitated, then gave in to temptation. 'I'm going out. I'll take your dad's car.'

'To see Jonathon?' Jenny asked.

Rosalind looked at her, startled.

Jenny blushed and said in a very low voice, 'I saw you kissing him at the fête.'

'How long ago that seems now.' It was important to set the record straight. 'We're not sleeping together, you know.'

'You don't need to tell me that. You wouldn't.'

But she'd wanted to, Rosalind thought. Heavens, she'd wanted much more than Jonathon's kisses. Did that make her as guilty as Paul? Did it matter? Did anything matter now?

At the door she turned. 'If your father asks, would you mind saying you think I've gone to see Harry? If he wants his car, ring Harry and explain.'

Jenny rushed forward to give her mother a hug, then watched her walk stiffly out of the house. Strange. She had expected her mother to crumble, not her father. She went to sit with Louise in the kitchen and pick at a sandwich. 'Ned's coming over tonight.'

'Good. I'm glad you've got him.'

'What about you?'

Louise looked at her blindly. 'I'd actually prefer to be on my own.'

She heard Ned arrive and go upstairs with Jenny, but sat on alone with her thoughts and memories. Tim had looked so peaceful in the morgue it had surprised her. 'Have you done anything to – to make him look better?' she had asked the assistant as they all stood there in that chilly room, gleaming with stainless steel and smelling of antiseptic – and of something else she didn't like to think about.

'No. We haven't touched his face at all. That's how he looked when he was found.'

At that moment Louise had known he was glad to be out of it and she even wondered if he'd done it on purpose, though she'd never say that to her mother, of course. He'd said a few times that he felt used up, exhausted. When she'd tried to talk about the future, he'd said simply that he couldn't see one.

But *she* had to carry on, and her future didn't look very rosy, either. She had to face her pain at losing her brother and also sort out her own life. Probably that'd mean rows with her father.

She wandered into the sitting room and stared down at him, taking the glass from his hand. He didn't move and she didn't try to rouse him.

*You've let her down,* she thought. *Mum needed you to be strong and you let her down. You should have gone with her today, then comforted her when she got back. I'm not going to be like you when I grow up.*

Tim was right. She still had a long way to go before she could consider herself mature. But she was sure of one thing: she was never, ever going to let anyone down again.

And then it all overwhelmed her in a great black wave of sorrow. She had to run up to her bedroom and bury her face in her pillow so that her father wouldn't be woken by her sobbing, so that her sister wouldn't come in.

# Eighteen

When someone hammered at the big front door of the Manor and kept on hammering, calling his name, Jonathon ran along the hall and flung the door open. He drew Rosalind into his arms. 'Oh, my love! My darling girl, come in!'

He took her into the small parlour and sat down beside her, his arm round her shoulders. This wasn't a time for large rooms and echoing spaces, but for the cosiness of the womb. As her grief eased, he poured them both a brandy, then they sat together quietly on the couch. When she looked at him, he said gently, 'No need to talk unless you wish to, my love.'

So she didn't try to speak at first, not until she had drawn enough solace from his presence. She simply sat there pressed against him, feeling his arm light yet strong round her back and clasping her hands round the brandy goblet as she soaked up the peace of Destan Manor. Nobody could bring Tim back, but friends could share your grief, acknowledge that you had borne and loved a son, and that his passing was momentous enough for them to stop their own busy lives for a moment or two.

She sipped the brandy from time to time and focused on small things to distract herself from the pain – the warmth of the liquid in her mouth and throat, the visual comfort of a wood fire flickering in the grate, the interesting textures in the worn fabric on the arm of the sofa. When at last she had pulled enough of herself together, she started to tell him what had happened over the past few days – quietly, not weeping, because tears wouldn't help. What did help was the warmth of this man's body next to hers and his unspoken offer of anything he could give her. It helped so much.

When she had finished the tale, they sat on in the quietness of the night, the dog lying nearby, sighing from time to time as if in sympathy. Once Jonathon got up to refill their glasses, later he dozed against her, his head on her shoulder, his fine, thinning hair tickling her cheek. The occasional grey strand filled her with compassion for the way the years marked them all. You could not go through life unscathed.

She didn't wake him because his presence was all she needed. She was deeply grateful that he'd made no attempt to fill the night with meaningless chatter, but she couldn't, she simply couldn't sleep. Not yet. This wakeful night was, in some strange way, her special tribute to her son.

Later still, Jonathon raised his head, blinked at her like a thin, nervous owl and said, 'Sorry. Didn't mean to fall asleep on you.'

She smiled and stretched out one hand to brush the soft hair from his eyes. 'What are you sorry for? You were still there for me.'

He caught that hand and raised it to his lips. 'Always.' But he didn't labour the point. After a few minutes, he yawned. 'It's nearly morning. Do you want a coffee? I've got your favourite brand.'

'I'd love one. And a piece of toast, perhaps?' The thought that he'd bought the plunger and coffee specially for her, since he much preferred tea, made her feel warm and loved. Of such details, she thought dreamily, were lives made. And relationships.

So they walked through the creaking, shifting old house to the kitchen and made coffee and toast, sitting at a scrubbed wooden table just as the first fingers of brightness were tearing the mourning veils from the sky and signalling the end of her darkest night.

Not until it was fully light did she leave. 'Thank you,' she told him, kissing his cheek and then fleetingly, impersonally, his lips. 'I can think better now. I have to go back and – and deal with it all.'

He could not help asking, 'Are you – do you think you'll stay with him?'

'I don't know. I can't decide that now.'

'No. Of course not. But – I do love you, Rosalind. And I want to be with you. Remember that, won't you?'

A fragile smile flickered briefly on her face. 'I will. And I love you, too, Jonathon. Very much.'

When Paul woke up, he couldn't think where he was for a moment. He winced at the stiffness of his body and groaned when he moved his head incautiously. A hangover started to thump behind his forehead, circling his skull with a leaden band and drumming a message of pain whenever he moved. He swallowed and grimaced at the sour taste in his mouth. Hell, what had made him tie one on?

Then he remembered.

Tim was dead.

He stood there, thumping his thighs with his clenched fists, until he had his damned emotions under control, then stumbled up the stairs to the master bedroom, stopping at the door in shock as he found it empty, the bed not even slept in. 'Ros?' He peered into the en suite but she wasn't there. He went pounding back downstairs into the kitchen, the dining room, the conservatory. Not a sign of her.

But there was a youngish man, a complete stranger, sleeping on the floor in the office. He mumbled in his sleep when the door opened, but didn't wake up.

Who the hell was he? Paul wondered as he closed the door quietly. The stranger looked familiar, but he couldn't quite place him, and he definitely didn't feel up to accosting the fellow and asking what he was doing there. Not till he'd had a strong coffee and put some food into his rumbling stomach. He never thought well when he was hungry. Now he came to think of it, he hadn't had any dinner last night. No wonder the drink had gone to his head.

Back upstairs. One room was full of her embroidery. Bloody stuff! He picked up the frame and as he saw what she was doing, he froze and stared down at it. He had never thought her good before, but this – it was clever, there was no denying that. She'd caught him perfectly, shown him as he liked to think of himself, confident, in control of himself. She'd caught herself, too, with those damned pale colours – he was going to take her to a fashion consultant before they went to the States, smarten her up. His eyes slid over the image of Jenny and that bloody dog of hers, then he saw the sketch of Tim.

A wave of anguish took him by surprise. Was that what Tim had become? That thin, haunted creature? He couldn't bear to look at it, even.

He tossed the frame down on the table, but it wasn't enough. The sketch of Tim was still there, still looking up at him accusingly. With a growl of anger, he knocked everything on the table flying, then kicked the frame with its stretch of canvas out of the way. It went spinning across the room and he was glad to hear the wood crack.

Where the hell was Rosalind? Tim's room! he thought suddenly. She'll be up there, mooning around. But there was no one in the attic. Tim's things were lying scattered around as if he'd just stepped out and that made Paul gulp and back out. He could feel tears filling his eyes again. Shit, you'd think he could control himself better than this!

He went and opened the front door and saw that his car was missing, which made him feel angry. He concentrated on the anger, which was better than the other emotion. What if she had an accident? Did no one in his family care about the liability of driving a car that wasn't insured for them? And where had she gone anyway?

He went back upstairs. Perhaps the girls would know.

'Jenny!' He shook his elder daughter awake.

She lay staring at him in surprise for a moment, then remembered Tim, sobbed and covered her swollen eyes with her arm.

He shook her again. If he let her cry, she'd start him off, and he wasn't, he definitely was not, going to parade his emotions like some sodding half-man of a poofter. 'Where's your mother gone? I can't find her anywhere. And she's taken my car.'

She had no trouble lying to him this time, she who normally blushed and stuttered if she even tried to fudge the truth slightly. 'She'll have gone to Harry's, I expect. They're good friends.'

'Harry?'

'Harriet Destan.'

Ah, he remembered now. Sister of the lord of the manor. 'Well, she has no *right* to go out and leave us. No right at all. Fine way of showing her grief that is!'

'It's better than getting drunk and *snoring*!'

'I do not snore.'

222

'You were rotten drunk when Mum came back from iden-
tifying Tim yesterday afternoon and you were definitely snoring. Loudly.' Like a hog, a disgusting hog.

'Well, that's neither here nor there. Get up and make me
some breakfast.'

She could not believe what she was hearing. 'Go and make
your own damn breakfast. I'm not Mum, waiting on you hand
and foot.'

'Get up, I said!' He hauled her out of bed.

After an involuntary squeal of surprise, she resisted him,
shouting and yelling.

Then Ned was there, pushing past her father to stand
between the two of them. 'Leave her alone, you bully!'

'Who the hell are you? And what are you doing in my house
anyway?'

Jenny clutched Ned's hand. 'He's here at my invitation.
This is Ned Didburin. We're engaged.'

'Well, well. I only had a drink to blur my grief, but you
brought someone round here to screw your troubles away.'

Whereupon Ned, peaceful, unaggressive Ned, punched him
on the jaw.

And Paul, unprepared for anyone so wimpy-looking to stand
up to him, rocketed backwards, crashed into the door frame
and overbalanced, to fall sprawling on the floor. He lay for a
moment, grunting, shaking his head.

Louise, woken by the noise, stepped over him and ranged
herself by her sister's side. 'What's caused this?'

'He wanted Mum. When he couldn't find her, he ordered
me to get up and make his breakfast. I didn't happen to feel
like waiting on him. I wanted to –' tears began to trickle out
of Jenny's eyes – 'stay here and p–pull myself together. So,
he tried to force me to get up. Then –' she gulped audibly –
'Ned came up to see what was happening and Dad accused
me of screwing him to – to block out what happened to Tim.'

'What a nasty sod he is!'

Ned was still standing dumbfounded, gaping down at his
fist, then goggling at Paul, who was pulling himself to his feet
with an ugly expression on his face.

Louise went to stand between them. 'Get out of here, Dad.
Jenny wants to get dressed.'

'Oh? And is lover boy going to stay here and help her, then?'

Jenny raised her chin and took a step forward, nudging her sister aside and facing not only her father, but the years of fearing him. Staring him in the eyes, she said, 'What Ned and Jenny do is none of your business.' Then she took her father by surprise by shoving him out on to the landing before he realized what she was doing. 'Leave them alone, Dad. If you need waiting on, I'll come and make your breakfast for you.'

Rosalind walked in just then. 'I'm back.' The door to Jenny's room opened again and Ned peered over the banisters.

'Good morning, Ned. I'm glad you came over to be with Jenny.' Rosalind went to kiss Jenny, then Louise, who gave her a watery smile. Still holding her, Rosalind turned to stare at her husband, who was glaring at her.

'I'll just have a quick shower and change my clothes, Paul, then I'll come and make breakfast. We'll leave Jenny and Louise to get up at their own pace.'

He grunted something which might have been agreement and followed her into the master bedroom.

She got out some clean clothes, the darkest garments she could find, though she owned nothing black. Pastels, she thought, looking along the neat row of hangars, they're nearly all pastels. She had a sudden longing for jewel tones, for shiny fabrics and rich patterns, for clothes with more *life* to them.

Paul flung himself into the small armchair in the bay window and watched her sourly. 'Where the hell have you been?'

'With friends.'

She walked into the bathroom and locked the door on him, needing a few quiet moments to pull herself together.

Paul sat down on the edge of the bed and closed his eyes, not sure what to do next.

At a nod from the inspector, Constable Thelma Simpton knocked on the front door. They waited, but no one came.

'Knock again!' he ordered.

Paul went to peer out of the window, muttering, 'Oh, sod it! Can't the bloody police leave us alone for a minute?'

In the bathroom the water cut off abruptly. Wrapping a

towel around herself, Rosalind went into the bedroom and joined Paul at the window. When he didn't move, she pushed it further open and looked down at the police officers. 'Yes?'

The inspector cleared his throat. 'Police here. Sorry to intrude on your grief again, madam, but could we come in and speak to you?' He gestured around him. 'This place is a bit public for a discussion.'

'The door's not locked. I'll be down as soon as I'm dressed.' Rosalind threw on her clothes at top speed and turned in surprise to Paul, who had flopped into the chair again and was sitting with his head in his hands. 'Aren't you coming down?'

'In a minute. And for Christ's sake, put some coffee on.'

As she went downstairs, she saw the two police officers waiting in the hall.

The inspector nodded. 'Sorry to intrude.'

'You have your job to do. Come through here.' She led the way into the sitting room. 'Sorry everything is in such a mess. We haven't had time to clear up yet this morning.'

He brightened. 'Does that mean no one's touched your son's room?'

'I don't think so.'

Behind them Louise said, 'No one's been in Tim's room except me, and I only stood in the doorway for a minute to see if he'd taken any money with him. Oh, and I think Dad went in when he was looking for Mum this morning.' She went to link an arm in her mother's.

Rosalind clasped her daughter's hand as it lay on her arm. Who would have expected Louise to be so steady and dependable in a crisis?

Paul came clattering down the stairs to join them, his tight business expression back on his face, the front of his hair damp. But he was still wearing the same crumpled clothes and his face looked ravaged. That touched Rosalind's heart a little. She couldn't have borne him to be unmoved by Tim's death.

'Would you mind if we checked your son's room, Mrs Stevenson. We need to find out if he's been storing drugs here.'

Paul breathed in deeply. 'Come upstairs, but I'll want to be there while you search Tim's room.'

225

'I'll come with you, too,' Rosalind added quietly. 'I know more about my son's possessions than my husband does. He didn't see Tim this time.' Alive or dead. And would presumably never see him again. None of them would. She felt the grief solidify in her chest as if ice was building up. She couldn't weep it out until it melted.

'Very helpful of you, madam. We're much obliged. If there's anything my officers can do to help, don't hesitate to ask.'

There wasn't, of course, but you said things like that to offer them comfort, make them feel you were on the ball – well, you said it to the nice ones, anyway.

He sighed as he walked downstairs again. There had been nothing in the room to show that the boy was a junkie, but judging from the condition of his arms, he'd been well into the stuff, though not recently.

Maybe he should take that early retirement after all. He'd seen too many grieving, bewildered families whom he'd wanted to help and couldn't, because the accountants had got into everything and the talk nowadays was all of bottom lines and staying within budgets, instead of service to the public.

When the inspector had left, Rosalind went into the kitchen and picked up the phone. Paul followed her and put his hand across the dialling pad. 'Who are you calling?'

'My mother.'

'Surely that can wait till after breakfast?'

'I don't want any breakfast. And I can't face cooking.' She pushed his hand aside and began to dial.

'I don't know where anything is in this house.'

'Try opening a few cupboard doors and looking. They're not locked. Ah, Mum.' Her voice was quite steady. 'I have some very sad news, I'm afraid . . .'

He watched her in disbelief as she told her mother about Tim, not weeping, speaking calmly, doing her best to console the older woman, whose sobbing was quite audible from where he stood. He kept expecting Ros to collapse, give way to her grief, but she hadn't done. He didn't understand how she could be so strong about this when she was so weak about everything else.

And as for Tim – Paul stood still and fought yet again to

contain his grief – as for Tim, well, that was over and done with. He didn't have a son any more. You just had to get on with things. But he'd make sure his daughters didn't go off the rails, by hell he would! And as for that chinless wimp Jenny said she was engaged to, they'd see about that. She was useless at picking men, absolutely useless.

After the phone call, Rosalind went up to do her hair and calm herself in the en suite with the door locked. By the time she came down again, Paul had made himself some toast and instant coffee, and was crunching an apple. The sound was obscene.

'The bathroom's free,' she told him and felt nothing but relief as he grunted an acknowledgement, took the plate of toast and ran lightly upstairs.

The phone rang. 'I'll get it,' she called. 'Yes?'

'Harry here. I'm so very sorry to hear about Tim. Anything I can do to help, Rosalind?'

'I'm not sure. I'll get back to you if I need you.' She heard someone else breathing and realized that Paul was listening in, spying on her. Anger filled her for a moment.

'You won't hesitate to call on us?'

'No, of course not. You and Jonathon have been good friends to me.'

'I told Alice Tuffin you'd ring if you wanted her. She'd be happy to help.'

'Thanks.'

'Jonathon sends his love. I'm with him now. You sure you're managing all right?'

'Yes. Thank him for me. Bye now.'

Upstairs, Paul frowned. Her voice had grown warm as she'd spoken to those damned friends of hers. But if this woman had to ring and ask how she was, Ros mustn't have gone to see her last night. Where had she been, then? He pulled his clothes off, leaving them scattered across the floor, and took a very long shower, emerging in full control of himself, thank goodness.

Downstairs Rosalind brewed some more coffee, taking a cup upstairs to Jenny.

'Where is he?'

'Showering.'

Jenny looked towards the master bedroom. 'We'll come down now. Can I get Ned something to eat?'

'Of course you can.' Rosalind nodded to him. 'I'm so glad Jenny's got you, Ned.' She felt warmed by the sight of their love. The lump of ice inside her cracked just a little.

Louise's bedroom door opened. 'All right if I go for a jog?' She lowered her voice. 'Don't want to face Dad yet.'

'Do whatever you need to.'

Louise hesitated, then came across to give her a hug. 'I love you, Mum.'

Rosalind's composure slipped for a minute and the ice cracked still further. 'I love you, too.' Her voice came out husky and she had to blink away the tears.

'Tim said I'd been a fool and he was right. I won't let you down again, Mum. Or him.'

'Good.' Rosalind flicked away a tear, but it was followed by another. Funny what set you off. 'You go for your run, love.'

Louise looked upstairs. 'Sure you'll be all right?'

'Yes.' She still had Paul to face about the other thing. But she wasn't going to have a confrontation about his infidelity with her son lying unburied.

She was nearly sure now that she was going to leave him. But not till all this – this main trouble was over.

It was a big decision to make. She couldn't rush it, had to be very sure of what she was doing.

# Themes

*The figurative characters . . . relate primarily to one of the following pictorial themes:*

*Biblical stories*
*Incidents from myths and legends*
*Allegorical themes*
*Single figures and groups*
*Commemorative events*

*(Hirst, pp.10–11)*

# Nineteen

Paul stared at Rosalind incredulously when she explained that Jenny and Ned had gone out for a while, and Louise had gone jogging.

'At a time like this? Her brother dies and all Jenny is concerned about is being with lover-boy. And who said they could get engaged? No one asked me.'

Rosalind was getting tired of him yelling. She kept trying to tell herself that it was just his way of dealing with this tragedy, but it was a way that took no account of others' needs. 'She hasn't been sleeping with him. He's been here offering her comfort and support.'

A nasty grin curved Paul's mouth. 'Don't you believe it, Ros. I know all about that sort of comfort. He was in her bedroom, helping her to dress, for heaven's sake. How naïve can you get?'

Pretty naïve, in her case. She nearly told him what she knew about him, but managed to turn away, taking several deep breaths. Not now. She had promised herself not to do or say anything about their marriage until after the funeral. 'I'm going out to the shops. We need something for tea.' It'd be a relief to get away from him.

'Why bother? We'll go out somewhere for a meal tonight.'

'You can go out if you want. I shan't. There's only the local pub to go to, anyway.' Rosalind didn't want to face a sea of sympathetic faces there.

'Well, all right, but be quick. I'll stay here in case the police want anything else.'

As if she needed his permission to go shopping!

In the minimart the staff and other customers left her alone, except for bobs of the head and sympathetic murmurs as they passed her. They didn't seem to expect a response, for which she was grateful. She slung food into the trolley as quickly as she could and when she was waved to the head of the small queue, she nodded her thanks, but didn't speak or make eye contact with anyone.

Back at the house, she put the groceries away and stayed in the kitchen wondering what to do with herself.

Paul came to join her. 'Fancy making us a cup of coffee?'

'No.' If she did that, he'd expect her to join him, and then she might blurt something out, like, *Was Liz a better screw than me?* She went upstairs to her embroidery.

When she saw what had happened there, however, she stopped dead, then rage boiled up in her, absolutely boiled. Paul had taken out his feelings on her things. 'Oh, you bastard!' she muttered under her breath. 'You nasty, rotten bastard!'

She went first to pick up the broken frame from the floor in the corner, checking every inch of the family embroidery carefully and breathing a sigh of relief when she found it intact. Had he even noticed the picture? Surely he'd have said something if he had, because his figure was very prominent in it, very recognizable and not at all flattering. No, he must just have hit out in blind fury.

She was picking up her skeins of thread when he poked his head in through the doorway. She turned to look at him and said loudly, 'If you ever touch my embroidery things again, I'll make interesting patterns on your business suits with my scissors.'

He scowled at her. 'I might have known you'd come here. You're sick, do you know that? Stuck in a bloody time warp, spending your life on an outmoded pastime that no one respects nowadays.' He slammed the door behind him.

Rosalind sat on the floor looking at her sketch of Tim, which had drifted under the work table. I'll do you justice, love, she thought. I really will. If I have to redo your figure a hundred times.

But she didn't have to. She mended the embroidery frame with insulation tape, then worked on her son's head. As it took shape, it turned into Tim, giving her his half-smile, looking rebellious, yet lost and afraid in a hostile world. A few tears fell and the ice that was weighing down her chest cracked a bit more.

She needed to finish the family embroidery, even though she knew she would never be able to hang it on the wall. It was too full of pain. All their pain.

But she needed to *know*.

That afternoon she rang up the police station. 'I was wondering how soon we could bury our son.'

'Have to be a post-morten, even though we know what he died of. Sorry about that, madam. Say three days, four at most. The undertakers will know what to do if you tell them what's happened. Munham's in Wareham are well thought of.'

'Thank you.'

Paul came out of the living room. 'What did they say?'

'Three or four days. There'll have to be a post-mortem.'

She started up the stairs.

'Is that all you're going to do? Sit and bloody embroider? Your son lies dead and you fiddle with embroidery silks?'

She paused only long enough to say, 'It's better than quarrelling, don't you think? If you want something to do with yourself, go and book the funeral.' She didn't care about the details. They were irrelevant. However they did it, it would be her son they buried. She had to stand very still for a moment on that thought. She had known of agony like this, but only intellectually. The reality was far worse, a bleak cliff of pain that she had to scale an inch at a time. She realized Paul was speaking.

'Yes. I'll go and do that. Where should I go, do you think?'

'Munham's. In Wareham. They're used to these cases, apparently. There's a local map book in my car and a phone directory in the kitchen.'

He strode off and started banging doors. She let some of the tension sift slowly out in a long breath, but her relief was short-lived. A few minutes later she became aware of him standing in the doorway. She covered the embroidery instinctively.

'I'm not going to touch your precious toys. I've seen what you're doing there. A pitiful attempt at a family portrait.'

'Did you want something?'

He scowled. 'I think you should come with me. I don't know anything about arranging funerals. You've just done one for that old witch.'

'*Don't–*' her voice was so sharp it surprised her as well as him – 'call Aunt Sophie that.'

In her bedroom, eavesdropping as usual, Louise grinned. *Good one, Mum. You tell him!*

'Don't be so bloody touchy! It's only a nickname.'

'Well, it's one I don't care for. I was extremely fond of my aunt.' Rosalind put down the sewing and shepherded him out of the room. 'Very well. We'll do this together.' She knocked on Louise's door. 'We're going to sort out the funeral. Do you want to come with us, love?'

Louise recognised the look of pleading in her mother's eyes and steeled herself. 'Yes. I'd like to be part of it, Mum.' And found to her surprise that it was the truth.

'Thanks.' Rosalind squeezed her daughter's hand.

Watching them, Paul thought how successful his methods had been with this child, at least. Louise had fallen into line, just as he'd known she would. 'You drive,' he said outside, waving a hand at Rosalind. 'You know the district.'

She couldn't remember the last time he'd asked her to drive him. And he was very quiet on the journey – amazingly quiet, for him – sitting staring out of the window with a grim look on his face.

Louise was just as quiet in the back.

When they got home, Rosalind fidgeted around the house then decided to go for a walk. She had to get out of this brooding atmosphere for a while, if she was to continue coping. As she came downstairs, dressed in her outdoor things, Paul peered out of his office, where he'd been making phone calls and sending faxes intermittently, as well as doing a lot of staring into space. 'Where are you going?'

'For a walk.'

'Where?'

'Just out.' She tried to pass him, but he grabbed her arm.

'I need to know where you'll be, in case the police want you.'

She had promised herself no confrontations till after Tim was buried, but suddenly she had had enough. She tore her arm out of his and shrieked, 'I'm going out and I don't *know* where. I just need a bit of peace, so damned well leave me alone!'

And she was gone before he could say anything, leaving him gaping, then angry at her for screaming like a fishwife.

In Western Australia Audrey decided to ring round her daughter's friends and let them know what had happened. 'Liz? Audrey Worth here. Yes, I'm fine. Liz – I have some bad news. Tim's dead.' Audrey took a deep breath. 'Drug overdose.'

Liz collapsed on to the nearest chair, speechless, shocked, her free hand pressed against her chest.

'Are you still there?'

'Yes. Mrs Worth. I just – I don't know what to say.'

Audrey's voice was thick with tears. 'I thought you might like to ring Rosalind. You two have always been so close. This is the number.'

'Um – yes. Yes, of course. Though I shan't know what to say.' Liz put the phone down and sat there, feeling numb. Then she looked at the clock. No, not a good time to ring.

When Bill came in, she was sitting in the kitchen with an empty mug in front of her. She didn't even look up.

'Something wrong? You haven't lost the baby?' He was getting quite used to the idea now, was looking forward to being a father. He would *make* himself the child's father, and let anyone try to say different. He'd been wondering about moving away from Perth, too. It'd been hinted lately that he needed to broaden his experience, work overseas for a while. If he found somewhere to go for a year or two, it'd get Liz out of the Stevensons' way, and keep the baby out of that bastard's hands, too.

Liz shook her head and managed a faint smile. 'No. No, it's not that. It's – oh, Bill, Tim Stevenson's dead, overdosed.' Her eyes filled with tears again. 'What must Rosalind be feeling?'

He came to stand beside her, his hand on her shoulder. 'You'll have to ring her.'

'I can't. Bill, I just can't face her.'

'You have to.'

So a little later, when it would be morning in England, she picked up the phone. 'Rosalind? Liz here. I just heard. I—'

'Go to hell, you cheating bitch!' Rosalind slammed the phone down.

Liz sank to the floor in the hall, burying her face in her hands. Rosalind knew. How long had she known? Had he told her? Surely even *he* wouldn't do that?

Bill peered out of the living room, saw her and rushed over. 'What's wrong?'

'Rosalind knows.'

'Oh, hell!'

Liz burst into tears and wept till she was so exhausted and wrung out that Bill was seriously thinking of calling out the doctor to sedate her.

When she stopped sobbing, he brought her a cup of camomile tea and sat beside her while she drank it, steadying her shaking hand round it at first, but not saying anything. What was there to say? The harm had been done. Nothing they could do would make things right again, not between Rosalind and Liz, anyway.

Hearing the phone, Paul came into the hall. 'Who was that?'

Rosalind stared at him blankly for a moment. 'What? Oh, wrong number.'

'But you told them to go to hell.'

'Nuisance call, then. What is this? The Inquisition?' She drifted up the stairs into her own room, not to embroider, no, just to sit and stroke the face she had made for Tim's figure. And wish this dreadful waiting time would end. Not until her son had had a proper funeral would she feel like facing the rest of her life.

A little later she went out in the car. Paul heard her go but didn't ask where she was going this time. He stood in the hall watching her drive away through the glass of the front door, feeling abandoned. They'd all gone out, Jenny with that fellow – God, she could certainly pick 'em, what a weak-looking prat! – Louise for a run – 'Keeping fit, Dad,' she had said brightly as she left – and now Ros. Didn't they realize he had feelings, too?

There was a knock on the door and he went to open it. A woman was there with a big arrangement of flowers in her hands.

'Special delivery,' she said in a hushed, sympathetic voice. He took them off her and she drove away. It was a while before he realized that he was still standing there, with the door wide open, clutching the damned things.

He set the flowers down on the hall table. What good did flowers do? But when he looked at the label, he felt a bit better. From the chairman himself. He studied them again. They must have cost a packet.

But the flowers didn't solve the problem of what he was going to do with himself for the rest of the day. He tried ringing work to catch up with a few things, see how the workshop had ended, but everyone insisted they could manage, speaking to him in gentle tones, as if he were ill.

He'd rather have worked. Much rather. It'd have stopped him thinking so much, stopped him regretting so much, too. He cut that thought short. He wasn't going to allow himself to get maudlin again. He'd follow Louise's example and go for a run.

It didn't help as much as he'd expected.

Rosalind drove for a long time, eyes blind with memories. Then she realized where she was and turned right. 'Why not?' she asked the wind as it buffeted the car. The cold spring was being featured on the news every night now – one of the coldest Mays on record. That suited her, somehow. It was much better than soft sunny days, which would have seemed to mock her grief.

Jonathon opened the door, glanced round and saw that she was alone, so simply opened his arms.

She walked into them, resting her head against his chest with a weary sigh. 'Can we go into one of your lovely rooms and just sit? The one with Araminta's embroidery, perhaps?'

'Of course.'

They walked along the hall arm in arm and she let him fuss her into an armchair near the fireplace.

He struck a match and soon flames were crackling in the hearth. 'Want a cup of coffee?'

'Mmm.'

When he got back, she was sitting there, staring into the fire with her hand on Dusty's head, stroking him absent-mindedly.

She looked up. 'I'm not very good company, I'm afraid.'

'I don't need entertaining. Would you like me to leave you alone here?'

She considered this, head on one side, then nodded. 'I would, actually. I love this room. I need to be alone and quiet. Paul's so – loud and demanding.'

'Want me to take the dog with me?'

She looked down and seemed surprised to see her hand lying on the soft fur. 'No. Leave him.'

'Come and join me when you feel like a bit of company. I'm varnishing the gallery floor upstairs.'

The peace and silence enfolded her like a lover's arms. Like Jonathon's arms. Only, she couldn't make him her lover. Well, not physically, anyway. And perhaps not in any way. During the long hours of the night she had woken several times and begun to worry about it, to wonder if she could leave Paul now.

She had to face the fact that she had lost some of her certainty about what she was going to do afterwards. There was no doubt Paul was upset in his own way. She had never seen him behaving so irrationally. He'd even looked at her pleadingly a couple of times. Could she just abandon him after all those years together? She didn't know.

Only – she didn't think she could continue as his wife, either. The thought of him touching her sexually after playing around with Liz made her feel like vomiting.

Dusty nudged her with his head, asking for more caresses and she obliged, finding the action soothing on herself as well as gratifying to the animal.

Oh, hell, she thought after a while, she didn't know anything any more. She had just been starting to get her act together, just been finding herself. And now she was lost again.

# Twenty

It was a long dreary week, whose only brightness for Rosalind was seeing Jenny and Ned's love for one another. Paul mocked the engagement when his daughter wasn't around, though he was more or less civil when Jenny brought her fiancé home.

Ned was never anything but stiffly polite to Paul, refusing to be provoked again and hiding behind that peculiarly glassy politeness at which the English are experts.

Rosalind took herself and her daughters into Bournemouth one day to buy some black clothes for the funeral. Afterwards they had lunch together then strolled along the promenade and cliffs, which were magnificent. They didn't say much, just enjoyed walking slowly along the miles of walkways that overlooked the water.

None of them mentioned a reluctance to return to Burraford. They didn't need to.

Paul was in a foul mood again when they got back. 'Didn't think to ask if I wanted to come, did you?' he snapped as soon as Rosalind walked through the door.

Her voice was cool and disinterested. 'No. I wanted to go with the girls.'

'I'll just put my things away, Mum,' Jenny murmured, hating the way he was glowering at them, then hesitating, feeling guilty for leaving her mother to face him. He was getting nastier by the day. She didn't know how her mother coped, she really didn't.

'Will you take my parcels upstairs, Louise?' Rosalind nudged her younger daughter. The girls might as well stay out of the firing line. She went to sit in the living room and he followed.

Coming in here with him is an act of bravery, she thought, and smiled briefly at herself.

'Have a big spend-up, did you?' He threw himself on a chair opposite her.

'We spent what was needed.'

'How did you pay for it?'

She was puzzled. 'By credit card, of course.'

'That's right, spend my money. I'd have thought you could start using your own now for clothes and things. You've certainly got plenty.'

'We've only just got probate. I haven't sorted out Aunt Sophie's money yet.'

'And you still don't intend to follow my suggestion of contesting the terms of the will?'

'Of course not. Aunt Sophie had a right to leave it how she wanted. And besides, I like having my own money.' She ignored his snort and got up, going to nip a couple of dead leaves off the plant in the window, which was struggling to cope with the nearby central-heating radiator. If he carried on like this, she'd walk out. She'd done that several times this week. Had sought refuge with Jonathon on two of those occasions, brief encounters that had nonetheless strengthened her backbone.

'Did you think to get me a black tie?' Paul threw at her.

She didn't turn round. 'No.' She had spent the day trying not even to think about him.

'Well, thanks for nothing.'

'If that's the sort of mood you're in, I'll go upstairs and unpack my new clothes.'

'That's right, run away. You're good at running away from trouble, always have been.'

She didn't turn to refute that, just walked out. Upstairs she sighed and sat on the bed with her head in her hands, making no attempt to open any of the parcels.

After a minute or two Jenny came in. 'Dad's in a foul mood today. Even worse than yesterday. I think I'll go over to Dorchester this evening, if you don't mind. I can catch the five-o'clock bus.'

'Yes.'

'Don't let him upset you, Mum.'

'No.'

Louise peered round the bedroom door, saw no sign of her father and joined them. 'It was good to get out of the house,' she said wistfully. 'Just us three.'

'Yes.' Rosalind gave each of them a quick hug. 'I'm glad I've got you two here. You're such a comfort.'

Of course, Jenny dissolved immediately in tears, but Louise nodded and said, 'Good,' in a gruff voice.

'Could – would one of you fetch me up a cup of hot chocolate? I think I'd like to lie down for a while. I'm not sleeping well.' She kept waking up and jerking away from any contact with Paul's body. If he had tried to touch her in that way – but he hadn't – which was not like him. She was too tired to puzzle that out now, though.

'I'll get it.' Louise left.

Jenny leaned against her mother. 'I hate the thought of the funeral,' she said. 'I don't know how I'll cope.'

Rosalind patted her hand. 'We'll face it together, love. And you'll have Ned for extra support.'

She was dreading tomorrow just as much as her daughters were, not only because of saying a final farewell to Tim, but because she'd decided to confront Paul afterwards. He was already speaking of getting back to work in London. Well, he wasn't leaving here without them having a serious talk about their future. Definitely not. If she had to, she'd lie down in front of his car to prevent him.

'Um, Jenny – after the funeral I'd like to talk to your father on my own. Do you think you and Ned could take Louise out somewhere? Give us a couple of hours to iron a few things out?'

'Yes, of course.' She began to fiddle with her skirt. 'Is something wrong?'

Rosalind hesitated, then said, 'Yes.'

'Are you going to leave him?'

'Would it matter to you if I did?' She glanced quickly sideways, wincing internally as she saw the anxiety on her daughter's face.

Jenny nodded. 'It would, rather. I know he's – difficult. But you're my parents and I've always been so glad you've stayed together. For better, for worse. Isn't that how the service goes?

And this is the worst our family has ever had, isn't it?'

Guilt speared through Rosalind.

Louise came back with a steaming mug. 'There.'

'Thanks. I think I'll have a rest now.'

The sisters went into Jenny's room to whisper together as Jenny got ready to go out and meet Ned.

'She wants to talk to *him* tomorrow after the funeral,' Jenny worried. 'On her own. She asked me and Ned to take you out somewhere for a couple of hours afterwards.'

'I hope she's going to tell him she's leaving him,' Louise said fiercely. 'And if she does, I'm going with her.'

Jenny began smoothing a corner of the bedspread. 'But why should she leave him after all these years. I mean – Tim's death isn't a reason to leave someone, is it?'

Louise chewed her bottom lip, then decided to put her sister in the know.

Jenny listened in horror to the tale of her father's infidelity with Liz and others. 'Oh, no!' she kept saying in a hoarse whisper. 'Oh, no! Not Mum's best friend. How could he?'

The door opened without so much as a by-your-leave and Paul stuck his head round it. 'Louise, I – Oh, hell! What's she upset about now?'

'Tim.' Louise jerked her head towards the door, hoping he'd take the hint.

He scowled but left.

'He just walks in without knocking,' Louise fumed. 'What if I'd been standing here naked, eh? I dare say he'd have enjoyed that, given his proclivities.'

When Jenny left, Louise accompanied her to the bus stop, calling, 'I'm going for a walk, Dad,' as they passed the living-room, just to be safe from recriminations when she returned.

But he didn't answer. He was pouring himself a glass of whisky.

'He's drinking a lot,' Louise said.

'Guilty conscience.'

Louise snorted. 'He doesn't know the meaning of the word. Oh, I do hope she's going to leave him. I do, I do.'

'Well, I don't.'

Louise stared at her. 'You still don't? Even knowing about Liz?'

'No.'

'Are you into sado-masochism or what? Get real, Jenny! And let Mum get a life.'

Left to herself, Rosalind lay down and tried to rest, but her thoughts were in a turmoil. She didn't want to hurt Jenny, who couldn't understand the sense of betrayal you felt when you realized you'd been living in a fool's paradise for nearly twenty-five years. Or the utter humiliation of finding that your husband had been unfaithful with your so-called best friend!

She knew Jonathon wanted her to leave Paul and she'd been secretly hoping he'd ask her to go and live with him. She felt so right with him, as if they'd known one another for ever. And she fancied him, too, loved his long lean body and his gentle hands. Since she'd started that embroidery, she hadn't really fancied Paul. And after finding out about him and Liz, she wondered if she ever would again.

But splitting up was such an irrevocable step to take. Jonathon wouldn't pressure her to leave Paul. She knew that. It would have to be her own choice for it to be right with him. And it would be, if – when she made the break.

But there were other things to consider as well. Did she want to leave Australia and spend the rest of her life in a foreign country, for a start? What about her mum? Then there were Jonathon's sons to think about. They'd seemed like nice lads at the fête, polite, well brought up, but with a certain liveliness. They'd got on well with Jenny, too. But how would they deal with a step-mother? And did she want to bring up step-sons? She hadn't made a brilliant success of bringing up Tim. At the thought of him she sucked in a long breath that was barbed with anguish too deep for tears, and it was a while before she could continue thinking things through.

She kept coming back to the same old question. Leaving Paul. Could she do it? Should she do it? After all, he had admitted their marriage was a bit shaky and had brought her here because he wanted to patch it up. That said something about his feelings for her, didn't it? She had to suppose the interlude with Liz meant nothing to him.

But it meant something to her. A double betrayal.

Oh, hell, what was she going to say to him tomorrow?

242

In the end she stopped trying to rest and went to her embroidery, starting on Louise, trying two or three sketches until she got the figure right. Tomboy looks, like Paul physically. Hands in the pockets of her jeans, short dark hair, chin jutting out as she scowled at the world. Yes, that was right.

She heard the front door slam and Paul's car drive away. He came back a short time later, presumably having found a black tie, but she didn't go down to him. And even when she heard him come upstairs and stop outside the closed door, she didn't call out to him as she once would have.

He went away without saying anything and she let a sigh of relief sift slowly out as she bent her head over her work again.

She didn't go to bed until long after he was asleep. The smell of whisky made her wrinkle her nose with disgust.

The following day they were all very self-conscious over breakfast. The funeral was to be held at ten o'clock, but no one mentioned it. No one ate much, except Paul, who ploughed through his usual cooked breakfast.

The smell of bacon sickened Rosalind and in the end she just had a piece of toast with a scrape of jam. Even that was too much for her to finish.

'I'll go and change,' she said when she had finished her coffee.

'I'll wash up,' said Jenny.

'I'll help,' Louise volunteered.

Paul wandered off into the small office, to sit there and scowl at the fax machine, drumming his fingers on the desk, staring into space, but seeing only his son's face, shouting defiance at him. That scene kept replaying in his mind. Again he fought for self-control, breathing deeply and clenching his fists.

Bloody hard, this. The worst. The pits. Fucking children! Were they worth it? He didn't know. He didn't know anything today.

Rosalind was relieved when the big black funeral limousine turned up. As it swallowed them up, it muted the colours of the landscape with its tinted windows. The grey upholstery heightened the sense of gloom.

In front of them, driving with agonizing slowness, the hearse carried Tim's body. Alone. Covered by flowers whose colours ran and blended together as tears welled in Rosalind's eyes. She didn't look at Paul, didn't even want to turn to him for comfort, and he made no attempt to touch her. But she saw that opposite them the girls were holding one another's hands and was glad of that.

Jonathon and Harry were parked at the end of the street and their car joined the funeral cortège.

'Who invited *them?*' snapped Paul, peering over his shoulder.

'I did,' said Rosalind, struggling to keep her voice quiet and even. 'They're good friends of mine.'

Behind them drove Ned, who'd also lingered outside rather than go into the house and face his future father-in-law's nasty remarks. Paul had refused point-blank to let Ned ride with the family, so Rosalind had suggested he come in his own car. That way he'd be able to take the girls out for an hour or two afterwards while she spoke to Paul.

The cemetery was small and Paul's voice seemed twice as loud as usual as he grumbled about the time it took the men to get the coffin out of the hearse.

'What do we do now?' he asked Rosalind in an undertone, scowling round. 'I hate this sort of mumbo-jumbo.'

'We follow the coffin into the chapel.' As they began to inch forward at a slow pace, she found Louise on her left side, holding her arm, but Paul made no attempt to touch her or to keep pace with anyone.

'The chairman offered to send someone to represent the company,' he said, too loudly, as they walked along. 'But I told him it wasn't worth it. They didn't know Tim, after all. But it was a nice gesture, don't you think?'

Rosalind didn't attempt to answer. She was watching her son's coffin, saying a mental farewell to his body, hoping his soul was now at peace.

It was Louise who surprised herself and everyone else by bursting into tears and sobbing so loudly that the last part of the ceremony came to a halt for a moment.

Rosalind sat with her arm round Louise's shaking shoulders, relieved when the service was over and the coffin had vanished downwards. What it contained wasn't really Tim any more. Her son was inside her now – in her heart, in her memories – there for ever.

From a short distance away Jonathon watched Rosalind whisper to the girl and hug her. He watched Paul lean over to say something in a low, angry voice and saw Louise wince. He wished – oh, how he wished he were able to share Rosalind's burdens on this terrible day.

Why do we do all this? he wondered, as he had wondered at his own parents' funerals. Why the hell do we put ourselves through the agony of a public performance at a time when we're still trying to come to terms with our grief in private?

He saw tears trickle down Harry's face. Funerals reminded her too much of her own husband, but she had made the effort to come today. He fumbled for her hand. She gripped his tightly and whispered, 'Damned shame!'

After the coffin had gone the small group of mourners gathered at the front of the chapel.

'So sorry,' said Harry. 'So very sorry, Rosalind.'

'Ros,' corrected Paul.

'Rosalind,' the owner of the name said firmly. 'You know I prefer my full name.'

'I've called you Ros all our married life,' he said, affronted that she would correct him in front of strangers.

'And I've preferred Rosalind all our married life, too.'

Jonathon had to content himself with holding her hand in his for a moment, meeting her eyes and hoping she would feel his love. As he stepped back, he murmured, 'If we can help in any way . . .'

'Very kind of you,' said Paul, seeing Rosalind neglecting her social duties, 'but we're going back to Australia soon.'

Every member of his family gaped at him.

'You never said anything about that before!' Louise blurted out.

'Why should I? It's my company who's paying for this jaunt. I've decided it's a waste of time and money, so we're going back.'

It was at that precise moment that Rosalind felt anger begin to take over from the sorrow. 'This isn't the place to discuss it,' she said in a chill voice, turned on her heel and walked over to the waiting limousine.

Paul started to apologize for her, but found himself look-ing at two backs as Harry and Jonathon Destan also moved away.

'We're going with Ned. We'll find our own way home, Father,' Jenny called.

He shrugged and walked after his wife.

'Let's go to the pub, eh?' said Ned, who was in the know about leaving Jenny's parents alone – and also why. He put an arm round Louise's shoulder as well as Jenny's as they walked to the car, and his future sister-in-law gave him a watery smile of gratitude.

'I wish I could be there to look after Mum,' Louise said. 'Dad's in a rotten mood. Foul. I hate him.' And that wasn't an exaggeration.

'She can look after herself,' Jenny said. 'She's grown very strong, Mum has.'

They both looked at her in surprise.

'We've all relied on her for years,' Jenny explained. 'I've been thinking about it. And I suddenly realized that she's always been the strong one where the family is concerned, though she doesn't brandish her strength at you or try to domi-nate you like Dad does. I wish . . .' Her voice faded for a moment.

'What do you wish?' Louise prompted.

'I wish I hadn't told her yesterday that they should stick together. You're right, Louise. She should leave him.' Tears came into her eyes. 'Did you see how Jonathon Destan looked at her? How she looked at him?'

They nodded.

'That's how couples should be. Dad's done nothing but snap at her since Tim died. What help is that?'

Louise could only shake her head.

'Come on,' said Ned as the silence lengthened into awkwardness. 'Let's go and have a drink, then decide what we want to do.'

They looked at him in puzzlement.

'If your family is going back to Australia, Jenny, you and I have to decide what we're going to do.'

'Heavens, yes!' Louise looked at them. 'Do you want me to leave you two on your own? I could go for a walk.' Though she didn't really want to. She needed company just now, needed it badly.

'No. You're part of my family, now, as well.' Ned gave her a hug to prove it. 'And you feel like family, too. But your bloody father doesn't.' And never would.

As the funeral limousine pulled away from the house and left them alone there, Paul stared at Rosalind. 'Why are the kids not coming back with us?'

'I asked them to leave us some space. We have to talk.'

'Oh? That makes a change. You usually go and hide in your little playroom to avoid talking to me.'

She ignored his gibe and walked into the living room, suddenly feeling clammy and apprehensive. But as she remembered how insensitive he'd been at the funeral, the anger began to rise again and she encouraged it. She would need its fire to carry her through this.

'I want to talk about your infidelity,' she began, as she had planned.

That made him sit very still. 'How the fuck did you find out?'

'What does that matter?'

He shrugged. 'Always like to understand the game, that's all.'

'*Game?* It's not a game! It's us, our whole life together!'

'Calling it a game is just a way of looking at things, for heaven's sake.'

'You want to understand so that you can *play* it better next time, I suppose?'

He shrugged.

She waited for an apology for the infidelity, but it didn't come. He just sat there with an assessing look on his face, watching her.

As the silence dragged on, Rosalind suddenly couldn't stand it any more. She didn't want to play games. The words exploded out of her mouth. 'You're not even going to offer me an apology, are you?'

'What for? I'm only human. We've had long spells away from one another. What happened was partly your fault for not moving around with me, so why should I be the one to apologize? *You* haven't apologized to me for your stick-in-the-mud attitude and that's what drove me to it.'

She ignored his accusation. 'You're not sorry at all, are you?'

'I'm sorry you found out. Sorry you're hurt.' He really was. It surprised him how much. He didn't want to hurt her. 'And to find out now of all times – well, I deeply regret that, Ros.'

'And that's all?'

'This is the twenty-first century. We're both grown ups. No one believes in fairy stories and happy ever afters nowadays.' Hell, he could do without this. Didn't she know he was upset, too? At least she had seen Tim. He hadn't. They hadn't even bothered to tell him his son was back.

Seeing how bright with tears her eyes were, he tried to explain, to soften the blow. 'The other women – well, they didn't make any difference to the way I felt about you, I promise you, Ros. It was just – opportunism. A man's physical needs are so much more pressing than a woman's. You know that.'

He was doing it again, Rosalind realized, twisting the argument his way, putting the blame on to someone else. 'Well, whether the women mattered to you or not, I'm leaving you.' She had the satisfaction of seeing his jaw drop.

'You're bloody not!'

'You can't stop me.'

'I can talk sense into you, though. We've lost one member of the family. This is not the time to break up the rest of us. For the girls' sake, if not for ours. Give yourself a few days, at least. Think things through. You'll see I'm right. And – and I do apologize for hurting you.'

'*Speak the speech, I pray you, as I pronounced it to you, trippingly on the tongue,*' she said scathingly. It was from Hamlet. Another tragedy. Very apt. The rest of the words she had once learned by heart for homework came back to her suddenly and she hurled them at him. '*If you mouth it as many of your players do, I had as lief the town crier spoke my lines.*'

'What the hell are you talking about?'

'I'm quoting the Bard. He was talking about actors and you were just acting out an apology.' She sucked in oxygen and tossed at him, 'How *could* you do it with Liz? Of all people, *Liz!*'

248

He stared at her in shock. She even knew about Liz. Oh, hell! After a minute of searching for words to put the best spin on things, he could only think of, 'She did it with me, too – was eager for it. To get back at Bill, she said.'

'And you couldn't resist seizing a freebie – even if it was with my best friend.' Rosalind's voice wobbled as she fought for control.

He shrugged. 'I suppose you're going to break up a life-long friendship now just for a few screws?'

'No. For the betrayal.'

'Betrayal!' He threw back his head and roared with laughter. 'Oh, my God, join the twenty-first century, will you, Ros?'

'*Rosalind!*' she screamed at him. 'I'm called Rosalind and that's how I think of myself and always have done. Rosalind, *Rosalind!*'

'Bit late to tell me that now.' He went across to the decanter and poured himself a large whisky. 'Want one?'

'No, I don't. But you go ahead and get drunk again. Your only son is dead, your marriage is over and you turn to the bottle. Very helpful, that.'

He could feel himself getting angry. He'd been very forbearing, but it took two to work out a reconciliation. Suddenly he wanted to wound her. 'Anyway, Tim might not be *my* only son. She's pregnant. Liz is, I mean.'

'*What?*'

'Yeah.' He patted his crotch. 'Everything's still working all right. Shook me when she told me, though.'

'Pregnant?' The word was a hiss of sound. '*Liz – is – pregnant?*'

'Yeah.' He raised his glass in an unvoiced toast. 'So I might still have a son.'

She could bear it no longer. He wasn't sorry for what he'd done, not in the least sorry, only sorry that she had found out. And for all her good intentions, she'd not handled it as firmly as she had hoped. That upset her, too. She turned and ran from him, not pausing to grab a coat, just snatching her handbag and throwing open the front door.

He set down his glass and followed her, but she had the car door open and the motor running before he could do anything. By the time he started down the porch steps, hands outstretched to stop her, the car was moving. He leaped in front of it.

And she kept moving, not caring whether she knocked him over. He had to jump sideways to avoid her.

'Damn you, you stupid bitch!' he yelled after her from where he lay sprawled among the dying daffodils.

'Jonathon!' She hammered on the door of Destan Manor. 'Jonathon, where are you? Jonathon, I need you.'

No one came to answer and she slid to the floor, sobbing and weeping loudly as a hurt child. The ice inside her was breaking up now in great chunks and pain was running like meltwater through her whole body. Harsh noises kept erupting from her throat and she couldn't stop them.

When Jonathon found her, he pulled her to her feet and supported her as she stumbled into the house. Then he held her while all the ice melted and she cried out her sorrow for her son and her marriage.

He understood what she was going through. He'd been there himself. And he knew better than to let her make any irremediable decisions in this frame of mind. If she came to him, she had to come for all the right reasons. Not because that insensitive shit of a husband had trampled all over her again.

# Twenty-One

'I'm not going back to Australia yet,' Jenny decided as they sat in the pub. She looked at Ned. 'You want me to stay here, don't you?'

'Of course I do. You can come and live with my family.'

'I don't think I'd better. I—'

He took hold of her hand, kissed it, then kissed her cheek for good measure. 'You've seen how happy all this is making my mother. She's been itching for me to get married. Besides, we've tons of room at home. You must definitely come and stay with us while you and I look for a house of our own. We'll get married as soon as we can. None of this fancy stuff. It's you I want.'

Louise excused herself and went to the ladies.

Jenny didn't notice her sister's departure, but sat smiling at the thought of having her own home, her own life. With him. Then it occurred to her that she'd be completely dependent on Ned and that thought didn't please her quite so much. 'There'll be formalities to go through. I'm an Australian citizen. And I'd like to find myself a job, though *not* as a trainee manager.'

'Fine, we'll go through the formalities together. No one will turn a gorgeous girl like you down. And if you want a job, I'll help you hunt for one.' He raised his glass and drank a silent toast to her. 'Though you can come and work in the gallery, if you like. It's hard to get part-time staff. Mum comes in sometimes when we're busy. You might enjoy it.'

She frowned. 'Is this a pretend job, or a real one?'

'It's as real as you care to make it, love. Up to you.'

Her face brightened. 'Then I accept. I always used to like art at school and I'd love to learn about antiques.'

Louise came back and sat down, smiling at them both. 'It makes me feel there's hope in the world, seeing you two

251

looking all smoochy.' Her smile faded and she stared down into her lemon, lime and bitters. 'I'm under age, though, and *he* still has power over me.'

'Only for a few weeks then you'll be eighteen,' Jenny said consolingly. 'At that age you're technically an adult – I think.'

'Yeah, but what do you live on, whether they call you an adult or not?'

'Mum has some money now.'

'I suppose so. Do you think she'd mind supporting me for a bit till I find my feet?'

'I think she'd love to.'

Louise began to look thoughtful. 'I'll still need to train for something. Perhaps nursing.' She blinked her eyes furiously. 'Tim suggested that and I think he was right.' She'd thought about it several times since his death and the idea pleased her greatly. It meant he would be with her in a sense, would have given her a permanent legacy. Then reality bit and she shook her head. 'Dad will find some way to stop me, you know he will. If Mum makes him mad enough, he'll do anything he can to hurt her – through me, if he has to.' She shivered. 'He frightens me when I'm on my own with him, you know. He thumped me around quite a bit when he came to get me in Perth.'

Jenny gasped. 'No!'

'Mind,' Louise allowed, 'I probably needed it. But he didn't need to enjoy it, which he definitely did. And I was terrified. Absolutely terrified,' she repeated, remembering that day with a shiver.

'He's always made me nervous. Tim used to say –' Jenny broke off for a moment, then continued unsteadily – 'that I should stand up to him. But I'm not like you two. I'm soft. Too soft. More like Mum, really.'

Ned frowned. 'I don't like your father, I must admit, but is he really so bad?'

Jenny nodded. 'Well, he does like to be the big boss man and make everyone's decisions for them, though to give the devil his due, he's always supported us in style. But he's had Mum under his thumb for years.' She paused, then added, 'Well, except for her embroidery, though she puts that away when he's home.'

Ned shook his head. 'He was very scornful about it when he was talking to my father, but she's a brilliant artist! How can he not see that?'

'That's probably the reason he hates it,' Louise said gloomily. 'He doesn't like anyone else to shine too brightly when he's around. You should see him perform at a party. Mr Wonderful in person.'

They stayed on in the pub until nearly three o'clock, then Louise sighed. 'I think we'd better get back, don't you? She might – you know, need us.'

'You drop us outside,' Jenny told Ned. 'No need to stir things up further by you and Dad having a confrontation.'

'Are you sure?'

'Yes. Very sure.' She linked her arm in Louise's. 'Besides, there are two of us, not one.'

'Three. Don't forget Mum.'

But their mother wasn't at home and their father was on the phone as usual, talking about – the two sisters looked at one another apprehensively – ending the lease on this house. At the sound of Ned's car driving away they edged towards one another, feeling suddenly vulnerable.

'Didn't she tell Dad?' Jenny whispered.

'I don't know.'

Paul came out of his little office. 'Come into the living room. I want a word with you two.' He waited until they sat down together on one of the sofas, then said, 'We're all going back to Australia as soon as I can book seats on a plane. Go and get me your return ticket, Jenny, and I'll re-book you with us – I presume you did have a return ticket?'

She took a deep breath. 'I think I'll stay on in England with Ned's family. We're going to get married quite soon.'

'You can get married later.' His smile became frosty at the edges. 'Your mother needs you at the moment. She's rather upset by all this. So go and get the ticket, there's a good girl.'

'I'm sorry, but I'm not going back with you.'

He glowered at her. 'Then I'll have to come and find it.'

Her mouth fell open. 'But—'

'I mean it, Jenny. What this family needs now is pulling together and I intend to do just that.' He set his hands on his

253

hips and stared at her challengingly. 'Well, are you going to get the ticket or am I?'

'I'll – it's in my room.' She stumbled upstairs wondering how to buy time, feeling as if she were living in a nightmare. Whatever had happened between her parents had made her father go all aggro. Had her mother given in to him again? Surely not? And where was she?

Jenny took out the plane ticket, looked at it and shook her head. She'd paid for it. It was hers and he had no right to take it off her. She tiptoed out on to the landing to see what was happening downstairs. He was shouting at Louise now, ranting on about people who went off for a drink in the pub at a time when the family should stick together.

'And with a stranger, too!' he roared.

'Ned's not a stranger. He's going to marry my sister.'

'Not if I have any say in the matter. I don't want a wimp like him for a son-in-law.'

Upstairs Jenny's hand flew up to her mouth. She knew her father and Ned had hardly had the most promising of introductions – but she had not thought even *he* would try to stop them getting married. If she went back to Australia, she'd be stuck there without the money to return. Well, she'd have the rest of her winnings, but why should she have to buy another ticket with it when she was here already.

So she wasn't going. She was legally an adult and was staying here to marry Ned. Letting out a long, slow breath, she murmured, 'Sorry, Mum. Time for me to leave.'

She stuffed the plane ticket into her handbag, together with all her remaining money. Then she shoved some underwear into a plastic carrier bag. After a hasty glance around to see if there was anything else she could grab quickly, she crept out on to the landing, ducking back with a gasp as her father came into the hall and shouted over his shoulder, 'And you, young lady, are going back to your studies next semester. *Business studies.* The only sort of qualification that gets people jobs nowadays. You can do better for yourself than nursing, by hell you can!' He stamped off towards the kitchen, not even glancing up the stairs, and there came the sound of running water and the kettle being switched on.

As cups rattled and cupboard doors slammed, Jenny tiptoed

downstairs. Passing the open door of the living room, she saw Louise sitting disconsolately on the sofa and paused, her heart going out to her sister. When Louise looked up, Jenny raised one hand in farewell and blew her a kiss.

Louise made shooing motions with her hand and tried to smile. For a moment, she thought of going too, then shook her head. No. Ned and his family had no responsibility for her. And besides, her mother needed someone here.

Jenny managed to get the front door open without her father hearing and didn't even try to close it behind her. Once outside she took off at a run, haring down the street as if pursued by all the demons from hell.

When she saw the Dorchester bus chugging round the corner towards her, it seemed as if fate was on her side. Hope springing up anew at this miracle, she sprinted to the pole with its little bus-stop sign at the top and its faded timetable under a pane of cracked glass, signalling to it to stop.

With a grin the driver pulled up. 'Nearly missed it there, young lady, didn't you? If I hadn't been running late, you'd have had to wait another hour.'

Joy filled Jenny. 'Yes. What a bit of luck! A single to Dorchester, please.' She slid into the seat and sat smiling out at the world. She wasn't going back to Australia yet. Not even for her mother's sake. And there was no way her father could make her.

If Ned's family didn't want her, she'd simply find somewhere else to stay and get a job. She had just cast her vote with her feet. Stuff you, Dad, she thought. Go and find someone else to bully.


When Rosalind's tears dried up, she poured out all the details of the encounter with her husband to Jonathon, then lay back on the couch, numb with tiredness and reaction.

'You needed to cry it out,' he said. 'You really did.'

'Yes.' The lump of ice inside her was gone now, but she was left with a sea of churning panic in its place. 'I'm going to leave him, Jonathon.'

'Are you sure about that?'

She nodded. 'Very sure.' She waited a minute and when he didn't say anything, she asked, 'Can I come here to you?'

When he didn't immediately reply, she looked sideways. 'Jonathon?'

'I want you to leave him, of course I do. And I want us to try living together. But I'm not sure . . .' he began to chew one corner of his lip.

'Not sure of what?'

'Of whether you really do want to make a life with me. Or whether you just want to leave him.'

'*Jonathon!*'

'And I don't think you're completely sure, either, which is more to the point. One doesn't break up a long marriage like yours in a fit of anger, as I know. If you want my opinion, you need to go back to Australia and make certain you really can leave everything – home, country, friends.' His eyes were shadowed. 'I've made one very serious mistake, Rosalind, and I'm not about to make another. Even to help you.'

'I thought –' her breath caught on a sob – 'you loved me.'

His gaze was warm. 'I do, very much indeed, but I'm too old and wary to toss everything aside because of it. That's not enough for me or for anyone. You, of all people, should know that. You loved Paul once. Greatly, if I'm any judge.'

More tears filled her eyes from the lake of meltwater within her. 'Yes.'

'So I'm not going to rush into anything – not even with you, my dearest Rosalind. When things have calmed down, when you've found your feet again, we could try living together. I'd really like to get to know you better in – in more normal circumstances.' He gave her a wry smile. 'And for you to get to know me, warts and all. I actually believe we stand a good chance of building a successful, and I hope long-term relationship – but not now, not while you're so upset with him. I won't be held responsible in future for breaking up your marriage, not by you or by anyone else.'

After a short silence, he gave her a hug, then put her resolutely away from him. 'Come to the kitchen. I'll get you a cup of coffee and a biscuit.'

She went with him, feeling shattered. She'd failed with Paul. Was she failing with Jonathon already?

Was he failing her?

*Or was he right?*

Did she need more time to come to terms with the failure of her marriage? She didn't know. She didn't feel as if she was very wise at all. The whole world, herself included, was a puzzle to her lately, incomprehensible as a high-walled maze that she'd strayed into by sheer chance.

'Thanks.' She sipped the coffee, avoiding his eyes.

He sat jiggling a teabag in his own cup, then fussing over the milk and sugar.

When the caffeine had started to kick in she stood up. 'I'd better get back, then.'

He stood up too and tried to take her in his arms.

'Don't.' She pushed at him. *'Don't!'*

He stood looking down at her, an anxious question in his eyes.

And suddenly she knew she would not be certain of anything until she got back to her own home and possessions, the home which had been the centre of her world for so long.

'You're right,' she said, turning to walk out of the house. At the front door she stood on tiptoe to kiss his cheek. 'I do need to go home before I commit to anything else. How wise you are! And there's Louise to sort out, as well. I can't abandon her.' She looked at him searchingly. 'I'll write. And phone. If you want me to.'

'I do.' He didn't have her Australian address and still he let her go, watching her drive away, aching to call her back. But he could not do that. Dare not. He wanted Rosalind wholeheartedly – or not at all.

He wanted to spend the rest of his life with her, to see her grow and expand her skills, to make her happy, to be happy himself.

Was that too much to ask?

He wouldn't try for anything less.


At home Rosalind found the mail on the floor in the hall. She picked it up and began to open her own letters, not wanting to see Paul yet. He was upstairs, packing his things, whistling. He knew she was back, but he didn't come down to see her.

There was a letter from her mother, written just after Tim died, which made her weep a little, and there was a letter from the solicitor in Southport to say they'd got probate. The money to which she was currently entitled would have been transferred into her account by the time she received this. The sum he mentioned was so large it made her gasp. She stuffed that letter hurriedly into her pocket. She and Paul had enough problems to sort out without the money.

Besides, this was her ticket to freedom – if she decided to leave him.

'I have to go up to London first thing tomorrow,' Paul said as she entered the bedroom.

He hadn't even turned his head to look at her, she thought resentfully.

'I've booked us three on a plane to Australia leaving Heathrow Saturday tea time. I wanted to book Jenny, too, but she ran out of the house and took her return ticket with her. Went off to join that twit, I suppose. So bugger her. She can fend for herself from now on.'

Rosalind felt a spurt of relief trickle through her. Jenny was safe, anyway. But there was still Louise to worry about. 'I think that's the right thing for Jenny,' she said carefully. 'Ned will look after her.'

'I don't agree. I think she should bloody well put family first at a time like this.'

She didn't state the obvious, that this was the first time he'd put family first in all their years together – if he was putting it first, if this wasn't part of some devious scheme or other. No, surely not! Even Paul wouldn't be scheming at a time like this. She contented herself with, 'Ned *is* her family, now.'

'Well, she needn't come to me to pay for a fancy wedding if she won't do the right thing by you.'

'She's doing exactly the right thing by me – marrying the man she loves.' And if Paul didn't pay for the wedding, Rosalind would. Not a huge extravagant one, but a nice wedding, which she'd certainly come back and attend. Oh, it felt so good to have Sophie's money behind her. 'I'll leave you to pack your things, then.'

He looked at the jumble in his suitcase. 'Could you just sort this out for me . . . ?'

'No, I couldn't. I'm exhausted.' And besides, she didn't want to touch his things. Or him.

What did that say?

'Thanks for nothing.' His lips curved in a particularly nasty grin. 'Wept all over your dear friends, have you?'

There was no point in denying the obvious. 'Yes.'

'Feel better for it?'

'Not really.' She turned partly away from him.

He paused halfway towards her, arms outstretched, then let his arms drop. 'I see. I'm still in the doghouse, eh?'

'Very much so.'

'Ros, I'm not going to beg you to stay with me, but I'll reiterate – what I've done doesn't make any difference to our marriage. It never has.'

She looked at him as if he were a stranger. He felt like a stranger. 'So you say. And my name's Rosalind. It always has been. And fidelity is something I value very highly indeed.'

He let out a long, aggrieved sigh and turned back to his case, cramming things in anyhow.

'I'll be back on Friday evening to pick you and Louise up and I'll drive us to Heathrow on Saturday morning. We'll get the hire firm to pick your car up from here.' He hesitated. 'You *are* coming back with me, aren't you?'

'Yes, I'm definitely coming back to Australia. I could perfectly well drive the car up to London myself, though. Save you a journey.'

'No need. I'll come and get you.' He zipped up the suit-case. 'Oh, and if Jenny comes to her senses, phone me through her flight details, will you? I can still change her ticket.' Scorn filled his eyes. 'That girl is too soft by far. We should have done something to toughen her up.'

'Why?'

'Because life, as you have recently found out, my dear sheltered wife, is never simple and one needs to be able to cope with it. I'd have thought the episode with Michael would have taught Jenny something, but no, she's walked straight into another relationship. I'm not a wicked ogre, as you all seem to think. I'm actually trying to look after my family, though a fat lot of thanks I get for it.'

He waited for her to say something and when she didn't, he added, 'Jenny's new relationship has been formed on the rebound, Ros – Rosalind. It won't last, you know it won't. And I don't like that Ned. He's as soft as she is. He'll not make a good husband for her. She needs someone stronger, someone who can look after her. As I've looked after you. That's why I wanted to get her back to Australia.'

She couldn't bear to listen to him making these ridiculous statements any longer, as if he had looked after her, when he'd spent so much time away from home and gone with other women. She walked out and went downstairs.

He came to the bedroom door and yelled after her, 'Stop walking out on me! We have to *talk!*'

She carried on, ending up outside in the garden, breathing in the fresh air in big gulps and blinking her eyes furiously. She wasn't going to cry any more. She was not.

He came out to see her. 'Pull yourself together, Ros. We have *got* to talk.' When she didn't answer, he reiterated, 'I definitely *don't* want us to split up. I never have wanted us to split up.'

She stood there numbly, waiting for him to speak.

'I'm coming back on Friday evening and if you're not here, I'll scour England for you. I mean that, Ros. We're going back to Australia together – you, Louise and I. I want us to remain a family. I *really* want that.'

She couldn't think what to say.

'After the funeral I wanted us to make up, get closer, not – not . . .' He paused to gulp back the emotion that welled up in him.

She stared in shock at the tears in his eyes.

'But no, you have to choose this moment to make a stand, *Rosalind*. See. I do remember what you want to be called. Well, I'm upset about Tim, too, and I've had it with this place.' He scowled around at the house as he fished out a handkerchief and blew his nose. 'We're not only going back to Australia, but we're going to sort things out between you and me. I want that. I really do.'

She nodded again, not having the energy to do anything else at the moment. Those were definitely tears in his eyes. She had not expected that, somehow, and it made her uncertain of what she wanted as nothing else could have done.

'Good,' he said in a softer voice. 'And tonight you and I are going out for a meal together. I've booked a table at a place I saw in Wareham.'

'I don't want to . . .'

'Just you and me. No children. Can't we even *try* spending time together? After all those years of being married?'

She opened her mouth to refuse, then closed it again and shrugged. 'All right.'

The restaurant in Wareham was small and discreetly lit. Waiters fussed over them. A candle flickered on the table next to a white rose in a slender bud vase. Rosalind stirred the food around on her plate and tried to look as if she was eating.

After the main course, however, Paul looked at her. 'This isn't working, is it?'

'Not really.'

'Want to leave now?' He pushed aside his plate, of which he'd eaten perhaps half.

She sighed in relief. 'Please.' It was such a parody of a romantic evening. And they had both been really struggling to find neutral subjects to talk about.

On the way home he stopped the car in the car park of Corfe Castle. As the engine died, he leaned his head on his hands for a moment, then looked sideways at her. 'I don't want us to break up, Ros – I really don't.' His voice broke.

She was shocked to see tears glinting on his cheeks again. 'Paul . . .' she said hesitantly, not sure what to do or say.

And suddenly he was weeping, harsh sounds that filled the car. She had not thought he *could* weep.

'I didn't even see him!' he sobbed. 'I never even saw Tim again! He was my son, too, you know!'

She took him in her arms and shushed him as if he was one of her children, and when he turned and clutched her, she let him, patting his back, murmuring meaningless words of comfort. It took a long time for the tears to stop.

'Oh, hell!' he said shakily at last. 'You must think me a real wimp.'

'No. I'm glad you cried for him.'

'Ros –' he gulped audibly – 'I can't lose you as well. You – you won't really leave me, will you? Please don't!'

'I can't promise anything yet. We'll have to – to see if we can grow together again.' And she'd have to see if she could forget Jonathon.

'But you'll give it a chance.'

'I'll try, yes.'

He rubbed at his eyes, gave a shamefaced laugh and asked, 'Got a handkerchief?'

She fumbled in her handbag and passed him the little packet of tissues she always carried. 'Here, use these.' She could hear how raw his breathing was and see an occasional tear tracking down his face.

She moved back a little and stared out of the window.

'Want to leave now?' he asked eventually.

When she nodded and looked at him, he reminded her for a moment of a much younger Paul, the man she had fallen in love with and married. But only for a moment. Perhaps it was a trick of the moonlight. But if it wasn't . . .

When they got in Paul went straight upstairs and Rosalind followed him slowly. She could hear Louise moving around her bedroom, the CD player making a faint rhythmic sound. Louise didn't call out and Rosalind didn't go in to see her.

But she had to force herself to follow Paul into the bedroom. She hesitated in the doorway. What she needed now was time to think. Away from him. Time to assess her own feelings. She felt as if the universe had heaved beneath her feet recently.

Paul looked at her with a frown. 'What are you doing?'

'Getting my night things.'

'Aren't you going to sleep here, with me?'

'No. Not yet.'

He bowed his head, his lips a tight thin line, his expression sad.

When he didn't try to persuade her, she nearly weakened, then shook her head in annoyance at herself. He hadn't been pretending to cry, he really had been racked with anguish for their son's death and she thought he truly wanted to stay married to her.

But did she truly want to stay married to him? She still wasn't sure she could trust him. Would he really try to change? *Could he?*

In the morning, Paul was very subdued, eating a rapid breakfast and leaving by six thirty. 'I'll ring you tonight, Ros – *Rosalind* – to check that everything is all right.'

He leaned forward as if about to kiss her cheek, but she pulled back, so he muttered something and turned on his heel.

Only when she had heard his car drive away did she start to think clearly again. She went back into the kitchen, breathed in the delightful lack of his presence, which always seemed to permeate the house when he was home, and put the kettle on.

She couldn't get the thought of his tears out of her mind, though.

A voice from behind her said hesitantly, 'Mum? Has Dad gone?'

'Yes. Come and have a cup of coffee with me, Louise. We need to talk.'

'Are you going to leave him?'

'I don't know. I shan't know till I get home.' Maybe not even then. She was torn every which way at the moment.

'Mum, don't let him persuade you. You deserve your own life now.'

'I won't let him over-persuade me,' Rosalind promised. 'But you don't lightly toss away twenty-five years of marriage, love.'

Jenny stared round the comfortable bedroom with its single bed. Mrs Didburin – Stella – had been kind to her, and so had Ned. She smiled involuntarily as she looked at the bar of chocolate by the side of the bed. He'd pressed it on her 'for comfort' last night. Dear Ned. What a lovely teddy bear of a man he was! But she felt very guilty for leaving her mother alone to face her father.

'Jenny!'

'Yes?' She poked her head out of the bedroom door and Stella's voice floated upstairs. 'Phone call for you. You can take it in the hall.'

'Who is it?' If it was her father, she wasn't going to speak to him, whether that was cowardly or not.

'Your mother.'

'Thanks. I'll be right down.' Jenny rushed downstairs. 'Hello? Mum, are you all right?'

'Yes, of course. Are *you* all right, love? Your father didn't hurt you yesterday, did he?'

'No. Of course he didn't hurt me. How are you – really?'

'I'm – oh, you know – coping.'

'I'm sorry to leave you in the lurch like that, Mum. I just couldn't take any more. He was going to take my ticket from me *by force.*'

'Leaving was probably the best thing for you to do, darling. I'm phoning to say your father's gone back to London. You and Ned had better come and collect the rest of your things today. I have to pack and close up the house. We're flying out on Saturday.'

'You're going back to him? After all he's done.' Disappointment flooded through Jenny's body, tasting bitter in her mouth.

'I'm going back to Australia. To my home. As to the other, I don't know.' She repeated the formula she had used for Louise. Bland words, masking a turmoil of contradictions that were tearing her apart. 'It's not an easy thing to do, you know, break up a marriage after all this time.'

She would telephone Jonathon later today and confirm that she was leaving on Saturday, give him her mother's address, so that he could write to her.

Jenny put the phone down and burst into tears on Ned's broad chest. 'She's going back to Australia with him! He'll smother her – he'll never let me see her again.'

The plane took off on time. Rosalind leaned back and sighed in mingled relief and tiredness. There had been so many things to sort out. Embroideries to discuss with George Didburin. Food remnants to go to Alice Tuffin. Other bits and pieces to Harry, to be disposed of as she saw fit.

By far the hardest of all had been sorting out Tim's few possessions. She and Louise had done that together, weeping over how little he had to show for his life.

And all the time Louise had kept begging her not to go back.

'I have to,' she'd kept repeating. 'I have to go back to my home and begin sorting out my life from there.' Because that was where it had all started. Because her home had always been so important to her!

She'd spoken to Jonathon on the phone, not daring to see him again till she was sure of herself. He had showed his usual understanding of her needs and in the end she'd had to say goodbye because she couldn't speak through her tears.

'Penny for them.' Beside her Paul smiled and patted her hand, but she couldn't return his smile and she pulled her hand away. She looked sideways at him, this man with whom she had spent all her adult life. Did she know him? Did anyone really know another person?

'You all right, Ros?' He saw her expression. 'Oh, very well, *Rosalind*, then. It'll take me a while to get used to it. Rosalind.' He sat with his head on one side and repeated it again, like a child learning a poem. 'Sounds quite good, actually. Dignified. I shall enjoy introducing you to people as *my wife, Rosalind Stevenson.*'

Trust him to make small concessions gracefully once he felt sure he'd won the major battle. She felt naked without her daughter there. You shouldn't need an intermediary with your own husband but she did. 'I wish you'd let Louise fly business class with us.'

'Whatever for? She's young enough to cope with those narrow seats and mass troughing conditions. Waste of money to pay double the fare for her.' He turned to smile at the hostess, who was offering him a glass of champagne. 'Thank you. Ros, do you want one?'

She shook her head. She needed to keep a clear head. Was he drinking more heavily because of Tim? Or had it been going on for a while and she'd not noticed before?

After the first meal he sat back, replete and mellow, sipping a glass of cognac now. 'What did you do with your embroidery things? I haven't seen any extra suitcases. Didn't you bring them back with you?'

'Just a couple of pieces I've been working on.' The family portrait was almost finished now, but she still had to complete her own figure. For that, she had to understand what she had become and where she was going.

His face brightened. 'I know you've done quite well with it, but I still think embroidery is a stupid occupation for the twentieth century. There are machines to do that sort of thing now. You just program them and they do it for you.'

A black mark for that, Paul, she thought. You can't even give me my own creative space, can you? She changed the subject. 'So – what are your plans for the coming year? Where is the chairman sending you next?'

'I've got a month's compassionate leave to see you settled in at home first. What with Tim and all. And talking of home, I have a small piece of news for you. I got a phone call from Australia yesterday.'

'Oh?'

'That fellow who attacked Jenny. Michael Whatsit.'

'What about him?'

'I put a private detective on to him, a good one. Rod followed him, caught him attacking another woman, knocked the bastard out and called the police. So, it's quite likely dear Michael will serve a prison sentence. I've informed the police that my daughter will be happy to make a statement to help the prosecution, but I suppose they can get that from England.' He smiled at Rosalind, waiting to be praised.

'I'm glad he's where he can't harm anyone else. That must have cost you a lot of money.'

He shrugged. 'No lowlife scum hurts *my* daughter and gets away with it.'

She nodded and let him take her response how he wanted. From the smugness of his expression, he had decided her reaction meant approval. Actually, she was trying not to ask whether he saw Jenny as a person in her own right, or only as *his* daughter. Whether he saw his wife as a person in her own right or only as *his* wife. The sort of questions she should have asked years ago.

But in the end she decided it'd do no good to ask. He wouldn't even understand the point she was making. She doubted he would ever understand such subtleties.

They took a taxi home from the airport, sitting in silence except when Paul commented on the beauty of the Perth foreshore. No one answered him. Louise was glowering out of the window. Rosalind was looking inwards, surprised how much a stranger she felt here now.

Perth in late May was cool. Almost winter. Another change of season, she thought ruefully, but one she had always liked far more than the hot summers. If only she could be sure what the right thing was to do.

266

Stay or go?

Forgive and forget?

Or remember and reject?

Twenty-five years of marriage was a long time. Jonathon was right. She did need to make her decision more carefully.

If Paul would let her. His cheerfulness on the flight back had come as something of a shock. Did he think things were settled now? Surely not?

At the house her mother was waiting, warned by Paul to expect them.

Rosalind surprised them all, herself included, by bursting into tears and throwing herself into her mother's arms. Then she noticed the man standing behind her mother. 'John. I didn't see you. Sorry to ignore you. I'm a bit – emotional.'

'You have every reason to be. I can wait in the car if you'd rather be alone with your mother.'

'No, no. Of course not!'

They all went inside. Rosalind excused herself to go up to the bathroom. She needed a moment before she could face them.

When she went down to the sitting room she viewed it with fresh eyes. It was like an ice cavern. Pale cool colours, chill marble floor, stark glass and brass. What a change from the small rooms in English houses, the busy wallpapers, the fussy ornaments! Even the big rooms in Jonathon's house were fussy compared to this one.

Her smile faltered for a moment as she thought of him, of Destan Manor and the village, of Jenny left behind with Ned, Jenny weeping as Ned drove her away the other night after she'd packed her things. Of Jenny trying not to accept the cheque her mother had given her, but in the end agreeing. Rosalind knew Sophie would have approved of that use of her money. 'You need some independence,' she'd told her daughter firmly. 'Even from Ned.'

As everyone sat down for a cup of coffee, Audrey and John looked at one another self-consciously. 'We have some news for you,' she said, reaching for his hand.

'Audrey has done me the honour of agreeing to become my wife,' he said in the fussy, precise way he always spoke.

But his expression was young and happy as he exchanged

267

smiles with Audrey and that delighted Rosalind. 'Oh, I'm so glad for you both!' She went across and hugged them ruthlessly.

Paul's congratulations were more temperate.

There was a ring at the door and when he went to answer it, a florist's van was parked outside.

'Delivery for Stevenson,' the woman said.

He carried the red roses back into the sitting room, smiling. It'd have been better timing if the flowers had arrived after Audrey and that moon-faced old fogy had left, but never mind. You played the cards you were dealt.

'For you,' he said to his wife, flourishing a bow as he presented them to her.

She stared. 'What?'

He felt a fool in that silly position and straightened up. 'Aren't you going to take them?'

She did so, setting them on the low table immediately, where the dark red of the roses was echoed in reflection as an even darker dried-blood colour. It made her shiver. 'To Ros with love from Paul,' she read aloud and gazed at him blankly. 'Oh.'

'Now, that's a nice touch,' Audrey said, leaning forward to examine the flowers. 'Beautiful, aren't they? Pity they don't have a perfume, though. I always think flowers should have a perfume.'

Louise didn't join in the chorus of admiration. Surely her mother wasn't going to fall for that old red roses trick? She was getting very worried about what was going on. Her father was looking smug, not chastened, and her mother had become very distant and vague again, like she'd been before they went to England. She'd seen where her mother had dumped her things when they'd arrived here, though. In one of the spare bedrooms. And seen her father's scowl as he'd watched her. So maybe there was still hope.

But these roses worried her. He was clearly trying to get back into her mother's bed again. Oh, hell, he was up to every trick in the book, that randy bastard was. And if her mother didn't leave him, Louise would be forced to stay with him, too, though not for long.

She would be eighteen soon and she wasn't going back to

business studies whatever he said. Nursing, she'd decided. Helping people who were sick, who really needed you – as she'd tried to help Tim, but hadn't been able to. She'd make up for that, though, by helping others. She really would. She'd make Tim proud of her but best of all she'd be proud of herself.

'Well, we'd better go and leave you three to settle in,' Audrey said, putting down her empty coffee cup. 'I'm sorry Jenny isn't here, but Ned certainly sounds a nice young man.'

'He's thirty,' Paul cut in, 'running to fat and already going bald. Not exactly young. And he's a typical public school wallah. No chin and no fire in his belly.'

'I like him,' Rosalind said, frowning at Paul. 'And I'm sure you will, too, when you meet him, Mum.'

'Are they coming over for a visit, then?' Audrey asked eagerly.

'No. But if you two are getting married, I'd like to offer you a trip to England as a wedding present. You could go there for a honeymoon. Check Ned out for yourself. Go up to Southport for a few days, perhaps. I haven't closed Sophie's house. Prue is going to caretake it for me. I think she's met a guy in Southport. I hope it works out for her.'

Louise nearly wet herself trying not to laugh at her father's outraged expression. He'd hate her mother spending that much money on a present, even if it wasn't his money. And he clearly didn't know about the house in Southport still being open.

She escorted her grandmother out to the car, but stopped outside the front door. 'I just want to say how sorry I am for how badly I behaved when I was staying with you, Gran. I was out of line and – well, I'm sorry. Tim told me I'd been a fool, but I had to –' her voice wobbled for a moment at the thought of her brother and the talks they'd had – 'had to realize that for myself.'

Audrey reached out to hug her. 'I'm really glad to have my granddaughter back.' She looked back towards the house. 'Are they all right? Paul and Rosalind, I mean? They seem a bit – strained.'

'I hope they're not all right. He's been rotten to her.' Louise looked over her shoulder to check that he wasn't nearby, and added, 'He's been unfaithful, actually. And she's very upset about it.'

Audrey's mouth dropped open in shock.

'Don't say I told you. I just thought that if you knew – if she needed help – you'd not say the wrong thing. You see – it was with Liz.'

There was a moment's silence, then Audrey whispered, '*Liz?*'

'Mmm. Him and Liz. And now she's having a baby – Dad's baby. It's so sordid.'

John cleared his throat. 'I'm glad you've told us, young lady. You can be sure it'll go no further. Your poor mother!' He shook his head. 'And having to face it at a time like this, too.' Then he coaxed a tearful Audrey into the car.

When they'd left, the thought that her mother wasn't completely under her father's thumb yet, that she'd had the courage to offer her own mother a big wedding gift, took Louise upstairs more cheerfully to unpack her things. It felt good to be back in her own room. But it felt awful to pass Tim's door. Not that he'd been there for ages, but still – it hurt knowing he'd never come back.

In the kitchen, Rosalind set about washing the dishes.

Paul came in with the box of roses. 'You haven't put them in water yet.'

She turned to him and her voice was like ice. 'Did you really think that cheap trick would win me over again?'

'It wasn't a cheap trick.'

'Oh, yes, it was! Believe me, the only way you'll get me to screw you at the moment will be by raping me!'

He threw the roses at her, muttering something which sounded like, 'Stupid bitch!' and slammed out of the house.

# Twenty-Two

The next morning, Rosalind went to the shops, partly to avoid Paul and partly because they needed some fresh fruit and vegetables. She was walking down an aisle in her favourite supermarket when she felt a hand on her arm. She looked up, saw Liz – and froze.

'Rosalind, could we talk?'

'No. There aren't any words which can possibly heal the way you've hurt me, Liz.'

Her ex-friend paused, tears starting to trickle down her cheeks. '*Please!*'

'No. I wish you well, I really do. And I hope the child brings you joy. Is Bill going to accept it?'

Liz nodded, her eyes welling with tears.

'I'll say goodbye, then.'

There was uncertainty in Liz's face now. 'You seem – different.'

'Well, a lot has happened to me lately, hasn't it? My whole life has changed.' And was still changing.

'I'm sorry about Tim.'

'Yes.' Determinedly she pushed Liz's trolley aside. 'Goodbye.' And walked away, her back straight. She could never forgive Liz for what she'd done. Not in a million years. And the encounter had made her realize that she couldn't forgive Paul, either. Just – could – not.

She cut short the shopping trip, feeling uncomfortable among the cheerful crowds.

When she got home, she saw a strange car outside the house with a sticker on its side saying DOOLIFFE & JONES – REAL ESTATE. She frowned as she drove into the garage. What was that doing here? Real-estate salesmen didn't usually call in person unless invited. Usually they pushed leaflets through

271

your letter box. Dozens of leaflets every year. It drove you mad.

When she went inside, Paul was sitting talking to a woman. She was blonde and ultra-smart, and there were papers – forms, they looked like – spread out all over the table.

She hated that table, Rosalind decided suddenly, hated its nasty chilly surface that took all the warmth out of people whose reflections were trapped in it.

Paul stood up. 'Ros! I didn't expect you back so soon.'

She looked from one to the other. 'Obviously.'

He turned to the woman. 'Please excuse me a minute.' Then he put his arm round Rosalind's shoulders and led her through into the kitchen. 'I was just getting a couple of valuations. I wouldn't have done anything without consulting you. But you need to think ahead when you're selling houses and—'

'You should have spoken to me first. I haven't decided anything yet.'

'I'll – um – ask her to leave.'

'Do that.'

When he'd left, she buried her face in her hands. He was walking on eggs, tiptoeing around her, but it wasn't working. It wouldn't work, either. They'd both changed too much, and neither would want to change back to the people they'd been when they first met.

Quite simply, it was too late to mend their marriage.

And she didn't want to. A vision of Jonathon floated in front of her and she smiled involuntarily. She wanted to be with him, needed a gentler man than Paul at this season of her life. It all seemed so much clearer now she was home. No, not home. This house wasn't her home and never would be.

But back here in Australia she knew where she stood, some-how.

When Paul came into the kitchen, he was rubbing his hands together, looking bright and cheerful. 'You're right. It's far too soon to put the house on the market. We'll look into all that together, once we've settled in.'

He sat down and smiled. Confidently. He was humouring her. 'Was I intended to find out yet about selling the house, Paul?'

'I wasn't selling it, just getting it valued. I told you.'

He came and put an arm round her, planting a kiss on her cheek. Impatiently she shook him off.

He looked at her through narrowed eyes. 'Something wrong?'

'Many things. You know that.'

'Oh, for heaven's sake, Ros, don't make such a meal of it. We've agreed to work things out, but we won't be able to do that if you keep taking a huff at the slightest thing. I can't change completely overnight.'

He moved towards the coffee plunger. 'There's something else we need to discuss. I didn't want to bother you yet – wanted to give you more time to get over things.'

'How kind!'

'But maybe we should lay all the cards on the table – No, you go and sit down. I'll deal with this. It's nice to be among our own possessions again, isn't it?'

'How would you know? You've spent very little time here. I'm amazed you could even find your way home from the airport.'

He clapped one hand to his chest as if wounded. 'Sharp, Ros. Bit *too* sharp, don't you think?'

'Rosalind.'

He rolled his eyes at the ceiling and said nothing.

When he came over to the table with a steaming mug, she shoved the bags of shopping aside impatiently. One fell on to the floor and glass tinkled as something broke.

'Steady on!'

She shrugged and took the cup, holding it in her hands as she waited for him to explain the 'something else'. And when he didn't, she didn't speak, either. She used his own tactic and waited him out this time. Enjoyed doing it, too.

In the end he sighed and said, 'The thing is, I've been offered a promotion.'

'So? What difference will that make to the house? Why do we need to sell it? You surely don't want somewhere bigger?'

'We need to sell it because the new job is in the old US of A. We'll have to live there, all of us. I'm on the chairman's senior team now. Can't get much higher than that. It's good news, isn't it?'

'Have you accepted the promotion already, then?'

'Of course I have. On the spot. You don't turn down an offer like that.'

'Without asking me.' She was stating a fact, not asking a question. He hadn't asked her when he had become the chairman's international rover, either.

'I was going to tell you after—'

'*Tell* me – not *ask* my opinion, let alone listen to my views.' She stared at him, feeling in control, for once.

He frowned. 'You wouldn't understand my career needs, hon. You have to trust me for that. And anyway, I thought you'd be glad to make a fresh start this time. On all counts.'

'In the USA.' She looked round slowly, making him wait, then said quietly, 'The answer is no.' She didn't need to shout any more. The last of her emotional shackles had fallen off today.

'Ros, you can't—'

'Rosalind.'

'Stop doing that, dammit! I'll get used to it. No need to snap at me every time I forget.' He picked up his mug of coffee.

'I saw Liz at the shops.' She saw the mug jerk away from his lips and coffee splash on to his hand. 'The baby doesn't show yet, but she has a softer look on her face. She wanted to talk. I refused.'

'Bit harsh of you. After all, none of us is perfect.'

'No. And I'm not setting myself up as perfect. Far from it. I'm just not able to consider her a friend any more.'

'Your choice. But think about this: Jenny's left the nest for good, your mother's getting married again, your best friend is lost to you. It seems to me a most appropriate time to make a move. Another change of season, eh? A big one, this time.'

She smiled at him, feeling sadness at this finale to a relationship that had started with so much hope. The biggest and most important of all the recent changes were inside her, and he hadn't really noticed them. She'd gained a little wisdom, she hoped – and some courage, too. 'It *is* time for us to move on, Paul. You're right about that.'

He gave his snarling tiger's smile of triumph. 'So, you'll come to the US with me, make a fresh start?'

274

Upstairs on the landing Louise clenched her fists, fighting not to burst into tears.

Rosalind let the silence drag on for a minute or two, till the smile on his face faded a little and puzzlement crept in. 'No, Paul. I won't be coming to the USA. I'm definitely leaving you. I'm going back to England to live in my aunt's house for a while and think about my options.'

Suddenly his expression was ugly. 'Oh, now that you have the money, you've suddenly got *options*, have you? I suppose you stayed with me before because I was the best *option* at the time – with the most money to offer you.'

She shrank away from him, he looked so vicious. Then she got angry with herself for reacting like that and sat up straighter, staring right back at him across the kitchen table. 'Actually, my favourite option has nothing to do with money. I met a man while I was over there, you see, Paul. A very kind man. We get on really well and . . .'

Upstairs Louise was weeping helplessly, relief turning her into a jelly. Oh, thank you, she kept murmuring. Thank you, thank you, God, or fate, or whatever you are up there. She's going to escape.

*And so am I.*

Paul's mouth dropped open, then he made a quick recovery, thumping the table with the edge of his clenched fist. 'So, you've been unfaithful to me, you bitch! And there you were, going on at me, treating me like a pariah.'

'No, I haven't been unfaithful. Not physically, anyway, which is the only thing you'd understand. I wouldn't do that while we were still together.'

'Who is it? Do I know him?' He snapped his fingers suddenly. 'Not that thin streak of nothing. That blue-blooded, waffly creature with the bossy sister?'

'Yes.' A smile suddenly overtook Rosalind at this description of Harry and she felt warmth spread through her. 'Yes. It's Jonathon.'

He thumped the table again and one of the coffee cups fell off it, shattering, scattering brown liquid on the grey and white tiled floor. Neither of them bothered to pick it up.

Face twisting with anger, Paul swiped at one of the carrier bags of food that was still sitting on the table, knocking that down on top of the coffee. 'Rich is he, your precious Jonathon? Richer than me? As well as better connected? You're more cunning than I'd realized, Ros. Made very sure of your options, didn't you, before you took the next step?'

She tried to explain, knowing it would be useless, but at least she tried. 'Jonathon's quite poor actually. That house of his is a sort of trust. No one can dispose of it, just guard it for future generations.' She would be proud to help with that if he'd let her, though she wanted to spend time in Australia, too, didn't think she could abandon her country entirely.

'So, *he's* after your money, then.'

She smiled, very certain of that. 'No, he isn't.'

'He is, you know.'

'Is that the only attraction I can offer him? I think not. Anyway I'm not going to live with him at first. I'm going back to Aunt Sophie's house.' She waved one hand around her, suddenly impatient to end this confrontation. 'To make things easy, I'll agree to sell this place as soon as you like and split our possessions down the middle. I've never really liked the house. It's cold and heartless. *You* chose it, not me.'

He folded his arms. 'Our younger daughter is staying with me, then.'

'No, I'm not.' Louise came into the room, trying to look calm, but actually feeling shivery inside. He was looking so black, like a thunderstorm about to crash down on them. She'd crept downstairs in case her mother needed help, but she wasn't having them decide her future without being there.

Rosalind stood up and Paul followed suit, moving to stand between her and her daughter.

Louise ducked away from him and darted across to join her mother.

'I doubt you'll get custody – even if you're foolish enough to try,' Rosalind said thoughtfully. 'I believe children get a say in such things these days as long as they're old enough to understand what's happening, which Louise clearly is. And anyway, she'll be eighteen in another month or so. You couldn't even get the case to court before her birthday.'

'I want to come with you,' Louise said. 'You will let me, won't you, Mum? I couldn't bear to live with *him*.'

He made an inarticulate noise and hit out, slapping Louise

276

across the side of her head. 'Don't you dare speak to me like that!'

'Stop that, Paul!'

When he swung round, looking as if he were about to attack her next, Rosalind reacted quickly, as her instructor had once taught her, taking him by surprise. She kneed Paul hard in the groin before jabbing the side of her hand into his neck. Then she stepped back and watched with intense satisfaction as he folded up with a quiet 'Oof!', rolling about on the floor in agony, unable to breathe properly.

'I went to self-defence classes one year, Paul. Don't you remember? I was worried because you were away so much and I felt nervous going out at night on my own. I've always wondered if I'd have the guts to use the techniques. Now I know.'

'Ros . . .' His voice was still half-choked and he was rocking about, his hands splayed protectively around his genitals.

'I think we've said everything there is to say. If you'll kindly move out of this house, I'll get it ready to sell. I can make a big difference to the price if I have things looking really nice – or if you won't move out, we can lose a lot of money. That's up to you.'

He glared at her as he tried to straighten up and couldn't.

She put an arm round her daughter's shoulders. 'Come on, love, let's go and tell my mother our news. Later today, when your father's moved out, we'll come back and start getting the place ready to sell.' She looked back at Paul, who had dragged himself to a chair, but was still clutching his crotch and looking shocked as well as winded.

'I'm sorry it's ended like this. You always did have a nasty temper. I've spent half my life placating you, more fool me. There's no hope of my staying with you, whether Jonathon and I work something out or not. You see, you don't seem to have learned *anything* from what's been happening. Didn't you see how alone you were in my family portrait? No one was standing near you, not even your wife.'

'What the hell has that sodding embroidery to do with this?'

'Everything. It mirrors our life.'

But he clearly didn't understand that. She'd take the family portrait with her when she went to her mother's, just for safety.

What a good thing most of her embroideries were still in England.

'I'll fight you – for everything,' he rasped. 'I've earned – the money that paid – for all this.'

'But I raised your children and played my part in the marriage. I believe the courts always take that into account.' She had seen a few of her friends' marriages break up over the years and knew the ropes. Had never expected to walk down the same path herself, but now found the prospect inviting. Very.

'You didn't do a good job with the children!' he snarled. 'Tim was a total failure. I blame *you* for that.'

Pain shafted through her, as it did every time she thought of her son. 'I blame myself, too, and I always shall, but I think I've time to make a difference with Louise.' She looked at her daughter, who was smiling proudly at her, not even looking at her father. 'I don't want to force you into anything, though, Lou.' She used the pet name Tim had sometimes called his sister by.

'I want to come with you, Mum. I need you.' For a moment, Louise's lips quivered, then she sniffed back the tears and managed a half-smile.

'I'm glad, darling. Will you nip up and fetch my suitcase? And yours. Just in case your father doesn't move out.'

Louise ran off.

As Rosalind turned to look at her husband, Paul found the breath suddenly to yell, 'Well, who wants an old-fashioned lump like you for a wife? I'll find myself a new one who's twice as smart – in every way!'

'I hope you do.' Then, as she heard Louise behind her in the hall, she turned her back and walked out.

After Rosalind pulled the front door closed behind her, however, she clutched her daughter's arm and took a deep shuddering breath. 'Get me to the car, Lou. I feel sick.'

'Hold on to me, Mum. Don't let him see that you're chucking a wobbly.'

They walked out together, arms linked, each carrying a suitcase.

'You'll have to drive. I'm shaking.' Rosalind slid into the front passenger seat. She sat up very straight until they'd turned the corner, then slumped down and began to weep noisily.

When Louise stopped the car and tried to cuddle her, she held on to her daughter for a few moments, then blinked away the tears. 'Changes as big as this hurt like hell,' she said huskily. 'But it's done now – well, the main decision is taken, anyway.'

'You – won't change your mind? About leaving him, I mean?'

'Oh, no. That is quite definite, whatever else happens. Only, I had to come here to – to close things off. How do you think you'll like living in England?'

Louise started up the engine again. 'I don't know. But it'll be better than living with him and I can always come back here one day if I want. I still intend to train as a nurse and I dare say I can do it there just as well as here.'

'I think you'll make a good nurse. I'll help you all I can.'

'Thanks, Mum. But until I can start training, I'll be getting a job. I'm going to stand on my own feet from now on.'

'I'm glad. It's what I want for you.' And for herself.

As they drove away, Rosalind not only felt closer to her daughter but at peace beneath the sadness. If it didn't work out with Jonathon, she'd still be better off without Paul. And she had her embroidery. George Didburin was very enthusiastic about her future as an artist. She meant to work very hard, really make something of herself. It was about time.

She sat up straighter. She'd begin another piece soon. A woman – on her own, head up, wind blowing. Herself. But not in pastel colours. That was what was wrong with the family portrait. Her own figure. She was such a faded creature in it. She would do another half-figure of herself in brighter colours and place the two Rosalinds back to back, as she'd once told Tim, almost like Siamese twins.

Then, and only then, when she'd seen herself as she had become, would she be finished with the past and ready to step forward into the future. Whatever that might be.

# Lifelike Effects

*Almost without exception, extant work reveals remark-able inventiveness and dexterity, displayed in a myriad of small embroidered slips and constructed artifacts, and an even greater ingenuity in their assembly into a finished piece of work.*

*(Hirst, p.8)*

# Assembling the Embroidery

*[Like life] A raised embroidery is built up in a series of layers . . . Succeeding layers must follow in the correct order of precedence. In reality, the process is a continuous one . . .*

*(Hirst, p.74)*